Sweeter than Honey

Sweeter than Honey

MARY B. MORRISON

Kensington Publishing Corp.
www.kensingtonbooks.com

DAFINA BOOKS are published by

Kensington Publishing Corp.
119 West 40th Street
New York, NY 10018

All Kensington Titles, Imprints, and Distributed Lines are available at special quantity discounts for bulk purchases for sales promotions, premiums, fund-raising, and educational or institutional use. Special book excerpts or customized printings can also be created to fit specific needs. For details, write or phone the office of the Kensington special sales manager: Kensington Publishing Corp., 119 West 40th Street, New York, NY 10018, attn: Special Sales Department, Phone: 1-800-221-2647.

Dafina and the Dafina logo Reg. U.S. Pat. & TM Off.

ISBN-13: 978-0-7582-1513-0
ISBN-10: 0-7582-1513-4

First hardcover printing: August 2007
First trade paperback printing: July 2008
First mass market printing: June 2009

10   9   8   7   6   5   4

Printed in the United States of America

Dedication

Dedicated in loving memory of Elester Noel, my mother, who committed suicide after being brutally battered by my father for years. My mother gave birth to eight—some say nine—children and she checked out of this world like many other battered women, not knowing her self-worth.

Acknowledgments

I thank God for the woman that I am and will become. I'm blessed beyond measure. I'm sexy, confident, intelligent, uninhibited, and most important, I love myself first, knowing that through God I will attain the greatness of all my desires. I'm fortunate to possess a passion to write and the determination to succeed.

Thanks and welcome to my new editor, Selena James. I'm looking forward to a long and prosperous relationship. I appreciate all the hard work and dedication of my entire Kensington family. Karen Thomas, my editor for life, I say unto you, "We are family and thanks for everything."

I absolutely love my author friend and writing partner, Carl Weber, aka the Prince of Drama. I experienced so much growth as a writer while we coauthored *She Ain't the One* and I can't wait to get started on *He Ain't the One*. While in New York collaborating on *She Ain't the One*, I had the opportunity to have lunch with Carl's wonderful wife, Martha, some of his staff at Urban Books, and also dined with a number of Carl's authors while we were on tour and I have no idea how

Carl finds time to write his *New York Times* best sellers. All I can say is, "Carl is a gentleman in the purest form."

Authors Naleighna Kai, Gloria Mallette, and Marissa Monteilh willingly opened up their hearts when I asked them to share with you very powerful and personal messages in the I Am Worthy section of this book, and I appreciate each of them. I hope their words inspire you to write in your own words why you feel worthy.

My son, Jesse Byrd, Jr., lights up my life. I'm so proud of him. As many of you know, Jesse is on a basketball scholarship and my wonderful godson, Robert "Chew" Owens, also is on a basketball scholarship, so you know I'm smiling from ear to ear.

I'm grateful that my fantastic siblings, Wayne, Andrea, Derrick, Regina Morrison, Margie Rickerson, Debra Noel, and Bryan Turner are so supportive of me, and I love my cousin Edward Allen.

Thanks to each of my fans. I want you to know beginning this new series, The Honey Diaries, wasn't easy because like you, I too was deeply in love for seven years with Darius and Fancy and Jada and Wellington and all of the characters from the Soul Mates Dissipate series; therefore, my new characters took time to develop.

I must thank my manuscript readers, Mother Bolton, my manager, Eve Lynne Robinson, and my awesome agent, Claudia Menza. Much love to Lou Richie, Bernard Henderson, Jerry Thompson, Michele Lewis, Vera Warren-Williams, Blanche Richardson, Karen Richardson, and Emma Rodgers.

I have the world's greatest manager and photographer, Eve Lynne Robinson. I thank Eve for enhancing my career, expanding my vision, and taking excellent care of me. Now my graphic Web designer/image brander, Kim Mason, is unequivocally second to none. I cannot thank these women enough.

Where Did I Go Wrong?

I know the bad things he does to me are my fault.

He's really a good man, and maybe if I would've shut up and not talked back he wouldn't have slapped me in my mouth. Maybe if I hadn't cursed him out or degraded his manhood, he wouldn't have yelled at me. Maybe if I had changed my dress instead of telling him what I wasn't going to wear, he would've allowed me to go out with my girlfriends. Maybe if I could learn to sex him better, suck his dick a little longer, or stopped telling him "no" more than I said "yes," he'd stop cheating on me.

What did I do to make him hate me so much when all I've done was try to love him? I need some answers. I'm lying in this emergency room: a broken heart this time. Maybe next time I won't be so lucky. Actually, if God cared about me at all, he'd bring me on home. I'm tired. I'm ready. I've been ready for quite some time now. Surely heaven can't be like this.

Getting my ass kicked on the regular is no way to live. Yep, I'm convinced that heaven has got to be a better place. Hell, hell has got to be a better place than living with him. All I ask is that my mother take care of my kids. I know she's tired too. Done, done her part and then some, but I ain't got nobody else to look after my babies.

Why didn't somebody see him hitting me? Kicking me? Biting me? Spitting on me? Raping me? Using my body for a punching bag? A doormat. My hair for a dishrag. If I hadn't made enough money to pay all the bills, I'm sure he would've bashed my face in again by now. Why was he cursing me? Shouting at me? Calling me bitch! Bitch! Bitch! So much that when anybody else calls me by my name, I don't even answer. Why is it that I can't do anything right to please him? No matter how hard I try.

I hope somebody cares because I sure don't. Not anymore. I'm ashamed to go around my family. I'm too embarrassed to confide in my friends. Outside of work I don't have a life. Haven't seen my folks in a minute. Lord, what happened to him to make him this way? Was it his mama? Was it me? He used to be nice to me. He used to say, "I love you." Actually he still does tell me he loves me, but I know he doesn't mean it. Does he? He can't possibly love me and treat me this way. Can he? I'm numb. I'm scared. In a world filled with people, some happy, others just like me, I feel so all alone.

Lord, I love You but if You don't save me this time, I'm going to have to repent in advance if that's possible, because I swear, if he hits me one, I swear, just one more time . . . I'ma kill him dead . . . or die trying.

The choice is yours, Lord.

* * *

I've never abandoned you. All I have to say unto you is . . . the choice to stay or leave is yours. Always has been. Always will be. How can you claim you love Me and at the same time not love yourself? I am you and you, my child, are Me. I've already set you free. It's already been done.

Freedom is a choice.

If you don't want My blessings, you won't receive My glory. I'll simply give your blessings to someone who's willing and ready to receive. You can't get My blessings if you continue relying upon him instead of Me. It's like winning the lottery but not knowing your numbers hit. My blessings unto you are useless if you don't acknowledge the fact that they are yours.

Knowing is not enough. You must accept My blessings in order to attain a better life. You must embrace a higher level of consciousness. Every time you walk out of your front door, you decide to return, unlock the door, and enter the house. Knowing he's there, knowing you haven't put him out, knowing he's going to continuously abuse you, yet you leave and then return day after day. Again and again you pray to Me, frantically begging that he'll change. Your prayers have been answered because each time he becomes more and more violent.

Oh yes, he has to answer to Me. But when are you going to see that you, My child, are the one who must change? Your willingness to transition into a greater consciousness will determine your happiness, your goodness, your blessings, your glory . . . all you have to do is flip on the light switch and stop living in darkness. The electricity is already there. Use it.

Trust in Me. Your ability to connect to Me is there. Focus your attention on yourself, not him. The time has come for you to stop believing that your relationship with him is the only one you are worthy of.

Stop hiding behind your contrived smile. Stop crying yourself to sleep at night. Stop acting like everything is all right. Stop putting him before your children. My child, let not your heart be troubled. When you come out of your conscious coma, awaken to truth, take responsibility for your life, or next time, honestly, there won't be a next time.

If you keep going back to him, I'll see you soon . . . real soon.

Welcome to Book #1 of my new series . . .

The Honey Diaries

Happiness is an acquired emotion.

Pussy is sweeter than honey and more valuable than money.

PROLOGUE

Lace St. Thomas

She's successful now. Money. Diamonds. Cars. Furs. To whom much was given, much was required. Let her tell it, and if anyone could've looked over her shoulder, I'm sure they would've agreed, not much was given unto her except grief and pain. She wasn't different from most folks. Everybody had a story to tell. Practically rearing herself, how did she ever survive? Her entire childhood, no matter how hard she tried to please her mother, she was never good enough to measure up to her baby sister.

What good was having a parent who constantly put her down? A mother who shattered her self-esteem, never believed in her dreams, always leaving her to pick herself up every time she fell. Why was each of her lessons learned the hard way? Unfamiliar family made her feel like a stranger in her own home. Nah, growing up she never had a home. It was more like a halfway house. No amount of bricks and mortar could encapsulate a loving environment.

Maybe her father could've showered her with the love that her mother didn't or simply wouldn't, but she doubted her father knew she was alive. They could've exchanged breaths or broken bread at the same restaurant table at separate times. Her on Wednesday. Him on Thursday. Her life was full of unknowns. And even as a woman, she had no idea where to find her daddy. Perhaps one day she'd really try.

Flagstaff, Arizona, a town with a population of less than sixty thousand, somebody had to know . . . what she didn't. His whereabouts. Without question the man who provided the seed to fertilize her mother's egg had to be better than the henpecked man her mother had anxiously agreed to marry. Her stepfather-to-be was a virtual vagabond who'd violated her not-so-sweet sixteen innocence and changed her life forever. Inevitable change left unforgettable scars on her soul. Many cold days and sleepless nights she wished she was either dead or never born.

Oh well, by every means necessary, she did survive. The worst, she prayed, was all behind her now, specifically the two men who wanted her dead: her ex-man and her ex-boss. Because she'd never had a positive male role model, all of her exes added to the long list of reasons why she didn't trust men. All the men in her life were satisfied as long as she gave them what they wanted. Did whatever they desired.

The johns who abused her were long gone too. Today, she was surrounded with good women she regretfully at times treated worse than . . . hm, let's not dwell on the negativity that learned behavior begets. For once, everything in her life was perfect, including her new man.

For once in her life she was happy more than she was sad.

What Happens Inside of Vegas . . .
Is a Damn Shame

CHAPTER 1

Lace

"**Y**ou're never going to be more than a trifflin', lyin' lil' slut! You make me sick! My God, I wish I woulda followed my first mind and aborted your ass instead of listening to that deadbeat lying-ass motherfuckin' daddy of yours. I can't believe you up in here under my nose tryna fuck my man! Why can't you be more like your sister? Get out of my house and this time stay the hell out!" were the last words I'd heard my mother say before she slammed the door in my face.

Was she referring to my baby sister? The golden can-do-no-wrong child?

What had I done this time?

It wasn't my fault that on my sixteenth birthday, my mother's fiancé saw in me what most men saw: a young, cute, innocent face, a firm, cellulite-free ass, perfect, plump, perky tits, and long legs stacked with a virgin cherry that they desperately wanted to burst. Well, he wasn't positive about the virgin part until his hard calluses, dirty hands, and jagged fingernails slipped inside my pink panties. His stale morning hadn't-brushed-his-yellowish-brown-teeth breath exhaled in my face as he squatted in front of my pussy. He poked, probed, gazed up at me, smiled, and then said, "Aw, man. You really are a preemie," kissing my virgin lips while checking twice for confirmation.

"Ow, you're hurting me," I said, shoving his forehead. As I crossed my legs, the scratches on my kitty stung worse than paper cuts.

That incident happened over thirteen years ago, but psychologically it hurts like he violated me yesterday. To this day I can't stand men with dirty or rough hands or bad breath or yellow teeth.

"I'ma tell Mama," my sister had said, standing in the doorway, covering her big mouth.

I snapped, "Stch. Go tell Mama 'cause I ain't do nothing wrong!"

Truth was I was very afraid, fearing Mama would side with Don and Honey. The only reason I'd let *him* find out I was untouched was that my mama constantly accused me of being a whore and a slut, so I wanted to prove her wrong. My sister was the fast one, sneaking boys into her room after Mama went to sleep, going to jail for petty theft, and staying out all night on the weekends smoking weed.

With any reason not to feed us or to have the house to herself with Don, Mama didn't care where we went or how long we stayed. I guess my being the opposite of my sister hanging around the house reading books or listening to music most of the time invaded Mama's privacy.

Don's eyes widened. He swiftly sucked air into his

mouth, snapping his head toward Honey. When he pushed me, I fell to the floor screaming, "Mama!"

My mother, Rita, raced into the family room, by-passing Honey. Rita stared down at me. Hatred narrowed her eyes that never blinked. I spread my legs, hoping she could see what Don had done to me. This was my chance to have him confess he was wrong and confirm I was pure. But he didn't. I lay there trying to figure out why a grown man would take advantage of a minor and why my mother would let him.

Sinking into the gray carpet, I felt my ignorance giving me away to the streets when my mother deemed me competition as opposed to her little girl. True, most times I was guilty of something, but not trying to have sex with my mother's man or the boys I went to Flagstaff High School with.

My heart exploded like a bomb when Mama believed her husband-to-be's words, "Rita, get rid of her . . . your tramp of a daughter just offered me her pussy," over mine. "Mama, I swear I didn't, he's lying. He stuck his finger between my legs. Go on, tell 'em I'm a virgin. Honey, you saw him. Tell Mama what he did," I cried, spreading my legs wider this time. Instantly I'd become a casualty of compassion.

Before my sister answered, the strands of my pony-tail wrapped around my mother's fist. Content that he was out of the spotlight, Don sat on the sofa with his lint-filled Afro and sagging gut gargling beer like mouth-wash while fingering the remote, flipping through channels like nothing was happening. Instead of helping me, Honey bent toward the floor, grabbing my white ankle socks. The tip of my brand-new tennis shoe slammed against her chin, knocking Honey on her ass.

It was an accident. I'd never done anything to hurt my sister. Honey was the only sibling I had.

Angrily, Mama dragged me faster. The rug beneath my butt felt like a flaming match frying through my skin. Frantically kicking the air, I yelled all the way to the door, "Bitch! Let me go! Grab his fuckin' ass!" I peeled my fingers from the door hinge, barely escaping the *slam!*

That wasn't my first time getting thrown out of the house, but it was my last time calling my mother what I'd wanted to call her for a long time. She was a bitch. Why I'd gotten kicked out every other month since I'd grown unusually large breasts twice the cup-size of my mother's and sister's put together, I didn't know. How could my mother carry me for nine months, birth me, then despise me for being molested by her man?

Dressed in pink shorts, and a white shirt with a pink cat on the front, I stood outside the door for fifteen minutes praying my mother would open it. When she didn't, I knew better than to bang on Rita's door. The smell of Mama frying Sunday morning bacon and baking homemade buttermilk biscuits made me hungry. Surely Rita would slide me a plate or a slice of my birthday cake so I wouldn't have to walk down the street to the Sunshine Rescue Mission.

I waited in vain, drifting off into thoughts about attending my first day of school tomorrow, celebrating with all the seniors, and getting my driver's license in the mail. Within seconds all of my hopes of becoming the youngest valedictorian had become dismal. I sat on the steps watching the heat waves float through the hot air in Flagstaff, Arizona. Our small town was a short drive from the Grand Canyon, where lots of tourists came to see one of the seven natural wonders of the world. As a homeless child, I felt like the eighth wonder that no one cared about. People drove by me waving but all of them kept going.

Sitting alone on the steps gave me lots of time to

daydream about the big city with bright lights. I'd heard lots of neighbors and students rave about Las Vegas, but I'd never been there. I heard that pretty girls made lots of money simply because they were cute like me. Vegas was over a hundred miles away from my house, too far for me to travel alone with no money.

The orange sunrays traded places with the blue moonlight. Gazing up at the stars, I questioned why I'd fallen into a bottomless pit so young, so innocent, and so afraid. Cursed for being beautiful, I slept on the ugly concrete porch until the break of dawn. The crackling of the front door startled me as I sadly looked up into my mother's piercing brown eyes.

"Mama, please, I'm sorry. If it'll make you feel better, I'll stay in my room after school whenever he's here, I promise."

Desperately seeking my mother's forgiveness, I apologized for Don's faults. I had no place else to go. Not permanently. With her silver spiked heels, my mother stepped on me like a doormat and kept walking as if I were invisible: incapable of being seen.

Years later, at times I still felt I wasn't perceptive to the human eye. Funny how back then I thought I was grown until I had to make it on my own. Over the past decade, I'd learned a lot about being a woman, not necessarily the easy way.

In my opinion, ninety-five percent of all women were abused at some point during their lifetime by their mothers, their fathers, their husbands, their boyfriends, strangers on the prowl seeking a rape victim or in my case all of the above. Living on the streets convinced me that the five percent who weren't abused died at birth. If only I could've been so lucky.

My sister to this day still lives at home with our mother. An old high school acquaintance said Honey was dying of some rare form of cancer and that I was

Honey's closest possible match for a donor. Was that God's way of paying my mother back? They didn't need me then and I don't need them now.

After my mother kicked me out I would've gone to live with my dad, but we never knew our father. And the way I saw it, any man who'd abandon his children was the worst type of abuser. Forget that lame bullshit about the mother keeping him away. I swore I was never having kids. My daddy had a choice! He could've fought for joint custody, weekends, supervised visitation, something. Anything was better than nothing. The one time we asked about our father, our mom cursed us out.

"Jean St. Thomas's green-eyed, slick-haired red ass ain't shit! Never was shit! Ain't never gon' be shit! Sorry-ass son of a bitch ain't never paid one damn dime to help me take care of y'all and if you ask me about him again I'ma beat y'all's ass! Now, get out of my face!" Then she mumbled, "That good-for-nothing-but-a-wet-dream bastard better not ever call me again asking to see y'all."

Daddy wanted to see us?

My green eyes filled with tears at the thought that my mother hated me but wouldn't let my daddy love me. I guess I was light-skinned with straight hair like my father, because my mom and sister had skin like dark brown sugar and hair equally coarse.

Whatever, I didn't need any of them. I was fine. Honestly I was. But it still hurts that after all these years Mama never inquired about where I was until Honey got sick. Mama didn't care if I never came back. If she could suction my marrow through a straw over the phone, she would do so, then hang up in my face without saying thanks. Maybe one day I'd go back to her in my white-on-white or my black-on-black Jaguar and show her how successful I'd become.

I still blamed and will never forgive my mother for the life I was forced to live after being kicked out. As an involuntary high school dropout, I'd hitchhiked and moved in with my instant twenty-three-year-old boyfriend who brutally stole my virginity, then yelled at my ass every other day like he was bipolar. He had me so screwed up in the head I jumped every time he spoke. I'd leave the house and forget to put on my shoes. I'd pour orange juice on his cereal instead of milk because I was so afraid he'd beat me if I didn't get him what he wanted fast enough. After six months together, I slept in the doghouse that was inside the garage just to stay out of the way of his fists.

At seventeen I ran away and married only what I could describe as Charles Manson's offspring. Brutally he stomped my ass daily, I think either for his amusement or for his daily thirty-minute workout. The reason I stayed was, once again, I didn't have any place to go, nor did I have any money. That was another lesson learned.

Men controlled women by making women dependent upon them for everything from food and clothes to shelter. So for an entire year, if my husband had a bad day, I had a worse night. But what I did have was enough sense to realize if I didn't find the courage to escape, one day a coroner would carry me out in a body bag and deliver me to Rita's, only for her to write *return to sender* on my toe tag.

Before leaving his ass I stole a blowup doll, inflated it, then doused his bed and the doll with six gallons of ketchup mixed with two gallons of gasoline, praying his ass would light one last cigarette.

I went to a pleasure store and stole four dildos that looked exactly like his dick, hiding them under my skirt. The first dick I chopped off the head with a butcher's knife, then sliced the shaft into tiny confetti-sized pieces and left the plastic floating in his toilet. The second one I set on fire on top of his gas-burning stove and left it there with a tent card that read *last meal*. The third one I ground in his blender on PUREE until the motor shot bluish red sparks into the smoky air. And the fourth one I poured fire-red fingernail polish over the head, watched it bleed down the sides, then drilled an ice pick into the piss hole and left it on his doorstep with a note, *Fuck and beat this, you piece of shit! If you come after me, your mother-fuckin' dick is next! I guarantee it!*

Needless to say I never heard from him again. Hopefully because he'd flicked that lighter and burned to death. If by some misfortune he was alive, his cruel abusive ass probably thought I was the crazy one.

On my eighteenth birthday, I moved into the Pussy-land Ranch and didn't move out until I was twenty-nine and went to work for Valentino James as a madam. Eleven grueling years on my back with my legs spread open was no easy feat, but where could I earn decent money with no diploma? After fucking a different john every day during my first three years at Pussyland, I became the top-requested girl. The high demand allowed me to establish a regular clientele, granting myself two days on and two days off. On holidays my nonnego-tiable rate of three hundred dollars an hour tripled.

Working for Valentino helped me maintain my san-ity and gave my body a much-needed rest. Instantly my twelve female escorts depended on me, and in re-turn I relied upon them for my five-figure monthly paycheck. I especially counted on my personal fa-vorite, Sunny Day.

There was something special about Sunny. Some-thing beyond her striking beauty. Something deeper than her almond-shaped eyes that beamed rays of light. Sunny was unique. She was young, vibrant, and enthusiastic about life. Sunny possessed the passion I lacked, and although she didn't know it, in many ways she'd helped me. I wasn't there yet, but occasionally I felt the desire to genuinely care about her and the other girls I'd hired. Kinda like how I wished my mother would've loved me. Sunny didn't have an old soul; she had a wise spirit beyond her years. Always happy, motivating the other girls, and willing to work extra hard to please her clients. Sunny's invincible, indispensable take-charge leadership personality reminded me of myself when I first started prostituting.

For me, prostitution provided a much-needed clean and safe place to live off of the hot, sweltering, or freezing snow-covered streets of Nevada. I wasn't always cold and callous. My God, I hoped Sunny didn't end up like me. She wouldn't. Tonight I'd decided Valentino could take Onyx or Starlet off the circuit for himself, but at the end of the month, three days from now, I was firing Sunny for her own good. Sunny needed to do what I couldn't . . . go home to a mother and father who loved her.

It was too late for me. I'd been in the game so long I didn't know how to get out. Didn't know what else I'd do. I'd been mentally, physically, sexually, spiritually, financially, you name it, taken advantage of. The only thing left for someone to take was my life and that's what was not going to happen without a fight. Whether I'd win or lose didn't matter to me as long as I never again voluntarily allowed anyone to beat me. I'd paid my dues. In some ways I was stronger. In many ways, wiser. Now it was my turn to take control of my life.

Abuse damaged me. Abuse was not cute and it took me a while to learn that abuse was not love. The next man who laid hands on Lace St. Thomas was one dead motherfucka.

CHAPTER 2

Lace

Day one of the seventy-two-hour countdown to Sunny's freedom, I envisioned Mommy sitting on the front row before a naughty professor raising her hand instead of spreading her legs to make a good impression. Sunny had the prettiest pussy of all my girls. The first time I peeled open her outer lips, I saw her slim pinkish shaft extending down to a mocha-ridged flap exposing a succulent pierced clitoris.

"Did this hurt?" I recalled asking while I teased the silver bar with pea-sized balls on both ends.

"Yes, Madam. Hell yes." Her wide smile flashed perfectly aligned teeth. "But it feels nice now, Madam. I like it. I have my own set of balls and they sure do drive men crazy."

Sunny started playing with her own pussy and she never flinched when I French-kissed her.

"Tell me why I should hire you?" I'd asked her, applying a drop of gel to my fingertip. Teasing her clit in a slow circular motion, I dripped another drop onto the bar, gliding my finger back and forth.

She smiled, held my hand, then slid my middle finger inside her incredibly hot, tight, juicy pussy, and replied, "Tell me why you shouldn't hire me, Madam."

Well, over my incredible year of being Sunny's boss, I had fallen in love with more than her personality. She was amazingly flawless. I could've waived Sunny's body inspection that day but I didn't. I couldn't resist experiencing the rest of her. Caressing her plump breasts, kissing her protruding nipples, massaging her firm ass, then putting her through my multiple orgasm tests— fucking her with a nine-inch dildo while finger-fucking her in the ass and savoring her sweet pussy with my tongue all at the same time—I'd come hard. Twice.

"I'm gonna miss Sunny," I whispered, strutting my red stilettos into the southside entrance at the newest and most extraordinary casino on the strip. I smiled at the thought of Sunny getting all As, then using her brain while maximizing her pussy power to make lots of money. For the first time, tonight I felt more like Sunny's big sister.

Working my hips into a figure eight, my red lace wraparound minidress slightly exposing my pussy pasty, I glided along the gold-marbled tiles. Men gawked and women pretended not to peep at the dollar sign between my legs.

Ignoring them, I glanced at shoppers inside Chanel to my right and Dior and Louis Vuitton to my left. I stopped at the Rolex store, bought a ladies' Presidential watch, and walked out.

Surrounded by trees decorated with thousands of sparkling white lights streaming from the roots to the trunks to the green leaves scattered amongst the limbs, I swung my long slick hair shoulder to shoulder, sashaying down the aisle as I showcased my diamond earrings, necklace, bracelet, and rings.

God, how I love being a woman, I thought, constantly reminding myself that women, not men, were the dominators of the universe.

I'd learned that the people with the least amount of control were more aggressive because they struggled to conquer that which they didn't have power over. Men beat women to make them submissive. Bosses demoted their smarter employees or gave them lower performance ratings to keep them as subordinates. And johns paid to fuck prostitutes because if only for five minutes, they felt they owned a bitch.

If reincarnation were possible, I'd definitely come back as a black widow spider or maybe a queen bee. Sad but true, men were only necessary for reproduction. Everything else, hell, I had that covered with no problems.

Admiring the horizontal patterns of the purple, green, and gold curtains that seemingly parted exclusively for me, I entered the upper level bar winking at a few of our regulars who were tossing back dirty martinis straight up, stirred, not shaken with blue-cheese-stuffed olives.

I knew the intricate intimate preferences of all my top-paying clients. I knew details that their wives and girlfriends either didn't want to know, or simply, like with most sneaky, freaky, down-low bisexual men, their women would never embrace the truth: Men were basic creatures.

"Hey, Daddy," I whispered in one of my client's ears. "Feel like predickting the forecast?"

"It's definitely a Sunny Day," he replied, then nodded in Sunny's direction before resuming conversation with his woman.

That stiff bitch cupped her drink with both hands, burying her face in a piña colada. I didn't give a fuck about her. Any bitch sipping a frozen drink wasn't a real woman unless she'd planned on having her man suck the pineapple and coconut juices through her pussy. I'd never let my girls drink that sweet-ass, make-you-sick-to-your-stomach shit unless they used it to make me money.

Men wanted to cum with lovers who were fun. Not some sexually repressed housewife curling under the covers draped in flannel pajamas with ridiculously fluffy slippers at their bedside who'd turn her back on him without saying good night, making both of his heads hurt while he stared at the hideous scarf hiding her hair.

I should salute boring bitches. Those were the types who made me successful. They were the kind of females who made their men cum running to me with her paycheck while she sat at home trying to figure out who her man was fucking. Women always asked the wrong questions like, "Who were you fucking?" or "Where were you all night?" The question women needed to answer was why their man was sticking his dick in somebody else.

With my mental sex Rolodex second in content only to a set of encyclopedias, I understood that most men enjoyed having their assholes licked while fucking, their balls squeezed while nutting, and having a dick in their ass while having their dick in an ass calling some face-less woman "Bitch." The right size butt plug or vibrator humming against a man's prostate with his woman sucking his dick or jacking him off would blow his fucking mind, but the average woman wasn't down with asking, doing, or hearing what her man honestly wanted in the bedroom.

That was why the streets of Vegas were filled with chicks sucking dicks in cars for twenty dollars a nut. An outdoor whore could never be on my team. Her standards were too low for me but higher than those of the women getting fucked for free by men who wouldn't get out of their beds at three o'clock in the daytime and surely not three in the morning to pick her up if she was stranded in the middle of Timbuktu.

The way I recruited new customers, I'd stroll the red carpet that divided the craps players from the blackjack gamblers. With a ten-thousand-dollar bet per hand on the open floor, it was easy to differentiate who had real money and why some men didn't mind paying ten grand an hour to get laid by a beautiful woman. Some of those guys needed to blast off after losing a hundred thousand dollars in less than fifteen minutes. The price of good pussy wasn't a problem for a high roller who could walk a short distance to the credit manager and cash a check for a million dollars.

That was the type of client my girls serviced at Immaculate Perception. Image was everything. If a woman dressed, spoke, or carried herself like she was poor, she shouldn't wonder why she attracted cheap-ass, broke-ass men. I dressed all of my girls in the best of what each designer had to offer.

I circled the bar where my twelve showgirls were seated on the orange polka-dot sofa and caramel leather seats facing the Niagara-sized waterfall flowing outside the panoramic window. Dressed in miniskirts, halters, and high heels, my girls laughed, chatted, and crossed their glowing legs while sipping champagne.

Bypassing the girls, I motioned for Sunny to come to me, then escorted her to the downstairs bar. We sat in the corner at a table for two. Covering her hands with mine, I said, "Sunny, you are so beautiful. You're smart and you're special."

I felt she needed to hear me say that because I so desperately wanted to hear my mother tell me the same. But Rita never did.

"Thanks, Madam," Sunny replied, tucking her long sandy-blond hair behind one ear.

"You've been reserved again tonight by one of your regulars. But, Sunny, sweetheart, I want to know, what do you want out of life?"

Sunny's mesmerizing large brown eyes traveled to the corners, then back at me as she replied, "Madam, I don't know. When I started in this business I wanted to work a few months, make some fast money, get out, and go to college. But now I'm not so sure. Why waste four years getting a degree only to make less money?"

"You can't do this forever, sweetheart, so tell me what you don't want," I said.

Crossing her giraffe-long legs, then folding her arms on the table, Sunny answered, "Madam, I don't want rich men treating me as though I don't have a brain, like I'm some inanimate sex object. You know, like a blowup doll."

Oh, how well did I know?

Briefly I digressed to the blowup doll I'd left on my ex-husband's bed. I should've known when he insisted on getting married at Graceland on Las Vegas Boulevard six hours after we'd met, I should've literally run for the hills yelling, "You ain't nothing but a hound dog!" Anybody who dressed like Elvis, acted like Elvis, and honestly believed that Elvis was still alive obviously didn't live in the real world. What I was sure of was any man constantly beating my ass was a reality I'd never repeat.

"And, Madam, I'd like to have a steady boyfriend, but what man is going to respect me being in this business?"

"Sunny, don't worry. I'll help you. All I ask is that you be patient in the process and trust me."

Gazing into my eyes as though she saw through me, Sunny asked, "Why should I put all my trust in you or anyone else in this business?"

That fucked me up. She was right. "One day soon, I promise you I'll explain. Now, you've told me before that you have family and you love them. If you don't want to trust me, then go home to the family you do trust. Sounds to me like your parents and sister would love to have you back in their lives."

Looking toward the ceiling, Sunny smiled. "Madam, this is a glamorous business. I feel like a big-time movie star like a Marilyn or Halle, but what sense does it make for me to pleasure these johns, then give my money to you and Valentino? I'm not thinking about going home. I'm thinking about going out on my own."

This girl was blinded by the bright lights of Las Vegas, but she wasn't the only one. There were lots of runaways, strays, and wannabe madams that didn't understand street prostitution, and drugs were territorial and addictive.

"You can't do that! Sunny, look at me!" Lowering my voice, I explained, "You're an escort, not a hooker, and certainly not a madam. You don't have a clue what happens to prostitutes on the street, especially the ones who have no pimp. And no street prostitute is going to let your pretty ass pimp them. Even with pimps whores get trains run on them, they get beat up. Sunny, what you're considering is dangerous. You could end up dead."

"Well, Madam. If anything happens to me, please contact my parents."

Once this young lady set her mind to doing something, it was virtually impossible for me to make her see things my way.

In order to gain Sunny's trust, I did what I'd never done before. I removed a business card from my purse, then wrote on the back *If you ever need me, call me,* along with my cell number and home number, and gave the card to her.

I was more convinced than ever I'd made the right decision to free this beautiful and innocent young lady, but I couldn't sever her from the venomous emotional attachment to prostitution. Only Sunny could free herself.

Looping Sunny's friendship present over her fingers, I released the Rolex bag. Sunny was mastering what it meant to become a woman. Knowing how to manipulate men and not relinquish pussy power separated the women from the girls. Women were confident and secure. Girls, some thirty, forty, and fifty-plus, played childish games like seeking passwords to check their lovers' voice mail messages.

Standing, I said, "Let's go. Nothing bad is going to happen to you, if you listen to me. And I'll pay all of your college tuition. Accept it. You are getting out of this business."

CHAPTER 3

Summer

Kneeling beside my sister's bed, I prayed, "Dear Lord, please bring my sister home soon. She's been gone too long and I miss her terribly. If Sunny does not find her way home tonight, then, Lord, I ask that you keep her safe from harm. Amen."

Every night I asked God to bring my sister home. Sunny had been gone for a year, but it felt like a lifetime. Standing by the window, I pulled the trigger on my lighter, setting ablaze the white eucalyptus candlewick.

This was my way of holding on to the hope that Sunny would come back to me. I didn't keep hope alive. Having hope kept me alive. The only other person I wanted back in my life was my first true love, Anthony James. At twenty-one he owned his house and had lots of money. He told me that his parents died unexpectedly and I felt sorry for him because my mother and father were alive and I couldn't imagine life without them.

Anthony was an entrepreneur. Drove a Benz. He spoiled me with clothes and my first diamonds. And oh my, could he kiss! His lips all over my body made me feel womanly. Anthony would pick me up around the corner from our home and take me to Foothill High School for my classes, and then he'd pick me up afterward. That was the only time I'd hid my relationship from my family, 'cause Anthony told me not to tell them.

He'd said, "Your parents don't know you like I do. You're becoming your own woman. They won't be happy for us. They'll try to break us up."

He was right. I wish I would never have told my parents the truth.

Back then Anthony was twenty-one and I was sixteen, but he made me feel all grown up inside, especially the way he was so patient and excited when he found out I was a virgin. The first time Anthony came inside me, I got pregnant. I was so scared until Anthony said he'd marry me and take care of us. When I told my parents, Daddy flipped out.

Now that I was almost twenty-one, hopefully I could find Anthony and maybe this time Daddy wouldn't run him away. If I ever saw Anthony again, I'd tell him my daddy was a Christian man and he didn't make me have an abortion. Our baby, Anthony James Day, was now four years old.

I wondered if someone had gotten my sister pregnant and that's why she'd left home. Did Sunny have a husband? Or if a man was loving my sister, did he make her feel the way Anthony did me? I wanted Sunny to be happy wherever she was, but I sensed she wasn't. Whoever she was with, he'd better treat her right or he'd have to deal with me.

Knock, knock. "Summer, you okay in there, baby?" Mama asked, slightly opening the door.

"Yeah, Mama. I'm all right. AJ asleep?"

"Yes, Nana's baby is sound asleep."

"Thanks, I miss my sister so much. I know she'll be home soon."

Grasping my hand, Mama sat me on the bed, then sat beside me. "Baby, you are identical but your twin sister is not like you. Sunny has always been independent. She's always done things her way. But the one thing both of you have in common is you're smart girls and you're good girls. When Sunny is ready, she'll come back home. And when she does, we'll shower her with love and take her to church every Sunday until she leaves again."

Why couldn't I have had the courage to go live with Anthony like he wanted me to?

"Mama. Do you think Daddy would let me see Anthony again? He is the father of my son. I mean, I am almost grown and I can't find any boy or young man to treat me the way Anthony did, not even the boys at church."

"Sshh. Hush, Summer. Now, you know that man was too old for you then and he's much older now. Besides, something wasn't right about his ways. He was impolite. Never came and introduced himself to your father even after you got pregnant. Always stayed outside in that there fancy automobile tootin' his horn for you. Nobody even knows what he looks like. The Lord will send you somebody. You just gotta be patient, baby."

Patience didn't have an expiration date, a due date, or an estimate.

"Mama, I could be old and gray and never have another baby or ever have a husband. Sunny seen him once. He's nice. She can vouch for me. Mama, please."

Mama stood smoothing out her robe. "I done spoke my peace, Summer. Don't wanna hear no more mention of Anthony James less you talkin' 'bout my grandbaby."

CHAPTER 4

Lace

L ast in. First out. I waited until my twelve escorts were comfortably inside the twenty-four-passenger white limousine. I nodded at my bodyguards, then watched the three men routinely secure black leather blindfolds over each of my bitches' eyes, except Sunny.

"You sure you know what you're doing?" Reynolds asked. "If Valentino finds out any of the girls know his location, we're all dead."

"I guess you're right. Do your job. Blindfold her too. But starting today," I announced to the others, "Sunny is promoted to wifee. Whatever Sunny demands of any of you girls, do not question her or you'll have to answer to me."

Listening to the girls continue their conversations until we reached Valentino's mansion, I had to give myself credit for hiring the baddest bitches in Nevada.

Women from all around the world traveled to Las Vegas. Some for fun. Some to get married. Others looking for love or the love of money.

When Valentino hired me, I fired all of his escorts and hired my own. Girl number one was five feet two inches and barely one hundred pounds. Chinadoll had long dark hair, slanted dark eyes, a tiny waist, shapely thighs, a cute butt, and the seven-foot basketball players loved her.

Girl two, Crème-d-licious, was of African descent, grew up in London, and was five foot ten with a body like Tyra Banks's. Big titties, juicy lips, curvaceous hips, and an English accent that made johns weak every time she spoke. Creamy, as I called her for short, was my squirter.

Girl three was my White Russian dominatrix and didn't hesitate to beat a man's ass. Four was my chameleon. Misty could be any nationality a man wanted and could imitate any woman from Condeleeza to Alicia to Omarosa to Little Bo Peep, but girl five was my biggest freak. I nicknamed her Bootylicious 'cause her ass made every man scream, "Damn!" A guy could lose his entire head with one booty clap.

Onyx, Starlet, and Sunny were the last hired because each of them exuded sex without trying. Onyx had raw beauty, black radiant skin, high butt cheeks and cheekbones. Her body was strong, solid, yet feminine. Starlet had mesmerizing eyes, short hair, gorgeous legs, and incredibly huge breasts. Out of all the girls, Sunny was my favorite because in addition to being beautiful with long natural blond hair that all the johns loved, she was what I wanted to be, a free spirit.

Sunny's mouth hung open the entire trip, still in shock, I supposed, from her unexpected promotion. When I nodded again, then stepped out of the limousine, my bodyguards escorted the girls inside to their dressing room, removed the blindfolds, and then waited at their assigned stations outside the door.

As I tilted my head up, down, then up again, my girls removed their clothes, showered, and promptly returned for their inspection. They all stood naked beside their vanities. "Sunny, you check 'em."

"But, Madam?"

"But what? Don't think small. Think big."

If Sunny was serious about being on the streets, I had to prepare her to become a real Madam, not a ho on the stroll begging to suck a dick for twenty dollars. Silently I stood next to Sunny waiting for her to get started.

Beginning with girl number one, Sunny spread her eyelids and checked for white crisp clarity. When Sunny nodded upward, girl number one opened her mouth wide. Leaning in close, Sunny did what I'd normally do. She probed with a wooden stick, checking for chipped teeth, canker sores, fever blisters, halitosis, and anything else out of the ordinary. Then she swiped the girl's mouth with an oral HIV test strip before placing it inside the sterile container.

"Excellent," I said.

Sunny circled her finger in the air and girl number one turned around, then bent over, touching the floor. Easing on a pair of rubber gloves, Sunny spread girl number one's cheeks and her lips, then sniffed, checking for any signs of malodor that would indicate the girl hadn't washed thoroughly. Slipping her finger inside the girl's pussy, Sunny scooped deep inside for any discolored discharge signaling a possible yeast infection or blood to see if the girl was beginning or ending her menstrual cycle.

Damn! I was impressed. Sunny really had this shit down.

Scanning the rest of the girls' bodies, from their hair follicles for lice to their fingernails for dirt to their toes for calluses, Sunny said, "Get dressed."

All except one of the girls got clearance from Sunny. I was seriously considering replacing this girl because she repeatedly cost us money. This time, she had a tiny puss-filled pimple on her ass and Sunny caught that shit, understanding that our clients paid megadollars for spotless girls.

This trick was testing my patience and trying to ruin my reputation for having the best escorts in Las Vegas, but I remained silent. Sunny looked at me. I hunched my shoulders.

"Girl six, you're dismissed. Go home," Sunny firmly said.

Oh, hell no! I intervened, "Girl six, what's up with your weekly breakouts?"

"Madam, I don't know why I—"

Before she finished, I backhand slapped her in the mouth. "You are costing us fifty thousand dollars a night every time I have to send your ass home. You've got one more time to have a rash, a cold sore, or a pimple, and I will beat your ass into the ground, then fire you. You make me sick! Get out of my face."

Raising my hand to strike girl six again, I glanced at Sunny. Our eyes met. Sunny shook her head. Sunny knew how to get her point across without disrespecting me or challenging my authority, but if Sunny was serious about doing this on her own, I wasn't sparing her.

Bam!

"Madam! Please stop! Don't! I'm sorry! I won't let this happen again," girl six cried. "Pleeeaasseeee, Madam, stop!"

Wham! Bam! Stomp! Kick!

Girl six balled into the fetal position, holding what I hoped was a few broken ribs. I looked at Sunny and whispered in her ear, "Is this what you want? No pimp or ho on the street is gonna call you an ambulance when some lunatic john kicks your ass. Step outside that door." I pointed, then continued. "And instruct security to take girl six back to the casino."

When Sunny left I said to girl six, "Put your clothes on and get the hell out. All you have to do is take care of yourself. If you're taking garlic tablets and papaya to keep your weight down, leave that shit alone. Garlic ain't for everybody and that shit will put pimples on the back of your thighs and your ass. Why do you keep disappointing me? Don't I pay you well?"

Girl six nodded.

"You've got exactly thirty minutes to get home and if you don't answer your home phone when I call you, you're gonna make Madam angrier."

Girl number ten, Onyx, rolled her eyes at me. She thought I didn't see her. The only reason I let her get away with so much was that she was my second highest producer next to Sunny and Sunny's friend, but Onyx wasn't above getting her ass kicked like girl six.

Nodding again, I gave the remaining girls permission to do their makeup, hair, and select their attire for the night. "Onyx, I want you to split girl six's johns with girl number two."

I felt the daggers shooting in my back. It was best I left without looking at Onyx, because if I had to walk over to her vanity, I'd smash her entire cosmetic tray in her face so hard she'd have instant foundation on her chin, eye shadow on her cheeks, and lipstick on her forehead.

Exiting the dressing room, I shut the door behind me and walked over to my boss's private study located on the opposite side of the mansion from the dressing room.

Valentino was layered in an all-white tailored suit,

smoking a cigar, with his black hair slicked back underneath a matching fedora.

"This is a change," I said, slanting Valentino's hat. "So, where are we going?"

Blowing smoke in my face, Valentino said, "Bitch, don't question me. I got shit to do. Keep your ass here. Watch, but don't touch, my money. I'll be back when I get back."

Valentino's hard-core attitude was a front for an empire that I'd taken over from day one, but I liked his arrogance. Waiting twenty minutes to make sure he was gone, I removed my audio recording from inside a book I'd placed on his shelf. I had to know everything that happened in Valentino's study while I was away in case his ass was planning to double-cross me.

While listening to the tape, I observed the girls getting dressed via the monitors in Valentino's study. Stiffening into a trance, I couldn't believe what I'd heard.

"Yeah, man. Straight. She's gotten too big too quick. It's barely been a year."

"For real, G. Fire her, dude."

Was that the voice of my security guard, Reynolds, suggesting my boss fire somebody?

"Straight, but I have to find another bitch to replace her first."

"What about me? I mean, I'm no female but I could be on your team. I protect your shit every night."

I stuck my finger in my ear and replayed the tape in disbelief.

Valentino replied, "I'll tell you what, kill her and job is yours."

CHAPTER 5

Sunny

Words were empty unless people gave them meaning.

Deep inside I believed most people wanted and some needed to feel appreciated. When Lace placed her business card in my hand, I felt an unspoken connection. And although I didn't need her approval to validate my work ethics, her small gesture made me feel important. But watching Lace beat girl number six scared me 'cause I'd never seen that side of my madam. Sure, she'd slapped all of us a time or two, but kicking and stomping? That was new.

After Lace left the dressing room, I sat at my vanity observing the other girls. While waiting for security to come get us, I opened the gift Lace had given me earlier. "Oh my God." What did this gorgeous sparkling Rolex mean? *I love it!* I thought, securing the watch on my wrist.

There was no sense in having Lace delegate authority to me if I wasn't going to use it. Outside of my parents, I cared about Onyx, Starlet, and my best friend, Sapphire Bleu, almost as much as I loved my twin sister, Summer, whom I hadn't seen in months or spoken with in weeks.

Sapphire knew more about prostitution than Lace, but there was no way I could tell my madam that my best friend was a cop. Sapphire and I talked two to three times a day. She was my mental support person, kinda like a therapist who'd allowed me to express my feelings without judgment. Sapphire admired my lifestyle while I envied hers. She was the hottest, sexiest, undercover female that got paid to arrest the types of men I serviced. Sapphire never had to suck a dick or turn a trick she didn't want to. But endangering our lives was the one thing we had in common. Almost every day Sapphire told me stories about missing prostitutes, generally teenage runaways, who were found dead on the streets or in hotel rooms in Las Vegas, so I was sure Sapphire would flip like Madam if I'd mention working the streets. I was no fool and definitely not serious about turning a twenty-dollar trick after watching Madam beat girl six.

I'm grateful that Sapphire has been my mentor and friend about as long as I've worked in this business. One day I'm gonna take her up on her offer and go with her to the firing range. Sapphire strongly stated, "Every woman needs two boyfriends: Smith and Wesson. If every woman knew how to handle a gun better than her man, I bet women wouldn't have to worry about men beating on them. Shoot his ass, then use the one line that works in any court of law: "I was in fear of my life. It's called self-defense."

Being ten years older and decades wiser, Sapphire helped me understand men better. "Against my recommendation, you can keep giving up your sweet pussy, Sunshine, but the one thing you must promise me you'll never do is give away your pussy power."

I'd heard that phrase a lot lately. Must be some new movement toward female empowerment.

Shaking my head, I wondered, *What does pussy power really mean?*

Before I asked, Sapphire had answered, "Pussy power has the same effect over men that kryptonite has over Superman. Every woman has kryptonite. It's your ability to control every man in any situation. You've got to believe you possess the power, Sunshine. You've got to believe in yourself, lovely."

I was glad I started talking to Sapphire at the bar that night, thinking she was one of Valentino's girls, or else we would never have met. Funny how your future best friend can be sitting right next to you and if you never say hello, you'll never know. Sapphire thought I was lying to her when I told her how much money I made.

"Dang, girl, you know how long it takes me to make that kind of money? Don't tell me anything else about this Valentino jerk, not even his last name, because it pisses me off how much money these so-called high-class pimps make off of women. What you make is cool and all, but I know it's nowhere near what he's getting paid. I wish I could arrest all of these opportunistic assholes, johns included, but then like on that television show we'd have to lock up the teachers, the preachers, the pimps, and the parents, and then we'd end up with a bunch of snotty-nose illiterate kids dropping out of school."

Sapphire had a sense of humor that could match her bad temperament, but Lace's sensitivity earlier tonight had taken me aback. Indirectly Lace reinforced what I'd been thinking, to do something that I wanted. But what did I want out of life? Surely prostitution didn't come with retirement benefits, and at my age, retirement seemed a lifetime away. In a few years there'd be someone prettier, smarter, and freakier to replace all of us.

Walking over to Onyx's vanity, I held her hand and said, "It's okay, O, don't let Lace get to you. You know me. I'm the wifee now and every girl here tonight will take care of the other. We're all picking up an extra fifteen to thirty minutes to cover girl six's johns. Including me."

Locking her arms around my neck, Onyx said, "Thanks, Sunny. I don't know what I'd do without you."

"O, you know what you really need to do. Leave that jealous-ass husband of yours. If he finds out what you're doing, he'll kill you. Then I'd have to have Sapphire kill him. Look," I said, easing the key to my new condo in Onyx's hand, "hold on to this. Don't ever give your husband my address, but if you need a safe place to stay, you don't have to ask. Just come. You don't have to call first or let me know in advance. I want you to be safe until you buy a place of your own. Preferably outside Nevada. Got it?"

Listen to me trying to advise my girl. Maybe helping others was my calling. I was a pretty good motivator. My mother always taught my sister and me that in every situation, we had to protect one another. I felt the same way about O and Starlet. Sapphire was my only friend who appeared to be in control all the time.

Onyx's eyes filled with tears as she hugged me tight. We didn't need to exchange another word. I'd duplicate the spare house key hidden under my car mat. For different reasons, Onyx, Starlet, and Sapphire each had a key to my condo.

Click.

Security opened the dressing room door. One by one

we piled back into the limo, where we were blind-folded again. I remained silent until we arrived at our nightly spot referred to as Immaculate Perception, but no one knew the street or the address. Once we heard a heavy gate close, the bodyguards removed our blind-folds. The cemented walls were so high the only thing I noticed in the distance was the glowing red needle-point that topped the Stratosphere Hotel and Casino.

Inside, there had to be at least fifty horny men of varying nationalities. The moment they saw us, lust filled their eyes. As usual the mumbling and pointing started immediately as we modeled along the sparkling platinum carpet that twinkled like stars.

Pointing out ten different men, I inquired about their preferences, paired them up with the girls of their choice, then listened to Reynolds instruct the remain-ders, "Make yourselves comfortable in the casino area, gentlemen, or at the bar. If you want to walk around, you are welcome to observe other couples, but you cannot participate unless invited. You are also re-stricted to activities on the second floor. The third floor is off-limits and reserved for private, top-paying *regu-lars*. If I catch you in unauthorized areas"—Reynolds flexed his biceps, then continued—"I'm throwing you out permanently. If you need a picker-upper of any kind, see me."

Utilizing the word *regular* was one of our incentives to have those egotesticle johns pay more for our ser-vices.

"Don't worry, we'll be back to fuck all of you too," I said with a wink, sashaying up the staircase. "At Im-maculate Perception you get what you pay for."

Those idiots stood down there cheering like they'd won the megalottery.

Making my way to the Presidential Suite on the third

floor, I entered a room so dark I couldn't see my hand in front of my face.

"I swear, the more money these guys pay, the stranger they are." Sometimes I wished I had normal johns like the other girls instead of servicing the highest-paying clients.

I tapped the light switch. "Oh, shit." This was a first. That fool had a black satin bag over his head gathered with a drawstring around his neck with a hat on his head. Two tiny holes were cropped so close all I saw were his dark pupils. Probably some preacher or deacon from my parents' church or a big-time baller with a wife and kids.

"I want you to dance for me," he said, reclining on the sofa while setting the white fedora next to him. Fingering his single-breasted jacket with one hand, he opened his white jacket, spreading his long-lean thighs, then massaged the crotch of his white pants.

Pressing the power button on the remote, I turned on the music and began swaying slowly in the space in front of him. Biting the tip of my nail, I lowered my gaze, then moaned, "Mmmm. I can't wait to taste you." Gliding my fingers over his slick bag, I wanted to yank it off.

"Don't touch my head, bitch. Just do as I say."

Relinquishing my kryptonite in exchange for my salary, I seductively straddled his lap, rotating my ass on his hard dick. "Tell me how hot you'd like me."

Sliding my thong to the side, he released his dick from behind the zipper and rubbed the head on my ass. I prayed, *Not another night of anal penetration.*

"Turn around. I want you on your knees, bitch. And I want you to take all of this dick," he said, squeezing his shaft at the base, then continued, "inside your hot mouth. I miss you, baby."

Whatever, freak.

Kneeling before him, I reached for the gold and black condom packet on the coffee table.

"Uh-uh. That's not how we do it. I want to feel you," he said, stroking his engorged head on my glossy lips.

Leaning my forehead into his stomach, I began licking, spitting, and groaning while working my hand up and down his shaft. Proudly I'd learned how to master giving a blowjob without letting them cum in my mouth.

He pulled my hair, lifting my head. "I said suck my dick. And lick my balls. I want it all. You're not clever, bitch. I want you hotter than a summer day in July. I paid fifty thousand dollars for five hours and I want you all to myself all night long. I want to feel my dick against your esophagus and I want you to swallow every drop of my cum. I'm gonna fuck you doggy-style, upside down, and I'm saving that swing over there for last or maybe I'll have you put those hot stones in my ass, then fuck the shit out of you on the balcony so everyone in North Las Vegas can hear you scream while I shoot this cream up your ass. I'm your daddy now, bitch. You do as I say."

Sadly enough I was immune to the profanity as it was part of many men's fantasy to call a woman a bitch while having their dick sucked.

Hmm, North Las Vegas, that's where I lived off Martin Luther King and Ann Road. They say most accidents happen within a one-mile radius of your home. Was I passing where I worked on my way to the strip?

Hmm, there was something about the way he said "summer" that made me think of my sister. Five fucking hours? So much for me helping out Onyx. This was gonna be one long-ass night. I knew what to do to his ass.

"Mmmm," I moaned, softly, kissing his plump head

oozing with precum. "You have the prettiest dick I've ever seen."

"Then lick it, bitch," he said, palming the back of my head.

"Like this?" I said, twirling my tongue around his balls. "Or like this?" I asked, slowly trailing a line of spit up his shaft. Desperately I wanted to snatch that bag off his damn head so I could see his face. I lowered my mouth over his head, sucking gently, then harder, then a lot harder.

"You want it rough and fast or slow and succulent?"

Before he answered, I eased my mouth over his entire shaft and swallowed hard several times.

"Oh, shit! Bitch, you making me cum without my permission. Back the fuck up."

Tightening my throat, I lifted my head, drawing all the cum out of him. His body shivered. I trickled his sperms back onto his dick as I continued stroking him.

"You taste so good," I lied. "Relax, you'll get your money's worth. I'll get him back up in a few minutes with this," I said, placing his hand on my bare pussy.

Making my way to the bathroom to spit out the sperms that didn't make it to my stomach, I heard him say, "Damn, baby, you've learned a lot."

CHAPTER 6

Sunny

What started out six months ago as a brilliant get-rich-quick scheme unexpectedly transitioned into the worst decision of my life! An epiphany, a paradigm shift—I didn't care what one called it, I wanted to quit! Who in the hell did I fuck last night? That bothered me all day because obviously he knew me.

What in the world was I thinking?

Voluntarily putting my pussy on auction to the highest bidder left me feeling slimier than a green snail crawling on its belly.

Preparing for another night of prostitution in the glitzy and oh-so-seemingly glamorous city of Las Vegas, I sat in front of my designated vanity—surrounded by lights and cameras—incapacitated by depression. Fear weighed so heavily on my neck and shoulders that my head practically hung in my lap. I wanted to lift my eyelids but I couldn't. What if I gazed into the mirror of my soul? What would I see? Who would I see? Definitely not the sweet, innocent little girl I . . . I paused, then exhaled.

The men I had sex with, like the one last night, never saw my inner beauty. All they wanted was "Action!" And as long as I was the center of attention, I allowed those men to do whatever they wanted, including making me feel worthless.

Take one! Take two! Cut! Action! Sunny, that's my girl, one more time, from the top. Move your ass. Let's go! Action, baby, action! You're a keeper, doll.

Yeah, but for how long?

Willingly I played the leading role, the fool, some may say, but they don't know me! I'm a good girl. Maybe too good.

Slowly I swiveled my vanity chair one hundred eighty degrees. I lifted my head, but I couldn't dare face the mirror 'cause I knew he was there. Not physically. Not visibly on my shoulder with a red pitchfork. His presence was mental. Ready and waiting to intimidate me once more. So instead of finding the courage to face my fears and quit what I never should've started, I listened to his haunting voice resounding in my ear.

Imagining how Valentino set his prices, the auctioneer inside my head shouted, "Can I get ten . . . ten . . . can I get fifteen for this fine specimen of a woman?. . . Fifteen to the gentleman in the corner . . . twenty up front . . . can I get twenty-five for a night of unforgettable pleasure?. . . Twenty-five to the man right here . . . can I get thirty if she gets real dirty?. . . Thirty to the distinguished man in the blue tailor-made suit . . . can I get thirty-five?. . . Thirty going once, going twice, sold, to the gentleman in the blue tailor-made suit for thirty thousand dollars!"

The john's filthy-rich salty spit licked onto my

grimy skin burning my self-esteem into green mush forcing me to crawl back into my shell. Forget him. Tonight this wasn't about him or them. It was about me.

Pivoting in my chair, I stared at the black-tinted windows surrounding the dressing room. I couldn't see a thing. No one could see in. None of us could see out. I was tired of this shit, knowing something was wrong when Lace hadn't shown up at the casino to meet us or at Valentino's mansion to do her job. I knew she couldn't be trusted. No one in this type of business can be trusted.

I whispered, "I hate myself." Refusing to do another inspection, I said to the group, "Y'all get dressed."

Why did I think I knew it all? Right now, I could've been at home in my room watching my favorite TV show, *Project Runway*, fixing my favorite cereal, Cocoa Puffs, waiting for the milk to turn chocolatey while chatting on the phone with Sapphire, or relaxing rereading my favorite book, *So You Call Yourself a Man*, by Carl Weber.

Why didn't I listen to my mother and stay home like my twin sister until I graduated from college? No, I had to open my big mouth. "Mom, you're too old to understand my generation. Things are different for us. We don't go to church three times a week. I got this. I can make it on my own . . . besides, I'm grown. Mom, please stop telling me what to do."

Dangling my red leather strapless diamond-heel stiletto on my French-pedicured toe, I laughed inside to keep from crying. Nodding, I thought, *You had to be a smart ass, didn't cha?* I'm entitled to make mistakes, aren't I? Right now all I want is to call my mommy and say, "I'm sorry." Oh my God, what if my dad answers the phone instead?

Retrieving my hot-pink cell phone from underneath the gold thong I was wearing, I watched them get ready, including my best friends, Onyx and Starlet. Everyone was oblivious of my "I can't do this anymore" attitude. Eleven drop-dead-gorgeous females scurried around the dressing room fussing over which high-priced outfits to wear.

I don't wanna be wifee anymore. Where's Lace? Where's my madam?

Discreetly, using my camera phone, I snapped a few pictures of the girls getting dressed. I sent Sapphire a quick text: *My place at 6 a.m.* Then I took pictures of the room and a few of myself sitting in front the bright mirror. This was my finale.

"I got myself into this mess. Surely I'm slick enough to get out." Quietly I reprimanded myself. *Stupid. Stupid. Stupid.*

Not so long ago someone cared about more than my wicked tongue, my beautiful spirit, and my exotic looks. I'd heard them say, "Is she black? Is she white? Man, with an ass like that she's gotta be Brazilian." Who honestly cared? My high school sweetheart, that's who. But his menial busboy income, ordinary looks, down-to-earth western drawl, and laid-back personality weren't enough for a girl like me who was told every single day, "Wow! You're gorgeous."

I wanted more out of life than a thirty-dollar date— more money, more clothes, more fun, and more drugs. Actually, I needed more and more XTC to get me through the night, nights of not so pleasant pleasantry. Tossing my head back, I swallowed two small pills.

Lost and confused, I hopelessly stood on an invisible auction block. No one made me stay, yet I couldn't take the necessary two steps down to walk away and leave this lifestyle forever.

What was I afraid of? Better question, who?

Hiding the metallic phone between my palms, I felt the mental shackles weighing heavily on my spirit. Incarcerated, held prisoner in my mind, all because Lace introduced me via a conference call to a man who'd told me he could show me how to make a quick dollar, quote unquote, some real money, utilizing the best asset God gave me: pussy, one of the few commodities I could simultaneously sell and maintain possession of my entire life.

Objectively I agreed but subjectively Sapphire was right. Why was I selling my pussy to make money for a man? A man I didn't know, hadn't seen, didn't love, and recently hated with such passion that vomit percolated in my throat like hot lava. During my initial telephone interview, that man, Valentino James, and that woman, Lace, whom I'd grown to like, failed to highlight my intellect, my loving spirit, or my independence. From my first day of work, they did all the thinking for me, including Lace telling me last night that I had to get out of the business. I felt Lace really cared about me. Maybe the talk we had at the casino bar was her discreet way of telling me she was quitting and leaving me in charge.

If I was supposedly, as they claimed, invaluable, then why was everything a secret? Valentino, a modern day Charlie from that throwback TV show *Charlie's Angels,* was a mystery man to all of his girls. Lace said I was her personal pick—girl number twelve. I was the last of her girls hired along with Onyx and Starlet, so she supposedly had some special affinity for me, for us. Like being in a gang, rumor had it, once hired, none of Valentino's girls could quit. Not alive. Maybe Lace was setting me up to get arrested or something. Naw, she wouldn't do that to me.

Glancing around the five-hundred-square-foot dressing room at my counterparts preparing for their fuck festival, I wondered, what made us do this? Top models who never quite made it to the top. Maybe it was the amazing layout of the space. A huge room bursting with the latest designer everything, perfect for an aspiring model's go-see: Tiffany's jewelry, clothes, shoes, Juicy Couture purses, underwear, wigs . . . everything a woman needed to wear in order to make a man look good right before stroking his ego, then sucking his dick. What hurt most was, we weren't permitted to keep any of this stuff. Especially not the semen-stained underwear that could be used as evidence against Valentino and Lace.

"You okay?" Starlet asked, sitting in her makeup chair next to mine.

Turning on my CD player, I said, "I can't do this anymore, Star." With trembling hands clinging to each armrest, I continued. "I'm tired of sleeping with strange men every night, letting them have their way with me. This is destroying my body and my self-esteem. Yours too. You know you don't like having these chauvinistic wealthy pigs waddle all in your pussy, especially the old farts, fucking us with everything except their dick. I want out. We started together. Let's quit together. Come with me, Star. And let's take O with us too."

Gasping, Starlet inhaled, then whispered, "Are you crazy? Is that a cell phone? You're gonna get all of us strip-searched if Valentino finds out. And Valentino's arranged strip searches are worse than getting fucked by a trick with a twelve-inch dick."

My eyes followed Starlet's stunning amber and gray ones around the room until Starlet looked toward the floor, then continued, "I'm going to pretend you didn't say no dumb stuff like quitting, Sunny." Gently, Starlet held my hands. "Listen, all we have to do is get these guys off for a few hours and we're done. I'll help you get through the night. I'll even do your tricks for you if you want me to. Just finish getting ready, okay?"

"Yeah, tonight, but what about tomorrow night, and the next night?" I countered.

"So what? You're the top girl and you make two grand flippin' tricks. Two grand a night cash and that's more money than any of us and more than you made flippin' burgers at In-and-Out, so what you complaining about?"

"I feel dirty, Star. Like I can't wash 'em off me. At least I could wash off the smell of beef patties and french fries. But the semen in my mouth"—I swallowed, digging my fingernails under my chin—"the sperm trickling down my throat"—I shrieked, clawing my nails down to my collarbone, peeling away layers of radiant flesh. "When they cum inside me, I can't get it, get them . . ." Fighting back tears, I blinked repeatedly, then sniffed, "Y'all go ahead without me."

Fluttering away her tears, Starlet squeezed my hands. "Stop it, Sunny. You're hurting yourself and me too." Starlet's bronzy-colored lips pressed against my forehead, then lingered for a moment. "I can't watch you do this to yourself. I gotta finish getting ready, but whatever you do, don't do anything stupid like break any more of Valentino's rules. You're in charge tonight. Do like Lace. Just chill right here until we get back."

"Fuck Valentino!" I shouted. "I hate his fuckin' ass!"

A wave of silence penetrated the entire room as eleven shoo-shooing females hushed in unison.

Starlet commented, "Where's Lace when we need her?"

Yeah, where was Lace?

I whispered, "I'm tired of men and all their fucking one-sided rules! What about me? Don't I have an opinion?! Don't I have some say in whose dick penetrates my pussy? I hope Valentino's balls fall off and roll across the floor like meatballs so I can crush 'em! Dirty bastard!"

One at a time the escorts resumed their conversations as I overheard girl six say, "Last hired. First fired. Sunny can't handle the pressure. At the rate she's going, she'll be dead before midnight. She's overpaid anyway. Listen to me, y'all use her as an example of what not to do."

Girl six had justification for her jealousy when Lace had announced, "Sunny is the new wifee. If there's a problem on the set, what Sunny says goes."

Was this girl six's way of showing animosity toward me? I wasn't the one who kicked her ass, yet she respected Lace while disrespecting me. I should find another pimple on girl six's ass and send her home for the hell of it.

Women hated on me worse than men. Women like girl six, who knew nothing about me, detested me simply because I was adorable, with light skin and blond hair. I knew I was a black woman and proud of it, but they thought that I felt I was white, I guess because I wasn't black enough to them. Girl six was remarkably picturesque, but like other women, she masked her low self-esteem by criticizing females.

A woman's self-induced inferiority complex could have me butt naked down on my knees sucking her man's dick the second I entered the room. Women considered me a serious threat to their relationship like I wanted their men when it was their men who wanted me, paid to fuck me, and sexed me to the best of their agility because I represented every man's fantasy fuck. Not to say he didn't want his woman, but when he showed up at IP, he preferred me.

Onyx hurried over and pleaded, "Sunny, hush, girl. Stop talking crazy and get dressed so we can get the hell up outta here. In a couple of hours Star and I can go to your new spot and talk about this privately, but this is not the time or place to go dumb." Onyx pivoted my chair, shifted her eyes toward the mirror, stared into mine, then said, "You know he's watching us. Oh my God, what happened to your neck?"

Ignoring Onyx, I said quietly, "I can't go." Jabbing my middle finger in the air toward the camera, I mouthed, "Screw you, Mr. Big Shot." I had to confront Valentino. Where in the hell did he get off living the lifestyle of the rich and infamous at our expense?

Onyx gasped as Starlet's eyes almost popped out of the sockets.

Calmly, lowering my hand to my lap, I promised, "I won't do anything else I shouldn't do. But if something happens to me"—my eyes filled with salty tears that flowed into my wounds—"swear to me you won't tell my parents the truth about what we do. I need y'all to cover for me tonight too. Star, you tell the limo driver I'm in charge tonight, and, O, you back her up confirming Lace will bring me over when she arrives."

Onyx's lips tightened. "If Valentino finds out about this, he'll kill each of us. You know that, right?"

With confidence I replied, "By the time he finds out, I might kill him."

Onyx shook her head and mumbled, "I give up," then walked away. Wasn't the first time someone had given up on me.

Easing from the makeup chair, I glanced at my plump shiny golden lips. Lips that men craved, then raved about having on their dicks. Confidently I whispered, "I'm nobody's whore anymore."

CHAPTER 7

Lace

"Lick my pussy, B."

Gripping Benito's ears, I shifted his mouth directly over my voluptuous pussy. "That's it. Right there. No, baby, not my clit. Not yet, Daddy." Slowly I swerved sideways, thrusting my precious pearl against his full sexy lips with each word. "Damn, your hard, hot tongue feels so fuckin' good, Daddy, I can't stop cumming."

Vigorously Benito's head shook side to side.

The leopard faux fur throw I'd sprawled on the living room floor puckered underneath my ass. Mimicking making a snow angel, I surrendered to the fluffy hairs, creating a cool breeze beneath my angel wings. Imagining flying high above clouds of joy, I envisioned heaven must feel like having a nonstop orgasm.

"You okay, baby?" B asked, interrupting my visual of doing to Sunny what he was doing to me.

"Uh-huh, I'm real good. You just keep licking. Stay focused. Stay focused."

My eyes scrolled toward my brows. Glancing at the plain white walls, I saw that no pictures hung in the living room of my cozy house with two master bedrooms and two and a half baths in upscale Windsor Estates. If there was a God, he had to know I'd had more than my fair share of hardships. I bought this cul-de-sac home for what it offered on the inside: privacy, peace, and serenity with an exterior backdrop of the rustic mountains hugging the city limits of North Las Vegas.

Relishing the tingling sensation between my thighs, I whispered, "That feels sooo good, B. You're the best, Daddy."

Although I truly loved B, I didn't trust myself to surrender and make love to him, so I simply enjoyed the moments we shared. For the first time in my life, I had sex whenever I wanted. For the first time in my life, sex was pleasurable. But many other facets of my life were not. Like pretending I was cool knowing my boss was plotting to have me killed.

Resuming swishing my arms in the softness, I wished I would've had the fortitude to torment the men that fucked me over. Why I tolerated so much abuse I had no idea. Getting real, I thought, *Yes, I do.* I accepted their abuse because I hadn't learned how to love myself. I'm not sure if I know how to love myself now but I'm working on it. And I've changed my mind about firing Sunny tomorrow night. Tonight was Sunny's last night, right after I finished my fantasy of being with her.

I was thankful those abusive days were gone for Sunny and me. All the things I'd done to please my ex-men I refused to do for Benito. No stripping, no role-playing, and definitely no massages. No cooking, cleaning the house, or washing clothes, like I'd done for the madam at Pussyland. To earn my full-time stay I became her part-time maid for eleven long arduous years. Now all of the chores in my home were Benito's job and the least he could do since I was our primary source of income and he was at my house all damn day.

"Your pussy tastes sweeter than honey. Um, um, um, so good, woman, I could eat your pussy forever," Benito mumbled, lapping his tongue between my lip and my shaft.

Hm, sweeter than honey. He was absolutely right.

My fingertips danced in B's short wavy hair. Why couldn't I love him completely? With B around all the time, I felt his love for me. I could stay with him forever, but never could I escape my past. All those years working at the ranch made me insensitive toward men.

I'd watched a john take his last breath while refusing to give him one of mine. I knew CPR and easily could've saved his life or at least tried. Instead I stared into his sunken blue eyes feeling no remorse. I'd secretly done the world a favor adding one less jerk to womankind. Deep inside, I knew I had a heart, but sometimes I wasn't sure if it was beating. If there truly was a heaven, I'm headed straight to hell, but hell would have to wait until I redeemed myself, and God knows how long that'll take.

I braced Benito's forehead with my palm. "Aw, shit," I hissed. "Slow down. You gon' make me cum too fast, Daddy. Oh yeah, wiggle the tip of your tongue inside me. Now up and down my shaft. Come on, B, go slower, baby."

There were so many more ways I could please Benito in bed, but the skills I possessed were supposedly reserved exclusively for sexperts and prostitutes with names like Tongue-a-luscious and Wonder Pussy.

Panting to catch my breath, I pinched my nipples, then watched those babies harden as I trembled with pleasure while B trickled warm drops of saliva on my clit.

"Tell me how you want it, Lace. I'm never satisfied until you've finished cuming," Benito groaned, burying his face in my Brazilian-waxed pussy.

At first I was scared to have the hairs snatched off my pussy, but now pain for me was pleasurable. The silkiness of my fresh pussy was amazingly orgasmic for both of us. My pussy felt so exhilarating I wanted to show her to the world. I cherished my kitty cat more than I loved B.

Rubbing B's face in my secretions, I relished his undying desire to please me in and out of the bedroom. B would do anything for me . . . including die. In return, I definitely had his back but not quite like that. I wasn't dying for anyone, especially a man.

Cuming a little, I grunted, "Yeah, B. Shit yeah. Move your tongue up my pussy, um, down the other side, yes, yes, baby, please go slower."

"Oh Lawd," I gasped when Benito's tongue made its way down the other side, then darted straight up the middle of my shaft, lightly fluttering on the tip of my clit, meshing his spit with my cum. "You are soooo wrong for that shit." My spine flattened against the floor, shooting my hips upward and stuffing my pussy deeper into B's mouth.

Benito hummed, "Mmmmm," as he flicked his tongue.

"Oh, baby. Suck her softly. Please," I begged, scratching the crown of Benito's head.

Brushing away my hands, Benito squeezed my breasts, forcing me to release another orgasm. My body tingled all over. This orgasm lasted longer than the one before. B's ultramoist succulent lips made my stomach rise. Arching my back, I enjoyed multiple orgasms. Embarking upon a major climatic explosion, I withheld releasing the big one, fearing I'd fall asleep afterward, but being late for work wasn't an option.

I was a perfectionist and Valentino was sporadically a loose cannon. He was the type of man who would act first, then say "Fuck it" later. Lately he'd mentioned starting a family. What kind of woman would marry a pimp? Or how could Valentino be a role model for children, including his own? His mind was set on Sunny, but Sunny deserved better. Valentino would never choose a woman like me. A woman he couldn't control. A woman smarter than him. Valentino wanted a nanny-trophy-beautiful wife to birth and rear his offspring, fuck him, feed him, never talk back, and not complicate his life.

Squeezing my upper vaginal muscles, I held back, careful not to allow the epileptic-like twitching inside my vaginal walls to travel to my G-spot. If I screwed up and did that shit I'd cum so hard my body would go into convulsions.

"Ease up just a little, B," I desperately urged.

"I know what you want," Benito said, yanking me closer. Grabbing his hard dick, he rubbed his head on my slushy pussy. Popping the head in two inches, B thrust upward into my G-spot.

Scooting backward, I screamed, "Ouch! What the fuck was that shit!" knocking B over as I leapt to my feet doing hopscotch in place.

Benito lay there looking up at me. Flip-flopping his hands back and forth, B inspected both sides. "What? My fingers? I was holding my dick."

"I told your dumb ass not to put your raggedy-ass nails anywhere near my pussy until you got a manicure!"

Rising on his knees, B yelled, "Get out of my face with that, Lace! I just got my nails done this morning."

Holding his hands high in the air, Benito rambled on, "See? Look at them. I even got two coats of clear just the way you like. I'm not going down this road with you again! I barely touched you!"

"You're just like Don, B! You're a good-for-nothing-but-a-wet-dream son of a bitch! I ask you to do one simple thing . . . tell the truth . . . and you can't even get that right! Dumb fuck."

B's dick hung south along with his chin. "How many times am I going to have to pay another man's debt? Huh? You won't tell me what he did to you, but I keep getting blamed. Serious, Lace, you need to see a psychiatrist."

"You callin' me crazy? Fuck you! You need to take your freeloading ass home! Oh yeah. That's right. What home!" I yelled in his face, staring down on him.

Whenever I threatened to kick B out, he conceded. But he was right. Don's jagged nails against my pussy left me emotionally scarred. Not a day went by when I didn't blame myself or Benito for what Don had done to me. I refused to look at B's nails, afraid that bad memories would resurface of how I obsessively filed my johns' fingernails before I allowed them to touch me. If it weren't for Don's lying ass, I'd probably have a good job at a respectable firm making a decent living.

Decent. The most judgmental word in the dictionary was meaningless in a so-called free country. People condemning one another as if their opinions were gospel when in fact their opinions didn't mean shit. Not to me anyway. Where in the hell were those dressed-in-all-white missionaries of the church when I was molested, then kicked out on the streets? Probably at Sunday morning service sitting a few pews ahead of another girl like me mumbling under their breath to one another about how indecent that little girl was.

I heard them shoo-shooing about me. "Uh-huh. I

heard she fast. Doing all them nasty things with grown mens . . . Amen! Hallelujah! All right, Rev, tell the truth and shame the devil! . . . Sister, where was I? Oh yeah, she almost stole her mama's husband. Somebody needs to tell her her kind ain't welcome in the House of the Lord."

What a difference a day makes? That one night sleeping on the porch and sitting in church changed my entire life. Weren't those missionaries supposed to help save me? A tear fell onto my cheek.

B wiped it away, then affectionately said, "I'm sorry, baby. I need to be more understanding," then gently placed his hands beside his hips. "Let me finish what I started."

Benito's eyes bypassed my navel as he stared up at me.

Did I just see B narrow his eyes before nestling his cheek into my pussy? Was that a look of disgust for me or the situation at hand? I made a mental note of that shit. I could look in a man's eyes and simultaneously know his intentions and his deepest desires. B was pissed at me but couldn't do shit to his satisfaction because he had no place to go.

A cutting of the eyes to the corners with a pensive frozen stare meant he was plotting his next move against me. Droopy eyes that softened indicated he needed my affection but didn't want to ask. He expected me to read his mind. And in that moment if I showed him affection, instantly he became submissive. That was the time when I could ask for the world, and he'd give me all he had to offer.

That window of opportunity for women lasted a split second. If she blinked, she missed it. And the look B just gave me signaled inner hatred suppressed behind his thoughts of bashing my face in for crushing his manhood. Most men didn't hide their anger. Too many women were busy trying to rescue abusive men. Oblivious of the warning signs, women blindly walked wide-eyed into danger.

There was so much I'd learned from observing a man's body language, listening to his speech patterns, and reading between his words that I could teach a class on how to recognize an abusive man before he strikes from the inside out.

Benito leaned closer, holding me firm, then gentle as a lamb as if he were asking for forgiveness of his thoughts. As I stepped back, my foot slid against a familiar piece of plastic that I must've forgotten to remove from the throw after peeling away the price tag.

There was no time for an apology. The money-millionaires were in town tonight and they were dropping C-notes like confetti, so I couldn't dare be late for work.

Glancing at the digital clock on the coffee table, I saw I had a good thirty minutes to spare. I moaned when Benito's lips kissed my clit, trying not to let my personal issues cloud my true feelings. The more I came uncontrollably, the more I wanted to spend the rest of my life with this man. I was completely aware of my emotional attachment to Benito and his insatiable appetite for me.

Benito was different. I was his fan long before Valentino introduced us. Watching Benito on TV in his tight football uniform, connecting his precision bombs to his running backs and wide receivers, and seeing him sport his championship ring on television made me fantasize about him many nights while he didn't know I existed.

B's stats during his ten years in the league were 197 touchdowns passing, 36 rushing, 26,259 yards passing, 3,700 rushing. I knew how many first, second, third, and fourth downs he'd gotten. I could give a play-by-play recount better than any commentator of all Benito's games. Now that he was mine, I wasn't sure how long I could keep him, but I was positive I was not going to a therapist.

At the end of the day, after working long hours through the night, I was grateful to have someone waiting at home for me. Benito was my star. In many ways my savior. Before Benito, no man had ever consistently cared about me. They weren't around long enough to. After our first month together I thought B would change. A year later, he still did all the things he'd done when we first met and more, including tolerate my relentless, selfish, won't-admit-when-I'm-wrong attitude. B did simple things like massage my feet, suck my toes, and run my bathwater every time I arrived home from work at five, sometimes six in the morning.

At first I resisted dating Benito because while professionally playing football, he was one of Valentino's top clients and I was the top-paid whore at Pussyland. The day Benito hung up his jersey, coincidentally I'd literally serviced my last john.

Valentino sat in my room at the Pussyland Ranch negotiating his fee like all the other tricks. Valentino was well known for stealing girls and hiring them to work for him. That evening we sat on my bed doing the usual back-and-forth.

"So, what would you like, handsome?" I'd asked him.

"What's your specialty?" he asked, tugging the straps on my lace bustier.

"I can suck you real good, fuck you until your dick falls off—"

He interrupted me, "Or?" staring at my ass.

"Or what?" I questioned with a frown, ready to have the madam escort his arrogant ass out of my room before I fucked him unconscious. Valentino was so fine he made my pussy drip every time he licked his lips like that L.L. hadn't-dropped-a-hit-in-a-minute Cool J, but who gave a fuck because he was still a sexy-as-hell rapper.

"You could let me fuck you in the ass."

"Anal sex is against the rules and out of the question. You can get that from your girls."

Pulling out a stack of hundreds, Valentino placed ten grand in my hands like it was my usual rate. He looked at me. I stared at him, then said, "Get the hell out," throwing the money in his face.

"Straight? You serious?" he asked, drawing his eyebrows together, his forehead buckling.

Standing over him, I replied, "Dead serious. I'm not compromising my livelihood for you or anyone else."

"Lace, I like your style. I guess it's true what I've heard about your no-nonsense reputation. You're exactly the type of madam I'm looking for."

Tightening my lips to conceal my interest, I thought, *Me? Madam?* Opening the door, I demanded, "Get the fuck out and stop playing games."

"Naw, straight. Come work for me and you'll never have to fuck another john. Here's my number. Keep the ten g's as a welcome bonus. I want you to start tomorrow night. Nine sharp. Not nine-oh-one." Tossing the money on my bed, Valentino walked out and I was right behind him.

"Lace, you ready for this dick? I have to get knee deep inside you, baby. My dick is so swollen he's getting a migraine. Let Daddy hit his pussy from the back."

"No way, not the back."

Benito went buck wild, slapping my ass like he was starring in a rodeo. Lying on the faux fur, I spread my legs wide, then pulled Benito's ass close to my pussy. Beads of sweat swished in his hairs slurping against my flesh. Benito wasn't my most creative lover, but what I really liked was how our chemistry sizzled, making him by far my best man. I guess I should thank Valentino.

Once Valentino discovered I was a huge fan of Benito Bannister, he surprised me with a blind date. I didn't know how to act! I mean, I'd never imagined sitting across the table from my brightest star let alone having him fall in love with me.

Benito's ass relaxed as he slowly stroked himself.

Pulling him closer, I yelled, "Stop playing, man, and give me this dick!"

Pressing his chest against my breasts, Benito got serious. "I looovvve you, Lace. Don't ever doubt my love for you."

The sparkle in my eyes shot toward his. After Benito's last game he reassured me he wanted to stop running women and settle down. I thought the real deal was he'd spent the majority of his money on maintaining a player's lifestyle and he was looking to freeload off me. When we first met, Benito owned a big house, fancy cars, and dated lots of women, but I wasn't sure how much money he had. I was still unsure how broke was broke, but he claimed he had his house up for sale and the cars in his garage were bought by one of his former teammates but he didn't sleep around anymore. I was his one and only woman.

B's dick slammed into my pussy so hard the penetration hurt, but that shit felt so good I wanted to cum so bad and he sensed it. Every time my body tensed, B quickly pulled back instead of thrusting like I wanted him to.

"Fuck you, B. Just fuck me deeper!" I yelled, ready to cum all over his dick. My mouth gaped open. I tried to inhale and gulped the air.

Careful not to let his fingernails touch me, B covered my lips and said, "Not yet, Lace. Relax. I know what you want. But I also know what you need. Trust me. Give me a few more minutes of pleasure before Daddy busts this big-ass nut inside you, baby."

Heat consumed my entire body as I tried to focus my energy outward. But I didn't want to lose my momentum. Plus, I had to get ready for work. Shit, I was at the edge of cuming and determined to have a vaginal orgasm instead of a clitoral one. Those clitoral orgasms zapped my energy. But the vaginal orgasm I eagerly awaited to release would boost my energy level so high I'd cum hours after Benito was done.

B swung his thick dick side to side, sticking to the bottom of my pussy with his head a few seconds each time. Instinctively when that next stroke hit, aw, shit! my legs clamped around B's waist, pulling him in closer. Arching my back this time, I pressed my breasts into his chest, burying my face against his sweaty neck and shoulders.

"Ow! Yes! B! Yes! Damn it, baby, I'm coming!" My legs trembled. My juices flowed in waves onto his thick muscular dick for a good sixty seconds. "Deeper, B. Cum with me, baby," I whispered, then screamed louder than before when a second orgasm hit harder than the first. I rotated my hips on his dick until I couldn't cum anymore.

B smiled, arching his back. "Whew, your ass is so good. I love you. But you know you cheated, Lace. You came too soon."

"You'd better quit fucking with me."

"Not this shit again, Lace," Benito said, grabbing my waist. "I'm not finished pleasing you. Come back here, woman."

"Fucking around with you, I'ma have to rush like hell."

"Tell Valentino I was puttin' it down. You can be late one time. For me. Can't cha?"

"No, I can't." I never wanted to find out what Valentino meant when he'd said, "Not nine-oh-one."

Sympathizing with B's desire to continue pleasing me, I said, "Aw, baby. Mama'll make it up to you when she gets back. Promise."

"But you won't be back for six hours. What am I supposed to do?"

Jack off! I don't care! "Get a job so you're not sitting around the house all day and night. Besides, you know what's going down this weekend. I may be three hours late."

"Three hours late!"

"Just like you, I was accustomed to a certain lifestyle before we met and I still am. Business before pleasure. Besides, somebody's gotta pay the bills," I said, tiptoeing to my bathroom. Closing the door, and then pressing the lock, I turned on the shower and waited for the steam to emerge. Before stepping inside the fog, I glanced over at my large white porcelain tub, wishing I had time to soak in some hot bubbly water.

Unexpectedly my thoughts shifted. I whispered, "What makes women cold-hearted toward men?"

Lathering my white exfoliating gloves, I wondered what could make a man so angry that he'd walk into a woman's job, a woman he once made love to, and hate her so much that he'd douse her with gasoline, strike a match, set her ablaze, then walk away like nothing happened. I was so pissed when I read that article on abuse in *Essence* magazine. Those women in Prince George's County living in big ol' beautiful mansions driving expensive cars had the same problems as me, a little girl who'd grown up way too fast in Flagstaff, Arizona.

One thing Sunny had taught me was that the stronger women had to protect weaker women from abusive men.

"Fuck!" A needlelike jolt darted through my breast. "What the hell was that?"

"You okay in there?" Benito asked, jiggling the doorknob.

"I'm fine. Too much hot water," I lied, stepping out of the shower, massaging my back.

I was glad I had B. The way he swaggered when he walked. Dragged certain words when he spoke like, "I love you, Lace." How he laughed deeply from his stomach each time I said something funny. And the way B grabbed my booty when I shook it in his face. No man's stroke of my silky hair was softer. I adored how Benito's muscles bulged when he voluntarily took out the trash. How his thigh muscles hardened when he picked me up. I liked the simple things about our relationship maybe because I'd never had a real relationship.

Rinsing my body, I lathered again, careful not to scrub too hard.

Benito was a charming motherfucka. Most athletes were. But eventually the charm wears off, the lies unfold, and a woman has to either be honest with herself or her whole life becomes one big lie. But I wasn't waiting in vain. Benito wasn't like that. He was honest with me all the time. B wasn't perfect but he was my perfect man.

Tearing a piece of floss, I glided the string between my teeth. Once I stopped wasting my time waiting for Benito to fuck up, our relationship grew stronger. The less I cared, the more he loved me.

Stepping out of the bathroom, I wrapped my body in an oversized towel, thankful I now lived a life better than most of the men I'd serviced. Watching Benito sprawled across my bed was divine. For once, a real man was in my bed. It was hard not to love B. But that was how dumb shit happened. Whenever I forgot, believing everything was right, shit happened. Usually to me.

I watched Benito with his thighs spread stroking his dick. Why did he do that shit every time he knew I had to go to work? His broke ass needed to earn his keep.

I smiled, then said, "I love you, B."

All six feet four inches, two hundred and twenty pounds with muscular quarterback thighs. Full succulent chocolate lips. Nice teeth that were slightly uneven but perfect to me. Although his NFL career was over, Benito still hadn't decided what he wanted to do. Open a nightclub or utilize his communication's degree and become a sports commentator.

Over the past twelve months, I watched Benito's sexy waistline grow from a solid thirty-two inches to a softer thirty-six. But he was still the most handsome sight I'd seen. His attentiveness and confidence held me by his side. The strangest thing about our communication or lack thereof was neither of us ever discussed our family.

"You know what your problem is." Benito paused, then said, "You work too damn much, Lace."

"Hardly enough," I replied, fastening my red garter strap to my sheer stockings, then glanced at the crystal chime clock Benito had given me on our second date. Five minutes.

"When are you going to slow down and give our relationship a real chance? You're not getting any younger, you know, and I want a son. I want us to start a family."

"Get real. What you really want isn't a son. You want a reason for me to gain weight, quit my job, and become your precious trophy wife. And that's what's not going to happen. I'm not ruining my perfect figure for you to marry, then divorce me like you did your ex-wife after she got fat from having the daughter you never take care of or talk to. You know how I feel about you. You're a deadbeat dad. But you're all that matters to me." At that precise moment B was honestly all that mattered. "Not a piece of paper or the promise of this expensive engagement ring on my finger and certainly not a baby," I said, wiggling into my red lace skirt.

"Yeah, whatever. All I have to do is finalize my marketing plan for my sports apparel business. You see, a black man—"

Lifting my eyebrows, I cut B off. "Not now, B. I don't want to hear another one of your soliloquies about the black man's plight, fight, or flight, okay? So, now you're starting a clothing line? Whatever, man."

B walked toward me. "Lace, don't. I don't downplay your ideas. Don't insult my manhood. I'm proud to have a woman like you by my side who's got her shit together." B crisscrossed his hands and said, "But after we get married, no more working at that whorehouse for Valentino. I don't give a damn how much he pays you, I refuse to have my son grow up around prostitutes."

Benito knew that bullshit only mattered because he was no longer in the spotlight. Newcomers had taken over the media and B was no longer an Immaculate Perception client.

I rebutted, "Married? Who said anything about getting married? We're engaged."

I know my thought process was unrealistic but I liked the idea of being engaged but dreaded the thought of a permanent commitment. What if B changed on me? I'd fucked many unhappily married men in my days, and if their wives knew the things they told me— "I hate that bitch! She can't fuck worth a shit! Fat slob done let herself go! I never loved her and wished I hadn't married her lazy trifling ass! I should kill her for the insurance money and buy me a sexy woman like you."—

they would've packed up and moved out while their husbands' dicks were deep inside my pussy.

Frowning, I glimpsed at the digital clock on my nightstand, stared at my watch as I fastened it around my wrist, then looked at B. "Did you change the clock? My watch has ten thirty and that clock," I said, pointing, "has eight thirty."

"Baby, I had to make a little extra time for us somehow. A few minutes won't hurt."

"A few what? You dumb fuck. I knew something didn't feel right. I really can't trust you."

Benito lay across my bed. His lips tightened, then curled upward. "I need you, Lace. More than Valentino. Can't you be okay with putting me first just once?"

"How many football games did you miss 'cause some groupie wanted to suck your dick? Huh?"

"You're not missing work, Lace. You're just a little late."

"Fuck you, B!" The home phone rang, interrupting my thoughts of slapping the shit out of this ignorant just-don't-get-it motherfucka. "If that's Valentino, tell him I'm on my way. I swear, B, you're a good-for-nothing sorry-ass bastard for that one," I yelled before slamming the bedroom door. "If I get fired, your fuckin' ass had best not be here when I get back!"

B yelled, "I love you, baby!"

CHAPTER 8

Sunny

Picking at my natural nails glued underneath the acrylic, Lace was the only person who could've changed my mind. But she was too late. For the first time since I'd started working for Lace, I had to protect myself and my girlfriends from men like Valentino.

"Shit!" I dug from one side to the other, popping off the white tip that flipped into my hair. Separating the strands, I found the piece of plastic and held it in my hand. Sticking my thumb in my mouth, I began wedging my teeth between the remaining acrylic that was fused to my nail. "Ouch! Ouch!" I was suffering so much on the inside, I no longer cared about the self-inflicted pain I'd caused.

Neither Onyx, Starlet, nor I should've accepted this job. But we were young and adventurous, hot and sexy. Onyx had an insanely jealous high school sweetheart whom she'd married knowing that she shouldn't have and he'd go ballistic if he had a clue he wasn't the only man Onyx had fucked. Starlet's fiancé, a professional surfer, who lived in Santa Barbara, California, would call off their wedding if he found out Starlet was a call girl, escort, hooker, prostitute, groupie, whatever someone would call either of us. They thought Onyx and Starlet worked at a casino serving drinks in a private high rollers' suite and the thousand dollars in cash they brought home every night was from tips.

If my girlfriends wouldn't quit for me, they'd quit because of me. I was putting a stop to Valentino's scandalous secret prostitution ring that masked as an image consulting firm and limousine service. That coward didn't have the decency to let us know the location of IP, claiming he didn't want any of us showing up on his doorstep unannounced with a wild hair up our ass. He was the ignorant one. Lace confided in me that Valentino lived in this mansion, not at IP. His residence was right on the other side of the door I stared at. The same door that Lace exited into from our dressing room led to Valentino's living quarters. But Lace refused to give me a physical address or phone number for either of Valentino's properties, saying, "Sunny, some things in life we're better off not knowing." Pausing, Lace seemed so sad when she said, "Some people too."

Scanning the clothes, the shoes, and the jewels one last time, I recalled the moment I saw this dressing room. Man, I freaked out with excitement believing I'd hit the jackpot without gambling. Once the thrill wore off, I realized the degradation wasn't worth the money. Never again before leaving the mansion would they cover my eyes until arriving at that isolated place near train tracks where I occasionally heard the familiar horn blowing in the background. Valentino must've forgotten to add soundproof windows. When I left tonight,

I'd be telling Sapphire Valentino's last name, his address that I was determined to get, and I'd be sketching her an image of what he looked like.

Sapphire was right. Ridiculous amounts of money poured into Valentino's pockets from clients I had to fuck. Each night while riding in the white stretch Hummer, the other girls gossiped about celebrity tricks' dicks but not me. I remained quiet. Maybe that's one reason Lace liked me.

Every trip I tried to learn something new. Transit time from the Strip to Valentino's—rate of speed times time times distance—meant Valentino's house had to be someplace within ten to twenty minutes of Las Vegas Boulevard. The Hummer's license plate, BITCHES, wasn't registered online in Nevada, Utah, Arizona, or California. The tag must've been blocked or something.

The pieces to Valentino's real identity weren't coming together fast enough. Waving at Onyx, I sat at my vanity and waited until everybody left. When the room became quiet, I recorded a quick video on my cellular.

"Whosoever finds this phone, my name is Sunny Day, I live at 555 Chestnut, number 201, in the city of . . . If I'm dead by the time you get this, go to the police and tell them Valentino James killed me. If I'm alive and Valentino is dead, thank me for killing that dirty bastard."

I pressed my lips against the cold .22-caliber gun Sapphire gave me yesterday for my shooting lessons tomorrow. Teary eyed, I saved the video, then speed-dialed my parents, surprised my mother answered on the first ring.

"Mama, I wanna come home."

"Honey, where are you? Your dad and I have been worried sick about you. You have to stop disappearing like this. We want you to come home too, baby."

I heard my identical twin sister, Summer, ask, "Is

that Sunny, Mama? Where is she? Let me talk to that girl."

This time I was glad I was wrong. My family hadn't given up on me. "Mama, I don't know where I'm at."

"What do you mean?"

Lowering my voice, I had to come clean and spare my God-fearing mother from embarrassment if her Bible-toting congregation discovered the truth first. I cried into the receiver, "I've been prostituting and—"

"You've been what! Yes, Lord Jesus! I must be losing my hearing!"

"Mama, please, this is not the time to yell at me. If I'm not home by midnight, call the police and report me missing. I bought a new condo. My address is 555 . . . and I left a note in my bedroom on the nightstand and be sure to give them the license plate BITCHES. Valentino's girls get picked up at bars on—"

All I heard on the opposite end of the phone was sobs before my mother yelled, "Danniiiieelll! Get in here! Now!"

"Mama, please don't call Daddy to the phone," I cried.

"Daniel, talk to your daughter. She's hangin' out with witches."

Shaking my head, my mama couldn't even bring herself to cuss.

"Baby girl, what's going on?"

"I'm sorry, Daddy. I'm so sorry. I'll be a good girl. Can I come home?"

"I'm on my way. Helen, get my car keys. Baby girl, where are you?"

I heard Summer adamantly say, "I'm going with you."

"I don't know, Daddy," I answered. Without any warning, my call dropped. "Nooooo!" I screamed into the dead receiver. I jabbed my gun into the power button, but nothing happened. "Shit!" This time I used my thumb to power on my phone. Nothing.

Sniffling, I left my cell phone inside Onyx's vanity drawer. Tucking the gun into the side pocket of my gold leather purse, I tiptoed to the forbidden exit door. Imitating Lace, I wrapped my fingers around the gold knob. Too late to turn back, I had to tell Valentino I was leaving and I wanted my money. All of it. Tonight. And not no measly two thousand dollars. I deserved more. A lot more.

I twisted the knob until it stopped, my eyes widening when I stepped into a spacious, never-ending hallway. Leaving the door ajar, removing my shoes, heel, toe, heel, toe, I crept along in my bare feet over the cold crystal-clear floor. Sharks swam beneath the glass crisscrossing under my footprints. My shoes dangled in one hand, my purse hung from my shoulder bouncing against my hip. Finally approaching a slightly opened door, I slowed my pace as I noticed, aw, shit! I was on three flat screens.

A man wearing pink socks, pink shoes, and nothing else sat in a large cinema-style chair viewing me on the monitors like he was at a theater. Without turning around he said, "Hello, Sunny. I've been expecting you."

My heart thumped in my throat at the sound of a familiar voice vividly recalling the last john I'd serviced. "I said suck my dick. And lick my balls. I want it all. You're not clever, bitch. I want you hotter than a summer day in July." Guessing he'd seen my every move, I prayed he hadn't heard my threats. I swallowed, then asked, "You're Valentino?"

Facing me, he yelled, "Bitch! Don't call my name!" When he stood, I saw that was definitely the dick I damn near swallowed last night. Thigh to thigh, his dick swayed with his every step from the caramel-colored chair to the black sectional sofa. Sitting, he leaned back on gold-plated fifty-cent pieces that were pressed into the leather like buttons, cradled his balls in his hand, and then spread his sagging nuts flat and wide. On contact with the cushion, Valentino's balls shrank and wrinkled, crawling toward his stomach.

Valentino had grown unbelievably handsome. He could have any woman he wanted except my sister. Oh my goodness. Now that I knew the truth, how was I going to tell Summer that Anthony Valentino James, her baby's daddy, was a pimp? My heart thumping, I questioned if I could carry out my mission to kill Valentino. Like it or not, he was family. But he was also a womanizing, low-down, dirty dog.

Focusing like Sapphire had taught me, I snapped a mental outline of the man I'd seen years ago. Dark eyes, thick eyebrows, long lashes, a well-trimmed thin mustache, a slender nose, mocha-colored lips, and a slim face. Six two, about one eighty, narrow shoulders, lustrous black wavy hair slicked to the back, and a dark, slightly raised mole beneath the outer left corner of his eye.

Sapphire once said, "I hate when a rape victim can't describe her assailant or point him out in a lineup. That leaves him free to rape, attack, or kill other women."

I jumped at Valentino's angry tone when he said, "I knew one of you bitches would try me. But I must admit I didn't think you were dumb enough to be the first motherfucka with balls bigger than mine, bitch."

Was this really the same guy my sister had a baby for? Rubbing my eyelids, I stuttered, "I, I, sorry, I didn't mean to disturb, you, Val, um, I—"

"Come. Sit," he calmly said, patting the smooth leather cushion beside his naked thigh.

My body froze in the doorway of his study. Another crystal floor covered more baby sharks. What was Valentino's fascination? I'd never seen anything like this in my life. My knees trembling, I knew I'd broken his rule, or rules. Fearing the rage oozing from Valentino's squinted eyes, I stared at his clenched teeth. Veins popped along the sides of his neck, making my chest hurt.

What would he do to me? Verbally reprimand me. Burn me with that cigar in the ashtray? Beat me with the heel of what looked like a size-fourteen salmon on his feet? Rip my ponytail away from my scalp? Or would he step on me like a doormat?

Nonsense. All the bad things I'd heard must've been rumored. Valentino had never laid a hand on any of his girls. That was Lace's job. And before today I'd never realized that in a way, he was family. I think. Maybe I was worried about nothing. But the tone of his voice was one all too familiar. Whatever Valentino had in mind, I wanted no part of it or him.

"Better yet, stand right there. Put on your shoes, then slowly remove your dress."

"But I, I really don't want to do this anymore. That's what I came—"

Valentino interrupted with a stern look. "Bitch! I'm not asking you."

Easing on my red stilettos, careful not to damage the diamonds, I lowered my spaghetti straps over my shoulders, then gently released my dress. Shimmering gold lace with red specks surrounded my ankles. I was virtually nude, the only items remaining my thong and high heels. Oh yeah, and my new Rolex watch.

Valentino eased from the sofa. Slowly approaching, he knelt before me. I shuttered as he inserted his fingers into my straps, then lowered my thong over my curvaceous hips, easing the elastic from between my ass.

"Turn around and bend over and spread this beautiful booty in my face."

Doing as I was told, I felt his moist lips press against my clit.

"Sweet. Straight sweet. Bitch, right now I should be getting paid for someone to lick this pretty pink cotton candy pussy."

Exhaling, I thought, if this was the worst of my punishment, I'd be okay. At least until Lace got here.

"Turn toward me," Valentino said, spreading my lips kind of the way Madam had done during my orientation. His tongue grazed my clit, then traveled up my shaft, momentarily resting in the crevice right before he softly sucked me.

My body trembled with delight.

"Oh, you like the way my tongue feels on your pussy, huh?" he asked, inserting his middle finger inside me with a come-hither motion.

None of this would've happened if I worked at a legal brothel. Legitimate prostitutes were independent contractors—well, somewhat—working in legal counties over sixty miles outside Las Vegas. Their problem was most johns didn't want to travel that far to get laid, which was how Valentino capitalized on us. In a way I envied the brothel-working ladies. Although I made more money, they got to set their own prices and work whenever they wanted.

Terrified, I nodded, too scared to open my mouth fearing I'd make him mad, or madder.

Contracted prostitutes never fucked in the ass. Their johns always wore condoms. Our johns seldom wore condoms and anal sex, while it did cost more, was available for the right price. The contractors got to do a thorough inspection of their johns' genitals before sex and had the right to reject them if the dick and balls had any signs of herpes, discharge, or anything contagious. Not us. If our johns paid Valentino enough money, they could fuck us in the ear.

"Ouch!"

Valentino's teeth clenched my clit tight and his soft hair slipped between my fingers when I tried to grip his hairy arms to stop him. If I took one step backward I'd be circumcised.

Releasing my pussy, Valentino stood, braced one arm behind my back, and the other underneath my knees. Carrying me to the sofa, he laid me down, stood over me, massaged his balls in my face, stroked his hard dick against my lips, then commanded, "Turn over on your stomach."

"But—"

Smack! Snap! Slap! Snap! Smack! Snap!

"Bitch! Shut the fuck up! Turn over!"

Reluctantly I obeyed. Not knowing what to expect next, I buried my face into the fresh leather.

The warmth of Valentino's strong body smothered me as his hot dick pressed between my thighs, quickly expanding. His head throbbed between my openings. Not knowing which hole he'd penetrate, I squeezed my cheeks as tight as I could, silently praying, *God, no. Please don't let him hurt me.*

"You do know my rules, don't you?" Valentino asked, pressing his dick harder into the spot between my pussy and my asshole.

Tears streamed down my chin and neck, making the leather slippery, reminding me of the scratches on my neck. "I remember you," I whispered. The more my bruises burned, the more I cried, praying Anthony Valentino James wouldn't ram his dick up my ass.

He must've thought I was Summer, but if he really knew Summer he would've known Summer would never sell her body to any man.

"Bitch, don't cry now. I hope you're glad. You finally saw my face. But I'm pissed that you're not at that afterparty. You know how much you're costing me.

I'm one bitch short and out of one hundred g's. So I suppose you'll have to make it up to me!" Valentino yelled.

Parting my lips, I prepared to scream . . . but didn't.

Valentino gently glided his dick inside my pussy.

"I see why my clients pay so much for you. I'm so disappointed in the lifestyle you chose, but your pussy is still incredibly tight, hot, and juicy. You're making me break my own rule. Damn, girl. I want you to know that I don't fuck my escorts."

Lying bastard.

"But since, aw, shit, you brought this pretty pussy back to me I can't resist. Aw, yeah, this is undoubtedly some of the, ou wee, best pussy I've had. Wouldn't you agree, Summer? I mean Sunny."

Protecting my sister, I didn't want to play his game, so I remained quiet as Valentino's big dick stroked in and out of me with intense passion almost like he was making love to me the way my sister said he made love to her. Although I tried not to, I started cuming and couldn't stop. The XTC I'd taken in preparation for my tricks controlled my orgasms.

"That's it, let it go," Valentino said. Looping his arm under my thighs, he massaged my clit as he continued fucking me.

I came long and slow with his deep penetrating strokes.

"I'm getting ready to cum inside you. You're special because I never cum inside any bitch without a condom. I was gonna take you off the circuit and make you mine again, but you straight fucked that up. Guess I'll have to choose your friend Onyx."

As he thrust his dick deep inside me, I felt the waves of semen leaving his body and entering mine. The Anthony I knew of never disrespected Summer. Maybe Valentino had a twin too.

Valentino's lips pressed against the nape of my neck. "Now, I want you to get up, get dressed, and think about what your punishment should be."

That wasn't punishment enough?

Easing into my dress, I stepped into my thong, covering my cum- soiled ass, then picked up my bag. Slowly I inched backward toward the door, keeping my eyes on Valentino.

"Bitch! Come back here! I ain't through with you yet!" Valentino yelled.

I flinched, dropping my purse beside my feet. Curling the hem of my minidress into my palms, I held my breath.

"Don't make me tell you again!" he shouted.

"Mama, Daddy, I'm sorry I didn't listen to you," I said, looking over my shoulder, praying Lace would walk through the door any second. "Please forgive me."

Valentino replied, "Daniel can't save you this time."

Should I run for the door? Scream as loud as I could? I realized doing anything was better than standing still. Something propelled me to move forward . . . one step, as my feet parted, then aligned side by side on the shiny floor. I stopped when I saw a baby shark circling below me like it was feeding time and I was his meal. Remembering how Daddy made Summer lie to Anthony about aborting his child, I understood why now.

What if Valentino had a secret button that would open the floor beneath my feet, drop me into the water, and drown me as the sharks ate away at my flesh? Trying not to give him any ideas, I glanced around the sparsely decorated room—a sofa now stained with our cum, two cinema chairs, three monitors in a row surrounded by a wall with built-in bookcases, and a high-back chair on wheels underneath a large desk.

Valentino's mansion was in alignment with the name of his business. A huge crystal chandelier with stars bursting like fireworks centered the study above an unoccupied pink Persian rug.

Desperately I wanted to leave, but I was here now. I was in charge, so I might as well speak my mind. Putting my hand on my hip, I asked, "Where's Lace? Oh, I get it. She's probably at the 'secret' location right now collecting your money, huh? Make that our money because everyone knows Lace is the one running this show and you're just her dirty lil' pimp ho."

I took a huge step back.

Valentino's silence spoke louder than any of the words he'd spoken. Fear crept up my spine, decomposing my backbone. How did I get myself into this abusive situation? This never would've happened to Summer. *Mama, did you hear me? I know Daddy is looking for me. Tell him his baby girl needs rescuing immediately.* He can follow the bright light flashing before my eyes.

Over the past year I hadn't communicated with my parents more than six times, terrified they'd find out what I was doing and make me come home. Summer knew everything about me except she'd faint if she knew the real name of Valentino I'd told her about was Anthony.

Praying for the best, fearing I might not make it out of Valentino's mansion alive, I was glad that yesterday I'd mailed a package to our family's Henderson home addressed to Summer. Inside were my condo key, my online bank account identification, password, and PIN. Hopefully sis wouldn't think it was junk mail and toss it into the trash.

Our life growing up in Henderson was boring, but Summer loved it. The biggest thrill back then was hanging out at Wal-Mart, where I'd met my first boyfriend. I tried dating like girls my age, but the guys were too insecure.

In my special way, I loved those guys. Not because they enjoyed licking my pussy until I couldn't cum anymore. No, that wasn't it. I loved each of them hard because my desire to be admired overruled my senses for true love.

After my exes would cheat on me or talk real indignant to me, they'd buy me pretty things or treat me extra nice. Kinda how Daddy did. Ever since I was a little girl, my daddy spoiled us. Gave us everything we wanted and more. I recalled my mother tapping our legs once or twice to command our attention, but my father would spank us, then apologize by giving us gifts. So in a way, my daddy prepped me for this cruel world full of sadistically abusive men.

"Bitch, if I have to get up, you'll be sorry. Summer, move your ass now!"

I couldn't. Maybe if I told him I wasn't Summer he'd let me go.

"Just beat me and get it over with! No matter what you say or do, I'm never gonna be yours, you dirty bastard!"

Valentino sat grinding his front teeth as though he was chewing coconut. He bit the tip off a fresh cigar, then lit it. Inhaling the fiery flames, he drew in smoke, then gently blew white cloudy rings into the air.

I wanted out. I'd made enough money, owned a big condo, a nice Benz, some designer clothes, and I had a decent six-figure bank account to hold me until I found a real job. Maybe when I turned twenty-one tomorrow I'd accept a job managing a clothing store inside one of the well-known casinos.

Valentino calmly whispered, "Summer. Baby girl. Come to Papa."

"I'm not your baby girl!" I shouted, hurling the

Rolex watch from my wrist like I was trying to strike him out on the first throw. I was sick of his bullshit. The white gold and diamonds cut through Valentino's hand, then sliced the mole on his face. "I'm sorry, Valentino. I never should've come over here. I quit."

Like before, whenever I was in bad situations there was no one to rescue me from my big mouth. My mother never rescued me from my father and my father couldn't rescue me from Valentino. I watched blood stream down Valentino's face and neck. Calmly he sat there staring at his hand, then shut his eyes.

This was my big chance.

For the first time tonight, I regretted not getting in the limo with Starlet and Onyx. I was sure there was a better way to quit. This was one day I should've stayed in my bed.

Quietly I knelt beside my bag, reached into the side pocket, and removed the .22 caliber. I'd never owned a gun. Never pulled a trigger. Every nerve in my body tensed as I shut my eyes tighter, pointing the gun at Valentino. I closed my eyes and quickly prayed, "God forgive me," but heard my mother's voice saying, "Thou shall not kill." Terrified beyond belief, I felt my arms, legs, stomach, and neck shuddering

Pow!

Valentino's fist crashed into the top of my head.

This was a time when having a Christian upbringing sucked. My life was in jeopardy and I was too scared to keep my eyes on Valentino and too afraid to pull the trigger. A wave of pain shot from my cranium to my feet. Everything became blurry. *This is it,* I thought as my body collapsed to the cold floor. I lay facedown, eye-to-eye with a gray shark beneath the glass.

"You think you bad, bitch?" Valentino asked, turning me over. "Done cut up my face and hand and shit. You can forget about leaving me, going to the police on me, or killing me! That's what's not going to happen! After all I've done for you, you ungrateful little bitch! Let's see how Mr. Daniel likes this shit."

My eyes fluttered, then closed as I watched Valentino's fist descending upon the one thing I admired so much . . . my face.

I screamed, "Ahhhhhhhhh!"

Like a fountain, blood squirted from my nose and mouth. My front teeth lodged in my throat.

It felt like a cement block fell on my face. If only I had the smarts to realize there was nothing wrong with working at In-and-Out Burger for minimum wage until I could do better. Living at home, like my sister, was far better than illegal prostitution. If only I had the strength to say no to Valentino's slick-talking ways. If only I could've stayed single long enough to get to know myself. Why did I feel I always had to have a man? Always had to have someone adoring me? With the exception of my busboy ex-boyfriend who I now realized was good to me, how did I always choose the wrong man?

Valentino removed my satin dress. My naked body caressed the floor. He covered the gun, placed the cold steel back in my palm, wrapped my pointing finger around the trigger, then pressed the barrel against my temple.

My head rattled. "No, please, don't." Blood slung from the corners of my mouth. "I'm sorry. I'll be good."

It's true what they say about your whole life flashing before you when you think you're dying. I saw lights brighter than the ones surrounding my vanity. Who was I? Who was Sunny Day?

"Bitch, I loved your ass. You could've had it all, including my baby. You fucked up." Valentino's voice faded into the airspace above me as his fingers rested atop mine. When his lips pressed against my forehead, his blood and tears rolled into my eyes. Valentino whispered, "Happy birthday, Summer. I love you."

Protecting my sister, I couldn't tell him the truth. Staring into Valentino's eyes, I found strength to ask what I already knew, "Anthony James?"

"Yes, baby. You know it's me," he whispered, then kissed my nose like Summer had told me he'd kissed hers before saying, "Good-bye, my love."

"Nooooo!" I screamed, spitting blood and teeth into Valentino's face. "You dirty bastard!" A train horn blowing like it was about to wreck into the mansion made me so nervous . . . I pulled the trigger.

Pow!

As I was fading to black, my life flashed before me . . . my purpose became clear. I was dying young so some little innocent naive know-it-all girl who was thinking about running away from home wouldn't. Not after she heard my story on the morning news. She'd listen to her parents because, contrary to her belief, she'd realize her parents were smarter.

I prayed my last prayer.

"Whoever you are, sweetheart, stay at home, go back home. If you insist on leaving, go someplace safe. Don't sell your body. No amount of money is worth it. Whatever you decide to do with your life, don't be like me. When they perform my autopsy, I'm sure they'll find a heart but no guts. Stand up for yourself. Don't let a man abuse you. Before I make my transition, promise me you won't become the next girl number twelve.

"P.S. Summer, Mommy, and Daddy, no matter what you hear, I was a good girl."

CHAPTER 9

Summer

The two shall become one.

Twins. Identical. The power of a combined yin-yang force describable as living an outer body experience from the moment of conception. A splitting image of indivisible spirits. Two hearts eternally beating as one . . . until one stops. Then the one heart must beat for two.

I didn't want to think, feel, or believe the worst, but I knew something terrible was happening to Sunny. Silently tears poured, drenching my lime cardigan sweater and black silk blouse. Smearing the saltiness into my cheeks, my mouth, and back into my eyes, I cried aloud.

"Daddy, let's go home. We don't have any idea where Sunny is and I don't feel so good."

Truth was I was afraid of what we'd see if we found Sunny. Ignoring me, my father aimlessly drove five miles an hour traveling west on Lake Mead Road. Glaring out my passenger window as we passed Wal-Mart, I didn't want to relive the fun times I had with my sister shopping when we were teenagers, fearing we may never shop together again.

After we graduated from high school, Sunny only went to Wal-Mart to appease me. She preferred to shop at Saks or Bloomingdales.

Honk! Honk!

Creeping in the slow lane, Daddy quietly sat behind the mahogany steering wheel peering through the windshield as he merged onto Interstate 15 heading north.

Unexpectedly moisture seeped between my thighs. As I clamped my buttocks, what felt like blood trickled into my panties and wouldn't stop. This was not a good sign.

"Daddy, please go back. Let's just go home," I pleaded, thankful I'd worn black slacks.

Lord, what's happening to my sister? I wondered.

I bit into a piece of sugarcoated ginger. "Ouch!" A sharp pain hit me. Staring at the dried fruit, I pinched my two front teeth to make sure they were there. Heavily my hand fell from my mouth to my lap like a piece of lead.

"Baby girl, with all your distractions you shoulda stayed home with your mama."

Daddy was oblivious of my uncharacteristic behavior. Mama would've read Sunny's signs through me and asked tons of questions by now. My daddy didn't know where to go, but I could tell he was determined to find Sunny and obviously we weren't going home until he did.

Each night at dinner, Daddy prayed at the table for Sunny's safe return. And precisely at ten o'clock before going to bed, I lit Sunny's favorite white eucalyptus fragrance candle and set it in the window, asking God to guide my sister home. It was after ten o'clock and the first night I wasn't able to leave a candle burning for Sunny.

Wringing my hands with the teardrops falling in my palms, I felt a burning sensation in my stomach. Trying not to think the worst, I recalled the stories Sunny told me about the celebrities she'd met and how they pampered her and gave her lots of money. Each time she sounded excited but her spirit was very sad. I sensed the haziness hovering over her heart. Her feelings spoke louder than her contrived laughter. That Valentino guy Sunny beamed about but had never met was the one I wanted her to marry.

My eyes were open but I couldn't see anything in front of me. Daddy drove so slow I imagined his foot being propped inches above the pedal.

One cold night about two months or so ago, Sunny told me, "Sis, I closed on my first condo. It's like a glorified apartment but I have lots of space. A huge living room with plush snow-white carpet. I just bought this crazy nice leather set. It's your favorite color, lime. My bedroom is my favorite color, green." She'd laughed but every time I asked she wouldn't tell me where her place was.

Buying her first home was one time when Sunny truly seemed happy. Oh, how she boasted about me having my own bedroom and how our rooms were decorated the same. Our family photo hung in the living room above her electrical fireplace. She had ceiling track lights with dimmers.

She continued. "We both have giant tubs and there's a new gas stove and a double-door refrigerator."

Sunny was a better cook than me but she'd never admit it. I never understood why she wanted more for me than herself. When I wanted to run away and go live with my ex-first boyfriend, Anthony, Sunny convinced me not to. But I couldn't do the same with her when she left home. "You gotta see it! I'ma pick you up in my new Benz. We gon' let down the top and let our long blond hair blow in the ... I take that back, we'll just cruise with the top up, put on our sunglasses, and act like celebrities."

I'm still waiting on that ride.

Sunny was more adventurous than me. She always wanted to travel the world. Embrace different cultures and learn foreign languages. International business was her desired field, while anthropology was my major.

Sunny could brush on mascara and smooth on foundation like her face was a canvas and she really was an artist. Her body was flawless. Mine too but Sunny's clothes were impeccable. All the whites, reds, greens, blacks, etc., still hung together in her bedroom closet at home. Her drawers were stuffed with a rainbow of panties that had to match her bras.

Personalitywise we differed in some ways. I was like Mother and loved going to church and praising the Lord. Sunny was like Daddy. She was spiritual in her own way but she didn't need a congregation to prove it. Her goodness shone from within.

Looking at the green and white freeway sign, I saw that the Tropicana Avenue exit was three miles away. The wind whistled at our windows, nudging the car sideways. Daddy's tires crunched along the cement as he remained silent. My tears dried to a crust, tightening my cheeks.

Mama said Sunny had mentioned something about a bar and witches, so the first place Daddy thought of was the Las Vegas Strip. "Oh my God!" I clamped both hands over my ears. "Daddy, stop the car!"

"Summer, what's wrong with you? I knew I shoulda left you at home. You're makin' me more nervous."

"My brain is on fire! Help me, Daddy! It hurts!" Leaning forward, I placed my hands over my temples.

My dad's eyes widened, then tightened, but didn't close as his mouth gaped open with enough space to shove in a double cheeseburger as he plunged the accelerator. Exiting the freeway, Daddy drove into the nearest parking lot at In-and-Out Burger. Daddy's chest flattened against my back. His arms covered my arms as he rocked me.

"It's okay, baby girl. I'ma find her. I promise you. Let's get you home."

"Thank you, Daddy," I said, feeling a little relieved.

Ever since Sunny and I were little—before we could speak a word—my parents told us we were one. When I was sick, Sunny was sick. When I was scared, Sunny got scared too. Didn't matter if we were in the same room or miles apart; we each knew how the other felt. The occurrences became more frequent after Sunny left home.

The green-illuminated numbers on the dash changed from 10:59 to 11:00. A bright light flashed before me. I closed my eyes and whispered, "It's too late, Daddy. I feel it's too late."

CHAPTER 10

Valentino

There was only one person I trusted more than Lace and that was her man, my boy, former MVP Benito Bannister. The real reason I hooked Lace up with Benito was that I couldn't risk having Lace get with some nosy-ass nigga who'd interfere with my sole proprietorship thinking he was smarter than the both of us because I'd have to kill his ass like this bitch right here in my office.

Summer, incognegro Sunny, had changed her name to get in the game and shit, but Sunny wasn't the bona fide bitch I had to worry about. Lace was gonna lose her motherfuckin' mind when she found out Sunny was dead.

Where in the fuck was Lace? I should fire her ass. If her ass was on time, Sunny would be making me money instead of . . . what the fuck ever. A G like me lives by the creed, no regrets. Hiring Lace to front my empire was the most intelligent decision I'd made. Quickly Lace became the mastermind behind my entire operation, installing surveillance cameras, monitors, and all that high-tech shit. She wiped out my computer records so the fuckin' law couldn't trace me. Incorporated Immaculate Perception, aka IP, so that tax nigga, Uncle Sam, wouldn't sweat me. Set up my cell phone so my outgoing and incoming calls didn't show up nowhere. Had a digitally activated fence built around my mansion near Ann Road and Rainbow Boulevard across from Walgreen so not even a golf ball from the Silver Stone or Painted Desert course could touch my property without my knowledge. And she had a wall installed around my IP joint down the way on Martin Luther King that was so high no one except Lace and my security guards got in or out unless I pressed a button. That bitch was so brilliant. The only things Lace couldn't fuck with were my dick and my money.

I didn't know how she kept so much shit in her head, but I was straight happy as a mug she was on my team. That bitch didn't have a degree, but her ass was a motherfuckin' genius! But I couldn't let her know dat shit. Bitches say some ig'nant shit when they think they know more than men. But as long as bitches bled from their pussies they'd always be subservient to a real G like me.

I ain't no gangsta with hard balls totin' a grip everywhere I go. I'm a hunter and gatherer of bitches and hos. Straight up. That's how I get down. Don't get me wrong. I'll bust a cap in a motherfucker's ass in a heartbeat if my life or livelihood is in jeopardy. Like this dead bitch bleeding all over my crystal floor. Right now a nigga needed some help. Straight up. And I knew just the man for the job.

Benito and I went way back to elementary school and shit. Football never was my strong suit. I was too busy running the ladies. That's what I called them in high school 'cause Moms and Dad, may they rest in peace, didn't tolerate no cussing in our home.

My parents were old as dirt when they decided to have me. So old that when they attended PTA meetings all my classmates laughed because they thought my grandparents were raising me. There were a couple of generation gaps between us. A solid fifty years. Don't sag. Comb your hair. Go iron those pants. Wash behind your ears. Brush your teeth before you go to bed. Moms would give me a stern look and I'd correct myself, then say to my father, "Yes, sir, or no, sir."

On top of all that shit, I had to go to church four days a week. The reason I joined the football team was so I didn't have to lip-synch at rehearsal. My dad was happy as hell 'cause my games got him out of Bible study on Tuesdays and Thursdays. They had some bitches in the choir who could've been on my team, but those holier-than-thou hos were too busy plotting long-term commitments like wanting to marry a G and shit.

I wish my mother woulda dodged that ig'nant-ass drunk driver the way I did those church girls. But Moms never saw him coming. Since the start of my freshman year, all she ever bragged about was my graduation ceremony. Six months prior to my walking across the stage at Valley High in my cap and gown, my mother was killed. That intoxicated motherfucka better be glad he wasn't on the scene when I arrived or I woulda straight stumped his face in the ground. I know that wouldn't have brought Moms back, but I sure as hell would've felt relief from my grief.

When Moms died Pops just lay on down beside her. Literally my old man had a heart attack at my mom's funeral and fell on top of the platinum coffin. After my parents' deaths, the only thing that kept me afloat was my bitches. Since I was an only child, I thought my peeps would've left me insurance money to take care of myself for a cool minute. All they had on those old-ass policies was enough to lay their bodies to rest properly. So a G like me, six months out from being legal, had to think quick. I refused to go live with any of my relatives in Arkansas, damn sure nuff wasn't gonna be homeless, and I had to pay rent to stay in the house I thought my parents owned.

The first thing I did was I applied for credit cards in my parents' names, glad as a mug they paid their bills on time. Then I threw out all that loud yellow, white, and blue plaid furniture that was wrapped in plastic that stuck to my ass whenever I wore shorts. With a twenty-five-thousand-dollar credit limit, I hooked up the place like a serious bachelor's pad with flat screens, stereos, new carpet, freshly painted white walls, and pillow-top king-sized mattresses so I didn't have to hear no sqeakin' 'n shit, and a state-of-the-art kitchen for my bitches to cook for those greedy-ass ballers. I traded in Dad's Honda for a used Benz-O. The next purchase was my wardrobe: tailor- and designer-made everything down to the gator shoes. All that fuss over my hygiene and appearance paid off. Big time.

Once I found out some nice threads, some smell good, a clean shave, and a precision haircut got me more pussy than risking breaking bones with some three-hundred-pound dude tackling me, then wiggling on top of me like a faggot, I straight gave up that rock.

Immediately I caught more fish than I could fuck, so I started hookin' up my boys on the team. Out of respect and shit I moved into my parents' bedroom and rented mine out to the fellas. Sure, they could get plenty of sleazy groupies to spit-shine their trophies, but ballers like Benito couldn't come close to scoring with the top-notch honeys I had on my team.

I was amazed to find out that bitches were loyal to me simply because I told them all the lame-ass shit they wanted to hear, treated them extra nice, and fucked them like I cared about them. So for the right amount of paper, and I don't mean loose leaf, I passed out pussies to all the ballers—basketball, football, hockey, golf, you name it, and the sweetest part about it was the honeys didn't know I was gettin' paid while they were gettin' laid.

Man, back then high schoolers had more discretionary resources than working adults because their parents, unlike mine, did without to make sure their kids kept up with the Joneses. So I stayed in school until I got my diploma, and then I bought this place. One of my bitches had an engineering degree and grandiose ideas for an underground fish tank, windows that dimmed to black, and all kinds of stuff, so I let her do her thang. Then she went to IP and created theme rooms like the electric chair room, the house of hot wax, and my favorite, the S and M gym.

The more money I made, the more sophisticated I became with my shit, so a nigga like me didn't need no college degree. I had beautiful broads: Asian, Caucasian, African, and African-American, Pacific Islanders, and Japanese. I mean the kind with triple-D breasts-stasis, tiny waists, and big ol' asses that made a nigga get whiplash and wreck his car at the same time. Only the finest bitches surrounded me on a daily.

It didn't take long to realize that when I started dressing my honeys in designer clothes, like Tupac said, *All Eyez on Me*, we commanded more attention than Jason Kidd's wife when she ran her ass down the street butt naked. We turned heads everywhere we went. I mean million-dollar heads. Which was why I'd been livin' large off my bitches for over ten years.

But the one thing I learned from my father, I never laid hands on any of my bitches. The one time my dad hit Moms, his ass was on lockdown for three days

straight calling the house beggin' Moms to get him out
of jail. I refused to beg a bitch for anything, so I kept
my hands to my motherfuckin' self and paid Lace well
enough to kick those bitches' asses whenever I said so.

A real playa didn't fight tricks. I didn't have to . . . I
was in their heads, big time. They knew who their
daddy was . . . until this ho trick tried me. Stupid bitch!

Stomping around my study, I started to pick up that
First Lady book that Lace put on my shelf and rip it to
pieces I was so mad at whatever the fuck Sunny's real
name was. I paid Sunny more than anyone else because before Lace hired her, Sunny was my heart, my
number-one lady. I wanted to take Sunny off the circuit her first day working for me for real and not just
because a year later Lace asked me to. I loved Summer. Even a guy like me knows when a lady is the one.

There was something special about her ass. Out of
all the bitches I'd had, when I met Summer, instantly I
knew she was unique. I didn't want to let her go, but
Summer was sixteen and I was twenty-six at that time
but had lied and told her I was twenty-one so I wouldn't
frighten her away. But that shit backfired on me. I had
to stop dating her when Mr. Daniel Day, as he introduced himself when he walked up to my Benz-O,
threatened to call the cops and have my black ass arrested.

Summer and I kicked it short but hard. So hard that
thoughts of her crossed my mind every day. We did
everything and nothing and we were happy. I hadn't
seen Summer in years until Lace hired her and introduced her as Sunny.

Pleased at the woman Summer had become, disappointed at the lifestyle she'd adopted, I had to see how
Summer would handle herself in the business before
making my final decision. That's why I fucked her.
Amazingly, she was the same free-spirited, sharp-minded

person. Being with Summer I cursed less and cared more about life. About being alive. A good woman could definitely make a man feel better about himself. Or worse. If I'd married Summer back then, Moms woulda been proud 'cause I would've quit pimping.

Still couldn't believe Summer had the mother-fuckin' audacity to pull a gun on a G like me! The P-I-M-P that fed her ass. Loved her ass. Made love to her a few hours ago. I'm the reason she was able to buy a condo and a nice Benz of her own. What more did she want?

Bitches were straight-up scandalous. "Well, take this."

Cocking the gun sideways, although she was already dead, *pow*, I shot Summer straight in her heart . . . for breaking mine.

CHAPTER 11

Benito

No matter how rich. No matter how poor. The only thing a black man owned free and clear in America was his black woman.

The black woman was the only entity the white man alienated to the point most black women couldn't imagine being—today they referred to it as being sexed. Back then it was called raped—at the command of a white man knowing he'd gladly screw her behind closed doors but never take her home to meet his family. The white man single-handedly prepared the black woman to accept her lashings while being obedient.

That was one way, the only way, the white man made life in the United States, a country where things were everything except united, easier for the black man. A black man could mentally and physically beat his black woman into submission. And why shouldn't he? It took a mere circus act by a jester for the black woman to obtain a restraining order against a black man who acted like a clown, but it required an act of Congress for a black man to unconditionally love a black woman. In less than three generations, the black woman went from being the white man's property to the black man's slave as she single-handedly cooked, cleaned, cared for the children, and paid the bills.

Now, me, I could have sex with a white woman in a heartbeat, even fall in love with her and let her buy me expensive things, but giving her anything more than sufficient cum to birth a blue-eyed, blond-haired black baby was a waste because the average white man who was by his own historical definition a black man would never let the black man own a white woman who was also a direct descendant of Africans who were the first humans on earth. But one wouldn't know that unless they drew blood, in which case getting a restraining order would be outlawed 'cause the majority of white people who claimed they were pure blood would probably commit suicide if they were forced to admit that they too were black.

What difference should the color of one's skin make when everyone's ethnicity was either African-American, African-Asian, African-European, or such?

White men were still angry at O.J. Simpson, and black men . . . we were happy for once, whether O.J. was innocent or guilty, to see the white man's system work in favor of a black man. The white man bought, never published, never sold—legally, that is—but stole copies of *If I Did It, Here's How It Happened* by O.J. while O.J. skipped with his nonreturnable advance all the way to the bank. And I was happy the woman I almost went to jail for having sex with, when she cried rape afterward, was intimidated by Valentino to keep her mouth shut. Otherwise, my black butt would be behind bars instead of chilling in Lace's house.

Like many black men I knew, I had way too many issues that I internally struggled with. I loved the fact that my woman was successful, made more money than me, owned her house, paid cash for two Jaguars, and looked and dressed like a supermodel. But at the same time Lace's lifestyle messed with my ego, my manhood. I felt like less of a man inside because there was nothing I could give her that she couldn't afford, but my pride thrust my chest forward and my lips spread wide when men gawked at Lace while she was on my arm. I loved Lace. But at times the green-eyed monster pacing before me and inside me made me hate her too. Or maybe I didn't like myself.

Sports taught me that the most manipulative component of the body was the mind. Control the mind. Control the man. I sought Webster's definition of a man, a bipedal primate mammal distinguished especially by notable development of the brain with a resultant capacity for articulate speech and abstract reasoning, and found the definition about as vague as the whole human race.

Development of the brain couldn't make me intelligent when society had already made me ignorant. Ignorant to the fact that the black man was a king before he became a slave. Ignorant to the fact that black men were hunters, gatherers, and providers for all of their wives and children before being stolen, shackled, and desensitized to everything, especially the black woman. Ignorant to the fact that Christopher Columbus, a white man, couldn't possibly have discovered America if the Indians occupied the land first. Ignorant to the fact that the black men in Rosewood lived better than plenty of white men before the 1920s. So well that the white man killed them off. Those who weren't killed fled to Gainesville. But that wasn't enough. In 1923 almost one hundred and fifty white men filled with racist supremacy returned to Rosewood and burned down whatever was left.

And society wants to question the black man's hatred.

If you'd ask me, not much is different today except the white man's fire burns in my brain like the crack pipes I see way too many of my brothas inhaling. Control the mind. Control the man.

Sure, I had the capacity for articulate speech, but some of the dumbest things came out of my mouth when I lost my self-control. Abstract reasoning is true because women can't attach anything concrete to what I say, so Lace drew her own conclusions, in most cases prematurely. One thing Webster and I agreed on was I lost all notable functions the first time I laid eyes on Lace.

Lace personified raw beauty. She always wore the sexiest lace outfits. If only I'd invested my money like the black men from Rosewood while I was playing football instead of trying to impress my teammates with the entourage surrounding me after every game, I could pay the mortgage every month.

The black man, myself included, has lost sight of what's important. We'd rather blow our money drinking and partying than pay child support. I didn't have a phat bank account, but most fellas, black or white, couldn't afford the incredible memories indelibly etched in my mind.

I may never have the money I used to when I played pro football, but my opinions are priceless. From Osama to Obama, I've got an answer for everybody about everything. At first Lace loved my thought-provoking comments. Now I think she tolerates my monologues, but pretty soon, just like my ex-wife, Tyra, she'll despise whatever comes out of my mouth if I don't smack Lace in her face for being such a smart-ass.

She doesn't talk down to me often, but when she does, I feel like I'm the woman and she's the man.

I'd had enough of being treated like a child well after I'd become a grown man. By my mother, I meant stepmother. I'm not sure what to call a white woman who adopts a black child, then marries a black man, has his baby, a son, and treats her adopted son like an orphan. To this day I don't understand why I hate the brotha Grant Hill. Can't bring myself to call him my brother, but honestly he's never done me wrong. I self-imposed my inferiority complex because his parents treated him better than me. That's why a black man has got to ditch the excuses and make his own way. For me, football saved my life. And when my so-called family relocated to Washington, D.C., while I was away at USC, the only person I could depend on for money was my best friend, Anthony Valentino James.

CHAPTER 12

Valentino

Dialing Lace's home number, I told myself, "Stop trippin', dog. You didn't kill Sunny. It was her gun. She broke the rules. She pulled the trigger. Sunny killed herself. Yeah, that's for real. The bitch committed suicide right in front of me."

"What's up, Valentino?" Benito answered, sounding all happy and shit.

For me, I had to keep shit movin' at light speed twenty-four-seven. Time was of the essence. Last time I'd checked, not nare a nigga was related to John D. Rockefeller. A nigga with too much time on his hands was lying up on a bitch with lint in his pockets or looking for a ho to lay his lazy, broke ass on. Like my boy Benito.

"Hey, look, B, where's your bitch?"

"Man, I keep telling you, Lace is my lady, she's not one of your tricks. Never has been, never will be, so check yourself with all that. She's on her way over to your spot."

Ig'nant niggas and assumptions fit like a hand in a glove. Benito was sleepin' with the biggest trick in Nevada and the nigga was clueless because the blood rushed from his head to his dick whenever Lace was around. All he had to do was Google the words *dicks* and *sucker* and watch his bitch's name pop up on damn near every link with a dick in her, sometimes two.

"Straight up. Whatever you say, lapdog. Looka here, I need you to make tracks over to my spot right away," I said.

Benito got quiet on me.

"Hold on just a sec." I put that nigga on hold and dialed the real man in his relationship, Lace.

She answered, "Hey, I'll be there in ten minutes."

"Correction. Go straight to IP, collect my money, then go straight home. I've already told security that when the girls are done to keep them at Immaculate. I've ordered a strip search."

Screechhh! Reclining in my bed fit for the king I am, I heard Lace's twenty-twos burn a quarter thread into the road. That's why a woman could never be president. Too many impulsive emotional reactions to shit.

"Valentino, no! You promised no more strip searches. Not again. Why? What happened this time?"

That bitch almost made me sit up. "Bitch, your ass is well over an hour late and you're questioning me. You'd better be thankful I haven't fired your ass yet. Listen. You don't have to handle this strip search. Your job tonight is to collect and protect my money."

"Wait, whatever you do," Lace pleaded, "you can't let them harm Sunny. We have a plan for her, remember. Do this one favor for me. Please."

"Bitch!" I said, leaping out of my bed. "Don't tell me what the fuck to do! You work for me! Just do as I say. I want you to lock my money in my safe at your house, then reprogram the combination to twenty-nine, seventeen, eighty-one, fifty-two, got it? And use our code to decode that shit."

"But—"

Opening my nightstand, I picked up my ivory-handled Colt .45. Imagining Lace's face in front of the barrel, I kissed the tip. Thumbing off the safety, I stretched out my arm, then aimed the gun sideways between her eyebrows.

"But my ass, get some rest tonight because tomorrow those bitches have a serious ass-whuppin' coming from you. Sunny included." I ended the call with Lace and resumed talking to Benito. "You still holding! Get your ass over here now, nigga."

"Man, you act like you done killed somebody," Benito said jokingly followed by a fake-ass laugh.

"Straight. Somethin' like that but it was self-defense," I replied, getting back in bed. I wanted to go into my study but I couldn't take looking at Summer, so I lay down staring up at the projector's image playing XXX porn on my bedroom ceiling, and continued. "The crazy bitch shot herself before I could. One of the girls waltzed her ass into my study like it was no big deal. When she saw my face, I laid hands on her but I didn't know she had a gun. Stupid bitch. I had to teach her a lesson. I was in fear for my life. If I'd let her get away with that shit, all of 'em bitches would've ganged up on me. Plus, the bitch fucked up my face and my hand, so bring me some Neosporin."

Whatever they put in that shit was the realist. Neosporin healed everything to perfection. Bitches and hos' bruises, burns, cuts, all of that shit. I knew all the right shit to say just in case my conversation was being recorded. But I also knew every cop from the chief to the streets in my city. Switching from the boring dick-sucking bitches to satellite television, I listened to my boy. As I stuck my hand in my mouth, the cut stung something fierce.

"Let me get this straight . . . and so what you call me for? Besides, how can a black man claim self-defense and allege suicide at the same time? That's reserved for white people."

"Nigga, don't get psychological on me and shit. I said I was in fear for my life. Don't forget who bailed your black ass out of that rape scandal. You should be locked up and getting fucked in your ass. And don't think if I get accused I won't send your ass up the river. I kept that video and the girl's cum-stained thong that you were too stupid to remove. And let's not mention all the free pussy I hooked you up with when your ass lost your endorsements, cars, and home to the IRS for filing fraudulent tax returns. If I drop that on Lace, your ass, my friend, will be homeless without shelter. You owe me—"

"You tryna blackmail *me?* Your boy?"

B was my friend, but if it came down to my freedom or his life, that shit was a no-brainer.

Propping my good hand behind my head, I said, "Straight. Plus—"

"Plus what? Plus the hell what! You're the one who introduced me to Lace, convinced her to let my broke ass move in while I pretended to have money. And speaking of money, don't forget that I still owe you twenty g's for the engagement ring you bought for me to give to Lace."

That motherfucka knew the deal. "Ya damn straight! Don't make me tell you again. Get your ass over here!"

"Naw, man. This ain't worth me going to jail. Hell, I'll take that rock off her finger tonight. You can have it back and I'll go back to playing ball before I get involved with your bullshit."

"Bullshit! Your sorry ass is washed up. Bad knees. Bad back. It's my miracle that got you a fine-ass woman.

Your tongue must do all the fuckin' 'cause that's the only thing you're working right now. I told your punk ass it was an accident, nigga! Look, I'll hook you up with a quarter of a mil and forgive your debt. I have a safe at Lace's house with the money in it. Memorize this combination twenty-nine, seventeen, eighty-one, fifty-two, then unscramble it with that decoding shit we used in high school. Then never tell Lace I gave the combination to you."

Right now, I needed to have every trick and dick close to me at my motherfuckin' mercy. That ludicrous talk about Lace handling my business—"Everyone knows Lace is the one running this show and you're just her dirty lil' pimp ho"—was all about to change. Lace's time had come to move on. But I wasn't letting her leave with my money or her dignity. If Lace hadn't brought Summer back into my life, she would've kept her job. Now I got a death on my hands because of Lace's poor judgment. How in the fuck did Summer get to me? I should've had Reynolds kill Lace months ago.

Interrupting my thoughts, Benito mumbled, "Say what? For real? A quarter of a *mil?*"

That dumb fuck would bury his white stepmother for two hundred and fifty g's. No matter how hard Benito tried, I knew he was never her favorite son anyway. That's another reason why I hooked him up with Lace. Two rejects automatically became legitimately blind codependents. Each one aware of the other one's faults. Both incognizant of their own baggage and shit.

My whole world was fucked up because my parents didn't love me. Whateva. Niggas with one fuckin' excuse after another needed to lie down and die, get the fuck bulldozed over, or get over their fucked-up childhoods and move on. Complaining and shit wasn't going to change a motherfuckin' thing. B would gladly take my dollar, but since he retired that mentally decapitated fuck wouldn't get up off his ass to make dime.

Easy money. That's why there were so many beautiful, brainless bitches waitin' for a G like me to rescue them from themselves. I could snatch an educated bitch off Wall Street and with the right incentives, make her walk a beat. And I had no regrets. If a trick was stupid enough to let me sell her pussy, I was just the man for the job.

In the worst way, Benito wished that white chick hadn't adopted him. Until he turned ten, he gave her someone to love. But then his mommy married a black man, and surprisingly got pregnant after the doc told her she couldn't have any children. Blah, blah, blah . . . so sad.

Then his stepbrother, her biological son, was one of those elitist Negroes. Half black, half white, utilizing whatever ethnicity was beneficial to him at the time. Benito was too proud and too black to follow his brother's lead, claiming one day he wanted to find his real parents because his adoptive mother never changed his adopted name. *Boo-hoo-hoo.* That was because she never wanted his ass in the first place. Benito needed to wise the hell up and man the fuck up.

But that trick couldn't wait to give her son his father's name, Grant Hill the second. If he wasn't Benito's brother, I would've paid somebody to whup his ass when we were in high school. I guess my boy should be thankful that white broad gave him a better life than his crackhead mammy and deadbeat pappy. And he should be grateful that I gave him somebody to love him back. Lace St. Thomas was the baddest, smartest, finest bitch in the state of Nevada. That was straight-up factual and too bad because I was exterminating Lace. No way she'd become more important to my operation than me.

"I don't know where no safe is. Besides, how you got a safe in my woman's house and I don't know about it?"

What a waste. That's why I couldn't put his ig'nant ass on my payroll.

"Straight. Trust me. I'll tell you after you finish this assignment. Man, I don't have anyone else I can trust. I have to get rid of this bitch before Lace gets back tomorrow, so get your ass over here now! And whatever you do, don't tell Lace. I can't afford for her nosy, analytical, wannabe, law-degree forensic scientific ass to get past my front door until this stiff trick disappears. Lace is worse than a bloodhound. You've got thirty minutes to get your ass over here or else."

"Whatever, I—"

Cutting Benito off, I placed the gun on the nightstand, sat on the side of my bed stroking my dick, then mumbled, "This shit never would've happened if I hadn't given Lace last night off."

When Benito got quiet, I knew I was in like a mug. Niggas were stupid. A hint that another man might've been banging their trick and their heads were all fucked up. Why niggas took another G's word over his bitch's was beyond me, but with a few simple lies, I had Benito right where I needed him.

Finally he spoke. "What? She told me she worked last night."

"Nigga, you slippin'. I'ma buy you a pussy pocket. See if you can keep track of that. You believe everything that comes out . . . and goes in Lace's mouth? You'd better start tappin' that ass and I don't mean with your dick. You gotta pimp smack the fuck outta her a time or two to prove your manhood, nigga. Check your woman. If you don't, next thing you know her balls will be bigger than yours. Oops, sorry, my brotha, they already are. I'll school your ass when you get here. Hurry the fuck up so you can get this decomposing bitch outta my house, and don't forget my ointment."

CHAPTER 13

Summer

When I arrived home with my father, all I wanted was to curl in Sunny's bed underneath the covers and pray my bad vibes were crossed with some sort of stomach virus. Unlacing my black tennis shoes, I left them at the front door.

Greeting us in the living room with AJ in her arms, Mama asked, "Well, Daniel, where's my baby?" One look at my snotty nose, red eyes, and droopy cheeks, and my mama screamed, "Lord, no! Say it isn't so!"

AJ yelled a piercing scream so I grabbed him.

"Calm down now, Helen, you upsetting our grandson. I'ma call the police," Daddy said. Picking up the cordless phone, he dialed three numbers and waited. "Yes, I'd like to report my daughter missing . . . uh-huh . . . okay . . . thanks."

Rocking my son, I watched Mama closely watching Daddy's mouth. "Well, what'd they say?" Mom's wide brown eyes bucked at Daddy as she eagerly anticipated a response.

"Helen, please, she's my baby too. Give me a minute before I forget the number." This time Daddy dialed seven digits, then repeated himself. "Uh-huh, okay, I'm on my way." Hanging up the phone, Daddy looked at Mom and said, "Helen, go get some pictures of Sunny and get your coat. Baby girl, I think it's best you stay here. We'll take the baby with us. We gotta go file a report."

Mama stared at me as Daddy took AJ. I tried to conceal my emotions, but when Mama hugged me I started crying on her shoulder.

"I'll get the pictures," Daddy said nervously, walking away, drying his eyes.

Sometimes it frightened me how connected Sunny and I were to my mother. Was I that obvious? "Mama, I don't know anything for sure. We didn't find her," I said, easing from her embrace before I had another breakdown.

Bypassing my room, I noticed a large insulated yellow envelope on my bed, so I backed up. I'd ordered identical charm bracelets online at www.italian-braceletcharms.com for Sunny and me to wear. That was gonna be my sentimental connection to her while we were apart. Each bracelet had twenty-one charms to celebrate our twenty-first birthday tomorrow. I'd bought links with our names, best friends, Daddy's girl, love Mom, a pink butterfly, angel wings, an emerald heart trimmed in gold, praying hands, Jesus loves me, and a cross embedded in a sunset because Sunny was my sunshine and I was the summer rain she loved to dance with to the song Luther Vandross sang about his father.

I flipped over the package to find the return address missing. Shaking the envelope, I smiled when I heard a jingle. Peeling away the tab, I peeped inside. Emptying the contents onto my comforter, I cried, unfolding the eight-and-a-half-by-eleven sheet of paper.

Sunny Day. Checking account number 000 . . . beginning monthly balance $276,000. There were twenty-five deposits of $2,000 each. Ending balance $326,000. PIN 6250, our birthday backward. I flipped over a business card with the name and number of a Sapphire Bleu. Sunny must've put this in here by mistake, I said, tossing the card into the empty waste basket beside my bed. Setting the bank statement on the pillow, I removed a green notecard from a lime-colored envelope.

> *Dear Summer,*
> *There's so many things I want to tell you I don't know where to start. How about I miss my Summer rain? I wish I was more like you. Isn't that silly considering you're my other half? If anything happens to me, I have a duplicate driver's license inside my Bible. Close my account, sell my condo, and keep the money. I've always wanted to travel abroad—Paris, Rome, South Africa, Italy. Promise me if I die first that you'll take a trip out of this country and carry my spirit with you. Don't try to keep or move into the condo or drive my Benz. You might be endangering yourself. If I make it out of this prostitution ring, and I'm told none of Valentino James's girls do so alive, I'm taking you on a trip far away from Henderson, Nevada, and I'm not accepting no for an answer.*
>
> *Your sunshine,*
> *Sunny*

I couldn't breathe, couldn't swallow, and couldn't stop the tears from falling. I had to find my sister and I knew just the ex-man to help me but had no idea where to find him.

In the upper left-side corner of the red, white, and blue statement was 555 Chestnut, number 201. Logging on to my laptop, I typed www.mapquest.com and got directions to a location near the North Las Vegas Airport where that small plane had recently crashed. Fortunately, no one in that accident was killed and I prayed Sunny was still alive.

I picked up Sunny's house key, slipped it into my purse with the bank statement, and exited out the back door to my two-door Honda. By the time my parents returned, I'd be at my destination.

Arriving at Sunny's condo, I parked in the lot on the back side in a space marked for visitors. The lighting was dim and her end unit was partially isolated. Climbing two flights of cement stairs to reach the second floor, I pulled the key out of my purse. Overcooked spaghetti couldn't have been softer than the muscles in my legs as I slid the key into the hole.

Locking the door behind me, I called out, "Sunshine, where are you? It's your Summer rain."

Total quietness surrounded me as I stood in the living room. The condo was as I'd pictured. Looked like a model unit. Decorative gold and emerald plates sat alongside a forest-colored table runner that was perfectly stretched across the middle. Five eucalyptus-scented candles were tiered on a brass holder freshening the entire condo.

The kitchen was spotless. The stove had plate covers with our family pictures on two and our toddler photos on the other two. I smiled at the image of Sunny and me hugging and grinning at our thirteenth birthday party. At first we couldn't wait to become teenagers; then we stayed up all night when we turned sixteen.

Suddenly I became sad again remembering our birthday was in an hour. The condo was freezing so I hugged myself praying my sister was safe. Entering the bedroom, I knew this had to be Sunny's. Artwork by a famous artist out of Oakland named Eve Lynne Robinson, a relative of Ray Charles Robinson, hung over Sunny's bed.

The bright orange canvas represented Sunny. The simple green dress represented me. And the poised dark-skinned woman with the golden hair reflected our Gemini personalities. As sweet as I was, I became a hundred percent evil whenever anyone messed with Sunny.

Noticing an envelope on her nightstand, I stuffed it in my purse. Whatever was inside, I was positive I couldn't handle knowing. Not right now anyway. Since the rooms were identical, I'd see my room later. Sunny's bed was where I wanted to lie. Clutching the Bible to my chest, I knelt beside Sunny's queen-sized canopy and silently prayed. Pulling back the comforter, I removed my tennis shoes and tucked myself in. If God heard me, Sunny would come home soon and I'd be here to welcome her with loving arms.

CHAPTER 14

Benito

"If I get fired, your fuckin' ass had best not be here when I get back!" were Lace's last words before slamming the door, and all I said was, "I love you, baby," which probably irritated her even more. But what Lace couldn't see was those words came from my heart, not my mouth.

I'm a man. A black man. A grown man. But what does being grown, black, and male mean in America? Oh, say, can you see? I have no factual documented history on this dirt or a desire to patronize a society that ostracizes me based on the color of my skin.

My jaded mind-set and countless issues were embedded in the DNA passed to me from my ancestors who were castrated and hanged for fun during slavery at picnics—which were literary pick-a-nigga-and-hang-his-ass gatherings—where white folks ate, drank, and were merry while the fat white dude in a red suit with a white beard called Ol' St. Nick, who fucked whomever he damn well pleased, including children, was someone I was taught to believe in because he brought me . . . toys?

Excuse me if I forget to laugh or hate the fact that my brother can pass for white while the devil robs my breath at night. I can't move. Can't yell. Although I'm alive I'm trapped in a hellhole, black hole, on hold.

My heart was so heavy, loving Lace helped balance my energy. But why couldn't my black woman understand I needed her to uplift me? To help me. For her to see me as more than what the white man denounced me to be.

Sitting in the living room, I flipped through over six hundred cable channels on Lace's flat screen and couldn't find one show that wasn't on a black station and had more than two black men with starring roles.

Yet a black man is expected to sing sweet land of liberty when the only thing he's free to do is die or be killed by a trigger-happy cop who plants a gun on the black man, then tells the sergeant it was self-defense while he vacations on administrative leave awaiting his reprieve.

Yes, I'm angry. Yes, I'm hostile. Yes, I'm a product of my environment, but all anyone ever sees when they look at me is a burly black man, which usually accompanies their predetermination of my being a monkey with a tail out on bail.

The white man sees a threat. The black man, like my boy Valentino, sees a debt due unto him. The white woman sees a big banana-sized dick that tastes ten times better than the white chocolate she has at home. And the black woman sees a quick hitch or overnight fix to repair her single parenthood into a family unit, not caring whether or not we are united. That's how I slipped up and married Tyra's ass.

But Lace was right. I needed to get out of the house or else I was gonna drive myself crazy with all this time to do nothing but think about rhetoric that most folks cared less about.

"What's wrong with me? Acting like a child." If Lace had mentioned buying me a pussy pocket, I would've exploded in her face the minute she walked through the door.

Powering off the television, I thought of Lace buying expensive stuff to come all over, then spending ridiculous money to have me take it to the dry cleaner's, how illogical and a waste of our money it all was. I could've used that change toward starting my business.

Lifting the leopard throw from the floor, I felt a hard object scraping my palm. Massaging the soft hairs, I discovered a piece of plastic attached.

"So this is what scratched Lace's pussy. I knew it wasn't me, I knew it. I can't wait until she gets home so I can shove this in her face and prove her know-it-all behind wrong."

Sounded all good but I knew I'd back down the minute Lace would raise her voice, then threaten to kick me out.

Rolling the vacuum cleaner back and forth, I did what I'd often do when Lace wasn't around, talked to myself. "Forget that idiot Valentino. I'm no fool. Sure Lace and I had problems in our relationship, but what couple doesn't? I'm a lucky man to have a woman who loves and financially supports me. A woman most men, married or single, would gladly screw if they could. Valentino wasn't slick. He probably wanted my woman too. I love Lace, but the thought of her giving my pussy to another man . . . is deeper than any woman could comprehend. Ou wee! I will beat the crap out of the dude if I catch him, but I could never slap my bread and butter. Lace knew I'd take care of her if I could afford to."

Wrapping the black cord around my fist, I yanked it from the socket.

"Where was she? She came in here last night acting like things were normal . . . was I hearing right? Did Valentino say two hundred *and* fifty g's? Maybe I shouldn't trip. Lace was a good woman . . . two hundred and fifty g's? Friend or no friend, a pimp like Valentino didn't give away money for free. Either he was bullshitin' or I . . . fuck that, where was Lace last night? That woman made me go against my own principles."

Tossing the cord to the floor, I abandoned the Kirby upright vacuum in the middle of the living room and marched into the bedroom. A black man separated from his biological mother at birth wanted to be, needed to be, but never felt completely loved by any woman. I had abandonment issues and suffered from separation anxiety. Didn't Lace see how desperately I tried to give her all of me? What I couldn't figure out was why she wouldn't or couldn't do the same. I bet it had something to do with that Don dude. Or the man she was giving my pussy to.

Shaking my head, I felt my shoulders tense as anger seeped into my protruding veins, stiffening my body. I had to change my thoughts before my brain pressed fast-forward. I was heated enough to ram my fist into the wall, rip out a baseboard, and crack it over Lace's head.

"Okay. All right. Relax, man. I'm good," I tried convincing myself, rubbing the back of my neck.

Why was it that whenever I found someone who cared about me, that was the woman I dated? Lace became my woman simply because she wanted me as her man. The same way Tyra had become my wife. I guess subconsciously as a black man I was accustomed to being hunted, conquered, and defeated, then placed on an auction block while my genitals, teeth, and strong muscular physique passed from the slave master to the black woman waiting for either to deem me valuable enough to take home.

When I was growing up, Valentino's mom, Mama Ruby Lee James, was a second mother to me. Everything she'd taught Valentino, I'd learned simply to gain her acceptance. Whenever she said, "Valentino, why can't you make straight As like Benito? Or get one of them scholarships like Benito? Or stay out of trouble like Benito?" I tried harder. The only thing I couldn't do well was handle rejection, which came in subtle and overt forms.

My parents gladly gave me hand-me-downs while Grant got the best of everything. After we graduated from Valley High, Grant went to Oxford and I went to USC, which some called the University of Second Chances, but they had the number-one football team in the nation and that's what I strived to become, number-one, until I retired. Now all of my fans are someone else's fans and everyone has forgotten about me.

Maybe I've caught that depression syndrome I saw on that commercial every day where people didn't want to do anything. Since I'd met Lace, that person was me. Somewhere along the way I'd lost my drive to be the best. Guess I was tired of always trying to please my fans, my parents, now my woman cleaning up her place like I'm the housewife. If Valentino honestly gave me the money he'd promised, I'd kick Lace down a grand or two, then leave, move to a small town, and do what I'd never done before. Find the real Benito Bannister trapped under this not-so-tough layer of thick skin.

·I'd never told anyone this before but how could a

masculine quarterback, a man amongst men, say "It's important to me that people like me" without sounding soft? Without seeming insecure? To this day I disliked swearing, not because I thought it was wrong, but because Mama James didn't allow cussing in her presence. Some things made me wanna say, "Fuck! Nigga! Bitch, kiss my black ass!" All that shit, but I'd seen how misdirected hostility made my angry black former teammates relentlessly beat their women, then end up in some anger management class designed by a white man.

Speed-dialing Lace's cell number, I ripped the lid off her white wicker hamper, tossed it to the floor, then removed the red lace thong she had on last night. Closely inspecting the crotch, I didn't see any come stains, soiled streaks, crust, or anything out of the norm, so I sniffed them. A light sweet scent hit my nose. Smelled fresh and clean as always. Lace was a classy woman. She wouldn't cheat on me. Not the way I held it down in the bedroom and licked her pussy dry.

Within five seconds I hung up and redialed her number. I'd repair the hamper later. "I'm giving her one more chance."

Hmm, Valentino must've mistaken my baby for one of his prostitutes. Back in my not so long ago days, I'd fuck a fine prostitute all night long but I'd never fall in love with a whore who screwed men for a living. Marrying a prostitute was one step below dating a stripper because I'd never be caught dead at the altar waiting for either one of them to walk down the aisle, then slide their tongue down my throat. Mama James wouldn't approve of me kissing a woman who sucked dicks like honey-filled Blow Pops.

My lips shrank to the shape of a quarter. "Fuck, I mean, darn." This time my call went straight to voice mail. Two hundred and fifty g's, huh? With the thought of that much money in my pockets, I relaxed a little. Lace could retire, stay home where I could keep an eye on her, and she could have my son, sons, who'd keep her busy twenty-four-seven while I hit the streets. "I wonder how my daughter is doing." My ex-wife, Tyra, could go to hell! Lace sent her two hundred dollars a week and she still complained that that wasn't enough.

"It's called child . . . support! Not pay for everything."

Whateva. A black man was damned, no matter what. If he didn't pay child support he went to jail. If a black man paid child support, his baby's mama raised hell, whining, "This ain't enough. What am I supposed to do with this, wipe my ass?"

Nothing a black man did for a black woman was ever enough. Best if the brotha left her, moved on, and got himself a white woman who was easily satisfied and eager to please him in and out of bed.

Lace was right. I'd never admit it but a white woman couldn't make me face my fears. I was a bit insecure 'cause my baby earned more than me, but I didn't give a fuck how much she made, I was the man of this house and if she fucked another man I'ma have to lay hands on her and prove to her once and for all who the man is.

Clamping my hands over my temples, I fell to my knees and yelled, "Fuck!" desperately needing to know who she gave my pussy to!

As I was imagining what Valentino would say if he saw me now, his voice resounded in my ear, "Nigga, get your punk ass up!"

Hopping toward the door on one foot, I shuffled on my black Jordan tennis shoes, tied the strings in my black sweatpants into a knot, grabbed the keys to my Jaguar off Lace's nightstand of pure ivory with eighteen-karat gold handles, then hurried into the garage.

Scared shitless wondering what the hell my boy Valentino was up to, I sped out of the driveway from zero to forty. The back end of my car fishtailed, skidding into the circular curb across the cul-de-sac. Gray clouds engulfed the rear window as the car slammed against the opposite curb. Turning the steering wheel in both directions, I regained control only to plunge the accelerator till I hit ninety miles an hour along Ann Road, racing through every red light. I damn near crashed into Valentino's twenty-inch-high black wrought-iron gate until the sensor lights blinded me.

"Slow down, man. Chill out," I told myself. "You don't know what your boy is up to."

I parked in the driveway, then sat staring at my dick. Shit always happens to me when I least expect it. I didn't mean to rape that girl. One minute she wanted to have sex; then she said stop. The next minute she was sucking my dick; then she stopped and just sat there like a zombie. The next thing I knew she was riding my dick like a jockey. She came. I came. Her pussy was wet. My dick was limp and happy as hell. She got up like nothing had happened, so I thought everything was copacetic until she asked for five hundred dollars. I laughed in her face so long she got dressed, then yanked the knob so hard she damn near took the hotel door with her. Next thing I knew some dude dressed in an LVPD uniform banged on room 5021 so furiously I was afraid to open up. When I did all I heard was, "Benito Bannister, you're under arrest."

Maybe I was wrong about white women making black men feel secure.

"Wait up, Officer," I protested, "I'm innocent."

With everything that happened that night with that girl, I just knew something would appear in the *Las Vegas Sun* or the national news like MVP BENITO BANNISTER ARRESTED FOR RAPE. Not a word was printed or spoken. But those handcuffs damn near cut off my circulation and my wrists. The man who knew the right people on the force and got me out of that hideous situation was Valentino. My boy never hesitated. He had my back to the point that I didn't have to explain anything to anybody, not even my stepmother. Grateful, I was in and out of central lockup before they did a body or a booty check, 'cause I'd pushed a lump of shit into my pants at the thought of a man's finger going up my ass.

I owed Valentino big time.

I abandoned Lace's black-on-black Jaguar in the driveway—oh yeah, if some illegal shit went down, this was not my ride. I stood outside for fifteen minutes contemplating if I should follow through with Valentino's demand. I had my share of wrongdoings, but nothing that would land me back behind bars. Rape was one thing but murder? That was against every law.

Walking up to the front door, I glided my finger toward the doorbell. Shockingly, Valentino opened the door before I pressed the button.

"Man, get your ass in here quick," Valentino said, locking the door behind me. Looking over his shoulder, he whispered, "Follow me."

Glancing around, I didn't see anything unusual. The joint was so quiet I heard myself breathing. Everything inside the mansion looked cool until—

"You gotta get this shit cleaned up in an hour before your bitch gets back to her spot and figures out something's wrong. We have to make sure every alibi is proper. I need you and that dead ho out of here before midnight."

Undigested steak and potatoes raced up my throat and out of my mouth, splattering onto the sparkling crystal when I saw a young girl's brains oozing out of the hole in her skull onto the floor. Backing up, I held my hands in the air. "Aw, fuck no, man. I ain't touching her. What the fuck did you do that for, G? I'm out."

"Out my ass!" Valentino yelled, placing a gun to my head. "You either clean this shit up so no one traces her back to me, or you join her and I'll pay somebody to dispose of yo' ass too, nigga. Don't believe me, try me." He shoved the barrel into my mouth.

Mumbling, I said, "I'm your boy, G."

"Nigga, that's why I called you. Now . . ." Valentino lowered the gun, then pointed at the girl.

Angrily biting my sore bottom lip, I felt sweat pouring from my forehead while vomit seeped into my mouth. Swallowing, I stooped closer to the body, then gasped, "My God, she's so beautiful and so young."

"If it makes you feel better, nigga, you can wish the bitch a happy birthday as you're burying her ass. She'll be twenty-one in an hour. The body bag is in the basement in the first closet to your left. Don't open shit else."

CHAPTER 15

Lace

Creeping along Las Vegas Boulevard in bumper-to-bumper traffic was every car from a hooptie to a Bentley glowing beneath a billion blinding nightlights. From the Stratosphere, Wynn, Treasure Island, and Harrahs, to Beuax Virage, Le Mirage, MGM Grand, Mandalay Bay, and the Hotel, to off in the distance at the Luxor, for miles all one saw was dazzling women and flashing lights: some sparkled between water beams, thunder, and fire while others caressed ships, lions, castles, or the pyramid.

Each casino strived to outdo the next by attracting gamblers with sideshows more spectacular than those performed by the automobile racers, but the outcomes were the same. Every outdoor show in Vegas created a traffic jam. No doubt Sin City was the premier attraction worth seeing at least once in everyone's lifetime, but right now all these damn cars needed to get the hell out of my way.

I contemplated abandoning my Jaguar in the middle of the street to get myself a stiff drink, but some shyster's ink would dry on the pawnshop's papers before I made it to the bar. One could buy or sell anything from sex, diamonds, furs, and cars, to the plasma in their blood because pawnshops, like prostitution, in Vegas were more plentiful than casinos.

Honk! Honk!

Leaning on my horn, I yelled out my window, "Unobservant, inconsiderate fuck! Just move up two damn inches so I can pull into the fuckin' driveway. My goodness. I can't take this tonight. Let me get off the Strip until these tourists finish their after-midnight sightseeing before I shoot somebody." I had to chill for a moment until I figured out what the two Negroes in my life were up to and why. A lot of unusual shit had happened over the last few hours and my gut instinct told me things were going to get a lot worse before they got better. Finally arriving at my destination, I refused to extend courtesy to the drivers ahead of me patiently waiting for assistance from the parking attendant.

Never giving a stranger access to all of my keys, I handed my car key and a fifty to the attendant at the Bellagio. I'd already locked Valentino's money in my trunk and activated the lock so no one could search the contents. Strutting inside, I stopped at the first place serving alcohol, the Fontana Bar, draped with a décor of blazing red curtains. Dian Diaz onstage singing "No more tears for you, and now I'm over you . . ." was perhaps a sign I needed to let Benito go and meet someone new. Any man who was devious enough to jeopardize my livelihood was an abusive, controlling bastard I needed to live without.

Should I wait until our relationship escalated to violence or do what I knew I had to? Embracing my inevitable breakup with Benito, I took the only empty seat at the bar next to a gorgeous woman wearing a blue sheer dress with a split parting damn near up to her pussy. Pulling back my stool, I gazed at the vivid red, green, and blue tones swirling throughout the cream-colored carpet. If I were in the mood to recruit girl number thirteen, I'd hire this diva-bitch on the spot, but quality superseded quantity.

My twelve perfect escorts were manageable and in the highest demand. Girl seven used to be a geisha. Men liked the way she draped herself in layers, painted her face highlighting her red lips, swooped her hair atop her head, and took small steps toward them. Girl eight had the bluest eyes, the blondest hair, and smiled, giggling at every word that came out of a man's mouth. Girl eight made her men feel smart and funny. Girl nine was a Polynesian double-jointed beauty.

Pimps and madams who recruited every available woman worked ten times harder than me and made only a fraction of the money I earned. Work smarter, not harder was a motto every woman should employ.

"What would you like?" the bartender asked in a tone insinuating I could have any top-shelf liquor in view or his fine sexy ass.

"A double beautiful heated," I requested, scanning the lounge. I recognized a dozen men who were my clients dining with their wives or girlfriends, but I pretended not to notice because some of them were probably wondering why I wasn't at IP. Irrespective of marital status, every high roller who frequented Vegas eventually made his way to IP for unforgettable nights of sexual pleasure. Men were shallow and I'd taught my girls how to make them feel extra special. Sunny was a natural at pleasing her johns, which unquestionably made her my top girl virtually overnight.

"But of course," the bartender replied, pivoting his nice firm butt toward me.

Of all days, why had Benito made me late for work today and why had Valentino demanded I go straight to Immaculate Perception, pick up his money, then go straight home? If Valentino weren't so busy trying to control everyone around him, he'd know that Lace danced to the beat of her own tune, not his. I'd go home whenever, if ever, I decided to go home. Retrieving my cell phone from my purse, I dialed Sunny's number.

The woman to my right glanced at the lighted display on my phone, then quickly looked away.

What was this bitch up to?

"Enjoy," the bartender said, flashing a smile and setting a glass of steamed water before me as he tilted the second snifter with Grand Marnier and Courvoisier atop.

Since I wouldn't see Sunny at work tonight, I'd wait for her at her condo and fire Sunny when she got off; then I'd go home. From this day forth, Lace St. Thomas was a woman of her every word. I was serious. This was Sunny's last day working for Valentino. But I could start up my own operation and hire Sunny as my personal assistant. That way I could keep Sunny close enough to make sure her impulsive ways didn't get her hurt. Or killed.

The call went directly to voice mail, so I redialed the number this time, flipping my phone over so the nosy trick seated to my right molesting the rim of her martini glass with her tongue wouldn't be up in my business.

Careful not to mention my name or Sunny's, I left a brief message, "Hey, give me a call as soon as you get this."

Whispering into the wind, the woman next to me said, "If you're not part of the solution, you're part of the problem."

Now, that bitch was certifiably insane. Where in the fuck did that come from? And who in the hell was she talking to? Probably trippin' over some man.

I shook my head. I'd learned a long time ago that women had to observe their surroundings at all times. Most women like the one beside me were victimized because they lived in their fucking heads, fantasizing about shit that was far from reality.

I made him hit me because I wouldn't shut up. He really is sorry this time. He loves me. He promised he'd never beat me again, so I'ma stay with him.

Until what? He beat her ass again or killed her? Every three seconds an American woman is beaten. And thirty percent of all female homicides in the U.S. are the results of domestic violence. So a battered woman swallows her poison every second she stays with her abuser. Some women perish slowly while others die instantly.

My having gone through that bullshit for years was the reason I kept my gun loaded. Most women couldn't tell if a fly on their nose regurgitated on them because they'd swat it away without thinking, feeling, or looking. That's why these fucked-up millionaires and billionaires and broke-ass men swarming around women like buzzards could prey upon any one of these whores for little or nothing. For real, deal or no deal, women would offer up pussy for free!

A woman would give her precious body to a complete stranger hoping he'd like her enough to, what? Buy her something pretty, give her a dollar or two, take her home to the wife he'd never mentioned, what? Most women didn't know and didn't think about what they wanted, so it didn't matter if a repulsive maggot dressed in a nice suit or sagging jeans devoured a piece of meat or degraded them. Same results. Women literally permitted men to dissolve them into manure and then those same low-life men could convince a woman that she wasn't smart enough to wipe the shit from her own ass without his permission.

A raspy voice resonated in my right ear, "You have beautiful green eyes."

"Huh? What?" I said, looking at the woman's hardened nipples showing through her thin blue dress. I'd had my share of threesomes, foursomes, and thensomes with both men and women and could tell from the way her plump red lips suctioned her middle finger before flicking her tongue on the tip of her nail that she knew how to please more than a dick. Her long, lean legs were now crossed. Toenails and fingernails nicely manicured. She tucked her long black artificial hair behind her ear. Nice wig but it didn't match the natural brown strands of her eyebrows that the black liner pencil had missed.

"I complimented you on your eyes. They're beautiful. Like you."

Damn, her deep voice was sexy. If I hired her to book appointments, every man in the bar would immediately drop off his date at the hotel and head straight to IP. If I had sex with her, we'd come until the sun set.

"Thanks," I said, turning away and sipping the warm brown liquor from the clear snifter.

What were Benito and Valentino up to? Whatever ship was getting ready to sink wasn't going down with me on it, because I traveled with my life preserver at all times.

My phone rang. On the caller ID the number showed *private*. I always ignored private calls, but it might've been Sunny so I answered, "Yes?"

"Don't yes me. This is your mother."

The heartbeat thumping in my throat practically knocked me off my stool. Composing myself, I casually replied, "You've got the wrong number."

Rita did have the wrong number. Giving birth didn't make a woman a mother. I hadn't been her daughter since conception. For a second, I thought about Jean, my father, wondering what he looked liked. Where he lived.

"You know I wouldn't call you if I didn't have to. I don't need a damn thing from you. Honey needs you. She's dying from cancer. I want you to take your un-grateful ass straight to the airport and get on the first plane into Flagstaff. Do you hear me?"

Once a bitch, always a bitch. I wanted to hang up in Rita's face. But I couldn't. "How'd you get my num-ber?"

"You still askin' dumb questions. I always know where you are."

Well, Rita's response clarified quite a few unan-swered questions I had. My mother didn't look for me because she didn't want me.

Shifting my focus to my sister, I asked, "How sick is she?"

"I just said she's dying. What are you, deaf or some-thing? We'll see you at eleven sharp at Flagstaff Med. There's a six fifty-five morning flight from LAS to FLG that stops in Phoenix and arrives at Flagstaff at ten forty. Oh, and come prepared to stay a few days. The doctor said we might need some of your bone mar-row or something. Honey is calling me, I gotta go," Rita said, hanging up the phone.

God, I hate her. But I love my sister. Always have. Al-ways will. I didn't want Honey to die without holding her, without telling her how much I love her. But lying up in a hospital volunteering for doctors to cut, re-move, then donate any parts of my flawless body was out of the question. Swallowing what was left of my drink, I tossed a twenty on the bar and pushed away from the counter.

The lady in blue seemed preoccupied as she looked across the lounge scanning the room for remnants of a prospective date.

"Good luck," I said, turning my back on the woman.

Then I heard her raspy voice echo, "Nice seeing you, Lace."

Aw, hell no!

Tapping her on the shoulder, I firmly asked, "What did you just say?"

"I said, 'Nice lace.' "

Before leaving, I took a long, hard look at that bitch's brown eyes peering beneath her gray contacts. I'd heard her right the first time. She'd called me Lace.

CHAPTER 16

Benito

"What are you doing with a body bag in your basement?" I asked Valentino, trying not to look at the dead body lying at my feet, wondering if my bloody shoes or soon-to-be bloody hands would become Exhibit A if I got charged with her death.

If I'd taken Lace's advice and gotten a job, I wouldn't have been so available to Valentino. Why did Johnnie Cochran have to die before I had a chance to hire him? I'd heard he'd done pro bono work. Surely he would've represented a national icon like me for free. I was certain Lace would let me rot behind bars before bailing me out believing I'd killed this girl.

"See, that's the difference between a sergeant and a general. A general prepares for war in time of peace. Get your monkey ass downstairs, nigga. Now!"

Some black men were worse than white men. Give a brotha a little power or authority and he thought he had to prove himself worthy of being the white man's equal. A black man in America would never be equal to the white man, but the black man would readily sacrifice another black man trying to make it. *See, boss, I done good. I caught this here nigga trying to be like us. I'm a good overseer. If ya wants me too, I's hang this nigga, boss.*

Didn't matter if the black man was Mike, Ike, Michael, Wesley, Red, or Richard, the white man had all of those brothas believing they'd made *it*, whatever it was, simply because those black men had become successful utilizing their talents. But those same black men still couldn't fight, sing, act, joke, or laugh without the white man's permission.

The white man giveth and the white man tooketh away whenever he felt like it. Black men were whitewashed. Selling the white man's drugs to black people in his own community. Shooting black mothers, babies, and his own brothers over territory the fools didn't even own. Killing people over the white man's drugs and white man's money while the white man vacationed in Europe off the currency he'd stolen from the stupid black man, then exchanged for euros while the black man sat behind bars serving twice the time for the same exact crime committed by a white man.

Didn't Valentino know that the white man could take all of his shit, lock his ass up, and swallow the key to his future? I sure did. When Uncle Sam slapped a for-sale notice on everything except my ass, Valentino bailed me out and introduced me to Lace.

Like a gofer, I'd raced to the basement and sure nuff discovered a stack of body bags behind door number one. Sweat streamed from my pores. "What the fuck am I getting myself into?" Counting from bottom to top, I mouthed, "One, two, three . . . twelve, thirteen." I closed my eyes praying that the eleven escorts plus

Lace's names were nowhere on the remaining bags. There were two more doors, but I was in the damn basement afraid that an alarm would sound if I tried to escape. "Fuck."

I stood there wondering how many black men were delivered through the back door to the U.S. from Iraq in body bags. Or dismembered? Or discharged, mentally unstable, left to their own devices to find a job or a black woman with a job? How many more soldiers would senselessly die before the war on black oil ended? If the president and Congress were so pro war, why didn't they pick up semiautomatic weapons, load their wives, husbands, and children in tanks, then roll through the hot-ass desert praying they didn't get blown the hell up?

Those who had the power made the laws, were above the law, and didn't have to abide by the law. Any black man who didn't vote or wasn't involved with politics quietly gave the white man control over his life, thereby surrendering all the rights his ancestors fought, marched, and died for.

Young black men barely eighteen were stripped away from their mother's bosom, good black family men were unconsciously taken away from their families, while single black men disappeared into the darkness of the night never again to date, marry, or love a black woman—all had one thing in common. They were all sold by Uncle Sam on a modified form of slavery with a license to kill or be killed while the white man watched or reported the highlights on CNN.

The stroke of a pen etching a signature, a commitment, a promise, encouraged by brainwashing lies of how a black man could pursue a career in music, obtain a communications degree, or receive a large cash bonus by serving his country was dangled in the black man's face like fried chicken. The underlying truth the government didn't tell the black man was he'd just signed up to manufacture one more body bag with his name on it. Maybe I didn't want to have sons after all. But how can the black man continue his legacy with a world absent of his kind?

Valentino yelled from upstairs, "Hurry up, nigga. I ain't got all night."

Snatching the thick black rubber bag from the top of the stack, I dragged the bag up the steps. Bleach, ammonia, and other cleaning products were next to a plastic bucket of steaming water waiting for me.

"You got gloves, man? That water looks hot."

"Not nearly as hot as your ass if I bust a cap in it."

The chemical mixture and damn near boiling water blistered my flesh while Valentino stood over me pointing.

"Get that last piece of meat, then get her."

As tears streamed down my face, I shoved the half-naked mutilated body into the bag, zipped it up, secured the straps across her breasts, waist, and legs, then asked, "What's her name?"

"This ain't *Who Wants to be a Millionaire*, nigga! Next thing I know you'll be asking to phone a friend for help and shit. You got one more time to ask one more question and that's yo' ass! Hurry up and move this bitch out!"

You think you know someone until they threaten your life to save theirs. That was supposed to be my boy. Can't say I ever did much for him other than be his friend. But he'd taken friendship too far.

Two hundred and fifty thousand wasn't worth this, but it was enough to find that small town I'd thought about relocating to.

Drying the floor as fast as I could, I accidentally splashed bleach everywhere, wiped everything up, then hurled the body bag over my shoulder and watched it fall to the floor.

"Damn. Sorry, miss."

"Nigga, drag her ass and take that gold bag too. Wait a minute," Valentino said, slightly unzipping the bag. "Here." He slapped the gun in my hand, then continued. "Toss this inside and bury all those cleaning supplies and her shit with her. Get some gasoline, then set her ass on fire before tossing dirt in her face."

Placing the purse on my shoulder, I decided I wasn't a mortician and wanted to ask where I should bury the body since I couldn't legally burn it within city limits. But I knew better than to question my boy, so I kept walking backward, dragging the body.

Valentino's eyes bulged. "Wait, have you ever done a strip search before?" he asked.

Hunching my shoulders, I shook my head, silently asking for Valentino's mother's forgiveness, certain Mama James was turning over in her grave like an overcooked rotisserie chicken.

"After you get rid of her, I'm sending you to my joint to strip-search these bitches. If you do a good job, I might hire you and fire your bitch. Call me when you're done with Summer, I mean Sunny. That's her name, Sunny. Then I'll teach you how to demand respect from bitches."

"Fuck, man! You tryna get me killed," I said, dropping the bag. "Sunny was Lace's favorite girl." I could use that job, but would I live long enough to report on the first day?

Valentino's eyes, lips, and forehead tightened. "Keep the ointment, nigga. You'll need it to lube your ass."

Good thing I didn't have the nerves to search for that gun. Friend or no friend, I'd shoot Valentino. Or maybe after burying Sunny, I should kill myself before Lace got a chance to.

Silently, I dumped the body bag in the trunk of Lace's car along with the purse, then sped down Rancho Road to the highway. Ten miles south on Interstate 15 as I headed toward . . . truth was I didn't know where I was headed, weaving in and out of the three lanes . . . red and blue lights proceeded by several bloops and I got pulled over to the side of the road listening to a cop blare from an intercom, "Do not get out of your car!"

If I were lucky, he'd shoot first and ask questions when it was too late for me to answer. Sweat drenched my body. I darn near pissed on myself, but the thought of Lace cussing me out for messing up her leather-ventilated seat made me hold it in.

Walking up to my window with his hand on his gun, the police asked, "Where you in such a hurry to go to that you just about ran me off the road?"

Temporarily taking advantage of the Fifth Amendment, I sat with my hands at four and eight on Lace's steering wheel so he couldn't see the skin bubbling on the back of my hands.

"Let me see your license and registration."

With my palm facing up, I cautiously handed him my driver's license, along with Lace's registration and insurance, refusing to speak unless I absolutely had to.

"Well, I'll be darned! You the same Benito Bannister that won that there national football championship?"

"That's me," I said, nervously rotating the diamond ring on my finger to prove it. Leaning back in my seat, I prayed the cop didn't see me sweating.

"Tell ya what, gimme that ring and I'll let you go with a warning," he said jokingly.

Forcing the ring off my finger, I wanted to scream like a bitch. I placed it in his hand, and eased my license and papers from between his fingers.

Frowning, he said, "Looks like there's blood on this ring."

"Yeah, I cut myself tossing a few balls. Gotta keep my arm strong just in case I come out of retirement. It's no big deal, I'm used to injuries."

"Guess you're right, else you'd still be playing. Here, hold on to it for me," he said, smiling. "But drive safe before you kill yourself or somebody else, ya hear?"

"Thanks, Officer."

I sat there wondering where to take Sunny. After I was positively sure the cop was gone, I unlocked the trunk, then rambled through her gold bag. Her driver's license had an address in North Las Vegas. "Hell, not only do I live in that area, I just left there."

When I glanced at her birth date, my chin damn near hit my neck. "Fuck! This girl really is turning twenty-one in less than an hour!"

Knowing Valentino, I'm the one taking the rap for this if the police find out. "Fuck this." I drove to the address on Chestnut, parked on the back side of the unit, and made sure the key worked before I returned to Lace's car to get the body. Checking out her living room, I saw Sunny was fanatical about cleanliness. Rummaging through her kitchen, I opened the cabinet and found exactly what I needed: alcohol—vodka, tequila, rum, cognac.

Peeling the metal strip off the cognac, I gulped until my throat burned. "Argh!" I sat on the leather sofa dreading getting that girl's body out of the trunk until my phone rang.

"You done, nigga?"

"Naw, man. Not yet," I said, swallowing and looking around the contemporarily decorated unit. "Don't you have a hookup or somebody who can take her off my hands?"

"You ain't no runner, nigga. You da man. Lookahere, after you're done dumping the body, this is how you do a strip search."

As I listened in disgust, I could tell clearly he didn't want any knowledge about where I was gonna bury this girl. I wanted to throw up again, but my aching stomach was on fire.

"I'll stall Lace so you'll get home before her. Finish both jobs, then call me when you're on your way home. And thanks, man. We're even," Valentino exclaimed.

"What about my job?"

"What job?" Valentino asked, ending the call.

I remained silent staring at the photo above the fireplace doubting there was any money involved for my services. Now he was playing mind games with me. "Damn." I pressed my thumb and middle finger into my eye sockets. "Is that Sunny? Am I drunk?" Or was I seeing doubles? Aw, hell no. Was this bitch a twin? "Argh! Fuck. Why me?" I yelled, finishing off the bottle.

Warm liquid streamed through my boxers, then down my thighs, soaking my sweatpants. Sliding off the pissy lime couch, I focused on what must've been their parents. They looked like such a lovely Christian family with their mother smiling and holding a Bible. Seemed like they'd raised them right, but where did Sunny's life go wrong? People who thought they knew me well would ask the same question not if but when I was arrested for murder.

Leaving to get her body out of the car, I closed the door but wasn't sure if I was returning upstairs, headed to Immaculate Perception, the police station, home, or straight to hell.

CHAPTER 17

Summer

Fluttering my sleepy eyes to the familiar sound of a key unlocking the front door followed by a squeak, then a soft thump, I exhaled, "Thank you, God, for answering my prayers." God had brought my sister home. I swung my legs over the side of the bed. My wobbling feet wiggled with excitement everywhere except inside my shoes as I tried to yell, "Sunny!" but no sound escaped my trembling lips.

Abandoning my tennis shoes, I rushed barefoot to the doorway, smiling ear to ear. I didn't want to scare Sunny so I peeped between the crack of the bedroom door, then gasped, cupping my mouth. Unless Sunny had grown muscles the size of watermelons, gained more than a hundred pounds, and had a sex change, that was not my sister.

Squinting at his frowning face, I recognized the well-groomed, casually dressed man crossing the threshold.

I'd seen him someplace, I just couldn't recall where. But why was he at my sister's home? Obviously she'd given him a key. Smiling again, I imagined he was Sunny's boyfriend. Might as well introduce myself and find out if he knew where Sunny was. As I moved to open the door, an invisible force like heavy hands braced my shoulders. My feet alternated moving in place.

Stepping backward into the bedroom, I stared at the space in front of me, then patted the air. The breeze was cold. I focused on the familiar-looking man in the living room. He made himself comfortable, then opened and began drinking from a full liquor bottle.

Answering his cell phone, he sat on the edge of the sofa guzzling alcohol like it was tea, then said, "Don't you have a hookup or somebody who can take her off my hands?"

You scandalous dog. No, you're not trying to ditch my sister in her house!

As I reached for the doorknob, a chilling gust of wind froze my hand. This time I did a three hundred-and-sixty-degree turn, gnawing the side of my palm.

Placing the empty liquor bottle on the coffee table, he closed the front door. My heart thumped against my breast as I cautiously reached for the knob, expecting another strange sensation. Easing into the living room, I crawled to the window and peeped at the silver emblem on the hood of a black car.

The muscular guy stood in front of the car looking to his left, then his right. Scanning the parking lot, he quickly glanced up at the window. Holding my breath, I kept the curtain still, praying he didn't see me. He frowned. I froze.

"God help me," I prayed.

He proceeded to unlock his trunk. The rear tire and side panel partially obscured my view. Why did visitors' parking have to be on the back side? How was anyone going to help me if they couldn't see me? Closing the trunk, he bent over, hoisted up, then dragged what resembled an unfolded garment bag toward the stairway.

Hurrying back into the bedroom, I closed the door. I pressed my ear against the white-painted wood, hearing what I assumed was him opening the front door again. Listening intently, I heard the squeak followed by a click, which reassured me the back door had closed and he was not on the outside.

I motioned to lock the bedroom door. Massaging the handle, I felt my heart thumping against my breast. *Oh no!* There was no lock or latch. Not knowing what to do, I hid in the worst possible but only available place, praying he wouldn't come into Sunny's room. When I heard the bedroom doorknob jiggle, my heart thumped and I silenced my cell phone. There was no inconspicuous place inside the closet where I could hide, so I quietly unscrewed the unlit bulb and pressed my body into the V of the corner, layering Sunny's long black mink over my head and bundling her comforter around my legs and feet, which reminded me I'd forgotten to put on my shoes.

Pressing my hands together, I prayed silently, "No weapon formed against me shall prosper. Yea, though I walk through the valley of the shadow of death, I will fear no evil." I was terrified, so I kept repeating the words hoping God heard me.

"Damn!" he yelled, opening the door.

The s*lush, slush, slush* sounds got louder and closer each time I heard him move.

"Please, God, don't let him come in the closet."

"Sunny's got a nice layout here. Too bad for her. With a house so neat, why was her bed unmade?" he said, opening the closet door and tossing something inside. A piece of heavy metal landed on my pinky toe. As he mumbled, "After this strip search, I'm done with Valentino. I wonder if he knows Sunny has a twin. Maybe he should hire her. Then no one would know Sunny is—" I wanted to scream but something caressed my foot and sealed my lips together.

Sunny was what? Finish the sentence.

The hairs on the mink tickled my nostril. *No. Not now. Please don't let me . . .* I held my breath as his cell phone rang. Before he'd stepped out of the closet his deep voice answered, "Hey, baby. No, I'm not out fucking around. Don't try to turn this on me. Look, I'm on my way home. Where are you?"

His voice faded as I heard the back door close.

Was my sister dating a married man? Maybe he was the reason she'd sent me her bank statement?

Waiting seemingly forever, I finally eased my way in front of a wardrobe, grasping the dangling sales tags attached to over half the clothes. Screwing in the lightbulb, I slipped, landing on top of the bag. "Ouch!" Furiously kicking, I hurt my sore toe, yelling louder, "Ouch!" Crawling around the bag this time to the bedroom window, I watched the same guy get into the Jag. Smashing his face against the windshield, he stared in my direction.

When he drove away, I retreated from the window, set my phone on the bed, and went back into the closet. With no lights, I couldn't see much so I flipped the switch, wishing I hadn't. The thickness of the material bubbled into a lump underneath that indicated garments were not in that bag. I pinched the long silver piece of metal and slightly unzipped the bag. I had to see what was inside.

Stooping closer, I tugged about an inch, then cried, "Oh my God!" as ammonia burned my nostrils, making me back away.

I stood staring at the bag before leaving the closet. "Okay, Summer, breathe in. Breathe out." Trying to stay calm and optimistic, I laced up my shoes, then grabbed my cell phone, Sunny's Bible, my car keys, Sunny's house key, and ran through the living room, bypassing the empty bottle. Stopping at the threshold, I retreated to the kitchen, yanked a Ziplock bag out of the drawer, sealed the liquor bottle, then hid the finger-printed evidence in the freezer.

I snatched open the back door and, "Ahhh!" there he was.

Slamming and locking the door, I sprinted into Sunny's bedroom closet, stuffing her Bible inside my shirt.

When I heard the front door open, he yelled out, "You can run but you can't hide."

I'd seen too many movies where the assailant over-powered the hopeless victim, and I started crying until something lifted me from the corner and whispered, "Go to the window." Faster than I imagined I could move, I opened that window, threw my purse down-stairs, crawled onto the small balcony, clamped my fingers around the rail, and hung with my feet dangling in midair.

His face appeared larger than the moon only this time without a helmet. He was the quarterback my father used to watch on television all the time. My dad had an autographed jersey and photo of this man framed in our computer room.

"You're not getting away," he said, reaching for my wrist.

"God, help me!" I screamed, letting go. The spongy thickness of my soles cushioned my landing. Watching him disappear into the bedroom, I scrambled, snatching my handbag from the sidewalk. My hands trembled so

badly I dropped my keys onto my car mat. Swiftly retrieving them, I started my engine.

Bam! His fist pounded on my hood.

Backing out, I didn't know how my car spun around
in one swoop, but I sped out of Sunny's parking lot,
onto the street, and couldn't remember anything else
except crying the entire time all the way home.

I was fairly certain my sister's body was in that bag,
so there was no way I was going to go back to Sunny's
condo alone. I needed to get the police and my parents
involved. What if my mom couldn't handle what I'd say
and suffered a heart attack and died?

God, why me?

Somebody else had to help me solve this mystery
without me upsetting Mom and Dad. Parked in my parents' driveway, I checked my cell. I'd missed ten calls.
Probably half were from Mom and the other half from
Dad. I scrolled to Anthony James's name, wondering if
his number was the same. Anthony was the type of
man who'd do anything for me. At least that was what
he'd said when we parted over five years ago.

What would I say to him after all these years? "Hi,
Anthony. This is Summer, remember me?" What if he
was married and his wife answered? Or I could say,
"Anthony, this is Summer. I need you." That *I need you*
line always worked on my dad when my mother used it.

A set of high beams flashed twice directly at my car,
then vanished.

"Oh my God. What was I thinking? Did he follow
me home all the way to Henderson?"

CHAPTER 18

Benito

Now that I knew where Sunny's twin lived, I'd deal with her later, but right now I had to get to Valentino's spot before he called me again. Cruising along Interstate 15 North, I clung to the steering wheel with aching hands. With the exception of Sunny's sister's home located in Henderson, Valentino's house, IP, Sunny's condo, Lace's and my place were all in North Las Vegas, each within a three-mile radius and in the same police jurisdiction.

Things were starting to make sense. No matter what went down, Valentino was protected, but my black ass was not. I was heated that a black man was either a test case, had to take a test, get tested, or be tested every second of his life.

In the Tuskegee Syphilis Study: six hundred dignified African-American men became human guinea pigs to the white scientists who played God, killing highly intelligent black military airmen who'd traveled from every region of the country—New York City, Los Angeles, Chicago, Philadelphia, Detroit—eager to serve their country.

White men didn't want to admit they were jealous of the fact, as I'd seen confirmed on *Oprah*, that black men had bigger dicks. So the white man went from cutting off the black man's dick to creating a sexually transmitted disease so that every time a black man fucked basically his time was up. From syphilis to the more life-threatening HIV/AIDS, by any means necessary the white man was willing to sacrifice a few of his own in hopes that black men from Africa to America would one day become exactly like dinosaurs: extinct.

Observing the speed limit, with multiple thoughts swarming in my mind, I was just trying to make my way across town without being stopped by the police.

The U.S. government not only denied 103 black Tuskegee officers entitled access to the Freeman Field Officers' Club, but also arrested the black officers, charged them with insubordination, and ordered each one to face court-martial. Oh, say, does that star-spangled banner yet wave, for the land of the free, which didn't include me, and the home of the, for whites, brave, for blacks, slaves?

Each day I was more convinced I shouldn't have any more children because the white man's development and implementation of the statewide high school exit examinations that more teachers than students failed were designed to deny the black man higher education while paying incompetent white men a salary to oversee the process.

An innocent black man who'd dropped out of high school could be convicted and sentenced to prison for decades simply because the white man knew the black man was worth more to him behind bars. A pardon and an apology were all the white man would offer in exchange for making $1.5 million off a black man incarcerated for forty years.

"Let's see. Hell, I'd be damn near seventy-five if I had to do that kind of time."

By design, the black man was robbed of forty years of freedom, forty years of voting, and forty acres while being the white man's mule. Forty years of free labor and the black man was supposed to be happy whenever the white man grinned and said, "Sorry, the jury mistakenly found you guilty. You're free to go, boy." Go where? To hell? Homeless on the streets? Or back to his mama's or some other black woman's house to eat and sleep until they stripped the shirt off his back or kicked his ass out.

No-fuckin'-body should question why a black man living in America was angry. The reason I could throw a football a hundred yards and hit a moving target wasn't that I was strong; I was pissed my ancestors weren't allowed to play professional sports and that schools like the University of San Francisco no longer had a football team because years ago white men refused to let a white coach with black standout players compete for the championship so the white coach did exactly what the white men wanted him to do. He gave up fighting for the black athletes' rights. To this day, USF still does not have a football team.

Maybe I was foolish for wanting justice in an unjust society when all I knew how to do was complain mainly to myself. One day I'd get mine and get the hell up out of America, but the only way for me to do so was to stop acting black and start thinking white. Irrespective of socioeconomic or political status, every white man felt superior to the black man. But the white man's offspring bought more hip-hop and learned how to bebop better than blacks.

Upon my arrival at IP, I parked in the first space closest to the entrance as Valentino had informed me that was Lace's spot. I entered as instructed and went directly to the second floor. Eleven girls were lined up naked, with their hands cuffed behind their backs, blindfolded, waiting for me. This was my first opportunity to prove my new manhood.

Thrusting my chest forward, I demanded, "Security, step outside until I'm done with these bitches," just the way Valentino had ordered me to.

Adrenaline rushed through my veins. Hearing myself say the word *bitch* made me feel empowered. Indirectly I had one murder that Valentino would attach to me and one premeditated murder brewing in my mind about Sunny's twin. That's how white men killed their victims, with forethought, planning, an alibi, and a witness who'd testify based on the time and place of the murder they couldn't have been at the scene of the crime. Figuring out how to make Lace my witness would be harder than killing anybody.

Fuck, what was wrong with me? Was this bullshit really happening? I must've been dreaming. Had I just dumped a dead body and followed a complete stranger home?

Focusing on the grand prize, I imagined what a black man with a soon-to-be warrant could do with two hundred and fifty g's before going to jail. It had been a while since I had that kind of cash. Maybe secretly Valentino was prepping me to be his right-hand man and handling these women was part two of my test before he'd hire me. Hopefully there wasn't a part three, but I'd bet giving me a quarter of a mil was Valentino's way of gauging my loyalty.

"Stand up straight. Now I want you tricks to tell me, who spoke with Sunny last night?" When I asked the question my stomach knotted up like a boxer hitting me below the belt.

Swallowing hard, grinding my back teeth, I was sure my guilty conscience had made me sick when Mama James's voice echoed in my ear, "Benito, baby, what are you doing?"

Ignoring the excruciating pain in my stomach and the pulsations in my head, I continued my assignment, glad the worst part was over. Sunny's body was where it was going to stay. Once I got paid, I was permanently moving to Rio de Janeiro, where the women treated black men like royalty and for two hundred dollars, I'd heard, I could have six of the most beautiful Brazilian women take turns sucking my dick.

Deepening my voice, I roughly demanded, "Okay, since nobody's talking, open your mouths wide."

I was sure they sensed I wasn't a true pimp and I was positive Mama James was turning in her grave watching me jab my finger down each of the girls' throats until they threw up. When I got to girl number six she said, "Onyx and Starlet are Sunny's friends. I'm sure one of them knows the real reason Sunny didn't make it in the limo."

"Who's Onyx and Starlet?"

Again no one spoke a word until girl six broke the silence answering, "Girl eleven is Starlet, and Onyx, the beautiful black bitch, is the perfect little ten."

The dark-complexioned one was incredibly gorgeous with flawless skin, perfect breasts, chocolate nipples, and a hairless pussy that I craved to stick my tongue in. She looked so damn good my dick got hard instantly as I imagined pouring thick warm chocolate all over her protruding pussy. As soon as my finger entered her mouth, she bit the hell out of me, splitting my nail across the flesh.

"Owwwwwww! Stupid bitch!"

Girl six snickered. "Beat her."

Without thinking I backhand slapped number ten so hard her head jerked. I'd never hit a woman before, but honestly it felt good. Moments later I felt bad and pissed off at the same time. Why did she make me do that to her?

Since none of the other girls could see me, I unzipped my pants, rubbed my stiff dick between Onyx's butt cheeks, then did what Lace wouldn't allow me to do in our bedroom. I finger-fucked Onyx until her pussy was nice and juicy, and then I slowly penetrated her wet pussy. My eyes scrolled to the back of my head. Passionately choking Onyx, I swear red velvet melt-in-your-mouth cake felt like sandpaper in comparison to this girl's incredible pussy. "Fuck!" Halfway in, her muscles clamped my dick so tight I froze. Loosening my fingers from around Onyx's throat, I came instantly.

Onyx whispered, "Satisfied, Benito Bannister?"

I yanked my sweats over my ass so fast, my now-jagged nail scraped my dick. "Ouch! See what the fuck you made me do!" I slapped Onyx hard across her opposite cheek.

The girl didn't flinch. Was she human or robot? She stood there as though she was accustomed to having her ass beaten.

Calmly she continued. "Right now you're probably wondering how I know you since I can't see you. I never forget a voice. The championship game afterparty. Your house. Hot tub. Remember now?"

Aw, shit! Actually I could recall the night but not her face.

"You were probably too wasted to remember me, but I'm sure you couldn't forget that awesome underwater blow job I gave you. You know, the one where you passed out afterward from drinking too much cognac—is it that I smell?"

Okay, now I can't kill all these bitches, I thought, pacing while staring at Onyx. Continuing my search so I could get the hell out of there, I bent the girls over one by one and stuck my finger up their pussies, then one by one up their assholes. All except girl number ten. When I got to the black beauty who had the memory of an elephant, I finger-fucked her real hard, kissed her pussy, then said, "Tomorrow Valentino has something special for you all. Six o'clock, don't be late."

I turned to walk away and heard Onyx ask, "Where's Sunny's body?"

Flashing back to when Valentino had that gun upside my head, I walked out wondering what the hell I'd gotten myself into. Now I understood how Valentino pulled that trigger on Sunny. That bitch Onyx was too fucking clever and as much as I'd hate to admit it, I was scared as hell.

Exiting the room, I looked at security and said, "Beat the hell out of girl six."

All my life my brother snitched on me. While I appreciated the information from girl six, I would've been better off not screwing Onyx and then getting fucked. I cupped my dick, and the stinging sensation made me wanna cry. I hadn't injured my dick since getting it stuck in my zipper in high school.

Starting Lace's engine, I dialed Valentino. "It's done. Don't ask me for shit else."

"I saw you. You done good, my nigga. Busted a nut and checked that ass at the same time. Go home and rest up. After Lace goes to sleep, you'll find the safe inside the shower walls. Stand on the built-in shower bench, then push in the center tile with the gold rose on it. The one on the ceiling. A door will slide open. You'll see a keypad. Unscramble, then punch in the code I gave you and the floor beneath you will part. Be careful not to slip your ass in, nigga, or it'll close and chop your fuckin' feet off. Remove the silver bag and there'll be two hundred fifty grand in it. It's all yours. Don't try to skip town on me 'cause I'll find you and kill you myself. Straight."

What was worse? Going to jail for forty years or following the explicit instructions Valentino had given me? I might take my chances, get the money, and leave the country as planned. But what about my girl, Lace?

"Wait up, Valentino. That trick Onyx knew me from a previous party. What if she goes to the police?"

Now I couldn't leave before finding a way to stop Onyx.

As I was opening my mouth to tell Valentino about the twin, he spoke first.

"I can hear your ass thinking, B. You'll be six feet under, nigga, faster than that electronic airline ticket is transmitted. Trust me, just like you, Onyx will keep her mouth shut, or you'll both end up . . ." Valentino paused as if I was supposed to fill in the blank before he hung up.

CHAPTER 19

Valentino

Pacing the floor in my kitchen, I ended the call with Benito's ig'nant ass and keyed in his bitch's number. Since I started pimpin' full-time, a G like me had to fix my own food. I couldn't risk hiring a cook, especially not a woman, and damn sure nuff, no set of balls bigger than mine were gonna crush my nuts or poison my soup. Where in the hell was Lace? She wasn't answering her home phone, so after dicing the red leaf lettuce and yellow bell peppers, tossing in dried cranberries and fresh pineapples, and sprinkling in walnuts, I speed-dialed her cell.

"Valentino, hey. What's up?" That bitch had the audacity to answer all cheerful and shit on the first ring.

"Don't what's up me. Why aren't you at home?" I demanded, massaging minced garlic into my Grade-A plump and juicy steak. Real men ate beef, not fish.

"Have a lot on my mind. Maybe you can help clear some things up for me."

Did this bitch fall, bump her head, and get amnesia forgetting who in the hell I was?

"Don't make me fuck up this nice center-cut steak," I said, closing the lid on my George Foreman grill. Inhaling the aroma of sizzling garlic with fresh onions, I said, "All you're going to do is go home and protect my money. Come in early tomorrow and bring all of my cash with you."

"Early? Hmmm. You do know the center cut is the cow's ass? Of course you do. Anyway, I might have to take a trip tomorrow. I'll get back with you on my availability."

Removing my Bluetooth, I wiggled my pointing finger inside my ear. Did I hear that bitch right? I swear my blood pressure could've deep-fried the Italian breaded chicken breast sprawled across my chopping board. I'ma have to expedite Reynolds's assignment and have this bitch terminated sooner than I'd intended.

Maybe once Lace was dead, I'd fire all her tricks and start over with eleven new bitches and retire Summer's number twelve. I'd give up this business if I thought it'd bring back Summer and she'd birth my babies. What good was it for me to have millions of dollars and no one to leave it to? But Summer was dead and trying to convince Lace I didn't pull the trigger wasn't going to fly and that nigga Benito couldn't be trusted to run a damn thing except his mouth.

Clipping on my headset, I stuffed the piece of ass in the garbage disposal and began deveining twelve tiger prawns. "Don't fuck with me. Have your ass here at six o'clock tomorrow night or find yourself another job."

I needed Lace but I had to put her ass on a tight leash until I found a replacement. Problem was no one else in my life was trustworthy or capable of running my entire empire.

"Hmm, interesting. I may take you up on that offer. I was actually thinking about quitting. Changing the subject, where's Sunny?"

"She's doing what you should be doing, getting fucked. Obviously Benito isn't servicing you well, because your ass is straight trippin'. What's gotten into you?"

"You," she answered.

I ignored that bitch. I already told her she couldn't fuck with my dick. It was bad enough she'd already fucked up my head. I wanted to fuck Lace so bad the night I'd hired her away from the Pussyland Ranch. I loved those beautiful green feisty eyes and she was so fuckin' assured of herself. Every bitch could be bought, but I loved Lace because she knew her price, was willing to fight for what she believed in, and her milky soft skin was wrapped around those big ol' creamy titties with gumdrop nipples. Her waist swooped in and her ass curved out into a perfect P. And that sweet black licorice hair flowed over her shoulders and down her back.

After cleaning the last prawn, I circled the six-by-four-foot island trying to stay ahead of her smart ass. I could've snatched one of the dozen skillets or pots dangling around my double-oven stove and batted Lace in her mouth with the steroid strength of Barry mother-fuckin' wannabe the leading home run hitter dressed in drag like a fuckin' fag Bozo.

Sighing, she said, "Let's leave B out of this. Why did you ask me to deviate from the norm tonight? If you fucked up, I'm the one you'd better tell."

"For a bitch who was late, you've got more questions than Alex on *Jeopardy*. I guess you have the thousand-dollar answer too, bitch."

Unwavering in her tone, she said, "You know what, I think you're right because tonight between you and Benito I hit the daily double. Either you tell me what's going on, or you find yourself another madam. And if you do hire another madam, with the press of a button, I'll send your entire client list to—"

I stabbed a butcher's knife into the wooden chopping board—that bitch was either lying or had lied to a G like me! She told me none of my shit was traceable and I believed her. But she never told me her shit wasn't documented. Tossing my prawn in behind the steak, I scraped the salad into the sink too. The china plate spun, screeching, until it rattled, then quietly settled in the stainless steel sink. This bitch had made me lose my appetite.

"Look, I can't talk about this shit over the phone. Tomorrow at six I'll tell you everything when I see you," I lied. I'd have a surprise waiting for her ass when she showed up without my money.

"Tonight."

"What the fuck?"

"It's after midnight, so technically you mean you'll tell me tonight at six. I'll see you then."

Trusting a bitch smarter than me, I should've known I'd eventually get fucked. Now I had to figure out if Lace was bluffing or if she really had a list and where she kept the information.

"Get some rest because you're gonna have to beat all of your whores tonight . . . Hello? Hello?"

Looking at the display on my phone, I thought, *did that bitch just hang up on Valentino James?*

CHAPTER 20

Lace

Valentino had lost his mind.

Dropping my cell phone into my purse, I made a U-turn and headed to Immaculate Perception. Me? Beat somebody's ass? Sure I'd done a few strip searches when I first started working for Valentino and put fear in all the girls, the kind of fear that with one lingering whisper in their ears sent a terrifying chill throughout their bodies. With the exception of girl six, I hadn't beaten any of my girls in months. Didn't have to.

A beat-down was brutal and I didn't know how to half-ass do anything, so if I commenced to whipping asses, all I could do is pray they didn't all end up in emergency like a few of my catfight victims at the Pussyland Ranch. If Valentino wanted a strip search done, his punk ass would have to do it himself.

I could tell something wasn't right by the controlling tone in Valentino's voice. That and he'd never been overly concerned about me collecting his money before his clients received their services. Valentino loved having everyone indebted to him. Hearing the insecurity in his voice, I felt the chill in my bones, but I was no fool. I'd definitely intimidated him.

Right now I knew he was pacing his floor questioning a lot of things. How much information I had. Where I kept it. How could he get it? How was he going to fire me? Who'd replace me? Whether or not to kill me.

I valued my life, and the strongest advantage I had over Valentino and Benito was that I was smarter than both of those egotistical morons put together. Deprogramming the signal, I remotely scrambled the pictures on Valentino's monitors beyond recognition. What I needed to do wouldn't take long, and by the time Valentino got here, I'd be gone.

Smoothing out my lace skirt to cover the gun in my garter holster, I parked next to . . . my own car? Okay, they made more than one black Jag, so I retrieved my electronic car key, pointed, then pressed the lock button. Sure enough, the lights silently flashed twice as I scanned my license plate.

Aw, hell no! Valentino was the only one at the mansion. I'd picked up his money early, was told to go home, and my man was here. Doing what? If Benito was in there fucking one of my girls, I was going to shoot his dick off.

Quietly unlocking the entrance to IP, I toured from room to room, starting with the Presidential Suite, to find Sunny. No one was there and the room was untouched, so I checked the S and M gym. Empty. Making certain my heels didn't *click-clack* on the marbled tiles, I peeped inside Fantasy Island, the House of Hot

Wax, and the other rooms. Now, this shit was weird. No Benito and nobody else. Fuck! That meant only thing.

Running as fast as I could, I darted down the stairs to the second floor to the room I hated the most, the discipline room. Opening the door, I saw the girls blindfolded and butt naked. "What the hell is going on in here?" I demanded.

"Business," Reynolds answered, hoisting up his pants.

I pulled my gun from under my skirt, placed it against his temple, and said, "Well, this here is personal." Tightening my finger against the trigger, I was so fucking mad I slammed the handle into his skull.

Placing my gun in my holster, I said, "Let this be a lesson to you," pointing to the other two security men. "You know the rules. If I hear that another one of you fucked one of my girls, your ass is mine, but I guarantee you I won't be as nice next time. Get his punk ass outta here. You're fired!" I said, stomping my stiletto into his dick and rewinding Valentino's message to Reynolds. A woman had to know how to turn on her poker face. Knowing Reynolds had been instructed to kill me, I had no compassion for him.

"You can't fire me, bitch! You're gonna pay for this!" Reynolds yelled, cupping his crotch.

"Hold up. Did somebody say something?" I said, intensely eyeing the other two guards, watching them shake their heads.

Reynolds shouted, "You heard me, bitch! You're gonna—"

Any man who talked that much needed to be shut the fuck up. Removing my gun from my garter, I pointed the barrel toward Reynolds's forehead.

"You don't have the balls," he said, leaning forward and reaching for his piece.

As I lowered my hand like a choir director signaling

to bring down the tone, my girls hung their head in unison.

I whispered, "You're right. I don't. But what I do have is pussy power, motherfucka."

Pow!

One bullet between Reynolds's eyebrows snapped his head to the floor.

"Burn his body, then bury him," I said to the two security guards standing with their mouths gaped open.

I could tell both of them wanted to say something, but they were too afraid because they knew pussy power was bigger than any set of balls.

"Now, where was I?"

Making sure all of my girls got dressed, I went downstairs and retrieved the silver case from my trunk. My black Jag was gone. Gathering the girls around the bar, I handed each of them five thousand in cash.

"Don't report to work tomorrow unless I call you." Whatever was going down, I needed each of my girls on my side, not Valentino's. "If I need you to report, I'll call Onyx tonight with the location and Onyx will call each of you."

Instead of sending them to Valentino's to change clothes, I instructed security, "Drop them off at the bar on Paradise and let them go home. Then get rid of Reynolds. And don't say a word to Valentino about any of this or I'll kill you too."

I knew they'd get rid of the body, but I also knew they'd tell Valentino everything because Valentino would torture them if they didn't.

"Onyx and Starlet, let me speak to you for a moment," I said, instructing the other girls to go outside and get in the limo. This was the first time any of them had stepped foot outside IP without blindfolds.

Onyx remained silent while Starlet answered, "Yes, Madam?"

For a moment I paused because Starlet sounded exactly like Sunny. "Call me Lace. I need to know what happened at the mansion tonight. Where's Sunny?"

Starlet looked to Onyx with wide eyes. Onyx wrapped her arm around Starlet's waist, then said, "It's okay, Star. Lace, we don't know anything."

"C'mon, I'm only trying to help Sunny," I pleaded. "Onyx, please tell me whatever it is you know."

Onyx heaved several times before she said, "You don't give a fuck about helping anyone but yourself. Besides, Benito Bannister told us where to meet tonight at six o'clock." A teardrop clung to her lash extension. "We feel that you're quitting and the only one you care enough to take with you is Sunny. What about the rest of us? Haven't we been good to you?"

Hearing Onyx speak my own words, I fanned my hand backward toward the door as my lips disappeared inside my mouth. Was that what she thought? Was that what she'd heard? I couldn't lie to Onyx or comfort her, because she was right. I had considered leaving and taking Sunny with me. Fighting back my own tears, I said, "Leave. Now."

Grabbing Starlet's hand, Onyx led her to the limo.

I stood in the doorway until the license plate BITCHES vanished beyond the gate. The more I worked with these girls, the more I knew I had to help not just Sunny but all of them find a way out of the business. But how? My relationship with my girls was like being in a sorority. I could handle them, but nobody else had better lay a hand on them.

I wanted to ask Onyx what part Benito played in all of this but didn't want to alert them that he was my man. I'd find out Benito's purpose for showing up here when I got home. Taking the remainder of the money, I'd tell Valentino that I deducted the fifty-five thousand dollars as part of my salary for the month.

I grabbed the case, locked the door, and walked to the parking area. I didn't have a reason to show up at Valentino's mansion, but if anything out of the ordinary went down I needed my voice recorder, which was hidden inside the *First Lady* book on Valentino's shelf. It wasn't like I ever had to worry about Valentino reading a book about a woman being a first anything. Behind that big blue hat and devious smile on the cover, underneath I'd collected enough evidence to send Valentino to prison for life.

No matter how secure a woman thought her position was, a woman had to be ten times smarter than every man around her. Listening to the recording tomorrow might be okay, but it also might be too late. Tonight was too risky. Driving off the premises, I checked my surroundings for Valentino's car and anything suspicious. MLK Boulevard was quiet. I restored Valentino's monitors to normal, then picked up my cell phone and dialed Benito.

"Hey, baby," he answered. "You wondering what I'm wondering?"

What was he talking about?

I answered, "Like why in the hell was your car at IP? Why were you there? Yes, I am wondering."

"Lace, don't start trippin' again. I've been home all night. Where are you?"

"So if I check my odometer on my car the meter will read the same as when I left home. Right?"

Benito became silent trying to figure out an answer to a question he didn't have the answer to. I learned a long time ago a woman could easily back a man into a corner, but she had to prepare herself if he came out fighting.

"I don't have to prove anything to you. We'll discuss this when you get home in a few."

Bingo! That was the kind of defensive reaction I'd predicted.

"I'm not coming straight home," I lied, "I'm working late."

"Lace, don't do this to me. Valentino said you were on your way. I've had more than I can handle tonight. Bring your ass home to me. Now."

"Pussy or luck? Don't answer that. Since when did Valentino start talking to you about my whereabouts?"

"Lace, bring your ass straight home," Benito said, then hung up the phone.

Benito's inability to be truthful with me definitely had him on the defense, so I had to plan my best offensive strategy.

Removing my stiletto, I glanced at the full moon, then plunged the accelerator. I know he did not hang up in my face, in my house.

Parking in my garage, I noticed my black Jag was parked with the trunk facing the garage door. "Damn, I told him to always back in just in case there was an emergency." In my line of business, the time difference between backing out and pulling out was life or death.

Entering the house, I watched in disgust as Benito lounged on the sofa watching television.

"What took you so long?" he asked with his arms folded high across his chest.

I set the silver case beside my feet. This wasn't the time to put his ass in check. I had business to handle first. "Hey, you," I said, slipping into B's embrace as he unlatched his arms. "I need a hug."

Benito's stare was cold and hard before he asked, "How was your day?" while massaging my back.

"It was good but not as good as you caressing me. And yours? I noticed my car faced in. You sure you didn't go somewhere?"

"I'm the man in this house. I ask the questions, I don't answer them."

Chuckling, I said, "Is that right? Then hand over my keys, my man," I demanded, opening my palm.

"You don't have to be so hard all the time. Damn, I went to the store and forgot to back in. Satisfied?"

"That's okay, I reversed it. My bathwater ready? I'm exhausted."

"Isn't it always?" Benito said, flopping on the sofa. "I need to talk to you. I'll be in in a sec. Soon as *The Wire* goes off."

"Take your time, baby," I said, picking up the money case.

I needed B to make love to me. No, what I really needed was a few big orgasms to take the edge off, but I had to handle business first. I locked myself in the bathroom, hid the money in the shower floor, then unlocked the door.

"Baby," I called out to B, "can you come rub my back?"

Walking in naked, B sat on the side of the tub, rubbing my worries away. Noticing a thin scratch on his dick, I walked my fingers from the head of his dick to his nuts.

Benito began scooting backward.

"What's wrong with you?" I asked, staring at the boils on the back of his hand.

Wiping his forehead, B answered, "I'm good. Just tired. Lace, look at me. I need you to tell me the truth." Staring into my eyes with grave concern, B asked, "Where were you last night?"

I laughed, relaxing into the suds. "With your dick and balls smelling fresh and clean and your body reeking of sweat, baby, what kind of question is that for you to ask me?"

"Don't play mind games with me tonight, goddamnit. Answer me, Lace. I wanna know where you were."

Exhaling I stared at Benito, then said, "You first."

He slammed the sponge into the suds, and bubbles splashed in my face and onto the floor. "Don't lie to me, Lace!" B paced the floor, almost slipping.

Holding in laughter, I hopped out of the tub, grabbed two oversized towels, tossed one to the floor, and wrapped the other around my body. "What's wrong with you?"

B's hands sprawled across his temples as he dropped to his knees in the fetal position, crying like a baby. This was more serious than I thought.

"What happened? Please tell me, B, what happened tonight?" I pleaded, squatting next to him. Shifting my eyes away from his split fingernail, I waited for his response.

B's jaw tightened. "I'ma ask you"—his hands fiercely trembled—"one more time." B choked the airspace above the tiles as he pronounced each word deliberately, pausing in between. "Where were you last night?"

At this point I stood, refusing to answer because whatever sick reverse psychology madness B had in his head, there was no way I was going to get suckered into it. So much for getting my pussy licked tonight.

"Baby, I'm tired. You're confused. I'm going to bed. Let me know when you're ready to answer your own questions, okay? Good night."

B's thick fingers locked around my biceps as he flung me to face him, pulling me to my knees. "Where in the fuck were you last night? And don't lie to me."

With me pounding on B's chest, slapping his face, then kicking him in the nuts, he shoved my back into the wet floor. I screamed, "Nigga, if you don't let me go!" wishing I had my gun.

"Get the fuck out of my face before I really hurt you,

bitch!" he grunted, slamming me against the side of the white porcelain tub.

"Ow!" I yelled, holding my side. I hadn't dealt with this kind of abuse in years and I sure as fuck wasn't about to let B pick up where my exes had left off.

Calmly I stood, looking down at B, seeing a split image of my ex-husband and wondering if I'd ever have a sane relationship with a black man. I'd never wanted to see B like this again. Leaving my towel on the floor, I whispered, "Get out of my house." I walked out of the bathroom. Water dripped from my naked body as I rubbed my aching side.

When I heard the bathroom door lock, I headed straight to my ivory nightstand, slid my sugar-cube-sized magnet out of the hidden latch, removed my Colt .45, and placed it under my pillow. Love or no love, if B handled me like that again, fuck a restraining order, I was going to put a bullet in his ass. Maybe two.

CHAPTER 21

Benito

Romance without finance was a nuisance. Going out of my mind, I sat on the edge of the tub for about an hour trying to analyze what I'd done to Lace and why. Was Valentino my true friend? What if I left Valentino's money where it was, apologized to my woman, and got a job or stopped talking about starting my business and did it? What was I afraid of?

Tyra had taught me once a woman stopped loving a man, there was nothing he could do to win back her heart. Jay-Z sang, "You can't turn a bad girl good, but once a good girl turns bad she's gone forever," in "Song Cry" and he was right.

The real reason I wasn't there for my daughter was that I couldn't stand seeing Tyra with another man: a man who made her smile brighter than the sun and laugh louder than her favorite comedian, Katt Williams.

A man who provided for my daughter and a man my little girl called daddy.

Breaking up with Lace wouldn't hurt me as much as Lace never loving me again. Could I erase the past twelve hours of my life and start anew? A second chance of sorts. What if I did everything Lace wanted the way she wanted me to? Would she love me unconditionally? How could a black man avoid a murder rap and getting killed at the same time?

Cracking the door, Lace was sound asleep on her back with both hands comfortably tucked underneath the pillow behind her head, so I locked the door, sat back on the tub, then stared at the shower for another hour.

Everything wasn't black or white, but some things were either wrong or right. I didn't kill Sunny, but I may as well have. Dropping to my knees, leaning over the tub where moments ago I'd pushed my woman, I cried, "My God, what is happening to me? I'm turning into everything Mama James taught me not to be."

Had I become what my white mother and black father anticipated? Maybe if I released the animosity in my heart against my brother, Grant, stopped being jealous of Lace, and stood up to Valentino like a man, irrespective of the outcomes, I could sleep with both eyes closed.

If I turned myself in, I could protect Lace and clear my conscience at the same time. But Valentino had inmate contacts that would hang my black behind in the cell with my own shoelaces before sunrise.

My body jerked as more tears poured into my palms. Skilled hands that could land a football through a field of husky men moving at the speed of lighting and hit my target right in the chest, precision hands that threw bombs ten yards at a time to gain a first down, loving hands that caressed my Lace every night since I'd met her, were covered with the blood of an innocent woman.

What would Jesus do?

When I'd dropped to my knees, spread my fingers, and motioned as though I was choking someone, God knew that person was not Lace. The person I visualized was me. I should've stopped there. I wish I'd never grabbed Lace's biceps and slammed her against the tub. This was the first and last time I'd put my hands on my baby like that. Next time, I'd leave until I came to my senses.

Shit happens, not overnight, within a matter of moments, minutes, seconds. I couldn't stay in the bathroom forever. Two hundred and fifty thousand dollars awaited me. How was I going to key in the combination without having my feet chopped off?

Not trusting Valentino's suggestion to stand on the built-in shower bench, I dragged the vanity chair to the shower, stood on the seat, and damn near slipped off.

"Shit!"

Grabbing my aching knee, I got extremely quiet expecting to hear, "You okay in there?" or "What the hell are you doing?"

The bedroom was silent but I cracked the door and checked again to see if my soon-to-be-ex was awake. She wasn't. The cover was up to her neck and her hands were still under the pillow. I'd deal with Lace later.

Locking the door again, I placed the wet bath mat rubber bottom atop the vanity stool, leaned over the top shower bar, and pushed upward on the golden rose tile. I entered the decoded code and sure enough the floor opened wide enough for my entire body to fall in. There was the shiny silver case Lace had brought in with her. Quickly I removed it seconds before metal blades shaped like shark teeth closed, followed by the tile.

"Shit!"

Valentino failed to mention the floor opening was on a timer. I almost lost my left hand. Looking inside the case, I saw, as promised, lots of cash. Too much for me to count. Replacing the mat and the stool, I wrapped the case in a white towel, unlocked the door, tiptoed out of the bedroom, and got in the black Jag, tossing the silver bag on the passenger seat beside me.

Driving a few miles, I arrived at Sunny's condo and parked on the back side where no other cars were in the visitors' stalls. Rushing inside, I saw the body bag was where I'd left it, and noticed her living room reeked of decomposing flesh. I placed the silver case on the coffee table and opened it.

My eyes widened. My heart raced with joy. I hadn't seen so much cash at one time in quite a while. Running my fingers over the edges of hundred-dollar bills made me feel good as I inhaled the breezy scent of crisp money. There was no way the only thing Valentino was selling was pussy. Maybe he'd killed Sunny because she knew what he was doing.

Taking a deep breath, I held it while unzipping the body bag. I rummaged through Sunny's purse but hadn't inhaled fast enough because her body smelled worse than a dead dog mixed with a skunk's spray and the sickening odor was trapped inside my nostrils. Guess it was all that bleach and ammonia that had fileted her flesh away from her bones. Quickly I snatched one of her credit cards, then watched the metal clasps overlap up to the top. Stumbling into the living room, I gulped, filling my lungs with air, unable to rid myself of the horrible stench. I flipped open my cell phone, dialed the number 1, then hung up, certain Valentino had bugged my phone.

Grabbing a paper towel from the kitchen, I wrapped it around the cordless receiver, then pressed the green-lighted buttons with my knuckles. "Yes, I'd like to book a reservation to Paraguay departing on the first flight available." Confirming with Sunny's security code from the back of her credit card, the expiration date, her name, address, and phone number, I gave the woman my middle and last names. Once I was on another continent I could rent a car and steal away into the night like the black African slaves that were transported to South America. Aw, shit! With the new white man's law of needing a passport to the U.S., was my passport current? Where was my passport? Aw, hell! One more obstacle but I was confident I'd find it later.

After scheduling my flight, I left the silver case in the closet with Sunny, knowing I'd pick up my money on my way to the airport in a few hours. Settling into the Jag, I forced gusts of air from my nose like a raging bull, blowing snot in an attempt to clear my sinuses of Sunny's sickening odor.

Returning home to apologize to my woman before my final departure, I parked next to Lace's car. I'd need a few pairs of clean underwear, toothpaste, a toothbrush. "Aw, hell no." How in the world was I going to get my money past customs without a declaration? Damn sure nuff wasn't checking in my cash at ticketing. "Fuck!"

Plan B. I could drive from Vegas to Bogalusa, Louisiana. That wouldn't work. It'd be my luck some old lady named Bertha Mae who'd never missed an episode of *Oprah* or *CSI* would recognize my face and alert the cops.

Best if I completely thought out my situation like a white man instead of impulsively reacting like a black man. Clearly my relationship with Lace was the best of my life and the last few hours were the worst. What if she wanted to work things out and I wasn't giving her the chance? I was the one who didn't deserve a chance. Lace was better off without me in her life.

Tiptoeing into the bedroom, I said, "I'm sorry, baby," then turned on the light.

Lace was gone.

CHAPTER 22

Summer

Quietly opening the front door I saw Mom and Dad kneeling in the living room in front of our small altar holding hands with AJ and praying. Seven white candles brightened their somber faces. I wasn't sure if they were upset with me until my mother stood and said, "Summer, you had us worried to death. You weren't answering your phone. Where'd you go, baby?"

"I went to . . ." I paused, debating on telling a small lie, the kind where I told the truth but not the whole truth by claiming I went to a friend's house. But what if Sunny's body was in that bag? "I went to Sunny's house, Mama."

Watching the twelve-inch candles melt onto the sterling silver cross, I hung my head like Jesus. That cross had been handed down to my mother from her great-great-grandmother, so I had to confess or the Lord wouldn't bless me for not honoring my parents.

"What!" my dad said, reaching for my mother to help him to his feet. "Come here, girl." Massaging his lower back, Dad continued. "You mean to tell me you let me drive all over Las Vegas when you knew where your sister lived all along?"

AJ ran to me. Holding my toddler in my arms, I stood behind the sofa to create distance between us and my parents, then replied in a "please don't punish me" tone, "I can explain, Daddy."

This was my worst birthday ever and the first one I wasn't celebrating with my twin. I know my parents didn't mean to overlook what should've been a joyous occasion, but there was no way I could party without Sunny. I'd hoped we could hit a few casinos tonight, gamble a little, and legally order our first drinks: a tequila sunrise for Sunny and a sunset for me. Sunny and I had done a lot of first things together before she left home. But I wasn't brave like Sunny. Taking my son and moving away from my parents was something I wasn't emotionally prepared to do.

"Before you say a word, did we hear you right? You went to *Sunny's* house?"

"Yes, Daddy. Sunny sent me a key to her condo." Focusing on the priority of finding my sister, I withheld telling my parents about the six figures in Sunny's bank account, the Benz, or that she'd told me to sell her condo. The one thing I had that Mother would want to keep was Sunny's Bible, which was on the dashboard in my car. "I just got it in the mail with this letter after we got back," I said, making sure that I pulled the right piece of paper from my purse. "I didn't know what to do and I had to find out if any of this was true."

"Summer, the Days are a family united in Christ."

"I know, Mama."

AJ said, "A family that prays together stays together."

"That's right, Nana's baby. Very good." Mama paused, then asked me, "Well. Did you go there?" while unfolding the letter. Silent tears streamed down my mother's face, smearing her mascara as her eyes scrolled back and forth.

"Helen, get my car keys," my dad insisted, taking the letter from Mother, then continued. "Summer is taking us to Sunny's house right now. We'll drop AJ off next door so he can play with his friend till we get back."

"Yeah!" AJ smiled.

Thank God none of this made sense to my baby.

"Wait, there's something else I have to say. Follow me," I insisted, stepping from behind the sofa. I led my parents into the family study and pointed at the framed photo hanging above my dad's computer. "The quarterback in that picture is romantically involved with Sunny. I don't know why, but he followed me home, and he might come back to k-i-l-l me because I saw him in Sunny's house."

Mama frowned at me, then softened her look at my father. "It's all right, Daniel." Cupping my face in her hands, Mother hissed, between clenched teeth, two inches from my lips, "Summer, stop it. Look at me. I know you're upset, sweetheart, but you know what the Bible says about blasphemy."

There was no way my words could prove I was right and Mother could quote a scripture from every book of the Bible from Genesis to Revelation for any response I'd give, but she'd taught me to have faith and I believed that God would reveal the truth when He was ready.

"Okay, then. If you don't believe me, let's go," I said, leading the way.

Once Dad dropped AJ off, I sat nervously on the backseat in Daddy's car wondering how to prepare them for the worst. Daddy parked in the space where the Jaguar was earlier.

"Wait a minute. I have to say something else before we go upstairs."

"Spit it out on the way up," Daddy said. "I gotta see my other baby and wish her . . . oh no. Not today, Lord." Daddy used the rail to support himself on one side, and Mother held him close on the other.

"No matter what we see, Daniel, the Lord's will has been done and we must remain strong in our faith knowing He will see us through—"

I blurted really fast, "Daddy, there's a black body bag inside Sunny's closet and I'm afraid she might be in the bag."

Snatching the keys from my hand, Daddy unlocked the door and rushed inside. Mother was right behind him until she collapsed across the threshold. Closing the door, I worried about my mother, but had to trail a few feet behind my father into Sunny's bedroom, expecting the worst.

"Well!" Mother yelled from the living room. "Is my baby dead in there, Daniel?"

I stepped inside the closet beside my father, my chin practically hitting my neck. The body bag was gone. I ran to my mother, knowing she was the one who'd believe me. Looking above the fireplace, I pointed, then cried, "Our family portrait is missing too."

Sitting on the lime leather sofa, Daddy pressed his lips together, interlocked his fingers, shook his head, then stared at me. "This sofa smells funny. Look, Summer. We understand you're under a lot of stress, honey, but this is not the time to make up stories or for you to protect Sunny. Now, how long have you known about this apartment? And where is your sister hiding and why?"

"Mommy, I don't understand. Daddy, I swear the

body bag was right in there," I said, revisiting the closet. Standing in the empty space, I ran to my mother. Quietly my mother's eyes shifted to the corners.

Hugging Mommy's neck like I was a baby, I said, "Mama, I didn't mean to swear. God forgive me but you've got to believe me. I'm not crazy. There really was a body bag in Sunny's closet."

CHAPTER 23

Lace

Exiting the US Airways/America West—whatever they wanted to call themselves—flight, I took ten steps down into the early winter freezing cold. Columbus Day had barely passed, but everything nowadays from the tsunami to 911 was unpredictable all over the world and I wanted to slap that bitch at Las Vegas's Homeland Security check-in who took my Oh Baby MAC lip gloss because I didn't have a Ziplock bag to put it in. What in the hell were the plastic bags protecting?

I couldn't tell if the chill in my bones was the nervousness numbing the inside of my body or the whistling wind, but my brown ankle-length mink coat and thigh-high chocolate boots weren't keeping me warm.

My gosh. Ignoring my burning cheeks, I glanced at

the smaller planes, realizing that I hadn't been back to Flagstaff in over ten years.

Rolling my overnight bag packed with one change of clothes, I hurried inside the small airport. Five hours was more than enough time to say hi to Honey without having to call Rita a bitch again. One thing I was sure of, my return flight was departing at 5:20 with me on-board. But I hadn't decided if I was going home once I arrived in Vegas to kick Benito's sorry ass out or going to confront Valentino. Both of them had good reasons to be very concerned about my next move.

Thankful there was no one waiting at the Hertz counter, I signed my contract, rushed outside to the small parking lot, got in the fanciest car they had available, a Ford Escape, and headed to Interstate 17 North. Merging onto U.S. 89, I was amazed to see new places like Quizno's, Cold Stone, Chili's, Target, Bed Bath & Beyond, a huge Barnes & Noble, and a drive-through Starbucks, and I was glad to see old places like Granny's Closet and the Buffet Restaurant were still in business.

I made my way around the bend onto the famous Route 66, passing South San Francisco Street where I'd gotten kicked out of the house literally one block from the Sunshine Rescue Mission and across the street from Northern Arizona University. Back then at the age of sixteen, I was too young to go to either. After Rita stepped on me, I bypassed the mission and made my way to Route 66 near the Visitors' Center where I'd hitched my first ride with my first abuser. I still prayed that he'd burned to death in his bed next to that blowup doll. If he hadn't, God only knew how many other women he'd beaten since I'd left him.

Zigzagging along a few side streets, I arrived at Flagstaff Medical with two minutes to spare. Smoothing out my mink, adjusting my designer sunglasses, swinging my expensive purse, I strutted my five-inch heels through the main entrance and up to Patient Information.

"Yes," I said, peering over my sunglasses while tucking my silky hair behind my ear, "I'm here to see Honey St. Thomas."

Smiling with a gap wide enough to slide her tongue through, the receptionist said, "What's your name, please?"

"Lace St. Thomas. I'm her sister."

"Oh yes. Yes, indeed," she said, shaking her finger while frowning. "I remember now. You're the one your mother said ran away from home. Well, I see you've done well for yourself. You look like a celebrity. Nice coat. Maybe you have a nonprofit that can donate some clothes or money to our battered women's or rape crisis unit before you go."

What did she think this was? Christmas in October? If I donated the mink off my back, she'd probably be first in line to steal it. Nobody helped me when I got my ass kicked on the regular, not even the hospital. Once I said I didn't have insurance, I sat in the emergency room damn near long enough for my wounds to heal.

One thing I was sure of, battered women needed psychiatric treatment more than medical because it didn't matter how many times a man would beat a woman's ass. If she wasn't mentally strong enough to leave him, the next woman lying in that hospital bed was just keeping the sheets warm until the battered woman returned.

Shifting my weight from one boot to the other, I exhaled, rolling my eyes toward the ceiling.

"Remember, Lace, it's more blessed to give than it is to receive. Take the skywalk over to the third floor. Here, you'll have to stick on this visitor's badge," the receptionist said, leaning toward my coat.

Snatching the tag before she stuck it onto my mink, I said, "Why don't I just hold on to it?"

Apprehensively clicking my heels against the white square tiles, I detoured and stopped at the gift shop, bought a bouquet of assorted flowers neatly arranged in a blue vase, then slowly made my way to Honey's room, wondering what I'd see.

When I cautiously opened the door, Rita was the first person I saw seated next to Honey's bed. Rita's eyes swooped from the *All My Children* soap opera toward me. She looked me up and down, then watched Ryan and Annie discuss what to do about their relationship and what was best for their child, Emma, and heard Krystal's baby was Tad's. Whatever. Rita could be in a soap opera her damn self.

As she exhaled through her nose, Rita's lips tightened while she grumbled at me, "Humph, you're late. What took you so long?"

Best that I ignored that evil woman before she'd need a room next to my sister's. Walking over to Honey, I kissed her forehead and softly said, "I miss you. You're gonna be just fine, sis. This is just a test and as I recall there wasn't a test you couldn't pass when you put your mind to it. You want some water?" I asked, tilting the small white plastic cup to her dry lips.

Honey's eyes swelled with tears and I repeatedly blinked to wash away mine. Opening my purse, I removed my gold-handled hairbrush and began stroking Honey's hair. Honey never said a word. She didn't have to. I knew my sister felt guilty for not helping me that day.

"No apology needed," I said. After a gazillion ass whippings by two exes, I turned out just fine.

What if a teenaged girl kicked out of the house had a safe, clean place to live? A community, not a system, to help her become successful? I thought, staring through

Rita. Barely forcing a half smile, I wanted to cry but I had to be strong for Honey.

Rita leapt from her seat, saying, "I'ma go get the papers so you can sign them for your test," as she hastily left the room. Rita must've guessed I was leaving sooner than she expected.

"She's still the same," I said, French-braiding the few strands of hair left on Honey's head.

"Don't sign anything she gives you," Honey said. "I have an advanced stage of cervical cancer and there's nothing you can donate to save me."

I was relieved because regardless of what Honey needed, I wasn't letting anybody cut on my perfect body. Laughing, I said, "Same ol' Rita, huh?"

"Lace," my sister whispered, forcing out the words, "I need to know that you forgive me."

"Hush, Honey. It wasn't your fault," I said. "I'm putting my business card inside this drawer. If you ever need anything, and I mean anything, including me, I'm just a phone call away."

"Thanks, Lace, but you've got to let me own up to my mistake. It was partially my fault. Maybe if I had stood up for you instead of trying to help Mama put you out," Honey cried out loud, "Don wouldn't have raped me."

"What!" I screamed, slamming the brush to the floor. Chunks of bristles attached to glistening fiberglass scattered in every direction. "That motherfucka did what!"

"Mama didn't kick me out. She just pretended like nothing was happening. My son is his son. If I don't make it, sis, promise me you won't let Rita steal my insurance money and that you'll take my son with you and give him the love I don't know how to because I'm so filled with hatred," Honey said, placing in my hand an envelope and a wallet-sized photo of the most handsome scrawny young man wearing a jersey with the number 1 on it. His smile was wide but dim. His lips were tight, eyes glossy. I felt the word *cheese* hidden behind his expression. I'd give him a C-plus for trying to look happy knowing he was truly sad, longing for his mother to love him and wondering why his father didn't claim him. The white envelope slipped away, fluttering at my feet.

Harboring those same feelings, I knew the look. Had seen it on the faces of many women pretending they were excited about their husbands or lovers when the truth was they wanted out of their relationships, but the magnetic codependency mentally fused them in a misery of distorted love.

Squeezing the picture, his shoulder pads touched. Affectionately I asked, "How old is he? What's his name?"

"I named him Jean St. Thomas, which pissed Mama off even more. He's ten years old and, Lace, he loves football."

Hesitantly I asked, almost knowing the answer, "What position does he play?"

"Quarterback. He's a straight-A student, a starter, and a star, just like you. You look so beautiful. You look like money."

"Sis, you are so beau—" was all I could say before Rita stormed in waving a white piece of paper like she'd won the lottery. Don trailed directly behind her.

That trifling nigga had the audacity to stroll his nasty balls into my sister's hospital room. What? Honey hadn't suffered enough? Or did this selfish dog feel no remorse?

"Here you go," Rita said, shoving the paper in my face. "Sign it."

Swatting Rita's hand out of the way, I kissed Honey

on the forehead and said, "You've got my word. I promise."

Stepping on the letter-sized envelope, not knowing what was inside, I instinctively reached down and put it in my purse along with Jean's picture. If I had to, I'd be the best mother to Jean and smother him with hugs and kisses every day. I'd go to all of his games, teach him street smarts, and make sure he never became a pimp. Maybe having Benito around would be a good thing. Benito wasn't right for me, but maybe he could be a good father figure and personal trainer for Jean.

Smiling as he walked toward me, Don enviously said, "Well, don't you look like a brand-new C-note fresh from the mint?"

"You dumb fuck. The U.S. Mint makes coins and protects over a hundred billion dollars of U.S. gold and silver assets. Paper currency is printed by the Bureau of Engraving and Printing in Washington, D.C., and Fort Worth, Texas."

"You tell him, sis," Honey said, clapping.

"I see all those years on your back at the Pussyland Ranch banged your head into more than just headboards." Then he seductively whispered in my ear, "How much, Miss Smart-Ass? Can I get the deep throat special?"

Without blinking or saying a word, I picked up the blue vase, smashed it in Don's face, pushed him to the floor, then stepped on his chest. "This is your lucky day. If I had my gun, you'd be one dead motherfucka." Removing my foot, I squinted, staring at Rita while repeatedly back-kicking the hell out of Don with my stiletto piercing into his side.

"Ow! Stop that, bitch!"

"What, Rita? You gon' take his side again? Say something, bitch. I dare you."

"Kick him again," Honey said, trying to yell.

Turning around, I jabbed my heel into Don's dick and left it there while he squealed like a pig, "Rita, get her!"

"Ha, ha, ha, my, oh, my," Honey laughed, holding her stomach.

The shit wasn't funny to me, but my sister had every right to laugh as long and as hard as she wanted. What I didn't understand was a woman who was assaulted by slime like Don, then felt sorry for the bastard when he got his just due. "Oh, he's a good person. He didn't mean to hurt me." What fucking script were these women being fed? And who in the hell determined it was okay to abuse precious women, the mothers of the universe, bearers of all children?

Before removing my foot, staring Don in his eyes, I twisted my spike into his nuts, watching him bleed and beg for mercy, "I'm sorry! Please stop!"

Rita screamed, "You crazy, good-for-nothing, just-like-your-daddy slut! What the hell are you doing to my man?"

I spoke to Don first saying, "You weren't fucking crying when you raped my sister. Shut the fuck up!" and giving him one final kick in his ass after he rolled over like a bitch.

"If I had a dildo, I'd shove it up your shitty ass, then down your throat, in that order, you coward."

"Rita, get her outta here," Don cried, cradling his nuts.

Swiftly I swept my sunglasses off. Two inches from Rita's face I stared deep into her eyes, then answered her question. "I'm doing what you should've been woman enough to do eleven years ago." Gurgling saliva, I spat in Rita's face.

Raising her hand, Rita said, "You—"

That was the only word she got out before I threw

her ass on top of Don. "Lay one finger on Honey or call the police and you don't have to worry about that sorry-ass bastard going to jail for rape. Both you and Don will be dead before the cops arrive. Oh, and, Rita, you are going to give me my real father's contact information. You've got my number and you've got," I said, standing in the doorway, "exactly twenty-four hours starting right this minute."

Facing my sister, I pressed my fingers against my lips, opened my palm, puckered, then affectionately blew in Honey's direction. "I love you and I will be back to see you."

Don hadn't gotten what he'd deserved. At least not yet. The worst for Don was coming soon. I wasn't prepared to take my nephew with me, but if Honey didn't win her battle with cancer I'd keep my word.

Briefly stopping at the receptionist desk, I slipped the lady my business card along with three one-hundred-dollar bills. "If *anything* happens to my sister, Honey St. Thomas, immediately notify me and only me as next of kin." Rita and Don had better not retaliate against Honey or try to collect on Honey's insurance policy. So that was probably why Rita wanted me to sign that paper.

Strutting with a volatile, "move, get the hell out of my way" step, bumping into a few people, I exited the hospital, drove directly to the Flagstaff Airport, parked the rental car curbside at one of the two spaces for Hertz return, then checked in early at one o'clock for the 2:13 departure. The attendant, who'd issued my boarding pass, was the same person who screened me at security check-in where the sign read TO ALL GATES when it should've read GATE HERE since there was only one.

Greeting him again, I handed the attendant my boarding pass. The flight attendant on board, who was thankfully someone else, politely asked, "Please do not sit in rows one through three as we have to distribute the weight on the plane safely."

As I sat in row four waiting for the do-it-all attendant to de-ice the plane, my cell phone rang.

The on-board attendant said, "Miss, don't answer that. You need to power off your phone immediately for takeoff."

With my heart pounding, I replied, "My sister is terminally ill. I have to take this call. I'll only be a second." Then I answered, "Yes?"

The caller on the opposite end said, "Sunny Day is dead. I've got her body," then hung up the phone.

CHAPTER 24

Benito

Twelve o'clock noon and Lace wasn't answering her damn phone again. This nonsense was getting old really fast. She was probably too busy doing whatever she refused to explain adding another chapter to my life story, "Things that make a black man wanna hurt somebody."

Maybe I should write a book with that being the title, but who would be my audience? The white man would boycott the release, the white woman would silently protest the sales, the black woman would have an "I coulda told you that" guide and the police would incorporate the reasons into some code blue justification to beat a black man's ass. I was sure a few brothas would read it and agree with me, but what good would that do us collectively?

Sitting on the edge of the bed, I imagined Lace looking at her caller ID, then placing the phone back in her purse. At least she hadn't pressed the ignore button, sending me directly into voice mail. She'd be sorry later wishing she would've answered my call. Double or nothing, I'd bet all my money on the fact that she was gonna beg me to come back to her. Too late for that. Lace blew her last chance. She should've been a woman and not have played little girl games with a grown-ass man.

I tugged on the nightstand drawer I promised Lace I'd never open, but it wouldn't budge. Why did she get to have an ivory nightstand when my side of the bed had a round table draped with a transparent cover? I wondered what Lace kept on her side of the bed that was so important she'd hidden it from me our entire relationship. "Well, I'ma find out today."

Gripping the gold handle, I pulled but the drawer didn't budge. I yanked, almost tipping the nightstand over, but the damn drawer wouldn't open. Going into the garage to get a hammer, I retuned to the bedroom. There was no lock, and no keyhole in sight, so I slammed the hammer into the back panel.

Boing!

Barely making a dent, it bounced back, so I hit harder, and harder, and then overlapped both hands into a giant fist. Squeezing the handle, I swung the hammer behind my head. *Wham!* I yelled, "Shit!"

An instant lump popped up on the back of my head. Determined to break in with all my strength, I banged again. My wrists snapped, jamming my thumbs into each socket.

"Fuck this." I slid the back panel back against the wall to hide the damages.

Frowning, I scratched the knot on my head. "I've never witnessed anything like this. I give up."

Lace had a nightstand that looked soft as ivory but was tougher than metal? I'd bet an automated teller machine was probably easier to break into. Maybe I needed some sorta decoded combination. I sat on the bed contemplating my next move while redialing Lace's cellular.

Lace had left home early, hadn't called me all day, and didn't say where she was going. Obviously shoving Lace wasn't aggressive enough to keep her from sucking the dick of another man. What difference should that make since I was the one ending our relationship? The only thing she did was convince me I'd made the right decision. But I needed to reject her first. See the pitiful expression on her face when I said, "I'm leaving you. Forever."

Surpassing "until death do you part," forever was the longest time. Maybe I'd have a change of heart and take her back in a few months after I got myself together or ran out of money, whichever came first. Then I'd make good on my promise to . . . damn, I'd forgotten all about my twenty-thousand-dollar engagement ring. Where was it? Lace didn't have it on last night. I swear if that man had my ring, I'd lose my mind.

Roaming throughout her house to find my ring, I already knew what pawnshop to take it to for the best deal. I wondered if Lace had any other secret hiding places where she kept money. I needed all the big-ticket items and cash I could get before departing on my one-way trip. When I first moved in with Lace, I'd been through almost every drawer, kitchen and bedroom, every closet, bedroom and living room, every box, jewelry and shoe, and every other place I came across in her house and her garage.

Obviously Lace was smart enough not to keep her valuables where I could find them. Sifting though her daily mail I never saw a bank, mortgage investment, credit card, medical statement, nor an electric, phone—cell or home—or water bill. Nothing. The only mail that came to her house was junk. Initially I was pissed, but now I was relieved that my name was nowhere on a single envelope.

"Fuck this," I said, giving up trying to find Lace's stash so I could steal it. Snatching a few mink coats from the walk-in closet, I figured I could recoup the money for my ring and call it even.

"Won't be needing these anymore," I mumbled, tossing Lace's house keys on the living room coffee table. Hurling the coats in the trunk, I noticed the box of alcohol in the garage and grabbed a few bottles of vodka as my cell phone rang.

Sitting in the Jaguar, I hoped it was Lace calling to change my mind, but the last person I wanted to speak with was on the other end. I answered, "What's up? What you want now?"

"Nigga, you need to straight drop the attitude. I ain't your bitch."

"And I'm not yours. What else do you want from me?"

"Oh, did you grow an extra set of balls, nigga? Get your ass over here. I need you to make a run for me right quick."

"I'm not your gofer. Get some—"

Exhaling, Valentino hung up.

Grinding my back teeth, I pressed my lips together, started the engine, and cruised out of the garage.

"Forget Valentino, I'm my own man. After picking up my money, I'll just drive and wherever I stop is where I'll stay, but it sure as hell won't be New Orleans."

That was messed up how President Bush called Katrina victims evacuees, refugees, everything except the United States citizens that they were in America. The damn dogs had better rescue efforts from animal rights' activists than the humans who died in their cars, attics, at the convention center, inside the Superdome, and with no place else to go, on the streets.

Strange how the president made his way to Mississippi to hug white people, then flew over New Orleans so he didn't have to touch folks like me. That's because a majority of the people living in New Orleans were black. And just like in the war in Iraq, military guards standing tall with fully loaded weapons were ready to aim, shoot, and kill. Unarmed residents who were almost over their heads in the muddy Mississippi River waters scraping for food and diapers for the innocent babies strapped to the back of their necks had become human targets for practice. Survival was ultimately through the eyes of the oppressor, not the oppressed, and every day a black man is reminded of his place in society. A new chapter in my book: a black man's place in the white man's race.

"Ignorant soldiers should've put the guns down and helped rescue the stranded. Just like I'm doing right now, if it were me stranded in New Orleans, I would've done whatever I had to to get to safety."

Sad, sad, sad, I bet a whole lot more bodies were pumped out of the city into the mucky waters of the Mississippi River than the statistics will show or loved ones will ever know. There was no closure for blacks in New Orleans on the whereabouts of their family members, but way too many foreclosures were generated by insurance companies refusing to settle legitimate claims in order to regain ownership of the black man's land that they'd resell to the white man for capital gain.

White folks in Mississippi and outside New Orleans got their one-hundred-and-fifty-thousand-dollar grant to rebuild their homes and their communities, young black wannabe gangstas in the Crescent City continued to kill one another for pennies on the dollar while white Americans reverted to their normal lifestyles: some trying to figure out how they could buy a house in New Orleans on the steps of City Hall once Nagin had cleared out most of the, as Valentino would say, niggas.

The shortage of cops wasn't the real problem. From big lips to diamonds in Africa to tans to bodacious booties to prime real estate property, by any means necessary white folks always wanted what the black man had. Everything except pride. The white man consciously took the black man's pride, rechanneling the energy into sometimes overt and at other moments covert white supremacy, then rammed his rules down the black man's throat, leaving a bitter taste in the black man's conscience and subconscious.

Stopping at the gas station, I began filling Lace's tank. Opening the trunk, I moved the minks aside, checking the car for bloodstains. There were a few crusty spots along with white speckles where the bleach had ruined the mat. Removing the mat, I carried it to the oversized Dumpster and looked over my shoulder before stuffing it in. When I got to a safe place, I'd sell Lace's car as is online, and buy me a Benz or used Bentley to park in front of my new house in Georgia. That way sistas like Lace would love me.

"Fifty dollars!" I shook my head. "Gas prices are ridiculous."

Paying the cashier, I headed to Sunny's condo to get my stash but not the body. I couldn't stomach the feeling of transporting a corpse. This was my first daylight trip to the condo. Parking across the street, I entered the property, observing my surroundings. A few kids were playing football in the open parking lot on the back side.

Halfway up the stairs I heard, "Hey, Mr. Bannister. Catch!"

Instinctively my hands reached out as the brown leather bomb fumbled in the air before settling in my chest.

"Can we get your autograph?" a kid barely five feet tall walking toward me asked.

"Next time, kid. I don't have a pen and I'm in a hurry."

"Oh, Benito. I have a Sharpie, sweetheart," a voice resounded from behind me.

As I turned to face an elderly woman sitting on the top step who was the spitting image of Mama James, my mouth hung open when the silhouette of the woman vanished with the wind.

I glanced up at Sunny's window and saw another image, this time her twin staring into my eyes before letting go of the balcony. Reluctantly taking the marker from the little boy, I scribbled on the ball with every intention of buying that fingerprinted football from him once I got my money from inside.

Dashing upstairs two at a time like it was goal and ten at the two-minute warning, I crossed the threshold, locked the door. and exhaled, "Fuck! If it weren't for bad luck, goddamn!"

Not knowing if Sunny's twin would show up, I hurried to the bedroom closet . . . the silver case . . . the body . . . both were missing? Gripping my tightening chest, I turned on the light to make sure. The clothes were gone too. A woman wasn't intelligent enough to do this. That negro, Valentino. *This is a setup,* I thought, ransacking the entire condo. "Fuck!" Racing out the door with the same twenty-dollar bill I had remaining after filling up the tank, I stopped at the top of the staircase staring in disbelief.

Looked like the entire peewee community team was seated at the bottom of the steps blocking my path. "Hey, Mr. Bannister. You house-sitting for Miss Sunny?

We haven't seen her in two days. She usually throws a few balls with us and tells us, 'Keep your heads up, your grades higher, and stay out of trouble.' Then she gives us a few dollars to keep an eye on her place. So why you here? She yo' new girlfriend?"

"Here, kid. Take this." Snatching the football, I continued. "Give me that."

Grasping the rail, I swung my legs over their heads and ran to my car.

"Twenty dollars! Come back here! Gimme back my ball! Mama!"

Speeding down Martin Luther King Boulevard, I thought, *What the fuck am I going to do now?* To keep my black ass out of prison, I'd have to kill all the whores, all the kids, Sunny's sister, whoever lived in that house with her, Valentino, and Lace.

There was only one thing to do. Go to Lace and tell her the truth about Sunny. Since she didn't know I was leaving, I didn't have to beg to stay. Shit! I'd left the garage door opener on the key chain with the keys. I could explain locking the keys in the house, but how could I explain having all of Lace's mink coats in the trunk?

Exiting the freeway, I made a U-turn, driving toward Valentino's mansion.

CHAPTER 25

Valentino

Pacing my study, I thought a G like me wasn't supposed to miss no female, especially Summer. It wasn't like we dated for years or she had my baby and shit and I couldn't see them. I hardly knew Summer. But no matter how hard I tried, I couldn't forget our powerful connection. Haven't met another woman that matched Summer's inner beauty.

Nobody knew what really went down except me. In the heat of the moment, I could've but I did not pull that trigger. Standing in the middle of my study, inches from the sofa where we'd made love, I covered my face. Tears flooded my hands. My parents didn't raise me this way.

They taught me to respect women and I did. All my pimpin' days I gave women the finer things. A safe, clean place to work. None of my girls had to suck a dirty dick or flip an alley trick by some cheap-ass nigga who would beat them down afterward to avoid paying for his services. Generously I gave my ladies a damn good salary. Set up weekly health physicals by a certified medical physician. Hired a madam they could look up to while I lay low in the background. Staying out of sight was my way of not fucking those fine-ass bitches. I was cool with strokin' my big dick every night while watching Summer get dressed. She had the prettiest, round, tight ass and those supple nipples. Just imagining them made my mouth water. None of my girls were forced to work for me; they wanted to. I had loyal and dedicated whores.

Sniffling, I was straight relieved that neither Lace, Benito, nor anybody else saw me all soft and shit with my head leaning and snot running onto my leather cinema chair. I had enough money to say, "Fuck this business," but I couldn't. Once I let those Mafia/police niggas plant Reynolds on my security staff to start selling drugs to my IP clients and supply XTC to my bitches, my revenue tripled, but this shit had gotten bigger than me and larger than Lace. I'd convinced Lace to groom Sunny so she could eventually replace Lace because Sunny was controllable. Lace was not.

Besides, I could never have a bitch in my space or face twenty-four-seven. If Sunny or anybody else were to marry me I'd build the bitch an in-law unit way across the street so I only had to see her ass when I sent for her.

If Sunny was serious about quitting, she wouldn't have shown up for work. Wasn't like I was gonna waste my time sending Reynolds to drag her in when I had a long list of younger replacements that looked just as hot. Some hotter.

Walking back and forth across my Persian rug, I wondered if Sunny wanted more of me too. Lately Lace had become too protective of Sunny. Why? How did Sunny know how to get to me? And why had she come all over my dick and then wanted to kill me? Damn, her pussy was pure silk. I would've been better off not fucking her.

Drying my hands underneath my shirt, I thought about how I gave that woman a better lifestyle than most women fantasized about. Fine clothes, a fancy car, her own place. If it weren't for me, Sunny would've had to work years to make the sixty grand I paid her every month.

Standing, I curled my hand into a fist. "I can't take this bitch in blue staring at me any longer. And why is this book of all the books Lace put on my shelves front and center?"

Landing my knuckles into her face, I knocked the First Lady on her ass. Missing the rug, the book crashed onto the hardwood floor. "Well, well, looka-here," I said, scooping up the recording device that fell from between the pages.

Sitting at my desk, inspecting the I-spy gadget, I worried how many other books were rigged. "So that bitch Lace thinks she's smarter than me, huh?"

Pressing the button on the recorder, I frowned, hit it again, then pressed and held the black dot. Gibberish. "What the fuck!" I couldn't understand one word, but I knew that bitch was setting me up for something. "That's okay. I got one for her ass," I said, locking the book in my safe.

"Bitch!" I yelled, dialing Reynolds's number.

"Yeah, boss," his right-hand man answered. "We took care of it."

"Nigga, put Reynolds on the phone."

"Aw, shit. You haven't heard? Lace said she'd handle everything, so we didn't bother notifying you or any-one else."

"Heard what, nigga? Stop wasting my time and put—"

"Reynolds is dead. Lace shot him in the head for fucking one of your girls."

"And your ig'nant ass didn't call me when this shit went down?" I was speechless for a moment, then said, "Don't say another motherfuckin' word. Get both of your asses over here. Now!"

As I made my way to answer the front door, my boy Benito looked spooked. Like he'd seen a ghost or some shit.

"Nigga, what took you so long? You ready to be down with my team or what?"

Leaning toward me, Benito said, "I—"

"Wait up, nigga, back the hell up," I said, covering my mouth. "What the fuck you been drinking this early?"

Slurring his words, Benito replied, "I didn't come here to transport no dead bodies or shit like that. I just came here to chill."

Oh, straight? Who did this nigga think he was? Mr. Biggs? That's what was not gon' happen. "Nah, nigga. This here is simple shit. All you have to do is spy on Lace. I wanna know everything that bitch says, every word she speaks, and every move she makes. For two grand a day, can you handle that?"

Benito's eyes lit up. He unrolled his pinky, ring, middle, pointing fingers, and his thumb.

I swatted his hand down to his hip, sorry I needed this depressed, incompetent Negro for backup, but his bitch Lace had taken the game to a whole new level.

"Take a seat," I demanded, sitting in one of my high-back Imperial chairs with the wide wooden arms. Motioning for Benito to sit in the other seat facing me, I stayed in the foyer so I wouldn't have far to go if I had to throw this intoxicated nigga out.

"First, I need to know what you did with Sunny's body," I said, staring directly into his eyes.

Aw, shit. Benito's face dropped, bouncing like a bobble-head. "I thought you said you didn't want me to tell you."

"I changed my mind. Your ass is sloppy and I can't have no more surprises. Already had enough of that shit for one day."

Wringing his lips, Benito mumbled, "I left it at her condo."

He said "it" like he'd forgotten a shirt or a camera.

"What!" I sat on the edge of my seat. "Somebody please tell me my ears are playing tricks on me before I shoot this nigga!"

"You didn't say what to do with her so I left her at her house. I ain't no mortician, man."

"Go get that bitch right now and bury her ass in the desert twelve feet deep."

"Twelve? Desert?" Benito shook his head. "I can't do that."

"Six, nigga, I don't care, just get it done!"

"No can do," he sang.

Oh! I swear I wanted to hurt Benito. "Can't, nigga, or won't? You're telling Valentino James what you not gon' do?"

"When I went back to get my money, the quarter of a mil you gave me and the body were gone. I think you set me up, man."

I had to sit back before I landed a stiff one in this punk-ass motherfucker's chest. "Your money! Nigga, that was my money. Start explaining from the second you left my house and don't skip a beat."

I couldn't believe what the fuck I was hearing. He thought I'd given him a quarter of a million dollars for losing track of a dead bitch. A bitch who according to him had either risen from the dead or had an identical twin sister that lived in Henderson? My money was gone. He honestly didn't know where the body was. That was his drunk-ass story and he wasn't changing it. I had to think fast.

"Where's your bitch, Benito?"

Hunching his shoulders, that nigga said, "Don't know. She was gone when I got back this morning and she won't answer my calls."

"Nigga, you fired! Get your bitch ass up outta my spot before I shoot you."

Slamming the door, I had to come up with something quick before this bitch Lace showed up at my door tonight and tried to kill me like she'd done Reynolds.

Angrier than a lonely, broke bitch in heat, I jumped in my Bentley, drag-raced up Ann Road over to Martin Luther King, and headed to the Strip. Barely coming to a complete stop, I tossed my key to a valet attendant at the casino.

"Wait for your claim ticket," he yelled, chasing me.

Reaching back for the piece of paper like I was the anchor in a relay, I headed to check-in and reserved a suite so I could fuck the first available dumb bitch I'd meet, then went straight to the bar and called Lace.

"Hey, how are you?" Lace answered all happy and shit.

The announcement in the background, "Last call for flight 172 to Miami is departing at gate C twelve," let me know I didn't need to ask where she was.

"Six o'clock. My place. Have my money and don't be late."

Glancing over at the bitch across the bar in a purple halter dress wearing more makeup than Prince, I thought she was exactly what I needed to destress.

"I'm a little tired, so how about I pick up the girls and see you at ten?"

"This ain't *My Wife and Kids,* bitch. Have your ass at my place by six o'clock sharp. I'll have somebody else pick up the girls . . . hello? Hello?"

"You seem a little tense, Daddy," a friendly voice echoed from behind. "Can I help you unwind?"

Damn, how did this ugly bitch in purple move so fast? One minute she was across the bar, and now she was sitting next to me. "One grand. No questions asked. Meet me in my private suite in ten minutes," I said, giving her my room number.

Strolling to the elevator, I let my shoulder lean sideways. Lace was lucky she wasn't within smacking distance. Her mouth was gonna get her kilt if her ass didn't beat her there first.

Sliding the key card downward, I lowered the lever. I left my shoes at the door, unbuttoned my shirt, unbuckled my slacks, then lay across the bed to relax for a moment.

Tap. Tap. Tap.

What was that desperate bitch doing? Following right behind me? I'd said ten minutes, not two seconds.

When I opened the door, she smiled wide without parting her lips, then said, "Hey there, handsome. Got something for me?"

I had something for her ass all right. I stepped back, giving her access to my room.

"This is nice. What's your name, good-lookin'?" she asked, casually strolling over to the minibar.

"Uh-uh. Over here," I said, pointing at my dick. "This is what I want in your mouth."

"Well, can a girl make herself comfortable first? Wet her throat?"

I swear my eyebrows touched my hairline.

"All right," she said, dropping to her knees. "As long

as you don't try leavin' without paying me, Daddy. I'll suck your dick real good."

As she stretched her mouth wide, I frowned. This bitch was a crackhead. Where in the fuck were her teeth? Fuck it. I was here now.

Her gums glided onto my head and for a moment I forgot all the bad shit when she clamped down on my dick. She gnawed my shaft and sucked my head, rotating her tongue underneath the tip, then let my precome form a slick line, then twirled her tongue around my fluids.

"That shit feels so good, bitch, you just don't know."

"Yes, I do, Daddy. Mama knows."

Her mouth opened wide. I locked my fingers into the tracks of her weave and gave her all the dick she could swallow. She gagged and that opened her throat enough for me to thrust in another inch or two.

Pulling her up by her hair, I led her to the dining table.

Placing my hand in her back, I pushed her over the chair, raised her dress to her back, and commanded, "Spread 'em wide."

Unrolling an XL condom over my dick, I spat on her pussy, then put the head in.

"Umm, that feels so good, Daddy. I love a big dick."

I let her pussy warm me up. In. Out. In. Out. I stroked that loose-ass pussy until it was oozing with come.

"Um, go deeper, Daddy. I want to feel all of you."

Bam!

I shoved my hard-ass dick past her stomach, trying to burst through her navel.

"Wait, not that deep!"

"Bitch, shut the fuck up!"

Bam! Bam! Bam! I couldn't stop banging the bitch. Come seeped into the condom.

The more I thought about Sunny the angrier I'd become.

"Stop! You're hurting me!"

"Make up your mind, bitch. One minute you want this big-ass dick and now you're begging me to stop. Fuck that."

I ignored her whining ass, ripped the back of her dress, threw the chair to the floor, sent the china plates, forks, spoons, and crystal glasses crashing to the floor, then leaned that bitch like a number 7 over the dining table.

Forcing her titties into the glass table, I rubbed my swollen head over her asshole.

She tried to protest, grunting, "Uh-uh," but I jammed her face against the table so she couldn't scream, and then I fucked her in the ass the same way I was gonna fuck Lace when I tied her up tonight.

"Think you gon' come up in my house," I said, giving this trick all of my dick, "and spy on me? Bitch, you'd better know who you're fucking with. Telling me what you not gon' do. You and that bitch-ass nigga of yours are worthless."

Bam! Bam! Damn, her ass was tight as fuck.

"Urgh! Yeah, take all of this, you slut! Urgh!" I released all my frustrations on this bitch I didn't know because she didn't mean shit to me. She was just another ho.

Tossing five hundred dollars on the bed, I left that bitch sprawled across the table, flushed my condom down the toilet, zipped up my pants, and walked out. I was through with that two-dollar trick. She'd gotten exactly what she deserved for pieking up a stranger.

CHAPTER 26

Summer

Lying in Sunny's bed at my house, curled underneath the comforter, I must've read her letter a hundred times praying some stranger hadn't raped and killed my sister. Picking up the yellow envelope beside my pillow, I retrieved the bank statement. If I procrastinated and my sister really was dead, it might be too late for me to get the $326,000. I blinked repeatedly to make sure it wasn't thirty-two or twenty-six thousand.

God only knew what my sister had to do to earn this kinda money. Expecting the worst, the feds would probably place a hold on her account and I'm sure the police would trace any transactions back to me. Be my luck to get dragged out of our house in handcuffs and with my son crying having to explain to my parents again that I'm not crazy as I'm being stuffed in the backseat of a patrol car. What if I closed Sunny's account and she was alive and needed her money?

I removed Sunny's birthday bracelet from my wrist and placed it on the windowsill next to the white candle. Looking down, I retrieved the business card from my wastebasket and held it in my hand. I wondered who was this person and if she knew my sister.

I dialed the number from our home phone, and a raspy voice answered, "I've been waiting for you to call."

Hesitantly I asked, "Who are you?"

"I'm a close friend of Sunny's. I can't talk to you over the phone. Meet me at Ruth's Chris Steakhouse on Tropicana Avenue in twenty minutes and don't bring your parents."

"My parents aren't speaking to me right now anyway. They're upset because I saw a body bag at Sunny's house and when I took them back to the condo, the body bag was gone. Benito Bannister followed me home and I'm sure he'll be back to try to kill me and now you're asking me to trust you when I don't even know you. Good-bye, I can't talk to you anymore. Why am I saying anything at all to you? Who are you? I think I'm going insane," I cried into the receiver.

"Wait. Do you know Anthony Valentino James? Don't answer that. We've said too much already. Just trust me. You're not going insane. I'll be waiting for you."

Placing the phone on the charger, I didn't know what to do so I eased farther under the covers. A gust of wind blew Sunny's bracelet onto my pillow. Fingering the charms, I thought I couldn't give up on Sunny. What if this person knew where my sister was?

Sneaking out the garage exit, I drove to the place on Tropicana. The restaurant was packed with diners and I didn't know who I was looking for so I sat at the bar.

"A tequila sunrise, please."

"Can I see your ID?" the bartender asked.

"Put it on my tab," a raspy voice echoed from behind me. "Hi, I'm Sapphire Bleu. Join me at my table. Harry, send her drink over."

Following this Sapphire woman dressed in a gray sweatsuit with a hoodie on her head, dark sunglasses, and white tennis shoes, I glanced at the food on the tables. The juicy steaks, fresh asparagus, mashed potatoes, and cheesecakes suddenly made me hungry.

Taking my drink from the waiter, I sipped through the straw, sat at the table, then asked, "Where's Sunny?"

Sapphire whispered, "There's so much we have to cover. Best if you listen and I talk." Removing her glasses, she let her eyes roam the room.

"How do you know—"

Her narrowed eyes interrupted my question as she asked, "How do you know Anthony Valentino James?"

"I don't." I lied to protect Anthony in case he was in trouble. I hadn't seen him in years, but recently I started missing him a lot.

Firmly she replied, staring into my eyes, "Well, Anthony killed your sister."

"You liar! Anthony could never kill anyone," I yelled, pushing my drink toward her and my seat away from the table.

The restaurant patrons became quiet.

"So you do know him," Sapphire said, placing her badge on the white linen tablecloth alongside her police identification. "I have no reason to lie to you, Summer Day."

She knew my name? "I'm confused," I cried, covering my eyes. "All I want is my sister."

"We can't bring Sunny back, but you can help bring justice to the man who killed her. Her body is at the morgue and someone will contact your parents tomorrow to identify her . . . Save your tears for the funeral. You have got to be strong for Sunny and the other girls who might end up like Sunny if you don't cooperate. Now, tell me exactly, how do you know Anthony Valentino James?"

I exhaled, my eyes darting in several directions before I looked at Sapphire. "He was the best boyfriend I ever had, but at the time I met him I was sixteen and he was twenty-one, so my father made me stop seeing him."

"Summer, stop being so naive. Valentino is ten years older than you, not five. Your father is a wise man. Too bad he couldn't protect Sunny, but the best parents can't always shield their children from harm. I see young, beautiful girls battered, murdered, or left for dead almost every day here in Las Vegas, but nobody publicizes the dark side of Sin City. Generally older men exploit younger women in some way or another. My research on Mr. James shows he's been pimping women since he was sixteen." Sapphire's voice became sultry as she continued. "So he knew all the right things to say to you. All the right places to touch you and make you feel really good."

Her hand caressed mine and my body tingled with weird pleasure.

"He probably gave you your first orgasm and I'm sure that blew your mind."

Drawing my hand to my glass, I knew she was right. I felt my face turning feverish. "How did he meet my sister? Did he think she was me?"

"Good question. Your sister was introduced to Valentino by a madam who hires young beautiful girls to prostitute. The same madam who's going to hire you. The lifestyle Valentino affords his girls is glamorous and the money is more than the girls could imagine making on their own."

"I don't need his money. Sunny gave me her bank—"

"Statement. Yes, I know, and I know exactly how

much is in that account. Sunny wants you to have everything she owned. I'll arrange a private banker and Realtor to assist you. But first I need for you to help me nail Valentino."

"I'm not a prostitute. What if someone kills me too?"

"Summer, this is bigger than you. I have a promotion riding on arresting this piece of slime and I'd love nothing more than getting revenge for your sister. I can't put you in a witness protection program, but I'll do my best to make sure you and your family are safe."

"Your best? What if your best isn't good enough?"

"You'll be the first to know. Don't call me again. I'll be in touch," Sapphire said as she walked away.

CHAPTER 27

Lace

After visiting my sister, Valentino could kiss my ass. I pretended I was happy to throw him off, but I had to hang up on Valentino before I started crying. Seeing Honey so frail instantly changed my perspective on life, on women's rights.

There should be a universal code of ethics that every woman upheld on how men must respect women. No respect. No pussy. I'd bet those no-good motherfuckers wouldn't seem so tough if they had to beat their meat, get fucked in the ass, or have another man suck their dicks. Those sorry asses who took pleasure in beating women should be thrown in cages with grizzly bears, then forced to fight their way out.

No man was perfect but some men were scum, and a few good men were better than the others. Benito had clearly made a mistake putting his hands on me. I wasn't accustomed to giving second chances, but B's misdirected anger was an accident I could learn to forgive him for but one he'd best not repeat. Fuck three strikes. If B valued his life, strike two meant his ass was going down in round one.

I didn't care where Benito had gone last night. Whatever he'd done was history. And no matter how much I complained, if I stayed I couldn't possibly undo whatever had happened at Immaculate Perception. Nor did I believe Sunny was dead. Sunny was alive. Honey was going to fully recover. I was safe and all that mattered was I kept my word to both of them.

Seeing Reynolds with his dick in Onyx reminded me of all the times I'd been taken against my will. Forced to bring pleasure to a man, men, I disliked, despised, downright detested. Hearing Honey say what Don had done to her re-filled my soul with hatred for Don and compassion for women.

Something inside me, for the first time, made me see Onyx and the other escorts as human beings instead of chattel. My vision, perhaps my heart, was becoming clear, or should I say clearer? I saw Onyx and the others as women worthy of having control over their bodies and their lives. Easily I could've killed Don like I'd done Reynolds. Not just because of what they'd done to Honey and Onyx. I could've killed Don for the same reason I'd killed Reynolds, because their outlook on how a woman should be treated was fucked up. But so was mine.

The sunset faded through my bedroom window. I sat staring at Benito's slightly rounded face, his cheeks blending into his chin. The broadness of his shoulder nestled into the mattress as his elbow curled under his side. His chocolate dick lay limp against the white sheet next to his hip. His muscular thighs stacked perfectly, bending at the knees, creating a V shape that resembled a check mark as his feet slanted upward. A wheezing whistle escaped his parted lips as he pulled the covers over his naked body as if he didn't want me watching him.

Poking his chest through the sheet, I said, "Wake up. We need to talk."

"Huh. What?" Frantically he scrambled the sheet into a ball. "I didn't do it! I swear I didn't touch that girl! She was already dead when I saw her!" he shouted before nestling back into the fluffy pillow, cuddling the sheet in his arms like it, or he, was a baby.

"What in the world are you dreaming about? Get up, B. Now. I need to talk to you." It was now or God knew when.

Slowly he sat up, propping the pillow behind his head. "Oh, I'm sorry. I had a bad dream," he said, trying to widen his closed eyelids.

"Me too," I said, folding my legs as I sat facing B, stroking his hand. "I feel like I've been in a twilight zone these past two days. What's wrong with you? You've changed a lot over the last forty-eight hours too. You never forget your house keys. And you've never taken my minks to the cleaner's."

Scooting away from me, B squinted, then said, "Ain't nothing wrong with me. I ain't changed. Whatever you're thinking, I didn't do it. You're the one acting like a black man can't ask questions in his own house. You the one out there giving my pussy away to some other nigga. I keep telling you you have no idea what it's like being a black man in America. And all you're doing is adding to my frustrations."

Patiently I waited until B got tired of hearing himself talk, then said, "I'm sick and tired of hearing black this and white that. B, I wish you were a real man. A real man doesn't lead with his mouth or by manhandling his woman the way you did me last night. By the way." I cleared my throat, then continued. "I wouldn't do that shit again if I were you. Anyway, where was I? Oh yeah. A real man handles his responsibilities, provides for his woman, and leads by example. If you want me to respect you, you have got to give me the same respect. Like it or not, this is my motherfuckin' house, not ours, and damn sure nuff not yours. I pay the mortgage, the bills, and put food on the table. All the things you do for me, B, I could hire Merry Maids . . . and sex, I can get that anywhere in Las Vegas from lots of men for, I mean with, tons of money. Look at this body. I know men go crazy over me, yet I pretend not to notice just so you won't feel insecure. Do you have any idea how much—"

Damn, I almost slipped on that one, flashing back to my Pussyland days.

This time B slid away from me toward the edge. Another inch and his ass was headed for a landing on the floor. Benito knew what I'd said was true; he just didn't want to hear the truth. Most black men didn't want to hear the truth, especially not from a black woman.

Black men thought that because they hit the gym, pumped iron, and looked good, every woman in the world wanted them. But that was that slavery mentality how the white master actually devalued everything the black man had on the inside. And because the black man accepted that his true value wasn't inside in heart, head, and soul but on the outside in his body and clothes, the black man's shallow view of himself made him worthless to the black woman. Maybe the sistas should cross over and forget about saving black men.

Um, um, um. I was starting to sound just like Benito.

B was satisfied living in fantasyland pretending he was the man, a man, while I was the one getting up every night going to work to support us. Glancing at the clock, I reached over to my nightstand and pressed the button on my cell to verify the time. I had a decent three hours before picking up the girls.

"Just like Valentino said, your balls are bigger than mine. I'll just pack my stuff and leave. That's what you obviously want."

B was masking more of his insecurities. Why couldn't he just say what he honestly felt? Motioning for B to come closer to me, I asked, "Why do you always have to get defensive? Valentino doesn't run shit over here. If you were to ask me what I want, I'd say, 'I want to get to know the real Benito Bannister. I want to talk to you. B, there's so much you don't know about me. I want you to know the truth about my past.' The reason I trip out about sex sometimes is because I've never forgiven my stepfather for molesting me. He stuck his raggedy-ass fingernail . . ." I paused for a moment feeling like that little sixteen-year-old girl again dressed in pink shorts. The memory of my mother stepping on me taught me that anyone was capable of walking all over me if I'd let them. Looking at B through watery eyes, I resumed my confession. "He finger-fucked my pussy, scratching the shit out of me only to find out I was a virgin. My mother took his word over mine and kicked me out." I wanted to tell B about my sister, my nephew who might come to live with us, my abusive exes, and how I sold myself for eleven years at a brothel, but I feared B might get defensive, then somehow blame me for being dishonest with him. Men always turned shit around, making it seem like they were the victim, so I got quiet for a while. I really don't know what came over me or why I felt the urge to share at this point in our relationship, but B and I had to get closer or I had to let him go and find someone else to help me raise Jean.

"Lace, baby, why you act so hard all the time? Talking down to a black man and stuff. I had problems growing up too. I never told you I was adopted. I haven't spoken with my adoptive parents in years, I don't know my biological parents at all, and I can't stand my step-brother."

Straddling B's lap, I hugged him, sinking into his childlike embrace.

B pressed his lips against mine, then said, "Baby, you know I never want to hurt you. If it'll make you feel better, I'll get a manicure every other day."

Yeah, but at my expense.

"And I promise to stop treating you like a child," I said as tears streamed down my face. I didn't know B had a stepbrother and I wasn't ready to talk about my conniving mother, Rita. I'd tried extremely hard to forget about my family on my plane ride back to Las Vegas. All of them except my father. And Honey, who made me afraid of losing my only sibling. I felt strange when Honey and I reunited.

Were we united because of Don's abuse, Rita's lack of love, or were we two broken hearts that needed one another to mend? Like B and me. I never knew he was adopted. Like breaking a toe and suppressing the pain, I wondered how many loved ones were secretly emotionally shattered into a million little pieces.

How could I tell B I thought he should try to make amends with his family when every cell—red, white, and other—in my body hated my mother?

Focusing on my man, I decided heart-to-heart confessions were a good place for B and me to start over. Although we'd lived together for more than a year, I realized we knew so little about the wounded children that lived inside our subconscious minds.

Ninety-seven percent of who we were was embedded in the subconscious. That's why folks say, "Once a whore, once a pimp, once a dog, always will be," because we manifest, successful or otherwise, our strongest desires or our deepest fears. Living a grown-up game of hide-and-go-seek, I hid behind my insecurities and B hid behind his inferiority. Neither of us felt good enough for the other. I didn't want Benito to leave, but no matter what I had to deal with we couldn't continue down this road of self-destruction.

"I don't want to lose you. I love you, B. But what's gotten into you? It's like you've changed overnight and I don't understand why. Am I not satisfying you?"

"Lace, no woman has ever made me happier than you."

"Don't tell me, B. Right now I need you to show me."

CHAPTER 28

Benito

Every time a black man took two steps forward, society knocked him on his ass. I wasn't prepared for Lace to get all sentimental on me and start spilling her guts. Now I wanted to spill mine. Not just to Lace but also to my adoptive mother. Most folks didn't change. My adoptive mother was probably living all happy and shit in her big house riding her big black dick every night, then going to her high-paying job promoting all her white employees. Yeah, white women wanted all the rich black men. When I had money, white women came in pairs and groups hanging around me all the time just for fun. But broke brothas, like I was now, had to kick it with sistas until we could afford to do better. I wanted my stepmother to know how fucked up she'd made me. A black man had to open up to somebody at some point in his life or he was gonna explode.

Boom!

Here I was, sharing the most beautiful moment of my relationship with the only woman who ever truly loved me, and I was ticking like a time bomb. All I could think of was the dead body and quarter of a mil that had disappeared. With that kinda money I could have a little free talk with Jesus and tell Him all about my problems.

Jesus was a brotha with special powers. He created me in His image so He had to understand my situation. The white man wanted me to believe Jesus had blond hair and blue eyes, and I did until I took a theology course in college. If cleanliness was close to godliness, then all my white college teammates were headed straight to hell with all that locker room talk about the bloodier the meat the better and they meant everything from prime ribs to pussy. So much stuff about religion was twisted to benefit the white man I'd gotten kicked out of class every day for proving the professor wrong. If a black man didn't know anything else, he knew his Bible.

In the New Testament book of Matthew, I prayed God would grant me immunity from the Parable of the Talents. ". . . Take the talent from him and give it to the one who has the ten talents. For everyone who has will be given more, and he will have an abundance. Whoever does not have, even what he has will be taken from him. And throw the worthless servant outside into the darkness, where there will be weeping and gnashing of teeth."

I felt like Lace was the one with all the talent and before our relationship would end God would probably give her everything except me. I may have not buried my cash like the guy in the Bible who had one talent, but I prayed God wouldn't take my money and give it to Lace. Getting my cash back was mandatory. But whosoever took Sunny did me a favor.

Did Lace have my money? Was she playing head

games with me? I bet she was in cahoots with her boss. Valentino said for me to pimp-slap her. Squinting, I thought about laying hands on her again for a minute, then stared at Lace for a few seconds trying to figure what she was thinking. Suddenly I came up with a brilliant idea. I'd fuck the shit out of her and make her confess while giving her the biggest orgasm she'd ever had, which would make her love me twice as much.

Taking Lace upon her word to show her, I tossed the comforter to the floor, grabbed both her ankles, and, "What the fuck!" Lace's foot slammed into my mouth.

"I'm so sorry, baby. I flashed, please don't stop," she begged. "Come up here."

Shaking my head to resume consciousness, I hesitantly planted soft, wet kisses all over her face, gradually moved down to her neck, then her collarbone, wondering why she'd done that shit. Navigating south, I lingered, alternating biting my woman's nipples thirty seconds at a time.

Lace had the most gorgeous cream-colored body. Praising her perfection gave my dick a craving. Her skin was smooth as liquid silk but at the same time firm as leather.

Lace moaned, "Mmmm, B, don't ever leave me. I need you."

Squeezing her plump, huge, coconut-sized titties together, I tried to fit both caramel-tasting nipples in my mouth at the same time, mumbling, "I need you too, baby."

As I parted my woman's thighs, she blossomed like a flower into a full split that a gymnast couldn't have done more gracefully. I cradled my tongue atop her lips, allowing her pussy to marinate in my mouth. Hardening, my dick grew an inch longer. Lace was sweet and fresh like coconut milk out of a shell. I was her worker bee and my mission was to eat her pretty pussy until she couldn't come another drop or speck of her nectar in my mouth. I cupped her ass, bringing her closer. As I lapped up her juices I felt a stronger connection between us. Once again, Lace was right. We needed to bond more. Open up to one another more. And learn to trust.

"You gon' make me come too soon, baby."

"You don't have to control everything, Lace. For once just let go and let me be in charge."

Her body relaxed, sinking into the mattress. Glancing at the clock, I asked, "Don't you have to be at work at six tonight? It's five, you know." I didn't want to piss Lace off by making the same mistake.

"I'm leaving at eight."

Crawling into the space beside my baby, I laid my head on her breast. "Can we be honest with one another, baby?"

"Yes, this is what I want us to do. I'm listening," Lace said, twirling her fingers through my hair.

"Baby, do you know what it's like to work hard all your life, become larger than life, then lose everything you worked for, everything you own?"

Lace rubbed her eyebrow, then kissed my cheek. "No, but I do know you need to get a—"

Smothering her lips with mine, I interrupted, "I'm scared, baby. What I need is you. Promise me when I tell you what I have to say, you won't leave me."

Lace held my hand next to her heart. "I really want to give our relationship a chance. Whatever it is we can work through it."

Valentino would kill me if I told Lace what happened and Lace would shoot me if she found out I knew but didn't tell her.

"Before you go in tonight, you should know . . ." I paused, tilting my head backward to see Lace's expression. Her eyes were closed, so I continued watching her, then confessed, "Sunny is dead."

CHAPTER 29

Lace

Legs trembling, pussy puckering, heart racing, I tip-toed quietly to the bathroom. Twice in one day I'd heard Sunny was dead. Never did I expect to hear those words come out of Benito's mouth, but at least he finally confessed the obvious, his ass was broke.

Benito spoke to my back. "Where're you going? Did you hear what I just said?"

Without turning around, I whispered, "Yes. Thanks for letting me know."

"Don't you have any questions or wanna know what happened to me? To Sunny?"

Facing Benito, I answered, "No, I don't."

Locking the bathroom door, I stepped into the shower, stood on the bench, then keyed in the combination. Nothing happened. I tried again and again but the floor wouldn't open. Taking a deep breath, I waited five minutes and tried one more time, thankful the floor parted.

Peeping inside, I saw the silver case was gone. I sat on the edge of the tub and turned on the hot water. Maybe this was some sort of life test.

Tap. Tap. Tap. "Are you okay, baby? Want me to wash your back or your hair?"

"I'm good. Just give me a minute alone. Bring me my cell phone, would you?"

Switching from hot water to cold, I cracked the door with enough room for Benito to slip me my slither cell phone, then twisted the lock.

Turning off the bathwater, I started the faucets to create background noise, and then I dialed the hospital.

"Thanks for calling Flagstaff Memorial, the medical facility that is your home away from home. How may I assist you?"

"This is Lace St. Thomas. Can you ring me through to Honey St. Thomas please?"

I just needed to hear a warm voice that was attached to someone who cared about me. I needed to talk to my sister. Honey was strong so I knew she'd be all right. She had to recover because although I'd given her my word, I wasn't prepared to raise my nephew.

"Oh, this is scary," the now familiar voice answered, then said, "I just picked up your card to call and notify you first like you'd asked. Honey passed away right after you left."

The cell phone slid between my fingers onto the rug. "Lying bitch!" I screamed into the mirror. "You can't take away my Honey," I cried, collapsing to my knees.

Bam! Bam! "Baby, you okay? Lace, open the door. Baby, please. What's wrong? Was it something I said?"

I lied, answering, "I'm good."

Easing into the steaming suds, I laid my head on the

inflated pillow and closed my eyes, wondering, *Why me?*

Why did nothing good ever happen to or for me? Now that Honey was dead, there was nobody to love me for me. Benito loved me because of what I could do for him. Valentino hired me for the same reason and now wanted to fire me, but he couldn't afford to. I figured Valentino knew I'd killed Reynolds, but what explanation would I give? Not only did I feel no remorse for shooting Reynolds, I'd practically forgotten it'd happened.

Plotting my strategy, I decided I'd take the first morning flight to Flagstaff and make funeral arrangements for Honey. But if I found out that Don and Rita were responsible for my sister's death, three coffins would lie side by side.

CHAPTER 30

Lace

I'd soaked in the tub almost sixty minutes, shedding enough tears to overflow my bathwater, but there was still another hour before heading to Valentino's. Recapping my day, I'd flown to Flagstaff, seen Honey for the last time alive, stomped Don's dick into his balls, spat in Rita's face, received an anonymous call during takeoff on a plane, and opened my heart to a man I now hated since listening to Benito tell me Sunny was dead.

My soul mourned my sister's death, but I felt relief in knowing the darkness of my spirit could still love someone. I was glad the hate I had for Rita and Don hadn't kept me from brushing my sister's hair or kissing her cheek. Holding on to the hopes of one day meeting my father and the terrifying responsibility of raising my nephew, I emerged from the water where every bubble had burst my dreams of getting to know Honey.

Wrapping a red fluffy oversized towel under my arms and around my breasts, I picked up my cell phone and opened the door, damn near bumping into Benito, who was on the other side waiting with open arms.

B's head and shoulders slumped toward his chest. "Lace, I'm so sorry." B started crying. His shaky hands hugged me so close my nostril suctioned his nipple. I couldn't breathed listening to B babble, "Please forgive me, baby."

For what? Being an idiot? Letting someone drop a murder charge in your hands? Was I supposed to be dumb and let you get me involved in your shit? I bet B's ass would let me go to jail and do twenty years while he lay up in my house watching Grey's Anatomy *and* 24.

Tucking my phone inside the towel, I cupped B's face into my palms, kissed his lips, then softly laid my moist lips against his neck right behind his ear. "Um, um. Can you get me a glass of water, baby? My throat is dry," I said, walking over to my ivory nightstand.

Slipping the magnet over the hidden latch, I glanced at the edges along the back panel . . ."What the hell?". . . dents. Not one, or two, but at least a dozen. That Negro tried to force his way in. See, that's why a woman had to be smarter than her man. Men were some of the nosiest motherfuckers on earth. Especially the broke ones. Quickly I removed what I needed, slid it under the pillow, then sat on the edge of the bed rubbing my neck.

Taking the goblet from B, I let a few drops of water trickle in and out of my mouth, then sat sucking on an ice cube until it completely dissolved. B sat on his side of the bed staring at the wall in silence.

"Thanks, baby." I set the glass on the nightstand, then patted the mattress. "Come lay with Mama for a moment. I need you."

Rolling B onto his back, I straddled him.

B's hands caressed my ass. "Baby, I love you," he cried, unwinding my towel.

I snatched that red cotton and flung it into the air, then watched the towel dangle from the canopy. "I love you too, B."

Gently I began kissing his lips, working my way to his neck, then down to his dick. Without touching B, I sucked his limp dick into my mouth, yanking him upward until he was fully erect, then gave him that deep throat special Don had requested.

My pussy pulsated with pleasure. Mounting B, I gave him something else he'd never had from me, my signature Pussyland rodeo ride. Taking my time, I rolled my hips forward and back, massaging his dick with my vaginal muscles. Grabbing the towel, I looped it around B's neck, suspending his head in the air.

"Yeah, Daddy. You like this wild pussy ride? You'd better hold the fuck on. You ready?"

B nodded, slapping my ass.

I transitioned to a figure eight, popping my pussy on the up stroke and gliding on the back stroke while increasing the pace.

"Damn, Lace. What's gotten into you? You got my dick . . . aw, shit . . . damn, baby!"

As I rode B like I was a jockey determined to come in first place, his body scooted upward each time I banged this good pussy against his dick. The only thing that prevented B from being knocked unconscious was the pillow between his head and the headboard.

B's words were broken, but the universal expression of a man coming was clear. B's mouth gaped open. "Ooouuuu weeeee! Ride your dick, cow girl!"

Turning to look at his feet, I noticed his toes were curled like he had on a pair of leprechaun shoes.

Watching his mouth relax, his eyebrows touch, and his forehead buckle, I slowed to a trot.

"Yeah, baby. This is my dick," I said. Laying my sweaty breasts against his chest, I sucked B's tongue into my mouth.

As I slid my fingernails from his armpits to his elbows and into his palms, B's body relaxed. I kissed his neck, curling my face between his dripping wet ear and salty, slushy shoulder. Releasing his hand, I eased mine under the pillow.

B was in a hypnotic trace. His eyes fluttered, then gave way right before his lips parted, exhaling a deep snore through his nostrils. Quietly I snapped the metal fur-lined handcuffs to the ivory bedposts, one on each side, and then I secured both of B's wrists in the other hoops, *click, click, click,* until they locked and tightened. Circling silk scarves around his ankles, I tied quadruple knots, then looped the same four knots to the foot of each post.

Straddling B, I raised my hand in the air.

Swoosh!

I descended upon B like a bitch who didn't have her pimp's money. *Wham!* I slapped B so hard I swore sparks flew from my hand the same way they'd shot out of that blender when I pureed that dildo.

"Wake your motherfuckin' ass up!"

"Aaahhhhh!" B yelled like a bitch, reaching for my hand that was wavering high in the air. He looked left at his wrist, then right at the other. Kicking his legs, B stared up at me.

Wham!

My backhand landed harder across the other side of his face. Calmly I whispered, "I'm only going to ask you one time and one time only, so listen carefully. What happened to Sunny?"

"Lace, please, baby, it wasn't my fault. What the

fuck you doin'? Get me outta this shit. I tried to tell you but—"

Balling my fist, I punched B in his mouth. "That one was for slamming me into the side of the bathtub last night. Nigga, don't make me ask you again." Reaching into my nightstand, I pulled out my .45, gripped it with both hands, and pointed the tip between B's brows.

"Valentino killed her! I swear! Sunny was dead when I got there!" B's entire body rattled. His eyes were wide and teary.

Kissing his dick with the gun next to his balls, I politely asked, "Got where, baby?"

B's head swung, alternating slamming his jaw into the mattress. "Uh, uh. No, baby, please don't fuck with my jewels. I swear you gotta believe me."

Pinching one of the most sensitive spots on a man's body, I dug my nails into B's inner thigh and yelled, "Answer the fuckin' question!"

"Got to Valentino's house! Fuck! Lace, c'mon now. You wouldn't like it if I scratched your pussy. Baby, please stop."

He was right.

Reaching for the goblet, I took a sip, then, *Splash!* threw the water in B's face along with the glass.

"Aahhh, then what happened," I asked, inserting the tip of the barrel in B's asshole. "Crying is not going to help you now. So, what did Valentino ask you to do?"

My aggression was for Honey, Sunny, and all the women who'd suffered any form of abuse by a low-life scumbag john, pimp, ex-anything, husband, or fiancé.

"I transported Sunny's body to her house, then left the body bag in the closet, but when I went back to get my money it was gone and Sunny too."

So these motherfuckers were really trying to play Lace St. Thomas for stupid. "Just because I have a pussy, motherfucka', don't mean I won't kill your ass."

The only way B could've taken the money was if Valentino . . .

"Shut up all that damn crying like a bitch!" I yelled. "I can't hear myself think."

As I pushed the gun farther up B's ass, he yelled, "Ow, that shit hurts! Lace, please stop it!"

"Okay," I said, propping a pillow underneath the gun. Then I left the barrel up B's ass.

I showered, dressed in front of B, then went into my closet. "Aw, hell no!" Storming over to B, I asked, "Where did you leave my mink coats?"

B exhaled heavily. "Lace, please, this is really fucked up. I don't deserve this. Please, baby, untie me and I'll get your coats and get the hell up outta your house."

I swear I wanted to laugh. B looked like a frog waiting for a circumcision. *Girl, let that thought go. That would be taking things too far.*

Rummaging through my nightstand, pretending I was searching for something else to torture B with, I found that everything was there. My bullets, my audiotapes from Valentino's, and a few XXX-rated videos I was paid to do but wished I hadn't while working at the Ranch.

"Okay, I already told you I was taking them to the cleaner's for you. Now can you please take the gun out of my ass?"

"Was taking or took?"

B said, "They're in the trunk of the black . . . aw, fuck."

I ran to my car, unlocked the trunk, then sighed in relief, thankful Sunny's body was not there, but neither was my car mat. Whatever, I'd deal with B's ass later. Closing the garage door, I drove to Valentino's, strategizing my move.

CHAPTER 31

Lace

"Okay, Lace, you've got to compose yourself, and accept the fact that Sunny is dead." Hearing myself speak those words, I felt like my heart had stopped beating. "But how? Why? What went wrong? How could I have failed Sunny in less than seventy-two hours?"

I asked myself question upon question until I was sick to my stomach. Parking my car at Valentino's mansion, I bit my bottom lip to keep from crying. Obviously I wasn't doing a decent job of controlling my feelings for Sunny. Emotions and prostitution didn't mix, so I rechanneled my energy.

I was certain my hidden recorder was loaded with invaluable information; this wasn't the best time for me to sneak the disc out of the *First Lady* book. First I'd have to find a way to get Valentino out of his study for a few minutes. "I've got it." When I got back, after the girls left Valentino's and headed to IP, I'd short-circuit the lighting and temperature controls on Valentino's precious shark tank. That'd send him frantically running to the basement.

Desperately I wanted to go inside and talk to Valentino before picking up the girls, but too many strange things had already happened. Plus, I was so angry with Benito's confession that I'd shoot Valentino in his face if he told me he'd killed Sunny.

Benito's voice echoed in my ear. "Lace, why you gotta be so hard all the time?"

All B's monologues about black this and white that, he should've understood black women were tired of being asexual. Having to go to work every night while B laid his lazy ass up in my bed betraying me after all I'd done for him. Fuck, that ungrateful son of a bitch. No, I didn't want to hear his sorry-ass excuse for being broke. Besides the obvious that he'd pissed off his money trying to impress others by buying friendships that ended when his last dollar was spent, the only way I could tell B was a man was that I was generous enough to have left his dick and balls attached to his body.

I smiled, thinking, *B must've prayed every minute of every hour that his nuts remained intact. I knew he was scared shitless that he'd make the wrong move, triggering a bullet up his ass.* I wondered how much time I'd have to serve if B died of a heart attack believing the gun was loaded.

Right now I had my own shit to deal with. Overcoming my life's obstacles since being kicked out of the house at sixteen was like jumping one huge hurdle after another with no time for rest. The two security guards were sitting in the limousine parked next to me. At this point I couldn't trust anybody, especially these guys.

Approaching the driver's-side window, I said, "Follow me to IP so I can leave my car there."

If any foolishness went down at IP tonight, I was out for good with a one-way ticket to Atlanta. Cruising along Martin Luther King Boulevard, I watched the guards in my rearview mirror. Were they talking about me? Worried if I'd shoot them like I'd done their boss? Or were they relieved that Reynolds was dead so they could fight over the head security position? Guys who were in gangs or worked for the Mafia always had one foot in prison and the other in the grave expecting to kill or be killed.

All over the world, men could shoot deer or ducks for recreation, so why shouldn't women be allowed to shoot men who were dogs and call it a sport? Just the way I'd killed Reynolds, without hesitation I'd have no problem getting rid of Valentino.

Parking my car at IP, I rode up front with the guys. I had to make sure they weren't plotting revenge against me, so I sat between them with my gun in my garter holster.

"Either of you tell Valentino what happened to Reynolds?" I asked, looking at one, then the other.

The driver answered, "He didn't want to know, so our boss told us not to say nothing. We didn't see nothing, and we don't know a damn thing."

The security guard to my right chimed in, "Not even where his body is buried."

Lying motherfuckers.

"I see," I said, noting that their lines were clearly rehearsed, which meant they'd had a lengthy discussion about Reynolds's death with their boss and Valentino. "Who did your boss say is Reynolds's replacement?" I casually inquired, using my peripheral vision to monitor their reactions.

Honestly I didn't believe there was a boss or anyone

else supporting these fools. Reynolds was probably a one-man operation who'd hired these guys off the street, then pretended to have an entire operation behind him so he could push his drugs in a safe environment.

Silence. The one to the right waited for the driver to answer and the driver looked straight ahead like I hadn't spoken a word. Whoa. Not at all what I'd expected. I tried to wait them out, but neither of them uttered a syllable.

"Okay, let me ask that another way. Which one of you is in charge?"

The driver spoke. "We decided we're fifty-fifty partners."

Just as I'd thought. I continued listening to his watered-down plan.

"You see, we didn't like the way Reynolds was cheating us out of our money anyway. Talkin' 'bout how all the revenue from the drugs was his. Only problem is, we didn't know Reynolds's supplier and we don't have one of our own."

Bullshit. If Reynolds had undercut either one of these unscrupulous four-legged animals, they would've bypassed me and gone directly to Valentino. And in order for Valentino to avoid dealing directly with Reynolds's boss, whoever that was, Valentino would've paid these guys to shut up and get out of his face. Ah yes, this situation was getting more complicated by the minute, but I loved when men challenged my intelligence.

"Valentino has connections. He already knows who's replacing Reynolds and I'm sure his new person, like Reynolds, has a supplier."

Fuck! That was it! Valentino wanted to be his own supplier. That's why he wasn't tripping over Reynolds's death. I'd done Valentino a favor. That slick motherfucker. Now I saw exactly how well his plan was going.

"Well, I'm going to make you guys a proposition you won't want to refuse. For a hundred thousand dollars each, you're on my team. Your priority is to protect me at all times. If some shit goes down, shoot first and don't ask any questions. I'll do all the talking."

The driver asked, "So, let me get this right. We're *your* personal bodyguards from here on?"

"Exactly," I said. "From now on you two report directly to me."

"Does Valentino know about this?" the driver asked.

"You're not listening. Valentino has hired his own men to replace you guys. That way he gets to keep all the money from drug sales. Y'all are demoted to chauffeurs," I lied, trying to confuse them. "What I'm offering you is huge. Take it or leave it, because at my price I can hire anyone else. If you're interested, I'll give you the details later. I gotta go inside and get the girls," I said, scooting out of the limo and strutting into the casino.

This pimpin' game had become like the United Nations and I needed every escort and security person to form an alliance with me against Valentino. Where was I going to get two hundred thousand dollars in cash to give away tonight without using Valentino's money? I had no idea.

Following the sparkling big red apple dangling from the ceiling, I entered the bar area, joining my escorts. Gathering them in a huddle, I said, "Ladies, I sincerely apologize for everything bad that happened to any of you yesterday and promise nothing like that will happen to you again."

"So, is this the 'You brought it on yourself' speech that you're giving us before you beat us, then shove your finger up our asses later?" girl six questioned.

The hairs on the back of my neck stood at attention. This trick had gotten bold. With the other ten girls awaiting my response, I remained calm, then said, "No, it's not and no, I'm not going to beat you. However, I do have to check all of you. But there will be some good changes coming really soon."

"I don't believe you. Maybe we should all find ourselves a new madam like Sunny did," girl six said, nodding toward the bar.

How in the fuck did I miss that? Covering my mouth, I felt like my heart stopped beating again. I felt the tears flooding my bottom lid, so I blinked repeatedly 'cause none of my girls had seen me weak. I knew Sunny was alive. I knew it. I knew it. I just knew it and I didn't care about her having a new . . . what the hell? Squinting, I stared at the woman seated next to Sunny. That was the trick in blue from the bar the other night who knew my name. All of the madness was like being trapped in a never-ending nightmare.

Onyx's pointing finger pressed against her lips as her chilling stare focused on Starlet's eyes.

Did Valentino get to my bitches before me? I didn't have time to entertain games with girl six or Onyx, who obviously wanted to provoke a response from me, so I gave all of them something to do in order to get these bitches out of my face before I leaned across the table and slapped the hell out of all of them with one long stroke.

"Onyx, escort the girls to the limo out back. Now."

I was happy, pissed, relieved, jealous, and angry all within five minutes of seeing Sunny. Approaching the bar, I smoothed my skirt, checking for my gun just in case. "Excuse me, ladies," I said, interrupting their conversation.

"Lace, hi. Good to see you. You look nice," Sunny said, twisting her torso in my direction.

"Good to see me? You're acting like you don't know

me. Like nothing has happened. Where were you last night and what's going on here?"

Frowning at me, Sunny said, "Oh, where are my manners? Lace, Sapphire. Sapphire, Lace."

Manners? Sunny introduced us like we were two of her girlfriends who simply hadn't met yet.

Whispering in Sunny's ear, I asked, "Are you on drugs? Is this woman holding you against your will?"

Pushing me away, Sunny smiled. "Don't be jealous because I have a new boss."

Firmly grasping Sunny's biceps, I eased her off the bar stool, insisting, "Let me speak to you in private."

This Sapphire woman opened her mouth when she should've kept it shut. "Lace, Sunny is with me now. And you have five seconds to get your hands off of her. Your job is done and so are you."

What the hell? That bitch didn't know who she was fucking with. I wanted to slap her ass just to make sure I wasn't dreaming. As I stared at Sunny, ignoring Sapphire, my eyes softened. Gently I touched Sunny's hand.

Drawing away, Sunny said, "I don't want to quit. If you let me come back to work, I promise I won't leave you again."

Whoa, what was with the sudden change of heart? I did want Sunny back, but that was too damn easy.

"What! You can't leave me like this!" Sapphire said, standing over Sunny.

Okay, I had two guys outside if I needed them. I could play along with Sapphire's game for a minute. "Hey, look." I wedged my body between the two of them. "You heard her. She doesn't want you, she wants me so back off," I said, pressing my thigh next to hers, making sure Sapphire felt my gun. To my surprise, she jammed her nipples in my eyes. Her pistol was wedged between her humongous titties with the handle touching my chin.

Sunny somberly asked, "So, can I work with you tonight, Lace?"

Too much was happening too fast. I didn't know who to trust or believe. My Sunny would've called me Madam. Maybe she didn't want to confuse me with this bitch.

Reluctantly I said, "Yes," to get Sunny away from this Sapphire woman, but I was checking Sunny's ass for wires when we got to Valentino's mansion.

Gulping a shot of alcohol, Sapphire handed me a business card. Staring into my eyes, she said, "If you value Sunny's life, call me at exactly ten-oh-four tonight. Not a minute before or after." Then she told Sunny, "You'll be back. And when you come back, know that you have an ass whipping waiting."

Sometimes saying less was better and it was best if I kept quiet at this point. We'd drawn enough attention from the bartenders and from the patrons who should've been watching the two men and two women who were singing onstage.

If Sapphire had pulled her gun, I would've drawn mine and every security person in the casino would've surrounded us at the bar. All I saw playing in my head was that *Gang of Roses* western starring Lil' Kim, Monica Calhoun, LisaRaye, Stacey Dash, and Macy Gray. Every bitch had a gun. That's how real life should be.

Exiting the casino, I rubbed Sunny's veins from her wrists to her shoulders. There was a lot different about Sunny's personality. Although I didn't see any tracks, she'd definitely taken something.

"Are you sure you're not on drugs?"

"No, I don't do drugs," Sunny said, stumbling into the limo.

That was odd too. My Sunny considered XTC her drug of choice. Now she was claiming she doesn't do drugs when her mood had swung from confident to peaceful in less than fifteen minutes. "Hmm," I said, trying to figure this shit out en route to Valentino's while Sunny danced in her seat the entire time singing, "Let's go, kitty kat," over and over. I wanted to scream, "Shut the fuck up!"

Arriving at the mansion, I instructed security, "I'll escort the girls inside. Keep Sunny in the limo and don't let her out of your sight."

CHAPTER 32

Valentino

Lounging in my cinema chair watching these bitches enter my dressing room with Lace, I stroked my dick wondering which one of them would try a G next. Obviously Lace was up to some foul shit, letting those tricks put on makeup and then get dressed without swiping their mouths or scooping their pussies.

Checking in with my boy, I dialed Lace's home number to speak with Benito, but the nigga didn't pick up so I called his cell. No motherfuckin' answer. Benito wasn't slick. His ass was either giving me a full report on Lace tonight or I was going to that fancy estate and personally whupping the black off his ass. Knowing that punk, he was probably tiptoeing across the border trying to pass as a Mexican right this minute.

"Fuck Benito. His leeching ass ain't never did shit for me." I called Lace on her cell.

"Yes?"

"Bitch, get your ass over here right now," I said, then hung up, not giving her a chance to end the call first.

I swear if these hos didn't make me so much money I'd fire all of 'em.

Three of my baby sharks swam in a perfect circle following each other. I pressed the button on my remote, and the feeding door retracted. I inhaled the salt water. Their jaws peeled outward, exposing their long, sharp teeth. I should've fed Sunny to them instead of trusting Benito to bury her, but I couldn't let my pets devour my love.

I didn't have love for Lace, but I did have lust and most importantly a G like me had dick control. One lie outta her tonight and I wouldn't have to feed my sharks for another week. At least she had sense enough to have Reynolds's body buried in the desert where the scorching sun would bake his ass into the sand and the desert ants would eat away his flesh. Reynolds's only remains, his bones and teeth, would crumble like dust if anyone touched him. That was the kind of wisdom I needed from Benito.

No doubt Lace would get away with that murder rap unless some new DA tryna gain popularity was assigned to the case. I'd be the first to slip an envelope full of money under the table and raise my right hand to testify 'cause the bitch scrambled my video signal that night long enough for her do damage, then flee the scene as though she were never there. Clever bitch did exactly what I'd wanted her to. Let's see how she gets past me tonight without trippin' over her lies.

If it weren't Sunny's body, I would've told Lace to dispose of her instead of Benito, but Lace had fucked up again by parking her car at IP.

"Knock, knock," Lace said, walking up to my study. She stood inside the doorway, letting her shoulder lean against the ledge.

"Come, in. Have a seat," I said, making sure she sat facing the bookshelves.

I followed her roaming eyes, until they stopped where the *First Lady* once stood, paused, then continued to the opening in the floor. Suddenly she looked away only to return her gaze to both locations seconds later. Then Lace's eyes scanned the bookshelves again.

"Something wrong?" I asked.

"No, naw. Other than the fact that you forgot to close your tank. Everything's good. I need to go do my inspections, what's up?"

"Don't!" I yelled, then whispered, "Play me for stupid. I watched you let them get dressed without doing any inspections. Where's Sunny?" I asked, walking over to Lace, watching her ass every second.

"Sunny's in the limo. Why?"

Oh, now this bitch really thought I was as dumb as her man. Grabbing her legs, I snatched her ass out of the chair. *Bam!* Her head, her ass, and her gun hit the floor at the same time.

"Bitch, stop lying! Where in the fuck is Sunny?"

"I told you, she's in the limo."

"Bitch!" I yelled, holding my heart.

Lace's stiletto was a motherfuckin' weapon. Falling backward, I almost landed in the tank. Lying on the floor, I looked up at this Wonder Woman, Cleopatra Jones bitch standing over me pointing a gun at my forehead, but she didn't scare me.

That was impossible for Sunny to be in the limo, but what if somehow, someway, Sunny was alive and I didn't kill her? What if the bullet only grazed her head and her heart? Maybe that's why Sunny's body was gone when Benito went back to get it. Stranger things had happened. I thought, *What the fuck are you trippin' off of, nigga? You put the second bullet in her, then watched her take her last breath.*

"You know something I don't? Or that I should?" Lace asked, putting away her gun while roaming through the shelves.

Standing up, I massaged the back of my neck, then said, "Okay, bitch. If she's in the limo, bring her to me."

Stopping less than an inch from my face, Lace said, "Sure." Her hands grasped my dick; then her lips met mine, as she meshed her gumdrops into my chest.

With her tongue swirling around in my mouth, there wasn't much I could say, but a lot I could feel. With me working with Lace's fine ass every day, secretly wanting her all the time, my dick must've felt like a piece of lead in her hand. Removing her thong, lifting her skirt, then tossing her leg into my arm, Lace opened my boxers and slipped my dick into her clambering pussy, then moaned, "I've always wanted you."

Here we were, two murderers in heat. Neither one of us trusted the other, but I had no fuckin' idea her pussy was this good. Hell, I should put her on a stroll. "Don't move," I insisted, lowering her leg. Retrieving a condom from my desk, I guided Lace to the caramel chair, put her face in the seat, and fucked her doggie-style because I hated looking into a woman's eyes while fucking. Doggie-style kept the focus on the orgasm, not the bitch. All that missionary fucking was too emotional.

Lace sucked my fingers and when she turned her face to the side, I couldn't believe I kissed her.

I stroked Lace long and deep until she started moaning, "Mmm, oh yes. Now, this is the dick of a real man. Oh yes. A real man."

Lace repeated those words like she was in a fuckin'

trance. But so was I. The deeper I fucked her, the larger my dick felt. I wanted to come so bad but didn't want to lose the sensation.

"You mind if I get this big-ass nut out of the way?"

"I'm ready whenever you are, Daddy. Come for Mama."

Speeding up the pace, I fucked the shit out of Lace, banging her head against the cushion until, "Urgh! Urgh!" My legs trembled, then became weak. Bracing my hands on the arms of the chair, I needed shoulder strength to lift my body.

When did all this shit happen? I thought, glancing at the now-closed tank and the place on the floor where Lace's gun was. This bitch was slick and my ass was too weak to challenge her.

Lace stood. Lowering her skirt, and fingering her hair, she said, "I'll be right back," glancing over her shoulder as she strutted in those stilettos that never left her feet.

Pouring a glass of scotch, I sat my naked ass in my theater chair reconsidering paying Benito to kill Lace tonight. I might want to hit that good pussy one more time.

"Here she is." Lace's voice resonated from behind me.

I really didn't want to turn around 'cause I knew Lace had probably hired some new bitch to replace Sunny.

"Well, you wanted to see her. She's here."

Slowly I swiveled my chair, facing her. "Aw, fuck no!" I scrambled in my seat, my feet shuffling on the Persian rug. Pointing at that bitch who couldn't possibly be Sunny, I backed into the bookcases. My arms spread wide, slamming into books. Pages fluttered as books splattered beside my feet. My heart punched my chest. "Oh, shit! You tryna kill me. Get that bitch outta here!" I yelled, gasping for air, holding my chest.

Softly she asked, "Anthony? Is it you?" letting me

know that was definitely Summer. Then who in the fuck had I killed?

I took a long deep breath until my stomach couldn't stretch out another inch, then exhaled. "Lace! What the fuck are you doing fucking with my heads?" I wanted to get my gun and shoot both of those bitches.

Pointing at Summer, I second-guessed whether the woman standing in front of me was truly Summer, then said, "Bitch, let me see your teeth. Fuck that. I don't need to see your fuckin' teeth. You killed yourself. What in the fuck is going on?" I yelled, "Get the fuck outta here. Both of you."

Opening her arms, Summer walked toward me. If I coulda slid between the pages of a book, I would've.

"I'm sorry I lied about killing our baby. My daddy made me do it. AJ is four years old now. He looks just like you, Anthony."

Lace interrupted and said, "Aw, hell no. Stop right there," just in time to save Summer, because I swore if Summer would've touched me I was bashing her face in.

"What, baby?" Lace questioned, frowing at me. "And who in the fuck is Anthony?" she asked, rattling Summer. "Now I know you're on drugs. Sunny, let's go."

"Yeah! Whoever she is, get that bitch outta here and don't bring her back! You're wrong for this shit, Lace! Dead wrong!"

CHAPTER 33

Summer

Lace was more than Anthony's madam; she acted more like his woman or his wife.

I didn't know much about the pimping industry, but I knew what having to hide my emotions of loving someone felt like. The way Lace escorted me into Anthony's office squeezing my biceps, the way Anthony sat there in front of us naked like he had more than his socks on. The way Lace tried to control me, standing beside me with her hands on her hips, exposed her insecurities. I felt Lace was questioning Anthony in her own way by using her body language to ask, "Do you want her? Or me?"

In my moment of standing in the presence of Lace and Anthony, I realized Sapphire was right. Anthony didn't kill Sunny, Lace did. Lace was jealous of Sunny, in love with Sunny, and in love with Anthony. She wanted it all, but I know Sunny, and my sister was no bisexual freak and she wasn't having it. That probably made Lace angry.

Lace wanted Anthony for herself and I felt like she wanted me too the way she'd frisked me all over. But did Sunny ever want Anthony? I couldn't blame any woman for falling for Anthoy. The minute I saw my baby's daddy, I wanted him back in my life and I wanted Anthony to meet his son. But the way Lace screamed, "What baby?" let me know for sure she was pissed at Anthony for not telling her he had a kid.

Lace was quiet during the ride to wherever we were on our way to next. With all the dizziness winding in my head, I couldn't figure out why she had so much to say earlier and nothing to say now. Maybe like me, Lace was trying to make sense of everything including why Anthony didn't have on his underwear. That was disrespectful.

The thing that frightened me the most were those sharks. The aquarium was beautiful, but when I saw those pointed teeth I wanted to scramble, but the shock on Anthony's face distracted me. An innocent, naive girl from a small town who had no idea what went on outside Henderson, Nevada, was coaxed overnight into prostitution. Sapphire had promised if everything went as planned I wouldn't have to do this again. But with so much happening so fast I had to remember to ask Sapphire where that football player was who'd followed me home.

I'd only been in this business for a few hours and I was ready to quit. I hoped this mystery of who killed my sister was resolved soon so I could get back to my parents, my baby, and my classes. I didn't mean to sound insensitive, but trying to mourn my sister's death in the midst of all this was giving me a migraine. The thought of being on track to graduate after completing my last semester gave me something positive to focus on. Grad school outside Las Vegas, hell, outside Nevada, was definitely appealing, but I didn't want to take my son with me and I couldn't leave him behind.

Thus far everything had worked out exactly how Sapphire explained it would. Sapphire was strikingly beautiful. Her small petite frame was perfect. I couldn't see that the first time we'd met at the steak house 'cause she had on that sweatshirt, but at the casino tonight she was dressed different. She had large, sexy eyes accented with a sparkling blue shadow. Her lips were a shiny but light shade of pink. And her hair floated over her shoulders. Sapphire reminded me of Jada Pinkett-Smith when I saw *The Matrix 3*. Sapphire was a woman who was strong, sexy, and feminine all at the same time.

When Sapphire took my family to identify Sunny's body, I cried for what must've been twenty-four hours straight. I was still crying on the inside. Or at least it felt like it. My stomach ached, my head hurt, and Lace was right, I was on drugs. But not crack or speed or cocaine or anything I'd become addicted to. I was on an unknown sedative that Sapphire said would control my emotions and prevent me from overreacting.

Before we arrived at the bar, Sapphire had rehearsed my script with me over and over like I was starring in a Broadway play, until I'd gotten every line memorized. But once Lace took me to the man she referred to as Valentino and I'd known as Anthony, I'd started ad-libbing. Hopefully I hadn't ruined anything for Sapphire. Maybe I could get the sex part right and remember what the john Sapphire brought to the hotel earlier this afternoon had taught me on how to please a man. I'd never sucked a dick before and thank God Sapphire didn't make me have anal sex like the guy tried to convince her.

"How's she supposed to give her clients some ass if

they ask for it? Come on, Sapphire, she's a virgin booty. Let me break her in."

Sapphire calmly said, "Forget it."

Before leaving the hotel room, he kissed me, then said, "You're a keeper, doll."

His words resounding in my head suddenly made me shivering cold. Now here I was in a limo full of prostitutes I didn't know except for Onyx and Starlet whom Sapphire had introduced me to on one occasion as Sunny's friends.

I kinda liked Onyx more because she took on the role of big sister when she'd said, "You can count on me. Here's your sister's cell phone. I'm sure she wants you to have it. Oh yeah, and Sunny told me to make sure her parents know she was a good girl. Relay the message for me, will you? My number is in there." She'd touched the phone one last time before I'd put it in my purse, and then she continued. "If you need me, call me. I got your back at all times."

I wondered if she meant it but prayed I'd never had to find out. Starlet was quiet and clearly took her direction from Onyx. The blindfold was too tight, so I was relieved when they escorted us into the whorehouse and removed the satin coverings.

Well, here I was in a sinful place silently praying to God asking for His forgiveness. I had to help Sapphire get her promotion by solving her biggest case. She said I'd be helping other girls not to end up dead like my sister. Although Lace, Sapphire, and Anthony had their own motives, I did this for Sunny.

When we entered the place, I'd never seen so many men in my life who were eagerly waiting to fuck women. Had my sister slept with all of these men? I wanted to cry but the drugs wouldn't let me. My pussy started twitching as Onyx led me to what she'd referred to as Sunny's room, the Presidential Suite.

"Wait here. Your john will be in in a minute. If you need help, just press this button on the phone. You won't hear anything, but I will."

I wobbled around the room in the highest pair of heels I'd ever worn. The shortest dress I'd never wear in public. And the most makeup I'd ever had on that Sapphire had painted my face with. My blond hair swayed behind my back and I still smelled the fresh strawberry fragrance the stylist conditioned my hair with. A few enhancements to my wardrobe and hair along with a body scrub to make my skin glisten and a massage made me feel like a woman.

Lounging in the swing, I wondered, *Was this my sister's?*

The drugs made me feel weird. Like another person was inside my body. Touching the silver thong wedged between my lips, I traced my new acrylic French-manicured nails over my pussy and I tingled all over with pleasure. My pussy got hot. Slipping my finger under the thong, I eased it inside me. I was wet. Really wet. Spreading the moisture on the tip of my clit in small circular motions, I started trembling.

"Oh my God. Oh my God, I'm coming?"

That was my first orgasm while playing with myself. Did my sister do this in front of a different man every night? I guess if that's all she had to do to save all the money she had in her bank account, this wasn't so bad.

"That's right, come for Daddy."

"Ah!" I leapt from the swing, tugging at my dress. My ankle twisted to the floor. "Who are you? Why do you have on that mask?" I asked, thrusting the swing in front of me.

"I came because I must know who you really are. Come to Daddy. I won't hurt you."

The voice was one I could never forget but had to ask, "Anthony James, is it you?"

CHAPTER 34

Lace

Men were simple.
I knew his fuckin' ass would show up unannounced to fuck Sunny. He couldn't wait to get here. I imagined the second we left his mansion, Valentino slid from his study all the way down his hallway straight into his shower still wearing his orange socks. A little extra attention to his genitals, underarms, and brushing his teeth, followed by gurgling. Ripping the cleaner's plastic off his clothes he would get dressed en route to his car. Shortly after security escorted the girls inside IP, Valentino came driving onto the property in his navy-colored Benz like he hadn't fucked me an hour ago.

Once I gave him some of this good pussy, I knew Valentino would feel empowered, but in actuality I had the power because whenever a man thought he had the upper hand, his game got real sloppy. Like B. Although

I didn't know exactly what made B slam me into the side of the tub, I knew something or someone had gotten into his head because B was weak. Any man who let a woman provide for all his needs was weak.

In retrospect I was an infatuated enabler. I was in love with the man B represented, not the man B was. Then when things obviously didn't go according to his plan, all of a sudden his confessions were supposed to make me forgive him. Fuck that. A bitch who forgets gets trapped in a maze of financial, emotional, spiritual, and sometimes physical ass kickings every day again and again until she figures out a way to outsmart her man.

Watching Valentino's jacket flap in the wind, I had to stop him before he skipped inside.

"Excuse me, you got a minute?"

Doing the sideways shuffle over to my car dressed in yellow from head to toe—hat, suit, tie, and shoes—he said, "I'm glad I caught you. Don't go anywhere near my house until I call you. You've got some serious explaining to do about seducing my dick. I told you never to fuck with my dick or my money. You must be tryna get fired."

Valentino massaged his thin mustache with his thumb and pointing finger, thrust out his chest, hoisted up his pants, then turned away.

"Wait!" I yelled to his back. "Why did you think Sunny was dead?"

"Straight up, because you know she is." Valentino went inside and slammed the front door.

Tears filled with anger streamed down my face. I wasn't supposed to develop feelings for Valentino. *Okay, Lace, pull yourself together. So, what . . . the part of your plan to fuck Valentino so he wouldn't fuck Sunny didn't work out.* But was Sunny dead or alive? Who in the hell did I pick up at that bar? *No, stop trip-*

ping. That was definitely Sunny inside and this was still her last night working no matter what Valentino said.

Glancing at my watch, I zoomed out of the gate and drove far away from Valentino's hidden cameras. Hell, I was the madam and I didn't give a damn about Valentino fucking any of my other girls, but I hoped security would keep their dicks in their pants and follow my instructions to protect Sunny.

Parking my Jaguar adjacent to the under-construction lot for Camino Al Norte Professional Center, I dialed 702-555 . . . calling this Sapphire woman at exactly 10:04 just in case she wasn't bluffin' about causing harm to Sunny.

"Good. You are a smart woman and your timing is impeccable. Meet me at Valentino's home in five minutes."

That trick was certifiably crazy. I questioned, "Why?"

"I can't say but you do have a choice. You can be on your way to the house or to jail, the choice is yours."

The moment Sapphire ended the call, I realized who she was but couldn't recall her last name. I'd seen her someplace else other than at the bars. Picturing her with no makeup and without the wig, I yelled, "Fuck!" banging my fist against the steering wheel, contemplating what to do next. Sapphire Bleu was the undercover cop my ex-madam had given me a picture of and warned me about.

I thought my madam was trippin', jealous, and trying to convince me it was safer to stay at Pussyland Ranch working for her for a measly raise of fifty dollars an hour. Scrolling through my mental Rolodex, I dialed my ex-madam's number.

"Pussyland Ranch, Triple D speaking."

"Madam, this is Lace. I need your help."

"Well, I haven't heard from you in over a decade. No hello, how you doing. Now you need me?"

"Please, Triple D, I don't have much time. I need you to tell me everything you know about Sapphire Bleu."

"So she finally caught up to Valentino, huh? I tried to warn him. I knew it was just a matter of time. Eventually she'll catch all the big-timers illegally running girls inside the county limits."

I didn't want to sound rude but I didn't have time to listen to all that shit. "Triple D, what can you tell me?"

"One, she likes women. Two, be afraid. Be very afraid. But if you need a safe, clean place to work, call me. I could use a skilled assistant." Triple D concluded, "I've got to go, my johns are arriving," then hung up.

"What a waste of my time." Not really, but there was no one else I could phone, which made me realize I didn't have the real alliances I needed in this business to protect myself. Triple D made a good point. I should've kept in touch with her over the years as opposed to calling her only because I needed her. Obviously Valentino had called her. Never had I been so confused. If I went to Valentino's, was I volunteering to wear an orange jumpsuit and a pair of handcuffs? If I went to jail, would Valentino let my ass stay in jail or bail me out? If I went to Valentino's, this might be my last day of freedom.

If I didn't go, my life might be in jeopardy. If they found Benito, his ass probably blew every whistle they stuck in his mouth telling them everything he knew. At this point I wasn't sure if Sunny was dead or at IP. That woman Valentino was probably fucking right now could be one of those Vegas lookalikes hired for this sting operation.

Cruising along Ann Road, approaching Valentino's home, I decreased my speed to three miles an hour. An unmarked van was in the Walgreen's parking lot. Yellow caution tape was wrapped around Valentino's mansion.

And a miniature SWAT team dressed in black gear with gas masks guarded the surroundings.

No fucking way, I thought, getting ready to slam my accelerator, when a blinding flashlight beamed through my windshield.

Someone yelled, "Get out of the car!"

Okay, I had one gun; they had God knows how many.

I stepped slowly out of my car, and the light vanished as Sapphire raced over, grabbed my arm, then rushed me past four security men inside the mansion.

"We don't have much time," she said. "Valentino is at Immaculate Perception fucking Summer. I've got two men posted outside the whorehouse to detain him, and if you help me find what I'm looking for we can slow our pace because NLVPD will arrest Valentino."

Prying away her fingers, I asked, "Who did you say he was fucking?"

"Huh? What? That's not important. I can explain that later. Right now we've got to keep it moving. Where does Valentino hide his drugs, his money, his guns, his surveillance videos, and his client list?"

Pacing back and forth atop the shark tank, I considered getting the remote, opening the floor beneath Sapphire, and drowning her ass, but somehow I felt she already had the controller in her possession. Asking her why she needed so much so quick would've been a waste of time, so I lied and said, "I don't know," when I knew where everything in Valentino's house was except my *First Lady* book.

"Bitch, I told you. You can be on my team or go down with his team starting with the deaths of Reynolds Washington and Sunny Day."

"Sunny is at IP like you instructed us, so how could I have killed her?"

"Get your asses in here and arrest this bitch! I don't have time to play games!"

Two of the four security men I saw outside raced into the room, grabbed my arms, then pulled out their handcuffs and flipped the metal loops open. This was not a smart time to pull out my gun. Triple D's voice echoed, *Be very afraid.*

"Okay, wait up. I'll cooperate."

Sapphire nodded and just like they had appeared, the security men vanished.

Reluctantly I told Sapphire, "Follow me," fearing my ass might still be arrested once she got what she wanted. I couldn't go to jail. I had to bury Honey.

Leading Sapphire to the basement, I opened doors number one, two, and three.

Searching inside the first closet, Sapphire said, "You wanna play games?"

"Step back," I told her, getting my gun out and firing two shots into the bottom body bags.

Cocaine poured like water. Struggling, I grabbed the sides of the middle bag and huffed until it collapsed the ones on top to the floor. While I unzipped several bags, Sapphire's eyes widened as wads of hundred dollar bills popped out of the bags.

"Now, that's what I'm talking about," Sapphire said, walking up to me. She swatted my ass, cupped my breast, kissed my lips, then whispered, "Good job. I'm gonna take real good care of you, Lace. I want you." Before I could answer, she yelled, "Down here, guys!"

Nervously, I unlatched the storage trunks inside closet two. Valentino had enough weapons and ammunition to employ an infantry division of more than five hundred men. Stepping inside the third closet, I screamed, "Aaahh! What the fuck! When did he get that coffin? And who's in it?"

"Lace, you done good. My squad will take it from

here. You're free to go but there's three things you can never do. One, you cannot go back to your house. Two, you cannot come back here or drive by Immaculate Perception. And three, you must never cross me. If you do, more than your ass will be mine. Every cop in town knows your cars and your license plates. And you cannot call me again. In exactly seventy-two hours I will call you."

"That's four."

"I told you you're smart. Now let's see if you're intelligent enough to figure out which ones you can do."

That was one of those tricky-ass statements. I looked at Sapphire and said, "One more question."

"Yes, Sunny is dead. No, her body is not inside that coffin. The woman you dropped off at IP is Sunny's twin sister, Summer."

"My God. Yes. Now it's starting to make sense. And Summer is the mother of Valentino's son. Does she know what she's doing? Is she—"

"Safe? We're doing our best to keep her that way."

Now I wished I hadn't asked so many questions, especially since I couldn't go anywhere near IP. On the way to my car, I bypassed the SWAT men posted outside the mansion. What a hellava way to end a fantastic operation. Valentino wasn't perfect, but he treated us better than most pimps did their madams, wives-in-law, and whores. I hated to see him go out like this, but whenever a woman had to choose between saving her ass and that of a man, she'd better use her pussy power.

I prayed Summer was okay, but the way that girl called Valentino Anthony, she was in love and in danger. If Sapphire couldn't guarantee Summer's safety and if Valentino's life was threatened, I doubted Summer would make it through the night. Alive.

CHAPTER 35

Valentino

"Anthony, please tell me what they're saying is a lie. Please tell me you didn't kill my sister."

Edging toward the swing, I thought a G like me wasn't supposed to get all soft and shit on the inside, but this was the same warm, loving, caring Summer I knew years ago. I removed the mask and said, "Summer, is my son really alive and do you really have a twin? Don't fuck with me. Straight, tell me what's going on."

"Yes, our son is alive and . . ." Summer paused, swallowing hard, then said, "But my twin sister, Sunny, is dead."

The more questions I asked the more I had. Why hadn't Summer mentioned a twin back when we were dating? Or was she lying? But I had watched a bitch kill herself. But how or why could Summer's twin end up working for me as religious as Mr. Daniel was?

"How do you know your twin is dead for sure?"

Tears streamed down Summer's flushed cheeks as she cried. "I saw her body."

"When? Where? Who showed it to you? Where's she at now?"

Hugging the swing, Summer started crying louder, but I didn't give a fuck about that sentimental bullshit right now. I needed my fuckin' questions answered. Cupping her hands, I begged, "Talk to Daddy. I have to know."

"Sapphire. Oops, I wasn't supposed to tell you her name. That's not her name. I can't remember what her name is. All I know is that I saw my sister at the morgue. She was shot twice. And I hope the bastard that killed her burns in hell! Her funeral is tomorrow. It's all my fault. I never should've let her leave home."

Summer backed into the corner. Her back slid against the wall until her ass touched the heels of her feet.

I wanted to reach around the leather straps, bend over, and slap the fuck out of Summer. Her emotions were all over the place and a G didn't have time for the nonsense. One minute calm, then screaming, then calm again, all the while crying every other word out of her mouth between sniffles.

"Baby, it's all right. What you should've done was told me five years ago that you had a twin and you really should've told me that you didn't abort my son."

If Summer had told me the truth back then, Sunny would be alive. Our lives would've been different. I would've been different.

Fuck. For once that nigga Benito wasn't lying. For once his dumb ass had his facts straight. I'd break him off something later for his loyalty.

Summer's voice deepened and her eyes widened, then scrolled up staring at me before disappearing behind her lids. I swear all I saw was the whites of her eyes and that shit freaked me the fuck out. That bitch looked possessed.

"Now answer a question for me," she growled angrily. "Did you or did you not kill my sister?"

Moving the swing from between us, I told the truth. "No, I swear I did not kill your sister."

"Then do you know who did? Because when I find out, I'm going to kill them the same way they killed Sunny."

Summer wasn't brave enough to hold a gun, let alone pull the trigger. She nestled her face between her knees.

Calmly I answered, "No, I don't. Look at me, Summer. All I know is I'm happy you came back to me. I need you. Let me hold you in my arms again. Come to Daddy. Let me make love to you, baby."

I knew just how to stoke Summer's cheeks, gently kiss her lips, massage her neck, which I could've snapped for her making that threat, but I cradled her into my arms because if only for one night this was the love I needed in my life. The strength I needed to hold on to in order to let all that other shit go. I led my baby to the bed, and we lay together in silence for a moment.

Interrupting the quietness, I said, "Summer, I'm gonna marry you. Let's make our own twins tonight." I searched Summer's body, relieved I didn't see any of those egg-killing birth control patches, then asked, "Are you on the pill?"

Summer shook her head as tears streamed from her beautiful big, brown, innocent eyes. I definitely recognized the personality difference from her sister, but if Sunny was here too, aw, shit, that would've been amazing to fuck both of them at the same time. Sunny was a woman. Summer was a girl trapped inside a woman's body. Great balance for a threesome.

Focusing on my baby, I was happy that Summer didn't resist me. Whatever drugs they'd given her to set me up worked in my favor.

Easing the straps over Summer's shoulders, I kissed her nipples, grazing my tongue over the tip. "Lie down, my love. I'm here for you and I'm never letting you get away from me again."

Removing the packet of white powder from my pocket, I saturated my tongue, parted Summer's thighs, then pressed the magic chemicals against her clit. Instantly Summer's juices flowed. Glancing up at *my* bitch, I watched her eyes roll to the back of her head. Lifting her hood with my tongue, I mashed more powder on her clit.

"Anthony, that feels so good I can't stop coming."

"I know, baby," I said, dabbing the powder on my dick before climbing on top of Summer.

Spreading her legs, I eased inside. "Damn, baby, you're tight."

Inching my dick along her cushioned walls, I wanted to make love to Summer, not hurt her. And I was serious, I wanted her to have my baby again. Just knowing I had a son made me proud. I couldn't wait to see him, hold him, toss that lil' sucker in the air. That was my seed and this was my lady.

My dick finally curved into Summer's pussy pocket. Pressing as deep as I could, I moaned, "Come with me, baby. Come for Daddy."

I didn't want to hold on to this nut. I wanted to explode every sperm in my nuts deep into her stomach.

Locking her legs around my ass and wrapping her arms around my shoulders, Summer kissed me. "I love you, Anthony. I never stopped thinking about you. You were always good to me."

"And you were always good for . . . Urgh!" I grunted

several times, shooting all the come I could thrust inside Summer, praying for her to have my child. "I love you too, Summer. Always have. Always will."

Gazing into my eyes, she asked, "You mean that?"

"Yes, I really do." And I did. In my special way.

Knock. Knock. Knock.

"Go the fuck away," I said. "A nigga can't have a moment of peace and relaxation. Whatever the fuck it is handle it. That's what I pay you motherfuckers for."

Knock. Knock. Knock. Knock. Knock. Knock.

"Stay right here, baby. Do not get up and spill my seeds. Let me see who the fuck needs an ass whuppin'."

Quietly stepping to the door, I leaned my eye over the peephole, then stood there for a moment. Shit outside the door was too fucking quiet for a G.

"Police! Valentino James, we know you're in there! Open up!"

Scrambling, I quickly put on my pants, shirt, and shoes. *Should I take this bitch with me as a hostage, or leave her ass here? Because her drugged ass is going to slow me down.*

"Hurry up," I said, tossing Summer her dress. "Put this on."

"What's going on?" Summer asked, trying to put on her shoes.

"Bitch, you gon' break your damn neck." If I didn't break it for her. "You can't walk, let alone run in those shoes. Here, put on my socks."

"They don't match my dress."

Bam! Bam! "You've got three seconds! One, two—"

By the time that fuckin' cop got to three, I'd slipped behind the clothes in the closet, made my way through my hidden door, down three flights of stairs, and to my underground tunnel.

"Hurry up, girl, you gon' get us killed," I told Summer, regretting I'd taken her with me.

Easing my way through the secret door, we stepped into my private home I'd never told anyone about, not even Lace's nosy ass. I bet that bitch was behind this shit. That or she'd fucked up and led the police to me, 'cause those motherfuckers knew my name and exactly where I was. I guess all my bitches were locked up by now too.

Or, I thought, staring at Summer, "Bitch, did you set me up? Think before you open your motherfuckin' mouth, because if you had anything to do with this, you're one dead bitch. Who in the fuck is Sapphire?"

CHAPTER 36

Lace

Life was less risky at the Pussyland Ranch. I'd be safe there, but there was no way at the age of thirty I could go back to fucking men to make a living.

I'd learned so much since Rita had kicked me out of her house. Girls who were given every material thing they wanted were cool as long as they didn't want their parents' love. True love, that is.

People, men, johns, families with money somehow thought they could buy affection, some saying, "Aw, honey, I'm sorry I have to fly off again but happy anniversary, I bought you a new car. Good-bye." Not caring, not even noticing if the person was truly happy with the car. She might have been happier with a candlelight dinner sitting next to, not across from him. A stroll in the park reminiscing and creating fond memories would've given her an emotional tune-up that might have exceeded the joy of her having yet another material object of affection while she struggled by herself to raise their children.

Some of my regular johns actually fell in love with me. Or so they'd said. But no amount of money can buy love. Happiness? Yes. Love? No. What I finally realized was it was okay to love somebody but longing to love and having no one to love created heartbreaks that caused death.

For the girls who were given love even though their parents might have not had money to buy them nice things, generally those girls grew into women who cared about themselves and others. Since I didn't have parents who gave me money or love, Sunny's death awakened me from my conscious coma. I wanted to love and be loved before I died. The way Sunny's family loved her. I knew I shouldn't go back to my house, Valentino's, or his mansion, but I wasn't relocating from Las Vegas to Atlanta until I was certain that Summer was safe. I owed Sunny and her family that much.

Thank God. If there was a God. I was smart while working for Valentino and over a one-year period was able to add more than a million dollars to my Sweeter than Honey business account.

Selecting my business name was a spiritual movement for me. Although I was a prostitute, I knew the work I'd done did not define me. Sometimes a woman has got to make a choice. And that choice may not always be one that she is proud of or the best in someone else's eyes, but those naysayers aren't the ones offering any type of support either. If all somebody had to give me was their opinion, I'd tell them, "Fuck you. Kiss my ass," to their faces, not behind their backs.

They didn't pay my bills and if I begged for food, most of them would walk by with leftovers in their hands shaking their heads while mumbling, "Get a job." Did they realize how fuckin' hard it was to get a job without an address? Live in a shelter sleeping on sheets where bugs ate away your flesh? Or what it was like to sleep on the streets and have no sheets at all? Waiting for someone to throw their food in the garbage, the same food they wouldn't hand you, just so you could fetch a meal? And the saddest part was that most of the ones who wouldn't help were women just like me . . . trying to fake it till they made it.

I'd started my business while working at Pussyland because regardless of whether I was a prostitute, a madam, or a whore on the street, I knew retiring from prostitution was a dream for most women but I made sure it became a reality for me.

I understood how difficult it was for women to sell their precious bodies for twenty, forty, or a few hundred dollars and struggle to make the mental transition to get a decent job paying minimum wage. That shit was hard and for most women in the game, illogical and impossible. I was once told a woman's only ways out of the game were incarceration, confinement to a mental institution, or death. I disagreed but at that time I wasn't prepared to make a difference. Now that my perspective has changed, I know that when I start providing consultation, a safe clean place for women in transition to live, and teaching women that their pussies have more brain cells than any other parts of their bodies, most women will get it . . . Pussy isn't about sex, it's about control. Not control over others but control and greater self-esteem for themselves.

As I approached airport security, folks around me started mumbling. An old lady pointed, then whispered in an old man's ear.

What was her problem?

Waiting at the gate to board my flight to Flagstaff, I sat next to a gentleman dressed in a gray suit. "You smell like you could use a friend. Soap," he said, abruptly standing.

Soap? A friend? Hmm. Both were something I didn't have. But what I did have was a lot of shit on my mind, so I'd left my car at the casino where'd I'd checked in last night and walked to the airport. As prideful as I was about my body the last thing I wanted was some guy twice my age making fun of my hygiene. Ignoring him as he walked away, I buried my face in the morning newspaper. I flipped to the local news section to see Summer's face . . . on the front page!

HENDERSON WOMAN ABDUCTED AND HELD HOSTAGE BY PIMP.

Fuck! Calmly I folded the paper over Valentino's picture, feeling torn knowing I had to bury my sister so I couldn't return immediately to help Summer, but there was something else I could do.

Walking to the nearest customer service counter, I handed the woman my credit card and driver's license, then said, "I'd like to purchase thirteen one-way open tickets from Las Vegas to Atlanta." One by one I gave her the names for each of my escorts, Summer, and myself.

Fumbling through my purse for a pen to sign for the charges, I noticed my nephew's photo. Where was I going to take him? How was I going to raise him? The envelope I stepped on at the hospital was crumbled. Smoothing the paper, I poked my finger between the opening, ripping apart the top.

Unfolding the paper, I saw it was Honey's birth certificate and mine. I'd never seen either before. Rita never showed it to me and Triple D, based on Rita's address, somehow got me a driver's license before I knew how to drive. The two most important leverages in life were people with power and people with money. The combination of both could circumvent any system. Oh well. At least Rita was our mother and Jean St. Thomas was our father.

Interrupting me, the ticketing agent said, "Excuse me, miss. You need to sign this. There's a line behind you."

Without looking up at her, I mumbled, "Oh, sure," scribbling my signature, then stuffed the electronic confirmations into my purse.

"Well, I'll be damned," I said, walking toward my gate. Next to our father's name was his address on South San Francisco Street only a few blocks away from Rita's house.

"Okay, Lace. Honey is dead. Summer is alive. There's nothing you can do to bring Honey back, but you can do your best to save Summer . . . but my daddy's address is right here and I could find out once and for all why he abandoned us . . . shit!"

I froze, standing between two rows of black vinyl seats. BREAKING NEWS! scrolled across the flat-screen television at my gate. I moved closer so I could hear the anchorwoman who announced, "The Henderson woman missing overnight was found an hour ago by Sergeant Sapphire Bleu. The victim, Summer Day, was unharmed. The pimp, Anthony Valentino James, who allegedly abducted Summer, is now under arrest for abduction, rape, illegal prostitution, and he's being charged with the murder of Summer's identical sister, Sunny Day, who was shot in the head and the heart. Her body was discovered days ago by Sergeant Bleu in Sunny's condo located in North Las Vegas.

"Sergeant Bleu, tell us how you solved this case."

"Well, there's a lot of illegal prostitution going on in Las Vegas. I figured why waste my time busting johns one at a time? My strategy was if I could arrest the pimps with the largest operations, I could prevent women like Sunny from being killed."

"That's highly commendable. We hear you're up for

a promotion. Well, after this case is settled you'll probably become chief. Before we return to our regularly scheduled program already in place, two more questions. What about the prostitutes who were working for Valentino— were any of them arrested? And are there any more people working for Valentino's operation that you're going to go after?"

I held my breath awaiting Sapphire's response.

"None of the prostitutes were arrested. Valentino's security guards are out on bail, and—" Sapphire looked directly into the camera as if she knew I was watching, then firmly said, "No. There's no one else involved. We've got our man."

Suddenly I heard, "Last call for Lace St. Thomas."

"Oh my." Tucking my purse under my arm, I raced to the ticket agent and handed him my boarding pass.

On my flights and my layover, I thought about meeting my father for the first time. Would he hug me? Hold me? Give me the love Rita couldn't or wouldn't? Anxiously, I wanted to drive directly to his house, but I had to go to the funeral home first and view Honey's body. Parking in the lot next to a stretch limousine, I sat still for a moment remembering some of the good times Honey and I had shared as little girls. I felt myself smiling. We played with dolls, watched scary movies, then slept on the living room floor together. The nerves in my shoulders crept up the nape of my neck, then stabbed the back of my head.

Getting out of the car, I wondered if I would ever forget that Sunday morning lying on the living room floor crying with my legs spread open. Even in the midst of good memories, the bad things that men had done to me made me angry and sad at the same time.

Entering the air-conditioned empty room, I saw Honey laid in a plain silver coffin dressed in a saggy black suit.

"You've got to change this," I said to the funeral director. "She's dead but she doesn't have to look it."

"Well," he replied, pinching his nostrils, "I'll see what we can do if you see what you can do. You know what I mean?"

Damn, I forgot about my appearance. Rushing to the Flagstaff Mall on the other side of town, I made several stops at Victoria's Secret, Bath & Body Works, Dillard's, and JC Penney to buy enough clothes for three days and an outfit for Honey. I'd decided to stay in Flagstaff until I received a call from Sapphire.

Hurrying to the Hilton on Highway 89, I showered, put on the best new clothes I'd bought, and drove back to the funeral home.

"Here, put this on her," I said, handing the director a beautiful honey-colored, long-sleeved lace dress with a matching head-wrap.

"This is beautiful but not nearly as heavenly as you," he said, staring at my juicy red lips.

Ignoring his comments, I replied, "I'll be back in a few hours for the services. You need to stay focused."

"I am focused," he said, nodding. "Oh, we need a copy of her birth certificate."

Digging in the envelope, I handed him the certificate, then walked away.

My next stop was my father's home. Matching Jean's address to one on . . . Honey's birth certificate? Oh, shit! I realized I'd given the director the wrong paper.

Or maybe not, I thought. My lips curved so high I swore they'd touch my nostrils.

Lace St. Thomas was officially dead, and Honey, middle name St. last name Thomas, was strutting up to my father's door to introduce myself.

CHAPTER 37

Benito

Bam! Bam!
"Aw, fuck! Lace, cut that shit out!" I yelled, lifting my ass, trying to keep the gun from shaking. I could've tightened my stomach muscles and pushed the barrel out a day ago, but I was scared I'd kill myself.

Lying naked, unable to move for almost twenty-four hours, I thought maybe if the gun did fire I would've been spared from starvation and dehydration.

Boom!

Tears streamed down my temples into my ears. "Please, Lace, please, stop it," I cried.

A woman dressed in a gray sweatsuit with a gun in her hand pointed it at me and yelled, "Don't move!" right before she fell on the floor laughing. "Y'all come in here. Ha, ha, ha. Oh my God, this is hilarious. And a first. Hurry up!"

I didn't see what the fuck was so funny. If I stuck that gun up her ass, she wouldn't be laughing at all.

"Ou wee! You got it funky up in here. Open all the windows guys, then get, hee, hee, hee, put on your rubber gloves and get that gun out of his ass, then untie him. Oh my gosh. Who did this to you?"

One of the guys said, "Hey, boss. The gun is empty."

There she went, falling to floor, holding her stomach, laughing so hard she'd started crying.

I bet if I were white they would've untied me first and I could've slapped her for making fun of me. But at least they hadn't shot me. Not yet. "Lace St. Thomas did this shit. I want her ass arrested and I'm pressing charges against that bitch!"

The smile on that woman's face turned upside down. Two inches from my face she hissed like a cobra, "You ain't gon' do shit but what the fuck I tell you. You got that? Whatever it was you did to piss her off that she'd do this to you is nothing compared to what I would've done. I'm Sergeant Bleu. Sapphire Bleu. Whatever the fuck you say can and will be held against you in my court of law . . ."

I was speechless. No, she was not reading me my rights while she was in the wrong. "I'm the one who was violated. Why are you reading me my rights?"

Throwing her head backward, she laughed, then said to another officer, "I can't believe how ignorant this man is. I bet he doesn't even know his rights. Get him in the tub quick. I can't even question him with him smelling like shit."

When Sapphire and her team broke down the door, I was grateful someone had finally rescued me. I was grateful I hadn't died in a pool of shit. Appreciative that Sergeant Bleu gave me permission and time to sit in a warm tub of water filled with Epsom salt to soak the soreness out of my rectum. "Ah," I said, leaning my head against Lace's inflatable pillow. "Hot water never felt so good."

It felt even better to put on deodorant, cologne, fresh underwear, and my best clean suit. Thankful simply to be alive, and free to go after questioning, I was too embarrassed to call any of my teammates or the women I'd bought nice things for but hadn't treated so well.

With no money in my pockets, Valentino behind bars, and Lace only God knows where, I had no money and no place to live after this Sapphire woman kicked me out of Lace's house, but I was grateful to be alive.

Fully cooperating with Sergeant Bleu, I told her everything I knew about Lace, which I realized wasn't as much information as I thought I had. I had no idea who Lace's parents were, how Lace met Valentino, or where Lace worked before I met her until Sergeant Bleu said, "Lace was a prostitute for eleven years before she became a madam."

Suddenly that Pussyland rodeo ride made sense.

I'd never trust closing both of my eyes around another female. After what Lace had done to me, I might be better off dating men. My manhood was violated. I seriously thought that gun was gonna go off in my ass. What had I done that was so bad that Lace would treat me like that?

Sure I'd made a mistake putting my hands on her. I was man enough to admit that. But I didn't kill Sunny. Sergeant Bleu said she could've arrested me as an accomplice, but instead I had twenty-four hours to get out of Nevada and never come back. I hoped they fucked the guts out of Valentino while he was behind bars. That wasn't my boy. No friend would've set me up like that. Try to let me take the rap.

With no place to go, I'd hitched a ride to the Strip,

then entered a Mexican restaurant on Tropicana Avenue near Terrible's gas station, picked up the pay phone, and dialed 0. It was hard to find a pay phone on the streets and ten times harder to find one with any privacy. Closing the booth, I motioned to hang up until I heard, "Operator, may I help you?"

"Um, yeah. Sure. Collect call to Washington, D.C., to a Mrs. Hill."

"From who, sir?"

"Um, yeah." I wanted to hang up, but what were my options?

"Sir, what's your name?"

"Benito. I'm her son."

"One moment please," the operator said.

After a few rings, a deep voice answered, "Hill's residence."

"This is the operator with a collect call from Mr. Benito. Will you accept?"

"Well, well—"

"Sir, I need to know if you accept."

"Yes, I accept. Put him through."

Nervously, I said, "Hey, I didn't expect you to answer," opening the booth. Suddenly when I'd heard Grant's voice it got hella hot in that tiny space and I could barely breathe.

"Man, you've got a lot of nerve calling my mother."

"*Your* mother?" I questioned.

Grant hadn't changed a bit. Still arrogant and elitist.

"That's right. She *was* your mother."

"Was? Mama isn't dead, is she?"

Had it been that long since I'd called her? It felt like my heart stopped beating.

"She might as well be dead to you. After all she's done for you. This is the thanks you give her, give us, by acting like you didn't know us when we came to your championship game."

I saw them. But they only came because they wanted a piece of my fame, not me.

"You were always her favorite, so what do you know about how I felt? Mr. Oxford."

"Man, I work hard. I don't apologize for my success. You should be grateful my mother took care of you. How do you think you got that scholarship? My mother adopted you when she was a single parent struggling by herself without a husband, and all you can see is what she didn't do."

"No, she adopted me when she thought she couldn't have you was more like it. But what do you know about being adopted? Not a damn thing."

I didn't need this bullshit. I would've hung up in Grant's face but I had no place to go.

"What do you know about respect? About love? Nothing. Now that your career is over and the IRS took all your possessions, what, you need my mother now? To help you? If it's money you need, I'll wire it to wherever you are as long as you promise not to set foot on my mother's property. Where are you?" Grant said in a demanding tone.

I told Grant what city and state I was in. Then I heard a warm, soft voice in the background and my heart began to cry.

"Mmm, good morning, sweetheart. Who are you talking to this early?"

"Nobody, Ma. Dad up yet?"

"Ma! It's me! It's Benito! Your son, Benito!"

"Grant, give me the phone."

The next voice I heard was my mother's. "Benito?"

"Yeah, Ma. It's me."

My mother started crying. "Why, Benito?"

"I'm sorry, Ma. Can I come home? I need you."

"I don't think that's a good idea, son." My mother cried harder.

"Who are you talking to?" I heard a deep voice ask.

"It's Benito, honey."

My stepfather commanded like a general in the military, "What you want, boy?"

"He wants to come home, honey," I heard my mother say.

"Then come. We need to talk to you face-to-face."

"You guys are too polite. Give me back the phone," I heard my brother say. "Look, I'm on way to my Atlanta office for a few weeks but I'll have my secretary wire you a thousand dollars today. Use it wisely."

Grant hung up before I could say *Thanks, I'll be there before you get back.*

A thousand dollars was enough to get a room for the night, and fly to Washington, D.C., first thing in the morning to see my mother, or maybe I'd surprise Tyra and my daughter instead. Tyra never could say no to me to my face.

CHAPTER 38

Lace

Matching the address on Honey's birth certificate to that on the white wooden-framed house I passed daily on my way to high school, I rang the bell, then took two steps backward.

The door opened and the man in the gray suit who'd practically jumped out of his seat at LAS after insulting me stood in the doorway.

"Oh, shit. I mean, hey, it's you. You clean up very well. Here," he said, reaching into his tailored pocket and handing me a ten-dollar bill.

I stared at his face in disbelief. How could I have overlooked his dazzling green eyes, slick dark hair, and fair complexion, just like mine?

"Are you Jean St. Thomas?" I asked, refusing to reach for the money.

"Are you from the IRS?" he questioned in a charming kind of way.

"No, I'm not."

"Then yes, I am."

I had so many questions I didn't know where to start. I expected some woman to come from behind him and ask who I was. That would've sped up my introduction and slowed the churning in my stomach.

"Um, do you know a Rita St. Thomas?" I asked, shifting my weight from one stiletto to the other. Smoothing my golden honey pantsuit from my hips to my thighs, I took a tiny step backward, wanting to turn and run away before he answered.

"Whatever Rita said is a lie. That woman has more issues than a black man on death row awaiting his last meal."

Moving closer to him, I spoke softly. "So I take it you know her very well."

"Unfortunately."

"Well enough to have had two children with her? Two daughters?"

"Um, look, I can't waste any more time with you. I've got things to do. You can take this ten dollars or leave it, but I'm not going to have this conversation with you."

Jean St. Thomas stepped inside, staring as if he were waiting for me to leave. It felt like my heart fell into my stomach. The bile percolated, decomposing my heart. *That was stupid, Lace! You never should've come here. Every time you let down your guard and try to have feelings for someone you get fucked, Lace. You should've waited until he showed up at Honey's funeral. That way he would've been more sentimental. Now you may never see him again.* I stood there chastising myself. I knew I should've said something before he motioned to close the door, but the words got stuck in my throat as the tears swelled, blinding my vision.

Click. The door shut.

My chin dropped to my neck. I felt like that sixteen-year-old girl again stranded on the porch, except this time I had enough money to go wherever I wanted.

Maybe I'd sit next to him at Honey's funeral, but I sure as hell wasn't going to wait on his steps much longer praying for Jean to have a change of heart.

My cell phone rang. Easing on my Bluetooth, I answered somberly, "Yes."

"Lace, this is Sapphire. Where are you?"

I exhaled, then said, "Flagstaff."

"Flagstaff? I need for you to meet me in Las Vegas by midnight. Not twelve-oh-one a.m. Midnight. I'll call you back in an hour with the location."

Checking the time on my watch, I knew the only way I could make it to Vegas by midnight was to drive. I hated driving the long continuous S-curves up and down the mountains in the daytime and I couldn't see shit at night.

I took a deep breath, and then my stilettos clanked down the wooden stairs onto the sidewalk in front of Jean's house. Gazing down the street, I could see the homeless people lined up outside the mission. I walked over to them, reached into my purse, and gave each of them a hundred dollar bill, then said, "It's not what you are, it's who you are."

CHAPTER 39

Summer

Bittersweet.

That was my life summed up in one word. I imagined most folks, whether Christians or atheist, felt the same way. Everyone had a story to tell that was so unbelievable that it would make for a great movie. That's what happened to me overnight.

My front-page story of being somewhat forced into prostitution in order to help find my identical twin sister's murderer, being drugged, kidnapped, raped—as the producer put it—then rescued, having brought my sister's assailant to justice, made me an instant millionaire.

Sitting on Sunny's bed with my son—oh yeah, I forgot about that part of the movie when I had Valentino's babies—I smiled knowing Sunny was pleased that Valentino was behind bars. Tears filled my eyes.

"Mommy, you okay. Don't cry. Nana said Auntie

went on a trip." AJ pointed out the window, then said, "To heaven."

These tears weren't for Sunny. If the home pregnancy test I'd taken earlier was right, the tears I cried were for the baby growing inside me. And I prayed for God not to give me twins.

Anthony always had his way with me. Looking up at the clouds, I thought maybe God had a bigger plan for Anthony Valentino James and I just couldn't see it. But the things I couldn't see, I could feel. Like the love in my heart for my son and his father.

Shifting my focus, I thought about Sapphire making sure Sunny's bank account read Summer Day. After I sold Sunny's condo, I was moving my family to Texas or someplace else outside Nevada to a churchgoing community. It felt good knowing I could afford to buy my parents a new home and retire them comfortably. It also felt good belonging. Belonging to a Christian family with morals, principles, and values for one another and others helped me to see that my daddy was right.

Quietly my son and I stared out the window. Nestling my cheek on his head, I rocked AJ in my arms. Just because Valentino was my son's father didn't automatically make Anthony entitled to see my son. What could Anthony have taught our child? How to be a pimp? How to disrespect women? How to sell drugs? How to get arrested? It was hard enough that one day I'd have to tell my babies that their daddy killed their aunt. Maybe I wouldn't tell them. Like my daddy said, "Summer, what good would knowing do for AJ?" Daddy was going to have a fit whenever I told him about the baby inside me. Maybe I should stay here in Henderson until the baby was born.

Tap. Tap.

"Baby, it's time to go."

"We're coming, Mama," I said, wearing Sunny's charm bracelet on one wrist and mine on the other.

Riding in the Town car to church—I never wanted to ride in a limo again—we sat in the back and I could feel Sunny's spirit surrounding us, especially me.

The driver double-parked in front of our church and it seemed like the entire community had come to say good-bye to Sunny. On a perfect day with the sun shining bright, I passed so many ladies of the evening with high heels and short skirts dressed like they'd come straight from work. But I didn't care. After all I'd been through, all my sister had dealt with, there was no way I'd judge or condemn these women. Whatever spirit moved them to come to church was all right with God and it was all right with me.

Sunny's casket was closed. There was nothing the morticians could do to make her look pretty on the outside, but my sister would always be beautiful to me. Sitting in the front pew, I motioned for Lace and Sapphire to join our family because they were our family.

CHAPTER 40

Lace as Honey

S ummer was Sunny.

Sitting in the front pew next to Summer, I knew that Sunny's body was inside the white coffin but her spirit resonated throughout the church. Glancing over my shoulder I saw there was standing room only. I wondered how many people would pay their respects when I died. Would I end up like Honey with my body lying in a funeral home instead of at the altar? Would a preacher, a friend, or a stranger read my eulogy?

Summer grasped my hand, interlocking her fingers between mine. How was it that a family who had every reason to hate me loved me and my family who had no reason to hate me disowned me?

Before leaving Flagstaff, I tried to keep my promise to Honey. After Honey's funeral, I asked that my nephew, Jean, be left in my custody.

The words Rita had spoken to me left me speechless. "Your sorry-ass father is raising him."

Frowning, I'd questioned Rita, "You mean my biological father?"

"Yeah, the one you saw earlier. I know y'all thought I was lying about y'all's daddy, but he didn't want the two of you or me," Rita had said with sadness.

I wasn't sure if Rita was sad because Honey was dead, sad because my father didn't love her after she'd given birth to two of his children, or both. I couldn't make sense of whether Rita was lying about my dad raising my nephew or my father really didn't want to meet me or she didn't want me to take my nephew, but I had to move on. Never again would I return to Flagstaff under any circumstances.

The real reason I allowed my thoughts to roam so much was that I didn't want to cry at Sunny's funeral. There'd be no sniffles. If I broke down in tears, someone would have to pick me up off the floor and carry me out along with Sunny. I felt responsible for Sunny's death. If I hadn't hired her, she'd be alive.

I was so glad when Sunny's funeral was over. Never in my life had I seen so many prostitutes in one place. I think Sunny's death made a lot of prostitutes think about changing their ways before it was too late.

Sapphire held my other hand and said, "It's time for you to gather your girls and come with me."

When I'd told Sapphire about the airline tickets I'd bought to get my ladies out of Las Vegas, surprisingly Sapphire commended me. Sucking in air, I couldn't exhale, wondering what Sapphire's intentions were.

"Relax." She smiled. "It's good news."

I hugged the Day family good-bye, signaled for my girls, and met Sapphire at a nearby casino in a private suite.

Grasping my hand, Sapphire said, "Lace, let me speak to you in private."

Walking into the adjoining bedroom, I sat on the bed next to Sapphire and waited for her to speak.

"Here, I want you to take this cashier's check and do something good. Take those airline tickets, get out of Las Vegas, and take all of those ladies in the next room with you."

Ladies. Not bitches, not whores, not prostitutes, not call girls, and never again escorts. Ladies. I blinked in disbelief, staring at the dollar amount on the cashier's check.

"Don't ask where it came from. Just know that you deserve it. And promise me you'll pay it forward," Sapphire said.

"Come with me," I said. "We can all get out of Sin City together."

Sapphire laughed. "Were you at the same church I was at?" Then she became serious. "Maybe when I retire, but right now I'm needed in Las Vegas."

"Well, just remember my house is your home anytime. No questions asked."

Sapphire stood, waved, and was gone like the wind as she disappeared out of the side door.

Sapphire's suggestion that I take my ladies reinforced that I'd done the right thing. Reaching into my purse, I pulled out one-way airline tickets for each of my ladies. "I'm leaving. Whoever wants a job can join me. A real job with wonderful benefits. There will be no more selling pussy or sucking dicks to make a living."

Onyx asked, "Then what exactly will we do if we follow you to—" She read her ticket, then said, "Atlanta, Georgia."

"Your first responsibility is to get yourselves together mentally, physically, and spiritually. Then your job will become to help other women get their lives in order."

Starlet spoke up, "So we can make the same amount of money that we made every night having sex?"

"No, definitely not. Don't be ridiculous. Working for me, you can make even more money. But you've got to earn it."

All of the ladies started mumbling.

Girl number two asked, "You think she's serious?"

Three replied, "I hope so, but I don't know if we can trust her."

I wasn't trying to convince any of them. What I was offering was an opportunity for each of them start over. "I've got a plane to catch. Y'all have my number."

Strutting out of the casino with a full heart and a fat wallet, I clicked my stilettos and yelled, "Yes!"

CHAPTER 41

Lace as Honey

Prostitution wasn't a job. Prostitution was a lifestyle. On the inside I was scared. I knew in my heart what I was doing was right, but what if I failed these ladies? Was I crazy asking them to leave their families, friends, environment, homes, and in Onyx's case, her husband? What if I couldn't deliver them from the land of easy money? Well, with a fifty-million-dollar cashier's check in my purse, I couldn't say I couldn't afford to.

"Good afternoon," the flight attendant said as I boarded my flight to Atlanta.

From this day forward, when any woman greeted me I'd smile. My lips parted, then curved as I replied, "Good afternoon," before taking my seat in first class.

Reflecting on things that had happened over the last year made me wanna laugh, cry, and scream out loud.

"Would you like something to drink?" the attendant asked.

"Yes, champagne, please." It was a little too early for hard liquor, but once I settled in my hotel room in Atlanta I was definitely having a real drink.

Sipping from the plastic flute, I chuckled, wondering where was Benito. I could only imagine what Sapphire had done to him, but oddly she hadn't mentioned him in any of our conversations.

No, I realized Benito was never the man for me. His insecurities and jealousies were destined to break us up. A man who was envious of his woman was a dangerous man. Maybe now Benito would get his life together, get a job, and not live off some other woman.

"Excuse me," a deep voice resounded.

Looking up, I instantly batted my eyes and smiled. "Certainly."

The fine-ass man who'd just sat next to me made my pussy pucker when he said, "Oh my. You are strikingly beautiful. Are those your natural color eyes?"

Was I blushing? When was the last time I'd taken notice of a man? Had sex with a man? Valentino's face popped into view and I immediately shoved him out of mind, knowing that if Atlanta was this handsome man's final destination, my next orgasms were a few hours away.

I focused on his tailor-made suit and shirt, platinum cuff links without diamonds, immaculate shoes, his large fingers with manicured nails, and big feet. His face was smooth and his teeth appeared whiter than his skin when he smiled and asked, "Where're you headed?"

"I'm relocating to Atlanta."

He nodded as if giving me an approval I didn't need. "You have plans for dinner tonight?"

I do now. Casually I said, "I'll have to check my schedule. I'm supposed to meet with a Realtor to discuss representation. You have a number where I can reach you?"

He smiled again, then said, "We'll get to that in a moment. I want to continue our conversation. So, tell me, what do you do for a living?"

Okay, casually offering to take me to dinner, not readily giving me his number or his card, what was this man interested in? Shit! I hadn't expected to answer that question so soon. Confidently I answered, "I own a consulting firm."

"What's the name?"

"Sweeter than Honey" rolled off my tongue like sugar.

For the first time, I dreamt aloud, sharing all the wonderful ways my new company would help women. Our flight arrived in Atlanta and he still hadn't given me his number.

"So, where're you staying?" he asked.

"Downtown, and you?"

"I own a place in Buckhead. Here's my card. Let me know if you're available for dinner. I can have my driver pick you up. Nice talking with you." He paused, extending his hand.

I smiled, then read, "Real estate developer, huh? You should've told me earlier."

Shaking his head, he said, "I never mix business with pleasure."

Squeezing his hand, I said, "I'm Honey. Honey Thomas," realizing out of all the information we'd exchanged I hadn't told him my name.

His cheeks rose high and I saw the most amazing smile in his eyes. "I think you need to change the name of your business. Nothing can be sweeter than Honey. I'm Grant. Grant Hill."

Well, I knew that from the card, but what I couldn't determine was if he was black, white, or Italian, and I didn't care. All I knew was I was getting some dick tonight and I was going to love living in Atlanta.

EPILOGUE

Lace as Honey

Keep your friends close and your enemies closer. Some will say, "I ain't mad at her." Others will mumble, "She did what she had to." And some would swear, "She should rot in jail. Nah, girl, forget jail, she should burn in hell for what she's done."

But if one were to ask me, I'd respond, "I was tired of men abusing women."

I also realized I couldn't help women who didn't want help. The ones who'd go back to their abusive lovers could stay. And while that may have seemed cold, truth was there were too many women who seriously wanted to get out of life-threatening situations. Those were the ones I'd commit to.

There was a better way to prove my position than killing every man who abused women, but if a man didn't have any respect for women knowing he came from a woman, then I believed he was better off dead.

After dinner I'd spent every night for two weeks in Buckhead giving and getting head while pussy-whupping and getting to know Grant. Good pussy did strange things to men. Actually I enjoyed being around Grant. He was polite, handsome, and he had his own businesses, one in Atlanta, the other in D.C.

In between spending time with Grant, he helped me find a mansion in Buckhead with fourteen bedrooms and just as many baths. All of my ladies came to me except girl six, but she had an open ticket and she always had a choice.

Onyx and Starlet became my top assistants and all the ladies worked diligently on putting together our business plan. I wanted them to trust me the way I was learning to trust Grant, so I gave each of my ladies equal profit shares in Sweeter than Honey.

Grant was different from Benito. He laughed, cracked jokes, spoke intelligently on any subject. He wasn't too proud to admit when he didn't know something or object to me teaching him things sexually. Grant opened doors, bought gifts, flowers, made plans, and paid for dinner. He was ready to settle down, get married, and have two kids. Grant offered all the things I'd dreamt about but never thought I would have. Once upon a time, I didn't believe I deserved to be loved. Grant was proving me wrong.

Good pussy did strange things to men. I couldn't believe that after I'd known Grant for only two weeks, he invited me to meet his mother. At my age of thirty, that was the first time any man had asked me to meet his mother, so of course I happily said yes.

When we arrived at his parents' home in Washington, D.C., I almost died when Grant said, "This is my mother, Sarah, my father, Grant, and my brother, Benito Bannister."

"Pleased to meet you, Mr. and Mrs. Hill," I said, staring at Benito.

"So this is why you left me, Lace!" Benito yelled.

Aw, damn. I didn't know what the fuck to do. Everyone was staring at me, including Grant.

"Who's Lace? Do you know Benito?" Grant asked.

Benito moved closer. The old Lace wanted to punch Benito in the face and shoot him in the ass for real.

"Know me? Man, that's the bitch that stuck a gun up my ass. Left me for dead and killed Reynolds."

"Grant, get her out of my house," Mrs. Hill said.

"Don't trust her, bro. And don't ever let that hooker bitch ride your dick like she's in a rodeo," Benito yelled.

"Benito, that's enough. Shut up!" Mr. Hill yelled, then calmly said, "Grant, you heard your mother."

Grant angrily escorted me to his car. Standing in the driveway, I was shocked when tears filled Grant's sad brown eyes. I expected him to yell, stomp, hit me, curse me, but he didn't. All he asked was, "Why me?"

"I'm so sorry," was all I could say.

Here I was with the man I wanted to marry, have his babies, and make him happy, and it was gone in an instant.

"Every time I trust a black woman," Grant began to cry, "I get hurt. It's my fault, not yours. Black women say they want a good man but y'all don't. You even lied to me about your name. Why?"

"I—"

"Don't answer that. Nothing you can say will ever make me trust you again."

Grant pressed two buttons on his red cell phone and said, "I need you to pick up Honey, Lace, whatever the hell her name is, from my parents' house. Now!"

My entire body tensed. I didn't know what to say, so I began crying. Grant didn't hold me. He wouldn't touch me. Turning his back, he didn't want to look at me. I guess I deserved that. Who was I fooling thinking I could get married, have a husband and a family? My own mother didn't want me. When the limousine parked in front of the house, Grant walked to his parents' front door.

All I said before leaving was the truth. "Grant Hill, I love you."

Once again in my deepest moment of needing to be loved, *Slam!* Another door was shut in my face.

BOOK CLUB DISCUSSION QUESTIONS

1. What is pussy power? How do you think you can control a man using pussy power? Do you enjoy sex? Why or why not?

2. What do you feel is behind the bitterness Rita has for Lace? Is their dynamic familiar in your own relationship with your mother? What is the relationship between you and your mother and how can it be improved?

3. Do you believe twins are connected in spirit, feel one another, know each other's pain? Why were Sunny's and Summer's lives so different? Or were they the same?

4. What is Benito's problem? Does Benito represent the black man's struggle in America today? What is the black man's major issue today? How can the black woman support the black man in this day and time without subjecting herself to abuse.

5. Why do some women give up their power and want to have a pimp control their life? Have you fantasized about being a prostitute? A madam? Have you used your pussy power to get a man or a husband?

6. Why did Lace take such an interest in Sunny? Are their similarities between Lace and Sunny?

7. Who are you most like in the book?

8. What is your opinion of Valentino and his fear of Lace? Was Valentino in love with Lace? Was Lace in love with Valentino?

9. Have you or anyone you know been mentally, physically, sexually, spiritually, or financially

abused? Were you or they able to leave or improve the situation? Did you or they leave only to end up in another abusive relationship? Do you or they make excuses (because there are no justifications) for staying in an abusive relationship?

10. If Summer would've married Valentino, do you think Valentino would've been a better man?

11. Considering the Days were a Christian family, do you think Summer's father, Mr. Daniel Day, made the right decision not to allow Summer to have a personal relationship with Valentino? Should her father have permitted Valentino to know about his son? Why wouldn't a Christian man approve of his pregnant daughter getting married?

12. Do you know of any young ladies who were reared in a loving household but weren't happy? Do you think Sunny was happy? Why do you think Sunny left home?

13. Do you feel worthy of happiness, success, unlimited blessings? Why or why not?

Affirmations for Women

1. I am beautiful inside and out.
2. I will love myself first.
3. I will learn something new about myself every day.
4. I will say no to any and all types of abuse.
5. I will plan for my future.
6. I will love those who love me.
7. I will say no whenever I want without feeling guilty.
8. I will have a personal bank account in my name only.

9. I will earn respect.
10. I will explore my sexuality.
11. I will dissociate myself from people who don't re-
    spect me.
12. I am sexy inside and out.
13. I will laugh from my heart every day.

Poetry Corner

Good Pussy

Can you keep a secret
I've got some real good pussy
Thinkin' about selling some
You know
For a couple of C-notes
Or by the hit
My pussy is so good
Men won't quit . . .

Cuming around sniffin'
Begging for a lickin'
My pussy ain't even trippin'

If all he's got to offer
Is his dick in his hand
Then this good pussy is moving on
In search of a real man
Who knows how to lick it
Hit it stick it and kick it

Kick me
Down with something tangible
A lifestyle that's manageable
Good pussy ain't never broke
Shit, I might start charging by the stroke

Pssttt
Let me whisper in your ear
Can you keep a secret
Good pussy drives men crazy
Make him claim your baby
Make him cum for more than fun
For pleasure
When and wherever
The pussy damn well please
Good pussy is a tease

Wanna know why my pussy is soooo good
I give her lots of treats
Eat something fresh and sweet
Pineapple one day
Coconut the next
Swipe her with a little honey
Then pop her in his mouth
A tiny mint on my clit
Definitely does the trick
For my pussy and his dick

Oh, I've got some good pussy
But don't you tell your man
I am what she eats
I stay away from all that beef
Drink lots of peppermint water
Or add some mint leaves to my salad
Then I let him toss me upside down
And go to work like Homey the Clown

I smother his face with savory juices
Then watch his lips spread ear to ear
My good pussy makes him cheer

Can you keep a secret
I'll share a little tip
Feed your pussy right
Then spread her on his lips
Keep your pussy tight
And he'll fuck you all night
Or pass out trying

Pssstt
I've got a secret
Wanna taste

In My Lifetime

All I ever wanted
Was to be loved
A caring hug
And to hear those three words
But as a child
My unspoken words
Were never heard

But I did find joy
In the arms of a boy
Or two
Who must've known
Deep inside I was blue

Quiet
Sometimes happy
Mostly sad
Or melancholy
One might add
To my long list of reasons
Why

Sometimes at night I'd cry
Praying for God to bring me home
No child should feel alone

But the next day
I'd play
With my brothers
With my friends
Wishing those days
Would never end
All I ever wanted
Was to be loved
A caring hug
Or to hear those three words

Why won't she hug me
Tell me she loves me
Where's my father
Who's my mother
Why can't I live with my sisters
Hang out more often with my friends
How much more must I endure
Before my sadness comes to an end

In my lifetime
All I ever wanted
Was to be free
To be me
And why shouldn't I be

Slowly I learned to love
I learned how to give hugs
To freely say I love you
Or I love you too
I learned to embrace
The things I wanted to say

And if unspoken words
Got lost along the way
That's when I learned I could
Write

Words on paper
Gave me power
When I was afraid to speak
Words in my heart flourished
Whenever I felt weak
No matter how challenging
No matter how hard
No matter how judgmental
Others were of me

The power of a voiceless voice
The split decision in making a choice
The spirit dancing in my heart
My words allowed me to stand apart
To be free
To be me
Knowing that I am Worthy

Speak up
Speak out
Have no doubt
Let your actions shout
In my lifetime
I am Worthy

Once Upon a Time I Was Happy

Today
is the last day
that I live with myself
without being myself

without being true to myself
pretending I'm someone else
naw, not pretending
convincing

Once upon a time before him
I had family
I had friends
I had the means to an end
a happy child
a magnetic smile
a swing in my hips
a curve in my lips

I laughed until I cried
I held my head high
never asked why
always asked why not
I yearned to learn a lot
had a zest for life
Once upon a time
I wanted to be his wife
strived to be his lover
determined to be his friend
Once upon a time with him
I was happy

Just to be alive
felt like a woman inside
we went on dates
we came home late
we woke up with the sun
we simply had fun
Once upon a time
I was happy

to hear his voice
to hold his hand
to caress his chin
to have a man
to put him first
to put my girlfriends on hold
just to hold him at night
to set the table by candlelight
to cook his dinner
to reassure him everything would be all right
to please his dick
to nurture him when he got sick

all those things I used to do
because I simply wanted to
have now become chores
I don't want to do them anymore

the more I give
the more he takes
the less he gives
the more I cry
the less he tries
the more I die inside

the harder I try
the more I die inside

the more my heart aches
the more I die inside

now I'm numb
but why
I no longer care to try
Once upon a time before him

I was happy
when did I stop
being happy

how did I lose myself
caring so much for someone else
why did my family and friends disappear
where did the time go
when did my spirit grow old
where was the person I used to know

as I look in the mirror
a stranger stares back at me
she's not me
she's cold
she's bitter
she's aged
she's sad
she's trapped inside herself
Once upon a time before him
I was happy by myself

I want to be happy again
I want to laugh with my friends
I want to dance, to sing, to smile again
I want to swing my hips
I want to curve my lips
Hug my child
I simply want to chill for a while

Smell the roses
be free
to love those
who love me
It's not too late
for me

to be me
again
I lost everything
trying to be his everything

but from this day forth
Today
is the last day
that I live with myself
without being myself
Once upon a time
has come
for me
to be
happy
again
I'm smiling
inside and out
because there's no doubt
I am worthy
of joy
of happiness
of love

Place of Pain

There's a place of pain
within my soul
that makes me want to cry
live another day
I heard Him say
and He'd make me whole again

There's a place of pain
inside my mind
that makes me tell lies

Be true to yourself
I heard Him say
and everything would be okay

There's a place of pain
inside my pride
that makes me want to kill
myself
more so than anyone else

There's a place of pain
inside my spirit
that makes me believe
I'm better off dead than alive
but if I can hold on
just one more day
to God's unchanging hand
I know God has got a plan

There's a place of pain
inside my heart
if I can survive another day
I know the pain will go away

I Am Worthy

While I was dining in Philadelphia with my mentor and friend, we stumbled across a very important topic for women: I am worthy. Asking ourselves and one another the question, "Why do we feel worthy?" we all had unique responses that paralleled in some aspects. The more we talked the more we thought, what makes us worthy?

I've asked several of my sisters-in-pen, Naleighna Kai, Gloria Mallette, and Marissa Monteilh, to share their views of worthiness. Before reading what they had to say, I strongly encourage you to take a moment and write about why you feel worthy.

I'd love to read your response and you can also encourage your family and friends to submit why they believe they are worthy of greatness. E-mail me from my Web site at www.MaryMorrison.com. Once a month I'm going to highlight a different person on my Web site along with a photo (optional of course) and your journey to worthiness. Submissions are limited to five hundred words.

As you read remember, money doesn't determine or sustain self-worth. I want to hear from you. At the end of each year, voters will determine which spotlighted woman will be honored at my I Am Worthy banquet. Women of all nationalities are welcome to attend this joyous celebration of Womanhood on Mary B. Morrison Day. For details, visit me online at www.MaryMorrison.com.

Mary B. Morrison Day is March 1. It's a day of recognition and appreciation not of me but from me to all women. I look forward to reading your submissions. And I look forward to meeting you. Without delay, here's what we'd like to share.

Naleighna Kai

I Am Worthy . . .

It has taken forty years for me to realize that I am worthy of many things—unconditional love, harmonious relationships, abundance, and prosperity—to know my purpose and to fulfill it during *this* lifetime. My experiences—from pain to pleasure and everything in between—have strengthened me, expanded my understanding, and made me a woman who knows I Am Worthy.

You Are Worthy . . .

Woman, you are worthy. You are a nurturer, lover, life-bearer; confidante, head of household, sports coach, organizer, maintainer, referee; you are all this and more. You understand that the Creator is your source—not a job, not a career, not family or friends, not the child support or alimony that has been as hard to get as pulling a lion's teeth. You are worthy because everything in your universe comes from the Divine; and you consistently acknowledge this through prayers, intentions, and affirmations that flow from your lips to God's ear. All it takes is a mere request and the angels, ancestors, teachers, and guides go before you and place people, resources, and the right situations in your path. All because . . . you are worthy.

As spiritual beings having human experiences, worthiness is not defined by our physical makeup. Your body is strictly a vessel in which you choose to enjoy the ride. You may have the luxury models (plus-size frames), SUV, or sports car edition. Either way is perfect, whole, and complete. So thank every lover/soul mate who caressed each curve, each roll, each inch, and appreciated the wonderful women we are in body, mind, and spirit.

You are worthy and deserve a relationship filled with compassion, friendship, and spiritual growth— the kind of relationship that is about respect, harmony, and balance; the kind of love that many admire, seldom attain. The kind of relationship that is defined only by the two interconnected parties. Your life, your choice, your love, your way. You are worthy of this and more.

I Am Worthy . . .

The fact that I am able to embrace those three words means I have overcome the biggest obstacles in my healing—not what was done to me, but what I felt as a result. I will share a bit of my story with you.

My birth certificate says: "Single Parent Adoption." My biological mother didn't take me home from the hospital; she decided that my interest, and hers, could be better served by passing the motherhood torch to someone else. Eighteen months later my biological mother stood in front of a judge, telling him that she had lied and wanted to adopt me back—not because she loved me or decided she had made a mistake. Fate had other plans that landed my "chosen mother" in a place she definitely did not want to be—jail. So I was back where I should have been in the first place—or maybe not. Years of abuse and a disconnectedness that no one could explain followed.

At fourteen I ran away from my mother to seek a safe haven with my father. What I found instead was a man with a sick mind who saw in me only the physical pleasure he could derive. I survived the dozens and dozens of the times that my innocence was stripped away by him and later another male relative who felt it necessary to take what I would never freely give to them. Those moments shaped the way I viewed myself, my body, and my worth, as well as my initial view of men.

Thankfully, the Creator does not leave anyone broken and splintered. A supervisor entered my life and she later became my minister, sexual abuse counselor, and friend. She pointed me to the tools and affirmations necessary to help me understand I deserve every good thing that comes to me. That redefining myself not by my pain, but by the fact that I can be and am healed of everything that has been done to me or any situation that has brought me low. The Creator makes me worthy.

And just to make sure I understood, the Creator gifted me with a son who has taught me more than being in any intimate relationship; a son who has caused me to take more risks than I would for myself. For every friend who has spoken an encouraging word, the type of friend who said, "If I have a dollar, then you've got fifty cents." Small things to some, but they have made me feel worthy and I love you with every ounce of my being.

We Are Worthy . . .

For some of us, healing may come in the form of a best friend, mother, grandmother, aunt, sister, cousin, minister, or a lover/soul mate who provides unconditional love. Someone who understands what we've been through and doesn't pass it off with a mere "get over it already" or "you're a black woman, we're stronger than all that." They realize there's more to it than strength alone. Support—real support—unwavering support is like pure gold. It might be in their words, or a book they have shared or music that touches the soul and soothes the inner pain. We are worthy.

Do we truly understand that our purpose is not about a job or what supplies a paycheck? It's not about outshining another human being, accumulating more wealth than we know what to do with, or human adoration or praise. It is about the spiritual path, the journey. And what a journey it has been.

It took the approval of several angels and ancestors for us to be here on the earth at this time. My being here is no accident, no coincidence. Your being here is in Divine Order. Through it all I can say I am worthy. If you really think about it, all experiences considered, you can definitely say the same.

Gloria Mallette

I like who I am, inside and out. Well, maybe I don't like my overly wide hips and big shapely legs so much. They've always been standouts, drawing many a gaze my way, but then again, I guess I adore them. They drew my husband to me, so I have to give them their due. Still, I know who I am, I know what I'm about. I didn't always know, I had to find out.

It's been a while, more like fifteen years, but I'll never forget the look in my best friend's eyes when she said, "I don't understand. Why do you always get everything you want?"

I was the one who didn't understand. Nothing in life was ever given to me. I had to work hard and still do for everything I have.

"What's that supposed to mean?" I asked. "What are you talking about?"

"You. I'm talking about you. You wanted a car, you got a car. You wanted a computer, you got a computer. You wanted a husband, you got a husband. You wanted a house, you got a house. I want all those things. I don't have them. Why you? How come you get everything you want?"

I was speechless. At that very moment, I didn't know how to answer that question. I didn't even know if there was an answer to that question, and in truth, I had to ask myself whether my "best friend" was my friend at all. Whatever I had was no different from what half the world had acquired. I think what my friend was really saying was that I wasn't deserving of anything I had, which hurt.

You see, I shared everything with "Tia." I told her all about my past, and as well about my hopes and dreams. After all, next to my husband, Tia was my best friend and she was closer to me than my own sisters. Not to mention that we worked together. So you can see how I didn't understand where Tia was coming from, especially when she had just about everything I had. She had a car, she had a computer. She traveled, she had money. Tia didn't have a house, but she did have an expensive co-op apartment. What Tia also didn't have was a husband, at least not a husband of her own. Tia had someone else's husband and she was madly in love with him. In Tia's bed, her lover committed adultery. In his wife's bed, he made love, he made his babies, he went to sleep, and he woke up to her stank morning breath, which he willingly inhaled and snuggled up to.

When Tia said those words to me, I wondered, was she jealous of me? Did she hate me because I had a man who had pledged fidelity to me? Or was she just angry that I had acquired or accomplished anything at all in my life? I questioned Tia about what she'd said, and she said she meant nothing at all, that I was being "too sensitive." Admittedly, my feelings were hurt, and if truth be told, I was sensitive and I had every right to be. I wanted to lash out at Tia.

I wanted to say, "Why don't you stop sleeping around with married men? Why is it that you can't get a man of your own?"

That's what I wanted to say, but I didn't. I don't have an evil spirit. Oh, I've told Tia before that it was wrong to go out with married men, that she should respect the sisterhood, and more important, I've told her that she deserved a man of her own who'd respect her and their relationship. But be that as it may, I took Tia's words personally, but I didn't stop speaking to her. I kept my feelings to myself, but I was more restrained with what I shared with her.

But then, two months later I accidently ran into Tia and her new "special" friend, whom I'd never met.

"You're very attractive," he said to me. "You must have had a lot of boyfriends loving you."

While I was flattered, the shocked look on Tia's face was nothing compared to the demeaning words she cruelly uttered. "You must be blind."

Both Tia's friend and I were stunned. I pulled my "friend" aside and asked, "What the hell did you mean by that?"

Without hesitation, Tia said, "You're so fat and black, I don't see what's attractive about that."

When I finally closed my mouth, I opened my mind. I finally understood my "best friend."

You see, as quiet as it's kept, through eyes like Tia's, I'm not supposed to have anything. Whereas Tia is supposed to have everything. I'm not supposed to be anything. You see, my skin isn't scorched brown from the sun; my dark chocolate skin comes courtesy of my birth. Just as Tia's high "yalla" skin comes of her second-generation mixed race parentage.

In this day and time, it's hard to believe that many, even in our own African-American community, see beauty in shades of skin tone. And me being short and dark, and, oh, not to mention at the time, well over two hundred and fifty pounds, I wasn't supposed to have a husband, much less a husband who was tall and as fine as wine, educated, and quite successful. Tia, who was slim and damn near white in complexion, couldn't understand how any man would find me attractive. Wow, go figure. But then again, as Tia well knew, until I was fifteen, I thought just as she did.

My mother died when I was two and a half years old. I am one of five children left to a young father who was ill-equipped experience-wise and financially to raise five babies—the youngest being eight months old and the oldest six years old. It was my father's sister who took us from him and from our home in Gadsden, Alabama, and brought us to the promised land of New York City. One would think my aunt, Auntie, as we called her, was going to give us a chance at the life my unskilled father was unable to. That was so far from the reality of what our lives would be with Auntie.

Auntie wanted her brother's motherless children because she was unable to have children of her own, and her husband wanted children. Through the court system, Auntie legally stole us from our father and then forbade him to ever see us. She put us up in a big house in Queens, New York, and to the world outside our front door, we were a loving, churchgoing family. We were blessed, our minister said, because Auntie had taken us in and given us a beautiful home. While we may have been blessed on one hand, on the other, we were damned. You see, behind closed doors, the Auntie we knew was so unlike the Auntie our minister, our neighbors, or our teachers knew. The Auntie we knew was the devil incarnate.

With my father out of the picture, and my uncle silenced by Auntie's vicious tongue, Auntie abused us. She beat us with electric cords, she deprived us of food, she locked us away in closets, and she kept us out of school. She had us so afraid of her, we knew she meant it when she said, "I'll kill you if you ever tell anyone what goes on in this house." We never got a pat on the back, a kiss on the cheek, or a kind word of encouragement. Our self-esteem was destroyed before it was even developed. We were three girls and two boys at the mercy of an aunt who herself had suffered the indignities of a childhood that had destroyed her self-esteem and planted the seeds of vindictiveness and anger in her soul.

In turn, Auntie took her anger out on innocent souls. She not only lashed us with the whip of physical abuse, she beat us down with her tongue of degradation. Auntie told my sisters and me that we would grow up to be whores and that men would use us and throw us away like day-old trash. According to Auntie, we would amount to nothing and no one would ever give us a helping hand. And me, in particular, the darkest of my siblings, no man would ever find me attractive, and no man would ever love me.

Oh, did I mention? Auntie was a light-skinned woman. Her father had been white. My father was her half brother; their skin color was not alike. If Auntie could have scrubbed the black off my skin, as she most definitely tried, she would have.

Auntie called me black when we as a people were still called Negroes or colored. As a ten-year-old, I was hurt by that word *black* and shamed as if it were a curse word. In the white elementary school I attended, I kept my eyes lowered, my dark arms covered, and if it had been at all possible, I would have covered my black face. For it wasn't just the white kids who taunted me, it was also the "colored kids." The lighter ones called me "tar baby" and "black." The few other kids who were as dark as me said nothing in my defense, for they too were called those names. We couldn't help each other, nor could I tell Auntie what was going on in school—she would not have cared.

I said my prayers, I talked to God, I asked him to see us through. I asked for a miracle that was not destined to come overnight. As young as I was, I understood that God might not answer my prayers when I wanted him to, but that he would answer when the time was right.

It wasn't until I was fifteen when my siblings and I got the courage to free ourselves. We ran away from my aunt and went to live with my mother's sister who was undoubtedly the answer to my prayers. My aunt Jimmie was our saving grace. She didn't take us to church as Auntie did, she took us to her heart—she was no hypocrite.

That fateful summer of 1968, James Brown had a hit song called "Say It Loud, I'm Black and I'm Proud." With all my heart, I felt that James Brown was singing that song just for me. From the first time to the hundredth time I heard that song, my whole outlook on who I was and how I looked changed. That summer, when I looked into my mirror at my black shiny face, I saw someone I had never seen before—a beautiful, bright-eyed black girl with short picky hair looking back at me. For the first time in my life, I smiled at my reflection. I wore my Afro with pride and reveled in my newfound freedom. Throughout that summer, I discovered me. I found a beautiful, strong, confident girl who would soon be a woman in control of her life. And to this day that is who I am.

I am God's child. Auntie didn't break me. I am a woman whom no man or woman can destroy. So to my "friend" Tia, I say, "Beauty is so much more than the face we see. Beauty is in the heart and soul of man. Look inward and discover the beauty you ought to be."

©2007 Gloria Mallette is the national best-selling author of *If There Be Pain, What's Done in the Dark, Distant Lover, The Honey Well, Promises to Keep, Weeping*

Willows Dance, Shades of Jade, and *When We Practice.*
Visit Gloria online at www.GloriaMallette.com.

Marissa Monteilh

They said, "You'll never sell your book, it's too
much like *How Stella Got Her Groove Back.*" They
said, "You'll never get an editor to buy your work, it
has too much sex." They said, "You can't afford to self-
publish, it's too expensive." I say, tell me something I
can't do and I'll show you something I can do.

The true essence of who we are is uncovered
through the actual journey of discovery of who we are.
Questions like who are we, what is our truth, what do
we believe, what is our gift, what is our love, and what
is our life's purpose, all come to mind. All because we
are a discovery in progress as we find the lesson in
each and every experience. Even in the worst of times,
in the deepest of criticisms, we're being led to a higher
good.

At an early age, though I was abandoned by my famous father, my mother, a strong black woman, raised
me and my two older brothers on her own. As a strong
black woman, she worked three jobs and still managed
to continue her education, later becoming an entrepreneur.

I found myself widowed at the age of thirty-three,
yet, as a strong black woman, I raised three kids, all the
while finding myself challenged by the fact that the
essence of who I was did not match well with all that
corporate America had to offer.

Once I discovered my love of words, I sat down to
write my life story after burying five family members
in ten years, and ended up with a novel. I researched

and wrote and inquired and focused and eventually, in spite of all the naysayers, I self-published. Six months later I signed a two-book deal offered by an editor at a major publishing house, and before I knew it, that dream some said would never happen, the dream to one day see my novel on the shelves of bookstores, was realized. And I became a full-time author. I followed God's pattern and sat in the manifestation of what was architecturally designed, which all unfolded in Divine order.

Surely the strength of my mother's independence planted ideals to never settle for less than what my spirit yearned to accommodate. I thank my mother for sparking the fire that burns inside me when I write, the same fire that warms my soul when I see women like Mary B. Morrison make profound strides in the world of publishing. Through it all, I have found out what my heart knew to be true, and I no longer have that divine discontent that nagged at my soul.

I, Marissa Monteilh, deserve success and happiness because I am worthy. I am worthy because along this journey, I have found my God-given gift.

I am a writer.

I have found my purpose.

My purpose is to create characters that people can see themselves through. And in having the courage to write my own personal book of life, the story of my own life journey, it is my dream that it will inspire and motivate others to say to themselves, "I too can do that."

The responsibility that comes with that is to pay it forward. We are blessed so that we can be a blessing to someone else. As we let our light shine, we give permission to others to do the same.

And as for my offspring, I have told my daughter to tell her daughter, to tell her daughter, that God has a bigger vision than was once thought of for colored girls. But in order to live God's dream for us, we must have faith, do the work, and stay ready. You must be in position to receive the possession.

Yes, I am worthy, meaning I am of more than sufficient value to be a woman who, like my mother, and like Mary B. Morrison, makes a mark, makes a difference, pays it forward, and liberates those who might ask, "Who am I to be brilliant, gorgeous, talented, and fabulous?" spreading the word that the answer is, "Who are you not to be?"

©2007 Marissa Monteilh is the national best-selling author of *Dr. Feelgood, Chocolate Ship, Hot Boyz, Make Me Hot,* and *May December Souls.* Visit Marissa online at: www. MarissaMonteilh.com.

Mary B. Morrison

I am worthy because my Creator has deemed it so.

No hesitations, reservations, conservations, limitations, justifications, imitations, deliberations, indeterminations, procrastinations, or dicktations . . . well, now, hold up, wait a minute, I do love the dick. But I won't allow anyone with or without a set of balls to control my destiny.

I learned at a very young age that most people are extremely judgmental. I thank God for my great-aunt, Ella Beatrice Turner, and her husband, Willie Frinkle. Considering they were only a few generations from slavery, I can only presume they did the best they knew how to rear me. And when my aunt placed a noose around my neck in the backyard, choking me while threatening to hang me from a tree, all I could do was cry as the neighbors watched but wouldn't help me.

For a plethora of reasons, I couldn't wait to leave New Orleans, Louisiana, and the hand-me-down southern slavery mentality among many blacks and whites was definitely reason number one. As a child, I was never hungry for food, yet I was never fed unconditional love.

I had to attend St. Paul's AME Church every Sunday with my great-aunt who held a position with the Eastern Stars, Isaac and Rebecca, and who was a missionary and on the stewardess board, etc. She was a woman who smiled in the faces of many and talked behind the backs of many more. But she talked about me to my face.

"You're not going to amount to anything. You're not going to be half the woman your mother was. You're going to be pregnant before the age of sixteen. You're trifling. You're ungrateful."

In part, she was right. I was the quiet and shy girl at McDonogh #35 High School in New Orleans, Louisiana, who became pregnant with my first child at the age of fourteen and miscarried shortly thereafter. No one at school ever knew. I wanted so badly to be loved by someone that the first boy who cared about me—who later became my husband and is also my son's father—that I was willing to open my heart and my legs. I was only a child but at the time I didn't feel worthy of being loved by him or anyone else.

I cried waterless tears for many years, harboring the kind of sadness that drowns the spirit of a child who suffers in silence. Giving birth to my son when I was twenty-one changed my perspective on life. God gave me somebody to love. Before the umbilical cord was cut, I felt a love that I didn't have for my mother, my father, my great-aunt and uncle, nor my, at that time, husband.

I made a promise to myself never to treat my son the

way I was treated. My connection to my son was so deep that out of all the babies crying in the hospital, I could tell when it was my son and I would comfort him. Today I'm still his proud Supermom. Some say I give him too much. I say I can never give my son enough—love, that is. The material things I give him are just that, things. At the end of the day, all most people want is to be loved.

Individuals, especially the loved one closest to us, can sometimes be mean and cruel for no apparent reason. My father chronically abused my mother. I'm told my mother slept with a butcher knife under her pillow and my mother's mother had threatened to kill my father if he ever came near my mom again. Eventually my mother committed suicide. So when my ex-husband beat me once, I divorced his ass immediately. I've been raped and also molested.

So how does a woman overcome an exorbitant amount of abuse and learn to love herself unconditionally? For me, I was able to separate my emotions from reality, believing God would protect me. People who hurt us don't love us. To me, it's just that simple.

I didn't have to relive my mother's pain and suffering in order to know that I'm worthy of being loved. I'm worthy of success. I deserve financial blessings. I embrace sexual liberation, and I am truly happy. And I don't need a man to define me. This is my life. This is my body. This is my brain. My heart. My soul.

I've learned that happiness is an acquired emotion. Now because I'm so laid-back, like most folk from N'awlins, those of you who know me can't always tell when I'm excited and that's okay. I've learned how to love me for me. I don't put myself down, nor do I give permission to anyone else to do so. I honestly believe there is nothing, and I mean nothing, that I cannot do, if I want to.

Soul Mates Dissipate is becoming a movie and I will walk the red carpet. And my next home, The HoneyB Playhouse, will be the female version of Hugh Hefner's Playboy Mansion. Everything in each room will be designed with sex in mind. Those are my next dreams.

I've lost a few so-called friends along my journey to happiness and you will too, but know that it's part of your growth process and it's okay. We must purge our lives of people who try to hold us back. You can't move forward if you allow others to steal your joy and that includes your spouses, family, and friends.

Once upon a time I had a friend. I bought her lunch almost every day for years when she couldn't afford to eat, gave her son money when he went to college, when he came home for Christmas, and even paid for her son to fly home from college, praise God, in time to see her mother, his grandmother, before his grandmother took her last breath. I feel good about the unselfish things I've done for others and I have zero regrets.

Along my journey to success this person said unto me, "You probably didn't notice I gave you fifty feet." Of course I'd noticed. But what I realized was her reason for distancing herself from me was her problem, not mine. After her mother passed, she gave me another fifty feet because I told her the truth. I didn't know how to be there for her and meet my publisher's deadline.

Writing for me requires tons of mental energy. After I finished my book, I called her and said, "I apologize. I'm done with my book. I want to know how you are. I want to hold you. Hug you. Call me." She didn't so I called her a few weeks later. She answered the phone and said, "I'm on the phone with my son. Let me call you back." To this day she has not dialed my number.

My point is, we can't be everything to everybody all the time. And sometimes no matter how much we do for some people, in their opinion it's never enough. She was my friend for a season, not a lifetime. If people cannot accept us for who we are, then we must learn to let go, not look back, and move forward.

Who decides what I'm worthy of? I do.

Who determines what you are worthy of? You do.

Life is all about choices. Claim your self-worth right now. Give thanks for what you have and freely ask the Creator, God, Buddha, or whatever higher power you believe in to provide your needs and fulfill your desires.

God wants us to be happy and we should be. So many folks walk around overlooking their blessings, complaining about what they don't have, trying to figure out how they can get what someone else has so they miss out on their blessings and God simply gives what coulda been theirs to those of us who are diligent, dedicated, and desirous.

I want you to start creating your success today. Be a positive thinker. Speak positive words. Selflessly help others achieve their goals. And more important, once you claim your worthiness do not question who your blessings will come from.

As an adult, I've never doubted my worthiness. But as a child who went to church every Sunday, I'd lie in my bed sometimes hugging the gray stuffed lanky monkey with big red lips wishing I was dead. Some of you may feel that way right now. But God had a different plan for me. And no matter how difficult your life may seem, He has a better plan for you.

"Live another day, Lil' Bea, I'll take care you," He promised and He did. And God has an even bigger plan for me, but I'm just not clear about what it is yet. This is why the more I get, the more I give. In my heart, I want you to be happy. There are so many of you that I don't know who contribute to my success each time you speak kind words about me, or buy one or all of my books, or e-mail my Web site to a friend. And I thank you.

The Honey Diaries are intended to entertain and at the same time help women who are suffering from low self-esteem and abuse. Now, I'm not suggesting you do like Lace and shoot a man or stick a gun up his ass, but it's time for women to stop tolerating violence. I'm serious. Lace St. Thomas is my modern day Foxy Brown for those of you blessed enough to remember. Foxy didn't take no shit off nobody, especially men. I'm not saying you have to be hard, but please, don't let anyone use your brain or your body for a punching bag.

If you are being battered, if you're unsure of your self-worth, then every morning and throughout the day I want you to say, "I am worthy of greatness." At first you may not believe it, but the more you say, "I am worthy of greatness," the more you will believe and realize that you are. The other thing I want you to say is, "I am loving myself first," and do it.

Stop pretending that you love God, that you love your man, that you love your kids when you haven't learned how to love yourself. Forget those snotty-nose, crumb-snatching dependents and the draining lovers who only share your bed and not your bills and kick 'em all to the curb.

Okay, although I'm allergic to kids under the age of eighteen, I'm kidding about the kicking-the-children-to-the-curb part. Hug your babies and tell them you love them, especially when you're upset. I have sixteen wonderful nieces and nephews and a beautiful son who's on his way to the NBA. I love kids. So much so that I've sponsored an anthology by thirty-three students entitled *Diverse Stories: From the Imaginations of Sixth Graders.*

You've got to learn to live, love, and laugh. But first

and foremost take care of number one. We are worthy of all we desire because our Creator has deemed it so.
                              And so it is.

Presented by Mary B. Morrison
Diverse Stories: From the Imaginations of Sixth Graders
(An anthology of fiction by Lou Richie's sixth grade class)

My SHIFT (Supporting Healthy Inner Freedom for Teens) Program is the proud sponsor of *Diverse Stories: From the Imaginations of Sixth Graders.* I know without a doubt the students in Lou Richie's class have made a SHIFT to greater self-esteem by becoming published authors. There are several future *New York Times* best-selling authors in the anthology. Writing allows students to explore and reveal how they view life based upon their frames of references.

There is no common theme in *Diverse Stories: From the Imaginations of Sixth Graders* because the students were allowed to write about whatever they wanted. How refreshing! The stories are equally as unique as the individual writers: some melancholy, some funny, some breathtaking, all fantastic.

The proceeds go to the Lou Richie Foundation to fund scholarships for students desiring to pursue a Catholic high school education when their parents cannot afford the tuition.

If your organization is interested in receiving information on the SHIFT Program, log on to www.MaryMorrison.com or call us toll free at (866) 469-6279.

Catch up with the daring and sexy Honey Thomas in
WHO'S LOVING YOU

Available now wherever books are sold!

CHAPTER 1

Honey

Love sucks! I swore on my sister's grave, I wished I'd never met him. His voice had lingered in my mind with crisp clarity every damn day, like he was standing behind me, leaning over my shoulder, whispering in my ear. But he wasn't. Not anymore.

"Baby," he used to say to me, and I would answer, barely above a whisper, "Yes?" Seductively, he'd say it again, "Baby," in a tone that quieted me. "Yes?" I'd say softly. We'd go back and forth; then his long fingers and strong hands would gently caress the side of my face and massage my ears.

I'd quiver whenever he'd moan, "Ummmm, you're fucking incredible. You know that? And I'm not talking about your bedroom skills. Baby, you are an amazing woman."

His eargasms would make cool waterfall secretions flow from my pussy, wetting my lips, before he'd ease his hand between my thighs, pressing his middle finger against my clit. He was left-handed. I'd heard Dr. Oz say on *Oprah* that left-handed people were smarter, more balanced, and better capable of processing information than those of us who were right-handed. His index and ring fingers would straddle my shaft, nestling in the crevices of my lips, as he strummed my black pearl with his middle finger. That was my favorite finger.

Gasping at the sound of his voice in my head, I knew . . . I was incredible. But no other man had told me that. No other man had said to me, "I love you." Grant was my first. I let the tears fall, then closed my eyes, visualizing our moments together, lifting my lids to see only me, surrounded by olive painted walls, bright lime cabinets, dark forest granite countertops, and a kitchen floor covered with new hundred-dollar bills that had been permanently laminated into clear ceramic tiles.

Green was my favorite color. I loved walking on men and money. I'd admit I was a little extravagant. A grand total of one million dollars—in hundred-dollar bills—was embedded in every floor of my home, including the bathrooms. Some preferred to walk on sunshine. Money was my visual reminder of where I'd come from. I wasn't proud of how I'd stepped on and over a countless number of people to get where I was. *Live and Let Die* was my favorite James Bond movie and my motto. Standing in front of the kitchen counter, I slid an already sharp knife along the steel sharpener.

Grant had been my joy. We'd loved sharing Cherry Garcia ice cream while watching *The Boondocks* DVD series, and making love. In between orgasms, we'd laugh at Huey, Riley, and their granddad. One time we stayed in bed all day, eating, sleeping, and fucking until we wobbled like ducks when we made our way to the bathroom for a much-needed piss.

"Quack, quack," I'd teased him.

"Quack, quack, quack," he'd tease me back.

Then, suddenly, our relationship had faded to dark. He was out of my life, as if I had frantically awakened from the best dream of my life. Shutting my eyes, I fought to go back to him, to go back to sleep and pick up where we had left off, before he left me. I tossed and wrestled with my empty bed. I opened my legs, easing the memory foam pillow between my thighs, then pulled my red satin sheet around my erect nipples, trying to forget he was no longer mine. Opening my eyes, I found myself standing in the kitchen, staring at a blue crystal bowl filled with red potatoes.

How could my past ruin my future? I had tried my damnedest to give that man my best, and he had slammed the door to his heart in my face, as though I was a Jehovah's Witness trying to save his spiritual behind so he would become the one-hundred forty-four thousandth person to make it . . . Where? To Heaven? Wherever that was. Who'd been there? What did they do to get in? Mistreat others?

From hot to cold, within seconds he had swatted me away like I was a fly landing on his food, regurgitating shit. I'd meant nothing to him. It was as though he'd truly awakened to a stranger.

Words were powerful beyond measure, but his silence hurt me more. He'd made me make myself go crazy. Wow. Love or the lack thereof could do that. Make one go crazy.

"Answer your damn phone. You wrong for this shit, Grant! Dead wrong!" I yelled. I grunted loud enough to release my frustrations, but not so loud that someone in the house would come running to my aid with a straight jacket. My house had thirteen bedrooms. Twelve upstairs. Mine was the only one downstairs.

"I should kill him. Goddammit, son of a bitch!" I

screamed. Sucking the stream of blood oozing from my finger, I threw the knife, the potatoes, and the crystal bowl in the damn trash can. "Fuck this shit!"

Love hadn't hurt me. I was clear that I'd hurt the one I loved. Now I was the one suffering. Every time I got angry, so angry that I could harm Grant, something bad happened to my ass. Unzipping the first-aid kit, I pulled out a bandage.

"He probably has some other bitch in his bed, sucking his dick right now, while I'm over here trippin' on unresolved issues that I can't control." *Not by myself.*

As I wrapped the Band-Aid tightly around my middle finger, thoughts of the way we had constantly been together replayed in my mind, reminding me of the irreplaceable love I'd lost. Where was I going to find another six-foot-five, 235-pound, twenty-eight-year-old, successful black man with a body sexier than any Chippendales dancer I'd ever seen? Grant was my man, and I'd be damned if I was gonna let him leave me. I just knew some ex-chick or someone hoping to be the next chick had been waiting for me to fuck up so she could move in on him, with him.

"Not on my watch, bitch! Get your own man!" I grunted.

Each morning I reached out my hand to touch him; rolled over, expecting to kiss him; opened my eyes, longing to see him. I called out his name, but he wasn't there to answer, "Yes, Honey?" as he had so affectionately done. Had he been sincere when he'd said, "You're the best thing that ever happened to me"? I wanted another chance. Hell, I deserved the opportunity to explain why I'd lied. Not everything I'd told him was a lie. Actually, most of what I'd shared about my past was the truth.

"Grant, listen to me," I said. "Are you seriously going to take someone else's word over mine? So what if

Benito is your brother! Hell, your own mama don't like his ass. I can't believe you're upset with me about something that happened before we met. You're not making any sense. Okay. Answer this one question. 'Do you still love me? Yes or no?' "

I wasn't getting the answer I wanted; he wasn't here to respond. All of this vacillating in the kitchen, talking to myself, had to stop. One minute I loved him; the same minute I hated his ass to death. I stood topless and barefoot in the middle of the kitchen, text messaging him: *Baby, it's not what you think. Please call me.* I was trying to give him the impression I was being patient with him, but my patience had run out a long fucking time ago.

CHAPTER 2

Grant

You thought you knew a woman; then you found out shit you wished you hadn't. The saying "What you don't know won't hurt you" could actually kill you. In retrospect, I wished our relationship would've remained platonic. That way even if our friendship hadn't flourished, I could have continued respecting her.

We consummated our acquaintance the first day we met. From the airport to dinner, to dicking her down really good, Honey was one sweet lady. Nah, she wasn't a lady; she was a woman. But was she that easy with every guy? Honey was hot and sexy, and my dick was hard and horny, and we clicked. My dick fit her pussy perfectly. I never wanted to wait to have sex with a woman I liked. What were we waiting for? The one thing I could've avoided this time, if I had waited, was having my heart broken. Broken heart and all, life went on. That was for sure.

Parking in my parents' driveway, I contemplated whether to go in. I didn't feel like pretending I was happy again today. Stopping by to check on my mom and dad was routine. As usual, my old man peeked out the front window; then he opened the door, motioning for me to get out of the car. I read Honey's text message, slipped my iPhone in the holder, then smiled at my father.

We walked up the seven steps to the house, with my arm over his broad shoulders. Five inches taller, I towered over him. My dad retired five years ago; Mom hadn't worked a day since they'd married. Her stay-at-home-wife job entailed taking care of my dad, my brother, and me, and although we could take care of ourselves, Mom still enjoyed taking care of us.

Inside the house, I greeted my old man, hugging him tight. "You got a class this morning, old man?" I asked my dad.

He lectured to high-school students during the day and taught entrepreneurial courses in the evening. I took over managing his rental properties when I opened my business, GH Property Management and Development, seven years ago. With Dad's guidance, I'd done well for a twenty-eight-year-old.

"Still trying to outdress me, huh, son? You gotta figure out where my new tailor is first. Close the door before one of those nasty flies creeps in."

I had the best mom and dad. I loved my parents. Would do anything for them. "Hi, my angel," I said to my mother, kissing her cheek. She hugged my waist, holding on a few seconds longer than usual. Mom's hugs reassured me that everything was good. The prolonged hug made me wonder if everything was okay.

Mom whispered, "It's already all right, son. Let go and let God. I know you want us to accept her, but she's not the one for you." Patting me on the back, she said, "You see your brother sitting over there? Speak."

Like I said, I would do anything for my parents.

Benito got up off the sofa and hugged me. Mom hadn't said anything about hugging that fool.

"Hey, bro," he said. "You dump Lace yet? I told Mom all about Lace's past. Take it from me, I keep telling you I dated her for three years. She's bad news."

Pushing him away, I said, "Her name is Honey, and I'm positive she'd plead temporary insanity for the entire three years." Distancing myself from my brother, I followed my dad into the dining room.

Benito was right behind us. "Whatever you wanna call her is cool, but I'm tellin' you—"

Dad interrupted him. "Benito, that's enough. Why don't you stop all the madness about that woman and tell us the truth about what's going on with you? We haven't seen you for twelve years, since you went off to college. And your mother just mailed Tyra a check for ten thousand dollars to pay your son's tuition. You haven't been home in a long time, but I raised you better. Even if your relationship with her is over, you need to go see your son. Now, why'd you come back here?"

Thank God. I wanted to keep the focus on Benito, so I asked him, "Yeah. Why?" I smiled, waiting for my brother to answer. Benito was two years older than me, but he looked forty. His years of partying and drinking were etched on his face. I wasn't having any kids until after I got married. I wanted two, maybe three. All boys.

"I told y'all I kinda made a few bad investments, lost all my money. Then Lace kicked me out. I just need to stay until things settle. A few months. No longer than a year or two," that fool said. Problem was he was serious.

My mother walked into the room, sat a plate in front of my dad, then me, and went back into the kitchen.

"What about me?" Benito yelled. "Why does Grant always have to be first?"

" 'Cause I check on my parents every day I'm in town," I said. "Your behind didn't call after you left, not until you needed us." I really wanted to say, "Nigga, your sorry black ass need to get up outta here and stop leeching," but my parents wouldn't have approved of that.

"Thank you, dear God, for this wonderful bounty, my mother, and my father. Amen," I said. I blessed my stack of pancakes, strips of peppered bacon, and scrambled eggs and started eating. I had a business to run. Benito didn't have shit else to do all day but lay up on my parents. I couldn't believe my mother had paid his cell phone bill. He knew better than to ask me to do anything for him.

Staring at my brother, my dad didn't blink once. Dad said, "You have one more time to disrespect my wife and you're outta here."

Benito was stupid, but not that stupid. He knew when to shut up. Mom walked back into the room and sat Benito's plate in front of him. No thank you, no grace, no comment. Benito started chewing with his mouth open.

"Man," I yelled at him, shoving his plate to the floor. "If you don't stop disrespecting my mother, I'ma beat your ass! Show some fucking appreciation for her. She ain't your damn maid!"

I stood over him, wishing he would push his chair back. My fists were tight. I wanted to punch him in his face. My dad scurried out of his chair and held my arms behind my back.

"Son, calm down. Sit. Finish your breakfast," said Dad.

Benito slid my plate in front of him and started eating my food. Through a mouthful of my pancakes, he said, "You not mad at me, bro. You pissed because you didn't know your sweet Honey baby was a hooker. Pass me the syrup, would ya?"

CHAPTER 3

Honey

The morning was three hours away from noon. The sun was too bright to go back to sleep. The red potatoes were in the trash, my finger was aching, and I was still in the kitchen.

I texted Grant again. *I give. You win.* I stared at my phone until the time and date confirmed exactly when my message was sent. I waited five minutes, then an additional ten minutes, for his reply.

"Ughhh. Motherfucker! What or who are you doing that's more important than me?" I yelled. Again, he had refused to answer. He was lucky I lived in Atlanta and not in D.C., or else . . . or else . . . What was his fucking problem? "Forget you, too, Grant. You're too old for this childish bullshit. A real man would have the decency to give closure to his relationship." Who was I fooling? I was angry because Grant was a real man. A real man with parents who loved him.

Lionel Richie's voice resonating through the kitchen's intercom created a much-welcomed distraction. One of the girls upstairs had decided to play songs, and since I insisted on the best, we had speakers in every room of the house, including the bathrooms. Softly, Lionel sang, "I do love you . . . still."

As Lionel's voice faded, I heard Luther singing, "Time rushes on. And it's not fair. When someone you used to love, is no longer there . . . now you're running back to me, to forgive you your mistake. Kinda makes me sad to say . . . it's a little too late."

Rushing into the spacious white-marbled foyer, I yelled up the U-shaped stairways. "Turn that shit off!"

Grant had helped me find this eight-thousand-square-foot home in Buckhead, which I'd paid cash for, so my escorts could quit fucking men for a living and for once be comfortable and focus on what they really wanted to do with their lives, and this was how they thanked me?

Whosoever had decided to play Luther Vandross at nine o'clock in the morning was lucky I hadn't raced upstairs and slapped the hell out of 'em. They knew Grant and I had recently broken up. I didn't need to hear that depressing-ass music right now. The feelings of rejection palpitating in my heart fluttered up to my throat, suffocating me. Fanning myself, I could hardly breathe.

"Damn," I whispered, wishing I had the courage to hop a flight to D.C., show up unannounced at Grant's front door, and make him talk to me. But I didn't. What if a woman opened his door? I'd kill 'em both. For real.

Clenching my teeth, I scratched my neck. I was so frustrated, I felt like taking my damn iPhone, raising my arm high above my head, then slamming the iPhone on the ceramic floor and watching it shatter, like my heart, into tiny splintered pieces. What good was a communication device when I couldn't get a response from the main person I wanted to hear from? Trembling, I exhaled heavily, then quietly sat my PDA on the counter and resumed cooking breakfast.

Flipping bacon in the frying pan, feeling lonely, I stood in my new home, inhaling the sweet aroma of thick strips of sizzling pork and watching grease specks splatter onto the stove. I hadn't had a normal appetite in almost two weeks. The burning energy in the pit of my stomach had melted away ten pounds in the fourteen days that I hadn't seen or spoken with Grant. I had gone from a size ten to an eight.

Outwardly, I struggled to appear calm so my girls wouldn't think I was going crazy, but inside, I'd lost control of the hatred raging through my body, knowing I could easily slap or curse, for no rational reason, the first person that said, "Good morning."

Onyx, my personal assistant, peeked her head inside the kitchen. When my eyes narrowed and shifted to the corners, I caught a glimpse of her disappearing into the foyer.

"Let me know when breakfast is ready," she blurted, quickly trotting upstairs.

After my favorite escort, Sunny, Onyx, with her sweet black-cherry pussy, had earned me the most money when I was their madam. Men of every nationality had lost their fucking minds when they saw Onyx in my lineup of whores. I was glad I wasn't exploiting women anymore.

I wasn't proud of my past, but I was one of the few lucky ones that had got out of the escort business before it was too late. I was thankful that I hadn't been arrested, like my ex-boss Valentino James, who was awaiting sentencing in a Nevada prison for thirteen counts of pimping and pandering, plus one count of first-degree murder. That could've easily been me sitting behind bars, facing the same charges.

There was such a thing called luck. With the help of a woman I barely knew, undercover police officer Sapphire Bleu, I'd escaped the prostitution arena in Las Vegas, and I'd avoided incarceration for the horrible things I'd done. Why she decided to help me, I wasn't sure. But I'd learned never to question where my help came from. Sometimes the person I least expected to help me helped me the most.

Footsteps crept over my head, reminding me my girls were safe upstairs in the entertainment room. I prayed none of them would ever have to revert to prostitution. Girl Six was my only escort who'd remained in Las Vegas. She was reluctant to come live with me in Atlanta. Couldn't say I blamed her, considering I'd kicked her in her stomach and fractured her ribs for showing up at work one day with a pimple on her ass.

Bam!

"Madam! Please stop! Don't! I'm sorry! I won't let this happen again," Girl Six had cried. "Pleeeeaaaseeee, Madam, stop!"

Wham! Bam! Stomp! Kick!

Girl Six had balled up into a fetal position, holding what I had hoped was a few broken ribs.

"You are costing us fifty thousand dollars a night every time I have to send your ass home. You've got one more time to have a rash, a cold sore, or a pimple, and I will beat your ass into the ground, then fire you. Put your clothes on, and get the hell out," I'd said, dismissing her.

Valentino had trusted me to run his multimillion dollar business, and the johns who paid ten grand an hour had demanded flawless women with beautiful bodies. At that time, my reputation meant more to me than sparing Girl Six's life. Today I felt remorseful. In my heart, Girl Six was now family, and I'd given her a one-way airline ticket to Atlanta, the same as I'd done with all my girls. I wasn't going to call her. She didn't need another invitation when she already had a standing welcome to join us.

Thinking about my top-producing escort, Sunny Day, I whispered, "I couldn't save them all."

CHAPTER 4

Grant

"I'm out. Bye, Dad. Bye, Mom," I said.

"Bye, bro. I'll see you later," Benito's sorry ass said, gnawing on a piece of my bacon.

Stopping in the restroom adjacent to the foyer, I took a piss, shook my dick, washed my hands, then left my parents' house. I got in my car. "Ooh-wee, I wish he wasn't my damn brother," I said, checking my messages. Honey had texted again, at nine o'clock. *I give. You win.*

"Good. No, great. Me too. I hope you mean it this time," I said. "I hate when Benito's fucking ass is right." I was angry at Honey. She had made me look like a fool in front of my parents. Wasn't she obligated to disclose beforehand situations that could embarrass us?

I pulled into Starbucks to get a grande soy White Chocolate Mocha Espresso, no whip, extra hot. I'd

stopped adding the whipped cream after Honey and I
broke up. The things she could do with whipped cream
made me shiver. *Damn*. The line was long. I'd wait.
Give myself time to cool off before getting to my office.
I swear, I wished I could've hit Benito's ass one time,
right in his big mouth.

"Ooh, he's got a nice big one," I heard the woman in
front of me tell the lady she was with.

Frowning, I thought, *Is she talking about me within
listening range?* D.C. women didn't hold back on anything, particularly on pursuing men.

Her friend turned around, looked at my dick, smiled,
then nodded. "He sure does, girl. Good looking out.
You don't miss anything. That's big enough to share. We
could double-dip fuck him at the same time."

The woman who'd checked me out first handed me
her business card. "Call me, on my cell. We're having a
private party tomorrow night. We'd love for you to
come with us."

I didn't want to embarrass her by saying, "I'm not
interested," so I took the card and said, "Thanks," putting it in my pocket.

Her opening line reminded me of a cheerleader I'd
met in Las Vegas damn near fourteen years ago. I was
fourteen years old at that time.

*"Ooh, you got a nice big one. Please let me suck this
pretty dick," she'd pleaded. "That is why you invited me
over, isn't it?"*

"Yeah, but—"

*"No buts, silly. Come here and shut up," she'd said,
peeling the plastic off of a small square pack of . . .
peanut butter?*

*Frowning, I'd stood by the edge of my hotel bed,
looking down at her. "What's that for?"*

"It's my favorite," she'd said.

A devious grin had crossed her face. She'd scooped

the peanut butter onto her tongue, smeared it all over my dick, then jokingly asked, "Got milk?" Then she'd opened a small packet of strawberry preserves. Layering the preserves over the peanut butter with her wet tongue, she'd put both of my nuts in her mouth at the same time.

"Ooh, my lord that feels good," I'd said, trying to control my shaky teenage legs.

Gripping my dick like a microphone, she'd spat on it, started singing like she was on stage, then licked everything off, including my cum. I'd recalled thinking, Girls in D.C. don't swallow.

"Sir, you're holding up the line," the cashier said. "May I please"—her eyes darted down to my dick—"take your order." She smiled a little too hard.

"Oh, sorry," I said, ordering my drink. I had to see what they were seeing. Damn! Those freaky-ass women. I had to start wearing underwear. One of them could've told me my dick was out. Tucking myself away, I dug into my pocket and pulled out a twenty.

The cashier held her hands up in the air. "Uh, that's okay. The ladies in front of you paid for whatever you wanted," she said, grinning. "Here's your Starbucks card. You have a ninety-five-dollar credit."

I was flattered but not convinced to call. Waiting for my mocha, I continued thinking. I'd never forget my first blow job. That shit felt ooh-wee! incredible, but I couldn't say I loved, strongly liked, or even knew the girl who'd done it. In fact, I lost respect for her because she didn't respect herself by going around and sucking dicks for fun while all the guys on our sophomore field trip in Las Vegas talked bad about her.

"Man, she'll suck your dick in the bathroom, in the hallway, in the stairway, anywhere you want," one guy had said. "All you have to do is pretend you like her ass, give her a few compliments, and that trick will drop to her knees and let your nuts bang against her chin until you cum in her mouth."

To see if they were telling the truth, I joined in the experience. I felt like shit immediately after I'd cum in Tiffany Davis's mouth. I doubted the other guys even knew her name. From that day forth, I promised myself I'd never disrespect another woman. If I didn't care anything about her, I wasn't putting my dick inside any part of her, no matter how attractive she was.

Tiffany was definitely not the type of woman I wanted to call my own or invite to my house to meet my parents. Damn! What made that girl do that shit? At times I wondered who or what had made Tiffany that way. What was she doing now? Probably somewhere prostituting. What had made my Honey fuck strange men for money?

"I guess I'll never know," I said aloud.

Honey's story continues in
UNCONDITIONALLY SINGLE

In stores August 2009!

PURPOSE OF BEING UNCONDITIONALLY SINGLE

Unconditionally single—a person who understands his/her relationship needs, communicates effectively, willingly compromises, refuses to settle

Before reading *Unconditionally Single,* I'd like for you to take a moment to identify your relationship needs. These are the things you must have in order to cultivate a healthy union with the person you'd like to marry or consider your life partner.

After identifying your needs, list your desires. These are the hobbies or things you enjoy and would love to do with your mate. Let your imagination explore the corners of your deepest fantasies.

I find that most individuals cannot readily identify their relationship needs. They kind of meet a person, stumble into like, trip into love, then fall into love/hate, never having asked of themselves or the other person, "What are your relationship needs?"

Somewhere along the way, perhaps months, maybe years later, they discover one another. Some find out that money is more important to their mate than love. The one with the most money is more powerful. Sex once a day, once a week, or once a month is either too much or not enough. In creeps infidelity and misery.

When a woman or teenage girl has an unplanned pregnancy, she automatically expects the man to do all the right things for her and their child. Most women hope the man will marry her because she's carrying his baby. Instead, the man stands on the fifty yard line for nine months like he's watching an uneventful football game—drinking beer, chilling with his boys, bragging about his other woman, what he did to and with her last night, while waiting for the fourth quarter to end— waiting for her third trimester to conclude. Then he prays for confirmation, his bet is good and he is not the father, mainly so he doesn't have to pay child support.

Clueless about how much daycare, diapers, and the daily cost of providing for a child is, she gives birth. Clueless that one night of pleasure can bring her a life-time of emotional and financial hardships. The natural progression of blind-love and lust, eventually heats up into resentment for both partners. Thus begins the battle of the sexes to see who can hurt the other the most. These relationship tragedies can be avoided or minimized through effective communication and safe sex, and more importantly, if both individuals enter the relationship knowing their needs.

Unconditionally single does not mean you don't desire marriage. I'm encouraging you to know what you need and desire before getting married or becoming involved with someone. Share what's important to you with your potential mate. I urge all men and women to read *The Honey Diaries* series before getting married.

* * *

On my way from the Antigua & Barbuda Literary Festival, I boarded the plane in Antigua to Miami, settled in my window seat. A newly married couple sat next to me. The wife, to my immediate right, her husband was seated at the aisle. The seemingly happy, giddy, constantly kissing couple couldn't keep their hands off one another. He lived in Canada. They were headed to Los Angeles to pack her belongings then drive to their new residence in Canada. Halfway through the flight, he pulls out two sandwiches. The husband looks at his wife and asks, "Do you like rye or would you prefer the other sandwich?"

My eyebrows raised as I continued reading Eric Jerome Dickey's *Sleeping with Strangers,* thinking, "They barely know one another." Obviously he likes rye, he'd purchased the sandwiches, and he didn't ask what she wanted. How well should a couple know one another before marrying? So many marriages end in divorce because people marry strangers.

Oh, well. That couple are probably of the majority who wander in and out of love, life, and relationships wondering why they keep choosing the wrong jobs and the wrong mates. What's your passion? Your talents? What excites you?

I hear some of you talking to yourself, asking, "What are Mary B. Morrison's needs since she has all the answers?"

Honestly, I don't have all the answers, but I am a thinking woman and I do know my passion, talents, what excites me, and I understand my eternal evolving needs. Like you, as I continue to emotionally grow, my needs change. But my *basic* needs are always clear.

I date openly, knowing that the man I will enter into a relationship with will show up. I don't have to build him, change him, or create him out of play dough. (But if I did build him, I'd use Steven A. Smith as my model.) I don't have to look under the covers or search the corporate boardroom for him. I meet men everywhere I go. I enjoy men. "I'm not reserving, preserving, or praying for God to send me Mr. Right. Waiting for "a good man" would be a waste of my time.

Here are my relationship needs:

- He must be intelligent, highly capable of expressing his views on politics, religion, sex, and sexuality.
- He must have friends. A man's friends tell you a lot about him.
- He cannot be a minimalist, satisfied with getting by or over to make his ends. Minimalists are underachieving, shiftless lazy leeches looking for handouts. I don't date cheap or selfish men. He can do bad on his own.
- He must be an entrepreneur or realistically striving to become his own boss. I don't mean the men who spit game about what they gon' do all the while they layin' up on a woman, burying her under his philosophical bullshit. "Baby let's buy a _____ to-ge-ther." Translation, his credit is fucked up.
- He cannot be envious of my success or my lifestyle. I work extremely hard. Trust me, lots of men are jealous, of successful independent women. I'm a full-time writer for two major publishers. I travel extensively. I own Mary B. Morrison, Incorporated, Sweeter than Honey, and Lift Every Voice and Write (my non-profit).
- He must have a sense of humor (this ranks at the top of my list). Know how to laugh; make me laugh. Have fun. And Lord knows he cannot be depressing, dragging around his garbage like he's

a sanitation engineer. I'm no comedian, but I love to make people laugh.

- Under no cir*cum*stances can he be broke. Hell-to-the-capital-N-O. I do not support men. A broke man should suck his own dick, then tuck his dick between his balls and fuck himself. Especially if he's sitting on his ass all day waiting for someone else to provide for him. I can't comprehend his mentality.

- He must be great sexually. Open to exploring new sexual territories.

- He must agree to an open relationship. Even if I never have sex with anyone except him, I can't commit to exclusivity because I might meet someone else that I decide to have sex with. No guilty pleasures for me.

- He must understand that he is my partner, not my dictator or dick-ta-tor. I have no need or desire for a second husband. Marriage is wonderful for those who need or want it. I don't. I'm happy and intend to stay this way.

Black women and men are not taught how to treat one another. We have generational relationship dysfunction. Our mothers' mothers' mothers' were raped of their virginity, their children, and their men. Our fathers' fathers' fathers' were used for breeding with no emotional attachment to family. We still deal with post slavery trauma. We still struggle to genuinely love and appreciate one another. Black men must stop running away from their paternal obligations. Black women must stop unconsciously opening their legs and their hearts. I know it's hard, but if we seriously think about the 'what ifs' before we become involved, our relationship will have a higher survival rate. We have to start someplace. You are the catalyst for change in your life.

Stop entering into relationships primarily to fill the voids of your ancestors. I encourage you to talk to our children about healthy relationships. Take time to embrace and express your needs and desires. Irrespective of your partner's views, your open and honest communication will prove productive in your relationship.

Be true to yourself.

PROLOGUE

Honey

Sometimes a woman had to kill herself to survive.
I came from nothing. My mother hated me. My father disowned me. Stepfather molested me. Johns used me. My ex-husbands abused me. I had scars on my heart. Blood on my hands. The one man who truly loved me for me, I'd pushed him away. I hadn't lived through countless trials and tribulations to exhale my last breath without dignity.

No way in hell was I going to die; not like this, in the back of a SUV staring down the barrel of his .22 caliber pistol. My ex-man Benito pointed the gun at the one place I was sure he would like to blast all his bullets, my mouth. Eradicate his troubles, his jealousy, his insecurities, his love, his hate, his pain by shutting my—scintillating, candid, sharp, sarcastic, independent—ass up for good.

Women living in fear died at the hands of men who

were never worthy of their love. Too many women emotionally buried alive, suffered in silence. Compromising their children, bartering their bodies, sacrificing their souls, their sanity in exchange for having a man. And in many cases, a man who didn't love, appreciate, respect, or deserve them.

I prayed, *Dear God, please don't let me become a statistic. Don't let me die without fulfilling my purpose to help save the women who'd given up on getting out of unhealthy relationships. Women who are living the way I used to. You gave me a brain, courage, and a heart. Now tell me which one to use first before I kill these fools.*

Benito accepted, though he seldom acknowledged, women were smarter than men. I was smarter than him. He hated my constant reminders that I was the one who'd paid the bills the three years he lived in my house. Didn't need him for much outside of sex. Proved it to him often. The day I'd tied him up, shoved a gun up his ass, left him in my bed in Las Vegas, I'd hoped was—the same as with my first and second husbands—the last time I'd see him.

A month ago, I saw Benito—my ex—again when I'd arrived at my current lover's parents' place in Washington, D.C. Benito was seated at the dinner table. Benito was worse than a bad penny, making my world smaller than I desired, in a bad luck kind of way. One step away from him, two back. Benito seldom talked about his family when we were together. Blamed his adopted mother for screwing up his life. Gave me no indication he had a half brother named Grant Hill. Now Benito was in my new hometown of Atlanta with my ex-boss, Valentino James, holding me hostage for ransom.

How much did Benito want from me? For me? Hadn't I given him enough? "Take this," I said, not knowing, not giving a fuck whose head I'd put a bullet in first. I fired my semi-automatic handgun at Benito and Valentino.

Pow! Pow! Pow! Pow!

My body pounded like a jackhammer. Stars danced in front of my eyes. I prayed I'd make it out of this situation alive. The sound of engines humming in the distance, too far away from us for drivers to distinguish gunfire from a car back-firing, gave little hope of my being rescued. Glancing at my wristwatch, both hands aligned directly on twelve. Too early for this nonsense. The sun, bright, blinding. I squinted at the sky, searching for an answer to my prayer. Brain? Courage? Heart?

I should've put each bullet in Benito's forehead. I couldn't. I once loved him. Still loved his brother Grant. This was not the time to have compassion for my enemies. Grant's abandonment of my heart made him my enemy too. He should've been man enough to come back to me.

"Ah!" Benito screamed soprano, ducked, covered his face, peeped at me between his fingers. His small gun fell, clacked three times on the pavement.

Pressing my lips togther, I swallowed my chuckle. I'd done right getting rid of him. Former pro-quarterback champion punking out in a shoot out. Why was I still protecting Benito? Kill Benito before he kills my chances of getting back with Grant.

Knees to chin. Heels cushioned into my butt cheeks. Lying in the trunk, messing up my red designer pantsuit, inhaling fumes of the new car, I aimed my gun at my target. Valentino's head.

Wiggling my fingers, I demanded "What the fuck is your problem, Valentino? Hand me your goddamn phone." I kept my gun and eyes fixed on him. My phone was underneath my side. The only person I'd phone was Sapphire Bleu, the one woman who could track down any man in America and wouldn't hesitate to kill him.

Left her a message not to call me back. I'd call her again. "Benito, if you bend over to pick up that gun, I'll slap you upside your head, then shoot you in your ass."

Benito squinted as though trying to figure out how I'd shoot him in the ass while he faced me. Maybe I should ask God to give him a brain.

"Nigga, I knew I shouldn't have trusted you with the gun. Fuck her. Pick up the gun and shoot her ass," Valentino commanded.

The last time I'd seen Valentino was the day he was arrested at his mansion in Las Vegas. Pimping and pandering was his vice. I got out of the business by choice. Circumstances beyond his control forced Valentino out. I had what he desperately needed. If he killed me, he'd never get what he'd come for.

Why did these lowdown dirty bastards agitate me to the point of wanting to blow their brains out? I could kill him. Kill them. Splatter the cells God intended as a masterpiece against the hot asphalt beneath their soles. No one would care but me. Didn't want to go to jail or go insane without having Grant in my life.

Curled in the fetal position, I pulled the trigger to scare Valentino. Waited a few seconds, pulled it again. Valentino dodged my first bullet. Escaped the second. Moved in the right direction both times.

"Slowly toss me the damn phone before I kill your ass for real," I said.

"Shoot her ass, nigga. Don't just stand there," Valentino yelled at Benito. "You want her to kill me?" he said, tossing his cellular inside the SUV.

I wanted to laugh. One toy gun between the two of them, and it was on the ground.

"Bitch, you gon' give me back my fifty mil, then I'm gon' personally kill you," Valentino said, curling his fingers into fists.

This time I had to do it. "Ha, ha, ha, ha, ha, ha, ha,"

I belted, keeping my gun aimed at Valentino. "Benito, get the gun. Give it to me," I said. Pressing the speaker on Valentino's phone, I kept my gun aimed at him.

Money was the root of evil for the person who didn't have any. The fifty million was mine. A gift. Sapphire had given me half of Valentino's money. He hadn't. I didn't owe Valentino shit. Neither did she. I'd given half of my half back to the women who'd earned it fucking Valentino's clients.

My assistant Onyx shouted through the phone, "Honey, where are you?"

Benito eased toward me, kicked the gun closer to Valentino. I shifted my aim to Benito, then quickly pointed the gun back between Valentino's eyes. Coldly stared at him. Eased back the trigger.

"One wrong move and you're dead." I dared him, "Try me."

"Let's go, nigga!" Valentino yelled. "That bitch is crazy."

No, I wasn't crazy.

I was a women who didn't take shit off of abusive men. Not any more. Two life-threatening marriages and these two fools here, I should be crazy, but I wasn't. The only person I was crazy about was Grant and my dead sister, Honey. I killed myself on paper, buried my birth name Lace St. Thomas, then resurrected my sister's name, Honey Thomas. Maybe if I were more like Honey, my past life of prostitution, being a madam, and killing Reynolds would perish, never return to haunt me.

"Onyx, I got this. Don't hang up. Stay with me," I said.

Valentino fell to the ground, crawled along side the car, yelling, "Lock that bitch in the trunk and let's go! I'ma personally kill her ass execution style!"

Always smarter than Valentino's wannabe pimp ass,

I'd organized and operated his escort service. Managed his thirteen girls for a year. Now they were my girls, all millionaires, no longer prostituting. Valentino had more than enough time to run like a bitch. All talk, no action. Valentino wasn't a coward. He was out gunned. He'd be back. I'd be prepared for his return. Next time I wouldn't have a heart. No talking. I'd shoot to kill.

I pointed my gun at Benito. He hadn't moved.

"Lace," Benito pleaded. His eyes softened. "Just give Valentino back his money. He'll give me half and I'll take care of you. You deserve that much from me. I met you first. My brother doesn't love you the way I do. I know you better than he ever will."

Valentino yelled, "Nigga, this ain't *Deal or No Deal*. Lock that bitch in and let's go."

Benito whispered, "Give us the money, Lace. I could never hurt you. Can't you see I still love you? I'd die before I'd kill you."

With no gun, he was right. Aim. Click. Turn. Fire. Four bullets shattered the front windshield.

Benito reached for my legs. Pulled me out of the car. Scrambled into the passenger's seat as Valentino sped off with the SUV trunk door in mid-air.

Damn, their gun was on the ground and Valentino's cell phone and mine were in the trunk of their SUV. "Huh."

No money. No phone. No transportation. Two guns. I stood in the middle of a deserted parking lot, placed my gun back in the holder. Tucked their gun behind my back, inside my pants.

"It's too hot for this shit."

Stilettos clicking against the black sweltering asphalt, sweat dripping from my head, rolling behind my ears, down my neck, I walked a mile through the Atlanta ninety-degree heat wave to the I-75 on-ramp and held up my thumb.

CHAPTER 1

Red Velvet

On my knees, I cried, "Noooo," holding on to Onyx's leg. Crawling up her body, I held Onyx's toned biceps, her jet-black skin flawless, nerves raveled. I screamed in her face, "Where is she? Tell me right now."

Gasping Onyx whispered, "Velvet, I'm so scared. Right before you walked in here I heard gunshots." Fueled with anger, Onyx's large eyes swept hard corner-to-corner. "Valentino demanded his money back. Wants me to get it. I don't know what to do . . . she might be . . ."

I let go of Onyx, matched the intensity of her hatred for a man I hadn't met, then asked, "Gunshots? Who the fuck is Valentino? Where is he? I'ma kick his ass."

Helpless. Standing in Honey's office of Sweeter than Honey, I had to rescue her. I owed her so much. I was grateful for Honey. I was her first client. She'd tracked down my son's father, gotten me seventy-two grand in back child support from Alphonso, the sleaze-bag who'd raped and impregnated me, then demanded I not call him ever again cause he didn't want his wife to know he'd fathered our son Ronnie. Honey believed in my dreams of starring in the movie *Something on the Side,* went with me to Los Angeles to confront Ronnie's father. I'd come to Honey's office to share my joy. I'd gotten the part. I had to thank her for all she'd done for me.

Onyx's eyes closed. Tears streamed over her cheeks, staining her sleeveless mint-green silk blouse. Her mouth opened. Blackberry lips parted, exposing chocolate gums and white teeth. Circling her long black ponytail in her palm, she jammed the phone to her ear. She was taking too long to say something. I snatched the cordless phone from her hand.

Frantically, Onyx waved her hands at me. "I was listening. Waiting. Don't hang up. Honey said, 'Don't hang up.' I think she's still on the other end. Oh, god help us please." Onyx paced the floor, circled her desk. Rubbed her palms on her skirt.

I pressed the phone to my ear. Heard a lot of static like someone was hissing, fumbling, or shuffling.

Onyx cried. "He's going to kill Honey if he doesn't get his money back."

"I'ma call Grant. Grant is a real man and he'll kick Valentino's ass," I said scrolling through my cell phone contact list.

Onyx shook her head. "I just talked to him before you got here. He's on his way."

"That's what's up. I'll call Sapphire then," I said, pressing the letter S.

"She's on her way too," Onyx said.

I yelled into the cordless, "Hey! Valentino! Answer this damn phone. This is Velvet, motherfucker."

The slamming stopped. Silence crept into my ear. Chills crawled up my spine tensing my neck. Then I heard a man's voice. "Who in the hell is this?"

"This is Red Velvet and I'm going to personally beat your ass if you harm Honey," I told him. "Punk."

Calmly, he said, "Put Onyx on the phone, Red Velvet."

"I'm running this show. You talk to me."

"Okay, Velvet. Is red your favorite color?" he asked.

"Yours?" I countered. "Stop wasting my time. Where in the hell is Honey?"

"You mean Lace. If we don't get our money, she's either dead or going to jail," he said. "I'll personally drop her ass off on the sidewalk in front of a mortuary and trust me, you won't be able to identify her body. Or I'll take her to the police station after I cut off her arms and legs. You decide since you're in charge. Or you can give me my money in exchange for your precious Lace St. Thomas or I'ma put your ass on a stroll until you earn my money."

I had to think this out fast. I gestured at Onyx. She took the phone.

"Valentino, give me forty-eight hours. You'll have your money wired to whatever account you give me. I can do a wire. I can't get cash out of Honey's account."

"What? Are you crazy?" I said, snatching the phone from Onyx. "We ain't giving your ass one dime, you hear me? No Honey. No money. You wanna talk? Meet us tonight at Stilettos Strip Club at eight o'clock and don't be late. I want to meet your retarded ass in person."

"You're a hot head. Liable to get yourself killed tonight. I'll be there. Eight o'clock but your forty-eight hours start right now," Valentino said, then hung up.

Onyx stopped crying, started sniffling.

"We need Sapphire Bleu," I said. "She'll take care of Valentino."

We had the law to protect us. Sapphire was a cop and she was Honey's friend.

Onyx sat on her desk. Held my hand, then said, "I owe Honey my life. We all do. The other eleven girls too."

"Where they at? The other girls. They could help us."

"Out working. Trying to convince prostitutes to stop selling their bodies. We were all escorts in Vegas. High paid escorts. And Honey was our madam. Honey started this business in Atlanta to help women get off their backs. Now she's the one who needs our help."

I exhaled trying to devise a plan to Honey. What if Valentino didn't bring her to Stilettos? What if he didn't show up?

Hoping to reassure Onyx, I said, "We'll find Honey. Believe that." I was fascinated, curious about Onyx. "What was that like? Being an escort. You know lots of females have sex for free, let men use them. Must be better getting paid. How much did you get paid?"

Onyx stared at me, cold, hard. "A woman would be better off auctioning her soul to the devil than letting a different man stick his dick in her mouth . . . pussy . . . asshole every night. Sometimes two, three, four men a night. Back-to-back-to-back. Two thousand a night isn't worth it when you end up shot in the head like my best friend Sunny. One day before her twenty-first birthday, Valentino killed her because she wanted out." Onyx broke down in tears.

Oh, damn. What if Valentino was serious about killing Honey?

I hugged Onyx. "I'm so sorry to hear that."

Onyx trembled in my arms, spoke as though she hadn't heard me. "Honey could've left us in Vegas, came to Atlanta by herself, took her millions, started a new life without us. But she didn't. Gave all of us airline tickets. We all came right away, except Girl 6." Onyx eyes widened. She picked up the cordless, dialed a number, then said, "Girl 6, get your ass back to the office. Now."

Eyes shifting. Bottom lip tucked between her teeth.

"You think Girl 6 set Honey up?" I asked.

"Don't know. But I'm definitely going to find out."

CHAPTER 2

Grant

The second Onyx told me Honey was in trouble, I was on my way to Atlanta.

Never got out of my car in front of my parents' home in D.C. Backed out of the driveway, drove to Washington/Dulles International, parked in the short-term lot, not caring how long my car would stay there. I owned a second home in Buckhead furnished with everything I'd need.

No luggage, hands free, I zigzagged across three lanes of congested airport traffic, slapped the hood of a car that almost hit me, woman looking down text messaging. Better keep her attention on the road before she killed someone. I ran to the ticket counter, pulled out my credit card.

Life without Honey wasn't happening.

I'd never met a woman with so much fire, enthusiasm, drive, determination, beauty, sex appeal, bedroom skills, and a bodacious booty. She'd ruined me for all other women. Honey was the only one for me.

The agent smiled, greeting me, "How may—" Before she said, "help," I handed her my driver's license.

"I have a life or death emergency. You've got to put me on your next direct flight to Atlanta. I don't mean your next available, let me make myself clear. I must be on your next flight leaving for Atlanta."

Her smile vanished. "Give me a minute, Mr. Hill." Her acrylic nails swiftly tapped the keys.

"I might not have a minute. Please, hurry."

Her head stayed bowed. Her eyes lift toward me. She continued typing.

"I apologize. The woman I want to marry is missing and I have to find her."

Her smile returned. She typed faster. "Here," she said, handing me a gold first class boarding pass along with my I.D. and credit card. "Wish we had more men like you. Your flight departs in twenty minutes. Hurry."

"Thanks!" I said, running to the security checkpoint. My jacket flapped under my arms like a bird taking flight. I emptied the contents of my pockets—wallet, cell phone, keys—in a white bowl, held on to my boarding pass.

My phone rang on the conveyor. I snatched the tray.

"Excuse me, sir, you can't reach into the X-ray machine," a man in a TSA uniform said.

Best to ignore him to avoid misdirecting my anger. I hadn't checked my caller I.D. before anxiously answering, "Hurry, I've got two minutes." I stepped aside allowing another passenger to go ahead of me.

"Hey, bro. Won't take but a minute," Benito said. "I need some money."

"Where are you?" I asked him.

"Hanging out in Atlanta for a few days. So can you help me out?" he asked.

"Atlanta?" I said.

"Yeah, I'm in the ATL, bro. You know me. I'm a transient. Atlanta. Vegas. D.C., never know where I'll show up."

I felt my blood pressure rising. Wanted to question him about Honey. Didn't want to give him time to make up lies if he knew the truth.

"I'll call you back in two hours," I said, then hung up.

Placing the bowl on the conveyor, along with my shoes, belt, and jacket, I walked through the metal detector. I had to get a secuity clear card. Should've been at my gate by now. I ran to the shuttle, stood the entire ride. The first one off the shuttle, I ran to my gate, barely beating the last call for my flight.

"Orange juice please," I told the flight attendant, settling into 1B, the same seat I'd sat in when I'd met my Honey for the first time. A different woman was next to me now.

Her black skin glistened. Long hair flowed over her shoulders. Skirt rose a few inches above her knees, exposing her bare legs. Open toe shoes revealed an impeccable pedicure. Hadn't seen black strips with diamonds across the tip of toenails. Elegant. She smelled sweet, like candy. The kind of fragrance that would ordinarily draw me real close to a woman. Make me introduce myself. Not today. Regardless how sweet she was, she wasn't sweeter than Honey.

"Here's you juice," the attendant said.

The cabin door closed. I fastened my seatbelt, shut my eyes. Wanted to cry. What good would that do? Wondered how much Benito knew about Honey's disappearance. If he was involved. Hated having to communicate with him, but my brother was my only lead.

I felt the lightest touch on my shoulder, opened my eyes.

"I don't mean to bother you, but you seem like a man who enjoys sports," the woman next to me said.

I exhaled. Nodded. Closed my eyes again.

"I'd like to offer you two box suite tickets to see my son play tomorrow night in Atlanta," she said.

Answering her without opening my eyes, I asked, "What's his name?"

Quietly, she said, "Darius Jones."

I sat up, looked at her, "You mean the Darius Williams who changed his last name to Jones?"

Her lips parted, smile captivated me. I took a deep breath.

She nodded. "Long story. Short version, my son changed his name back to Jones after my husband died. His biological father is—"

I interrupted her, "I know Darryl Williams, pro-basketball player." I smiled back at her. "You are gorgeous. Stunning."

"Thanks. My name is Jada Diamond Tanner," she said, handing me her card.

I dug in my jacket pocket, handed her my card. "I'm going to Atlanta on an emergency. The woman I want to marry is in danger. I have to do all I can to save her. I love her."

Jada's eyes filled with tears. "My husband felt that way about me before he died. My Wellington wasn't a perfect man, but the one thing I knew for sure was my husband loved me with all his heart. Doubt I'll ever love like that again, but I haven't given up. If there's anything I can do to help you find her, you have my number."

Had no idea what compelled me, but I leaned Jada's head on my shoulder, held her hand in mine, and comforted her until our flight arrived in Atlanta. My instincts indicated Jada was one special woman.

Everything happened for a reason. Was I in search of Honey to have a wife? Or is my heart simply in search of a true love?